Also by Marie Harte

THE MCCAULEY BROTHERS

The Troublemaker Next Door

How to Handle a Heartbreaker

Ruining Mr. Perfect

What to Do with a Bad Boy

BODY SHOP BAD BOYS

Test Drive

Roadside Assistance

Zero to Sixty

Collision Course

THE DONNIGANS

A Sure Thing

Just the Thing

The Only Thing

MOVIN' ON

The Whole Package

All I Want for Halloween

The Whole Package

MARIE HARTE

sourcebooks
casablanca

Published by Sourcebooks Casablanca, an imprint of Sourcebooks, Inc.
P.O. Box 4410, Naperville, Illinois 60567-4410
(630) 961-3900
Fax: (630) 961-2168
sourcebooks.com

Printed and bound in Canada.
MBP 10 9 8 7 6 5 4 3 2 1

To D&R, as always, I love you.

And to all those who have served and are serving our country, thank you!

Chapter 1

SO MUCH FOR A RELAXING EVENING AT HOME AFTER A hellacious day at work. Reid Griffith bolted upright in his chair and stared wide-eyed at the television. "What the hell?" He leaned closer to the set. "Is that *you*?"

"Huh?" His older brother lay sprawled sideways on the sofa, taking up the entire couch, his back propped up on a few pillows and the armrest. His size-thirteen feet hung over the opposite edge while he downed a beer and shoved a hand in the family-size bag of chips that would serve as Cash's one-sitting snack.

"You. On the news."

Cash shrugged. "Thought I told you about that when I got home." He shoved a handful of potato chips in his mouth.

"No, you didn't." Reid stared at the television in horror. All the work they'd been doing to grow the business, all the effort to dress as a team, to act and appear professional, to ignore rude customers while delivering quality service to the stressed-out Seattleites planning a local move.

All of it out the window as his brother let fly with f-bombs and violence while he beat the crap out of two strangers, broadcast for everyone to see on the *local news*—spotlight to come.

"You're such an asshole," Reid growled, his patience worn thin. "Didn't I tell you to keep it together? Who the hell is going to hire us if you keep—"

Cash, still eating, turned up the sound and drowned Reid out.

"It's an amazing story," the newswoman was saying at a volume that hurt to hear. She turned to the old woman standing next to her and shoved a microphone in her face. "Tell us, in your own words, Reva, what happened."

Reid snapped, "Turn it down, damn it."

Cash did, and Reid watched as the excited old lady waved her hands around, gesticulating wildly, and nearly smacked into her teenage grandson. "I couldn't believe it. I was supervising the movers when I—"

"When we, Grandma," Reva's grandson cut in. He had shaggy hair and wore grungy clothes. A typical young Seattle hipster.

"Yes, *we* noticed some commotion across the street. The de Gruyters were broken into already once earlier this year. So when Asher pointed out the men going in and out of their house and moved in to take a closer look—way too close, young man," she addressed her grandson before turning back to the reporter. "I knew there'd be trouble. I yelled for him to come back and started calling the police. Then one of those criminals saw Asher watching and dragged him close. I think he was going to hold him hostage or something. He shoved a knife in my grandson's face!"

The boy brightened. "He did. That guy totally tried to cut me. But I moved back just as Cash and Hector came in. They took those guys down like it was nothing."

Reva continued, "They raced right over there, not

even thinking twice. They saved my grandson and stopped a burglary before the police arrived."

Behind them, the white moving van with a bold VETS ON THE GO! logo was clearly visible. Whether that remained a good thing or a bad thing was yet to be determined.

"Your *movers* tackled the assailants?" the reporter asked with a glance at the many people standing around, their focus on the movers and the spectacle of police cars. "Let's see that footage your neighbor captured."

The station played it once again, bleeping out the obscenities. Reid watched as his brother disarmed two men then put them down, hard. Hector grabbed the third man before he could escape, clotheslining him then shoving him face-first into the sidewalk. Then they duct-taped the trio together and waited for the police to show.

Flash forward back to Reva, the reporter, and the police. "I can't believe how fortunate we were," the old lady was saying, fanning herself. "Not everyone would've stepped in to save my grandson. Those thieves had a knife and who knows what else."

"And a gun, if I'm not mistaken," the reporter commented. "But your *movers* disarmed the thieves pretty easily. Amazing. Let's see that again."

The footage replayed in slo-mo. Yep, there went Cash charging in to save the day and pounding the crap out of two guys while Hector held the other criminal down easily. With any luck, the burglars wouldn't sue Cash and end up sinking the company. Reid sighed. Cash had done the right thing. If only it hadn't been caught on camera.

"I look good," Cash rumbled smugly.

"You look lethal. I hope we don't lose clients because they're scared of us." Reid waited out the rest of the segment as the reporter interviewed a few more witnesses.

She tossed her long blond hair and nodded at the van. "What makes this story so fascinating is that Vets on the Go! is a local moving company that only employs veterans." She walked up to Cash and Hector, who'd been talking to a cop.

Reid glanced over at the lug lying on the couch.

"Man, we really look badass," Cash said, smiling.

"Shut up."

On TV, the cop left Cash and Hector to the reporter, who asked, "Cash Griffith? You run Vets on the Go!, is that right?"

Cash nodded. Said nothing.

The reporter tried again. "So you employ veterans?"

"Yep. Vets know how to follow orders and get the job done. We're honest, and we don't mess around." Cash planted his hands on his hips, and Reid saw bloody knuckles. At least the dark shirts they wore didn't show stains. Then Cash added, capping the interview, "Semper f**kin' Fi."

Lovely how he'd had to be bleeped on the news. Next to him, Hector laughed.

More bleeping followed as Cash added, "Mother***kers think they can rob honest people. What horse***t. I'd love to kick their a**es all over again."

The reporter gave a weak smile, but she stayed close to Cash all the same. Reid hated to admit it, but his brother *did* look good on camera. If he could just shut up and keep looking big and strong, they might actually reap something positive out of this mess, like more business they could desperately use.

Hector cleared his throat, and the reporter gratefully turned to him. "You know, it's tough for a lot of military folks to find civilian jobs after they get out. You leave the service and return home with nothing lined up. Vets on the Go! gave me and my brother a job, and we love it. We work hard, and we do the job right."

"Thank God someone has a brain," Reid muttered and ignored the finger Cash shot him.

The reporter looked at Hector in awe. Nearly as large as Cash but much more affable, Hector drew notice without trying. His dark skin showed off his bulging biceps. Whereas Cash looked like a bruiser you wouldn't want to meet in a dark alley, Hector had the look of a guy you wanted to trust. That smile nailed it.

The reporter took a step closer to him, and Cash ducked away, ignoring the cameras to return to work. Hector continued to schmooze the reporter while Cash lifted boxes and moved furniture into the van. He moved at a steady pace, and watching him, Reid admitted to being impressed at how much his brother could carry.

Thank God he'd insisted the team start wearing the new Vets on the Go! shirts last week. They were dark blue with red-and-white lettering, which showed a lot less mess than the white shirts they'd started with.

The reporter wrapped up the segment, and Cash yelled for Hector to "Hurry the hell up and help; we haven't got all damn day."

Reid groaned again. Next to him, Cash chuckled. "What? He was taking forever flirting up that chick."

"Please tell me you didn't call her a chick to her face."

"Not to her face. But maybe I did later, when we got hot and heavy after the broadcast."

Reid blinked. "Are you serious?"

Cash snorted. "No, dumbass. I was too busy moving shit to hit on the woman. Look, we had a job to do. Sorry if I wasn't as smooth about it as you would have been. But that mess put us behind schedule. We have to go over tomorrow morning and finish up, so we won't get to our next job until the afternoon."

"Great." Reid blew out a heavy breath. "Well, with any luck, we won't lose customers because of your inability to resist a fight."

"Hey."

That wasn't fair, and Reid knew it, but today was just one more "incident" to add to the bucketful belonging to Cash.

After fourteen years, Cash had separated from the Marine Corps due to a hell of a mess with some commanding officers. Though Cash had no doubt been in the right, he'd mouthed off at the wrong time and offended someone with influential friends.

Reid had known Cash would need help on the outside, so he'd left the Corps as well. Truth be told, though he missed it, he liked the challenge of adapting to the civilian sector. He'd done well since leaving the military. Cash, not so much. Creating Vets on the Go! had begun as a way to help Cash earn a living. That it also provided jobs for other vets was a bonus.

Reid and Cash had brainstormed the idea and used Reid's savings to invest. Their cousin had fronted them more funds to get started, and Cash put in what little he could. Five trucks later and the demand was growing. Now they just had to adjust to their tenuous new growth…before Cash ruined the business with his big mouth and even bigger fists.

"It's not that I have a problem with you stopping a robbery," Reid said. "That was great. It's just that you manage to find trouble wherever you go." And had since he was a kid.

"It's a gift."

"That just keeps on giving." Reid groaned. "With any luck, this too shall pass." He got no response from his brother and sighed. "Don't forget you have someone to interview tomorrow. The background check is good. With this one, we'll have our last hire to round out the team."

"Yeah, yeah." Cash waved his concerns away. "Jordan something-or-other. I'll get to him after the job. Or you could—?"

"Nope. We've talked about this. I screen 'em on paper, you interview 'em in person. And that way I don't have to hear you bitching about the idiots that you have to work next to." A complaint Reid had addressed before. Cash hated anything he considered administrative. *I'm a field Marine, not an office jockey*, he liked to say. "Besides," Reid added. "I'm busy enough as it is making sure we don't miss anything. This company is a logistical nightmare without the right supplies on hand, the right scheduling, the—"

"You lost me after 'Nope.'" Cash crunched his way through the rest of the newscast.

"Asshole." A picture of their moving van flashed on the screen, their phone number in big red numbers. The reporter turned back to Hector, who had the presence of mind to talk up the company as trustworthy and disciplined. Then he made a comment about sacrificing even their safety to protect their clients' prized possessions, which made the reporter laugh and the camera zoom in once again on the criminals being arrested.

Bull's-eye. Something good finally *had* come out of Cash's ability to land in the thick of things. Not only had he saved the kid, but he'd made the company look heroic by stopping a robbery. Movers who cared enough about your possessions to put themselves in jeopardy. Reid could spin that.

He considered the new branding ideas he'd been tossing around. Vets on the Go! needed something more to sell it than just hiring veterans. Perhaps with time, he'd—

His cell phone buzzed. He didn't recognize the number. "Hello?"

"Hi. Just saw you guys on the news. Way to go helping out that woman and her grandson."

Reid realized he hadn't taken the office phone off forward from earlier, when he'd had to leave for an appointment during work hours. After-hours calls typically went to the company's voicemail. "Oh, yeah, thanks."

"We're moving out of Seattle to Tacoma and have been looking for someone reputable to move us." The guy gave Reid details, which had Reid scrambling to take notes. After hanging up, he noticed he'd missed a call.

"See?" Cash threw a chip at his head. "You should be thanking me for looking so fine while doing my civic duty. Got us a new customer."

"Whatever."

Cash just grinned at him before changing the channel to a reality show that made Reid want to leave the room. Cash guzzled his beer then tossed the empty on the cluttered coffee table with a *thunk*. "Oh man. Chandra did not just tell Buffy to step off."

Reid rolled his eyes and went into the spare bedroom he'd set up as a study. Sharing the three-bedroom house with his brother had been a practical decision. They could better afford it, and living together just made sense, since they poured all their efforts and money into the business. In the year and a half they'd been up and running, they'd managed to buy two more trucks, giving them a total of five, and added five employees.

But if—

His phone buzzed again. Great. Now he'd missed two calls and had someone trying to get through while he checked. It seemed Cash's citizen's arrest had done the trick. Reid didn't recognize any of the numbers coming through. He took the next call, then listened to the messages on his cell.

Every one of them had been a request for moving services and a "well done" for stepping up to protect young Asher.

And the calls kept coming. He grinned, vowing to make it up to Cash with pizza at the end of the week. He answered the next call and scheduled in another family needing reputable movers. And then another.

Hmm. Make that an extra-large pizza with all the trimmings…

—∿∿—

Naomi Starr stared at the television and could almost feel the hamster in her brain running in his big wheel pick up pace. The little bugger was racing like mad.

She tried to thread a hand through her hair, but it got

caught in the tangled mass. A glance down at her holey sweatpants only confirmed the sloth of her rare day off. God, she had so much to do. What had she been thinking to take a day to herself? Especially since her self-care of yoga and a smoothie had devolved into chocolate and couch lounging while she channel surfed.

Doubts that her business would ever rocket out of its current orbit as boutique and "good for its size" returned.

Rex, the cat, gave her a baleful look, as if reading her mind. Then he set to ignoring her and licked himself, not even deigning to flick an ear her way.

She tugged at her tangles. "Look, you have no room to judge. You sleep twenty hours a day. I'm entitled to relax." *So why do I feel so guilty?*

She ate another square of chocolate and forced herself to enjoy every bit of it. On TV, she watched some behemoth of a hunk single-handedly stop two burglars in broad daylight while his equally muscle-bound friend stopped a third.

The hamster in her brain shot off the wheel as inspiration struck. Vets on the Go! had "opportunity" written all over it.

Quickly googling the company, she took inventory of all its website did and didn't show her. It looked like a small company. But her sixth sense told her it was sitting on a gold mine and didn't know it.

Yet.

She felt a spark in the embers of her enthusiasm that had cooled since getting screwed over—both literally *and* figuratively—by her ex-boss. *No. Not going there again.* She was done dwelling on Tanner. And good riddance.

Instead, Naomi jotted down a few ideas and made notes.

She just needed a boost to take her business to the next level. She used to be a marketing and PR high roller who'd rubbed elbows with the bigwigs in Seattle. She'd helped professional athletes, CEOs, and celebrity chefs launch their brands. And she'd assisted with marketing strategies, advertising, and public relations solutions for her clients and left them satisfied with success.

An executive at Paulson, Pierce & Ryan, Naomi had worked her tail off to be seen as an intelligent go-getter, not just a great face for the company. As a leggy redhead with boobs, she was used to attention. It took hard work to be seen as more than a pretty girl who had a nice smile.

She'd been smart, never mixing business with pleasure. Then her older sister had scored one more victory in the family tally, putting Naomi *way* behind on the chart to success. Not that she ever thought she might catch up to her older siblings. She didn't save lives or defend people from going to jail. She helped businesses grow for a living. As did her sister, Harley. But with Harley's huge coup over some stupid account, Naomi had once again been left in the dust.

So Tanner's attention had been welcome, a boost to her flagging ego. She'd known sleeping with the boss would be a bad idea. And she'd been right.

It had been a year and a half since she'd left PP&R and all that went with it. She dated sparingly, just to prove that she could. Mostly she poured all her effort into her new firm, Starr PR. She worked eighty-hour weeks since it was just her, Liz, and Leo doing everything. Fortunately, Naomi still had friends and contacts, and she used them to her advantage.

Word had spread. Starr PR was getting a reputation as thorough and easy to work with. They got results. Liz, her assistant, and Leo, their IT specialist, worked their tails off as it was. Naomi planned on adding a marketing expert to her tiny team soon. She had the funds to do it, but she needed to continue finding new clients to keep the momentum rolling.

She already had her eye on a cash cow, one that would put her fears of fading into oblivion to bed. Chris Jennings, CEO of a new and rising tech company, was her ticket back into the big leagues. A friend had clued her in that Chris was looking for someone to help him reach the next level. He'd been vocal about serving proudly in the Marine Corps, so she knew he had a soft spot for veterans.

Helping to make Vets on the Go! the huge business she had the feeling it could be would be just the thing to get Chris Jennings's notice. Naomi had a nose for potential. Hunky men who'd served their country and stopped crime would be her ticket to the top.

She'd make them into a huge business, grab Jennings's attention, and get the funds she needed to expand Starr PR into the powerhouse it should be. Then she'd take back the clients Paulson, Pierce & Ryan had stolen from her.

Because yes, she was petty in her need for revenge. And hell, she needed to prove herself. Sometimes she hated being the youngest in a family of overachievers. Ignoring another call from her mother checking in, she threw off her proverbial mantle of sloth and jumped on the treadmill in her spare room. Sweating out her frustrations, she planned.

And knew just how she'd introduce herself to the hunky vets, long legs and all.

Chapter 2

HER INTRODUCTION TO HER FUTURE CLIENT DIDN'T GO exactly as planned. Nearly tackled by the African American man she'd seen on the television the day prior, Naomi had to dart off the stairs into the hallway to avoid being flattened, only to run into him somehow ahead of her.

"Twins," the new guy offered with a gorgeous smile. "I'm Lafayette, the better-looking one."

Sexy twins with muscles and a sense of humor. She could sell that.

"Sorry about that. I didn't see you there." The guy behind her put down the huge box he'd been carrying and joined her in the second-floor hallway with his brother. He sheepishly held out a hand. "Hector Jackson."

Since he'd been carrying a box she wouldn't have been able to lift let alone see beyond, she forgave him. "No problem. I'm Naomi Starr. I'm looking for the Vets on the Go! office."

"That's where we're heading. Come on." Lafayette motioned for her to follow him down the corridor. The warehouse had a large office on the ground floor that had been closed for repair, directing foot traffic up the stairs. She passed a watch repair company and a computer repair shop on the right, and on the other side of the hallway a small specialty clothing store that didn't seem to belong. The building itself stood in a decent enough location in northwest Seattle, and she liked what she'd seen thus far.

But as she walked down the hall, she heard raised voices and a lot of swearing, no doubt coming from the open door on the left.

Next to her, Hector cringed. "Ah, that's just Cash and Reid, um, discussing some stuff."

A deep voice accused, "You can't not hire someone who's qualified just because she's a woman!"

Oh, Naomi wanted to hear this.

"Bullshit. You told me I'm the one doing the interviewing. So butt out."

"Ah, excuse me," a husky, feminine voice cut in. "Do I get a vote?"

"Yes."

"Hell no."

"I think I'll see if I can help," Lafayette murmured. "Naomi, Hector will take you to the main office."

"Sure." She followed Hector slowly, wanting to hear more from the open doorway.

As she passed, she caught a glimpse of the big man she'd seen yesterday on camera—Cash Griffith. Next to him stood a slight woman who looked vaguely annoyed, and facing the pair, Naomi caught the back of yet another giant. The Reid who'd been mentioned. Likely Reid Griffith, the other owner.

Naomi stood five foot eight, five eleven in her power heels, yet in this place, she felt small. Especially following Hector, who wasn't so much tall as he was broad. And not an ounce of fat on him that she'd seen.

"Jordan, please forgive my brother," she overheard

Reid saying, his voice rich and smooth. "He's a little less than enlightened."

"I figured," Jordan answered. "But he was a Marine, so I didn't expect much better."

Ahead of Naomi, Hector laughed.

"Was? *Am*, honey," Cash answered. He sounded like a grizzly with his paw caught in a trap. Angry and growly. She hoped like hell she could deal with someone else, like his brother, who spoke calmly by comparison.

"My name's Jordan, you jarhead. Not honey," Jordan snapped back.

Naomi liked her already.

Lafayette cleared his throat. "Yo, we got people in the hall. You might want to keep it down, or at least close the door."

She lost the rest of the conversation when the door closed and continued to follow Hector into the main office at the end of the corridor.

Inside the large space was a waiting room and, in the center, a grand reception desk. Against the far wall were three closed office doors, and off to the left of the sitting area, where three people sat leafing through magazines, she noticed a table with fixings for coffee and several plates of baked goods.

Behind the reception desk, a blond man sat talking on the phone and writing on a yellow notepad, ignoring the computer, and her, completely.

The tasteful decor of the office surprised her, as did the fact the place wasn't tacky or filled with vending machines. Cream-colored walls had been decorated with patriotic photographs of the flag and members of various services. And on one particular wall hung a framed

photo with a Vets on the Go! truck and a line of employees standing proudly in front of the vehicle.

The office had a professional feel not quite in
tune with the brutish men and loud voices she'd just
overheard.

Hector set the box on the reception counter and
turned to her. "Sorry about that. We're still growing.
Got so much attention from that thing on the news that
it's total chaos lately."

Hector turned to the people waiting. "Hey, folks.
Reid'll be right with you." To Naomi, he said, "Reid's
the guy you want to talk to."

Thank God. She nodded her thanks.

Hector took his box through one of the closed doors,
then reappeared and grabbed a clipboard the blond man
at the desk handed him. Hector looked at it, mumbled
something under his breath, then left in a hurry.

The man and woman on the couch, probably a
couple, continued to peruse their magazines. The older
man across from them noticed Naomi's gaze, shrugged,
and said, "Got nothing but time."

Behind the desk, the lanky blond finished his call, his
gaze now glued to her. He hung up and smiled. "Well,
hello. How can I help you?"

The way his gaze subtly traveled over her, lingering
on her face instead of her curvier assets, along with that
charming smile, made her feel appreciated instead of
leered at, which she found amusing. The guy had looks
and charisma and worked them to his advantage.

She continued to catalog the strengths and weaknesses in the place as she answered, "Hi. I'd like to talk
to Reid Griffith if he's available. I'm here to help with

your marketing and PR needs." She didn't want to be confused with another client needing a move.

"Do you have an appointment?"

"I couldn't get through on the phone. It just kept ringing."

"Damn it," came a growl from behind her. "I knew this would be a problem."

She turned to see a dark-haired man with light-gray eyes striding into the office. Reid, apparently. Naomi could only stare as his magnetic pull made it impossible to look away. He barely gave her any notice, glancing instead at the people waiting. "Sorry, folks. Finley will be right with you." He gazed at the blond man, one dark, arched brow raised.

"So I'm done manning the phones?"

Reid groaned. "The phones are killing me. Yeah. Thanks, but I need you to help the people waiting *here*. Use office 2A."

Finley nodded and stood. Geez, did they hire anyone small around here? Unlike the other men she'd seen, Finley had a more streamlined appearance. If he was an athlete, she'd think him a runner or cyclist.

He stepped around the desk, gave her a wink, then smiled at the couple. "Okay, Mr. and Mrs. Barnett. Come with me, and we'll get you scheduled."

Reid walked over to the older man. "Mr. Thompson, sorry for the long wait. Would you come with me?"

The gentleman grabbed a black Vietnam vet ball cap, placed it on his head, and stood with a grin. "See what happens when you save the day? Get too popular to handle yourselves."

Reid ran a hand through his short dark-brown hair.

"You got that right. Sorry again for the wait." He spared Naomi a glance and gave a clipped smile. "I'll be with you after Mr. Thompson, ma'am."

She blinked and nodded, still staring like an idiot.

Then he turned and escorted Mr. Thompson into one of the empty offices.

She sat, trying to gather her thoughts.

The amount of eye candy around the place had thrown her. It was like an office for supermodel buff guys. Normally, Naomi was the one drawing the eye. But in this place, she didn't feel as if she stood out. It didn't help that Reid had barely spared her a look before leaving with Mr. Thompson.

Her ego aside, the thought of using all that muscle and sex appeal for branding purposes was like being handed a gift. If the men of Vets on the Go! photographed well, she could easily envision more business flying through the door.

On the surface, Vets on the Go! seemed too good to be true—busy, inefficient, and totally needing her help.

Two more moving people came in. A male redhead about her height walked next to a bigger man with plain features. They nodded at her, then each grabbed a clipboard from the desk before leaving again.

Jordan, the woman who'd been arguing with Cash, entered the office, followed by Cash and Lafayette.

"Look, I'm sorry, okay?" Cash rumbled. "You're big and strong and not at all girly. You win."

Jordan shot daggers at him while Lafayette grinned behind the pair.

Everyone froze when they saw Naomi sitting and waiting.

"Hel-lo there." Cash looked her over with a directness she might have found refreshing if she hadn't overheard him talking down to the woman next to him. "And how can I help *you*?"

Naomi rose to her feet. "I'm looking to speak to the owners of Vets on the Go! to talk about your marketing strategies and targets. I was told to ask for Reid Griffith?" She did her best to sound pleasant while mentally castigating the big bastard for his machismo. "I'm Naomi Starr of Starr PR." She held out a hand, and Cash shook it, his large hand engulfing her much smaller one.

Up close, she felt the power of his green-eyed stare and might have felt overwhelmed…if she hadn't been used to dealing with alpha business types. She met his gaze and smiled, giving the appearance of being unperturbed.

"Cash Griffith." He frowned a little then let go of her hand. He hadn't squeezed too hard or been rough, which she thought a good sign. Maybe the lout had potential after all. "Ah, if you're talking business stuff, you want Reid."

She nodded. "He's in with a client."

Lafayette turned to the woman with him. "Hey, Jordan. Let me show you around, okay?"

She gave Cash a glare, turned to dismiss him, which he clearly didn't like by the large scowl on his face, and motioned for Lafayette to lead the way. "Sounds good. I'm ready to start whenever Mr. Macho here lets me."

Cash growled. It made Naomi want to laugh to see the big guy defensive. "Come on, you two. There's shit we can be doing while Reid takes care of all this." He waved his hand at the office and left, brushing by everyone in a huff.

"What's his problem?" Jordan asked Lafayette.

"What problem? This is Cash on a good day." He grinned. "Sure you want the job?"

She sighed. "Unfortunately, I do."

Naomi sensed a story there, but then they left. All alone, she sat once more and went through her phone, checking things off on her calendar while coordinating with Liz and Leo about two of their current clients.

Twenty minutes later, Mr. Thompson walked out with Reid behind him, the pair laughing as they shook hands.

The old man smiled. "Take care, Gunny. I'll see you guys in a month."

"Will do, Dan. It was a pleasure to meet you."

Dan Thompson left with a pep in his step and a smile on his face. "Ma'am," he said and tipped his hat at her as he passed.

She stood and managed a professional nod at Reid, aware of her racing pulse that had as much to do with involuntary attraction as it did with nerves. No matter how handsome she might find him, she couldn't screw this up.

Reid didn't give her the once-over his brother had. He met her gaze and smiled. "I'm sorry you had to wait. I didn't see an appointment...?"

She shook her head, pleased to see him follow the motion of her deliberately styled waves. "I'm Naomi Starr of Starr PR. I saw you on the news and thought you might need some help. I think you have the potential to grow."

Reid nodded, his gaze focused on her. Good Lord, it was like being studied under a microscope.

She felt breathless and hated herself for it.

"Why don't you come in and we'll talk?" He motioned for her to walk with him into his office.

When she passed, he put a gentle hand on the small of her back, and a zing of heat spiraled throughout her body. Totally weird.

He removed his hand upon entering and seated her across from his desk before taking his own chair. "Would you like something to drink?"

"No, thank you."

He nodded, took a huge gulp from the large insulated cup on his desk, then kicked back and laced his hands behind his head. Which showed off his impressive chest and amazingly toned arms. *Hurray for spring and men in short sleeves.* "So, how can you help me, Ms. Starr?"

A loaded question for sure, she thought, wishing she'd sensed something off about the man—but no, she hadn't seen a ring on that finger and he still wasn't flirting. Unfortunately, nothing he'd done dampened her need to be found attractive by him.

She cleared her throat. "Naomi, please." Naomi took a subtle breath and let it out slowly. She was an amazing strategist. She could do this. Even better, his firm needed her. She could help him achieve the greatness buried just under the surface. "Mr. Griffith, I—"

"Reid is fine."

"Reid," she continued. "I saw your company on the news yesterday and was drawn to your concept: veterans helping other veterans and in turn helping out the community. You offer a sense of pride and a dedication to helping people who are in a vulnerable state of transition. But your website is a little hard to manage. You have no automated scheduling, which might be losing you potential customers. And you're a small company trying to compete with larger firms in a city this size. It can't be easy."

He sighed. "It's not."

"I'm here because I'm also part of a small firm competing against bigger but not necessarily better PR firms. I run a boutique agency, meaning we focus on smaller companies we know we can help. I think Vets on the Go! has enormous potential. And I'd like to help you achieve success."

He watched her like a wolf sizing up prey. She squelched a shiver, reminding herself she'd worked with bigger, badder versions of dominant men. *But none of them nearly so attractive…*

Reid lowered his hands to the desk as he sat forward, his gaze penetrating. "So you saw our spotlight on TV and out of the blue decided to come down here and pitch your services." The gaze he swept over her, *finally*, surprised her. It felt less than flattering.

"I did. I actually called to talk to you, but I couldn't get through."

"Oh. Sorry about that." He sounded nothing but polite once more. Perhaps she'd misread the look he'd given her? "Since my brother and Hector decided to play superhero, the phones haven't stopped ringing. I mean, I'm glad they helped people out. And the publicity has been great. It's not helping in that we can't keep up with the demand."

"That's kind of what I thought."

"And there have been a number of women showing up with plates of cookies, cakes, and brownies. Are you sure I can't get you something? We had two pans of blondies a few hours ago."

She paused, suddenly understanding, and tried to bite back a grin. "Ah. Well, I didn't bring you any cookies. I'm just here about business."

"Thank God."

She chuckled, not at all offended. "Hey, at least you're attracting people in the door."

"I guess there is that." He gave her a tired smile. "We've been in business the past year and a half, and it's been a struggle to get going. Part of why we're doing better than our small-business competitors is we only hire people we vet, so to speak. They pass a background check before we even think about hiring them. They have to jibe with Cash and our motto of *always faithful*. It's not just a Marine thing."

"That, right there, is what you need."

"What I need are two more of me to handle the work-load," he muttered. "What exactly do you think I need?"

"To refine your brand. *Always faithful* is a great tag-line for your business."

"You're saying we need help with PR and marketing?"

"Exactly. Have you used anyone before?"

He shook his head. "It's been all me. I've been mean-ing to hire someone, but we never had the funds or the time to look into it. Frankly, it's pricey. I'm sure you're not here out of the goodness of your heart to provide a free service."

"No, but I get the feeling you can't afford *not* to work with someone. I'm hoping we can help each other." She smiled at him and noted a subtle change in his expres-sion, though she still couldn't read him. Naomi prayed she didn't look as attracted as she felt. "Do you know the difference between public relations and marketing?"

"No."

"A PR professional creates awareness. We use social media, like your website, Twitter, Facebook, Instagram, etcetera, to get people to notice you. Marketers create demand. So whereas a PR professional works on your brand and makes you shiny to new customers, a marketer will use social media to increase the demand for your services."

"I need more coffee." He downed what was left in his cup.

"I don't mean to confuse you. PR and marketing really go hand in hand. It's like"—she glanced at his cup—"say you're really desperate for coffee, but you don't know there's a coffee shop across the street from you. You're thirsty but don't know where to go to sate that need."

Was it her imagination, or did his eyes just grow darker?

"Then, too, you might be thirsty for something but not realize coffee is what you're hankering for, that caffeine jolt to push you through your day. With the right balance of marketing and PR, we can show you that coffee is what you want, and that you can find that coffee right across the street. Does that make sense?"

"Sure, but people know if they need a moving company."

"But they don't know that they need *your* moving company. And they might not see it since there are so many other companies offering a similar service and experience. With my firm's help, we can convince them that what they need is you. Then we convince them to tell all their friends about you, and that you're exactly what they need now and in the future."

He watched her, and she sensed a keen intelligence behind those light-gray eyes. "You're pretty good, aren't you?"

"The best." She smiled and reached into her purse. "Here's my card." She laid it on his desk. "When you work with us, you see results. We know a lot of people in town and like to refer locally. You need help. We both know it. This publicity push from TV will either make you or break you. It's time to capitalize on what you've got. If you can't keep up with current demand, you'll start to see all that good buzz go south."

"Tell me something I don't know."

"Look at it this way. We can run a trial partnership, and I'll be happy to go over the contract with you. We'll make it a short run, say, three months, to see if what we offer is what you need. *I* know we can help you, but you have to be satisfied with our services. And three months is long enough that we can help you see some results."

She waited for him to respond.

"How much are we talking?" he said after a moment.

To her consternation, his gaze moved to her mouth.

She fought the urge to lick her dry lips, not wanting him to think she was coming on to him. And how bizarre to have so many sexual thoughts about a client. Naomi never did that. Sleeping with her boss had been her one and only foray—mistake—into unprofessional behavior.

She gave Reid a ballpark figure that was more than competitive with other like-minded firms. "We'll work through details on the contract so you'll know exactly how much you'll be paying once we iron out how much time you think you'll need and what you want from us. We're worth the investment, Reid."

He watched her for a moment then nodded. "And I'd be working with you or someone else?"

"I'd be your primary contact. As I said, we're a boutique firm. I have an assistant and a data expert, and we'll soon be hiring a marketing professional. Right now, I handle all that." She nodded to her card. "Please look us up. Our clients will be happy to talk to you about what we did for them. We've got references, testimonials. Feel free to talk to people who know us."

"I will." He picked up her card and held it in his large, graceful hand. "Can I call you once we figure out our budget?"

"Please." Sensing her time had ended, she stood.

He stood as well and crossed to guide her out of the office. Once again, he put a hand against her back.

She didn't know how to feel about it other than annoyingly aroused. At the exit to the main office door, she turned and took the hand he offered.

He held it a moment longer than she would have, but nothing about his behavior was anything other than that of a gentleman.

"Thanks, Naomi. I'll be in touch."

As she drove to her office, she made a mental note to add in even more exercise time to work off her sudden bout of nervous energy. And to get back on that dating site. Reacting so strongly to a client couldn't be normal.

Then again, when confronted by a perfect package like Reid Griffith, a girl could be excused for being impressed.

Chapter 3

AT THE END OF THE DAY, REID FOUND CASH ARGUING WITH three of their employees, including their new hire, Jordan, in the warehouse downstairs. The large space housed their trucks and moving supplies. They shared the downstairs with a bakery chain, which stored its trucks on the other side of the barricade. But Reid knew Vets on the Go! could easily add a few more vans and still have room to spare.

As always, when vets from different parts of the military mixed, the age-old debate of which military service was superior started. As if the discussion ever needed to happen. Everyone knew the Marines to be the best of the best.

He lounged against the wall as Jordan tore into his brother. Reid wasn't sure how he felt about hiring Jordan as a mover yet. He knew looks were deceiving, but next to his brother, she looked downright tiny. The company was an equal opportunity employer, and she had an exemplary military record. Just because she didn't look like she could lift five hundred pounds didn't mean she couldn't bench her weight. Finley and Martin weren't overly muscular and still did their fair share. He tried ignoring any sense of gallantry and forced himself to acknowledge Jordan had the right to pass or fail on her own, without his bias. Too bad Cash wouldn't see it the same way.

"I think you're scared of someone who can outthink you is all," Jordan was saying. "Not your fault you're a big, burly Marine with a tiny brain."

Hector guffawed, then quickly coughed when Cash turned a murderous stare his way. "Honesty hurts, big guy."

Jordan snickered.

"Tiny brain, right." Cash snorted. "You're prejudiced because you're jealous of these guns."

Reid rolled his eyes as his brother started flexing. Because that started Hector and Lafayette posing. Then Jordan shocked the group by shrugging off her windbreaker to showcase toned muscles under her own short-sleeved shirt.

"Well, day-um," Hector said on a laugh. "Little Army's got her own set of ammo."

"Told you." She smirked at the group, and Reid liked her for the team. She fit, like a piece of their growing puzzle.

He watched the group, not surprised to see everyone gravitate around Cash. It had nothing to do with Cash owning part of the business and everything to do with his natural ability to lead. No matter how much experience others possessed, the guys in the units they'd been with in the Marines had always looked to Cash for what to do. The man would lead a squad out of danger, know where and when to attack. Cash was the go-to for getting things done…especially if that meant working under the radar, not following the rules.

It sometimes made being in the same room with him tough because Reid felt like that proverbial wallflower at the dance, overshadowed by his prettier debutante of a brother. And just thinking that made him want to laugh.

As the gang continued to try to out-flex each other, the

mood easy and fun among them, Reid decided to make his presence known. He clapped, and they all froze.

Jordan quickly put her arms down and flushed.

Cash snickered. "Little Army is right."

"Shut up," she muttered.

Reid walked over to them. "You guys did great today. We're back on track since Jordan helped with the last job. Good work," he told her.

She smiled. "Yes, sir."

"Please." Cash shook his head. "He was an E-7. Don't call him *sir*."

"Yeah, don't." Reid grimaced. "I worked for a living." He'd been enlisted, not an officer, though not for lack of opportunity, something he'd never shared with Cash. "So, Jordan, you're on probation while we see how you fit with the team. Cash will make sure you learn what you need to know to start. And like we went over in the office, paychecks come the first and fifteenth, just like the service."

"Nice," she said.

"Yeah." Lafayette nodded. "It helps. Yo, Reid, so what was up with the looker in the office this morning?"

Everyone watched Reid, curious.

"You mean Naomi Starr of Starr PR?" he asked.

"Naomi Starr. Sounds like a porn name. What?" Cash asked him, seeing his frown. "I'm just saying."

"Jesus, is he housebroken at least?" Jordan asked the twins, thumbing at Cash over her shoulder.

"Not yet," Lafayette said, "but we're working on it."

Cash shrugged. "PR? Do we really need to hire someone for that?"

"Probably yeah, due to all the business you're picking

up from that spot on television," Jordan said. "The Starr woman looked classy. Was she smart?"

"Yes," Reid answered. And sexy and someone who'd shot his latent libido into the stratosphere. He'd had to put on his disinterested, serious face when dealing with her so she wouldn't realize how badly he'd wanted to bend her over the desk. That was more Cash's style. Not exactly sophisticated or professional.

"So, what? We're celebrities now?" Cash grinned.

"Not quite." Though they'd gotten a call from another television station requesting an interview. He needed to know how to handle it.

Naomi had said all the right things and come at just the right time. Finding someone to help with marketing had been on his long to-do list since they'd opened. This thing with Cash and Hector had sped up the timeline.

"I have to talk to Evan. You guys should go home for the day. We just added six more confirmed jobs that want in as soon as we can get to them. Jordan, are you good to come back tomorrow at six?"

She blinked. "In the morning?"

"Duh," Cash said.

She glared at him but said to Reid, "Ah, sure. I'll be here."

"Great. Cash, set her up with a few shirts and give her the schedule. I think we have something that can fit her."

Jordan beamed. Reid saw Cash and Hector noticing her with more than platonic interest, cleared his throat, then gave them a knowing look. Lafayette put his brother in a headlock and walked him away, leaving Cash and Reid alone with Jordan. Cash tried to ignore him.

"Cash, a word?" Reid said.

"I'll be right back," Cash said to Jordan.

"Ohhh, I can't wait," she deadpanned, and Reid had to laugh.

Well away from the woman, Reid dragged his brother close and whispered, "She's a teammate. Not a possible conquest. Stay out of her pants."

"Please. I'm not thinking that at all."

"Yeah?" Reid knew his brother. Cash liked women. A little too much. He never went where he wasn't invited, but Reid knew they'd have to be careful about stepping over any lines, especially since they were now in charge. It was a lot like being back in the military where fraternization was a huge no-no. "Well, then keep *not* thinking it. Jordan is clearly capable. Take her through her paces, and make sure she's a good fit. I like that she's not afraid of you. But let's hope she still understands a command structure."

"Hey," Cash whispered back, affronted, "*I* didn't want to hire her. *You* made me."

"Bullshit." Kind of. "It helps to have a woman on the team. She's a fellow vet, and she looks damn good on paper. See how she works out—not in bed but on the job."

"I should be saying the same thing to you. I saw you eye-fucking that redhead earlier."

"I was not." He hoped he hadn't been obvious about checking her out.

"Nah, man. I know you. She's just your type."

"Smart and pretty?"

"See? You noticed."

"So did everyone else." Naomi Starr had looks and grace. And breasts. Good Christ. Reid focused on

relaxing his sudden tension. "Look, just play nice with
Jordan. Stop pissing her off so much, and treat her like
one of the guys."

"I am."

"Really? You never looked at Martin like you want
to do him."

Cash bit back a grin. "Yeah, okay. Right."

"Get her settled, and lock the place up. I'll see you at
home. I'm going to swing by Evan's first to talk about
hiring Naomi."

Cash nodded, shoved past Reid, then barked a few
orders at Jordan.

Reid shook his head and went back upstairs. After
confirming a meeting with Evan at a local restaurant, he
finished finalizing a few scheduling conflicts.

To his surprised pleasure, all this extra business had
been just what they needed. But his fear they'd soon
outpace themselves continued to rear.

An hour later, he sat with his cousin at a downtown
bar in Queen Anne. They'd both started on their second
rounds—beer for Reid, soda for Evan. Poor Evan looked
the way Reid felt.

"Bad day?" he asked his cousin.

Evan's and Reid's fathers had been brothers. Both
had passed within a year of each other. Evan, like all the
Griffith men, had that tall and good-looking thing going
for him. Evan, though, seemed to have been born with a
natural ability to charm anyone out of a bad mood. Hell,
even Cash liked the guy, and Cash didn't like many
people outside of Reid.

"Bad day?" Evan repeated, laughing a little
hysterically—totally out of character for the chill guy.

"God, it's not over. I'm just on a break. Man, I hate my job."

"Not good, considering it's your livelihood."

"Yeah." Evan downed the rest of his soda. "Shit, Reid. I've been thinking about ditching the job and joining you guys full-time. I'd rather move couches than tally numbers. I'm so sick of tax season."

"Um, it's May." Reid felt like a moron when Evan shot him a look.

"Because we only worry about taxes through April fifteenth? Do you have any idea how many extensions were filed this year? And Vanessa Campbell-McCauley, you remember my workaholic boss, has been busting my balls on a regular basis. She is the biggest pain in my ass…"

Reid felt for the guy. Evan's boss, the blond dragon, whom Reid had once made the mistake of complimenting within his cousin's earshot, seemed to live to make Evan miserable.

"I thought she was grooming you to be a partner someday. That's a good thing, right?"

"She is. And yes, you'd think being a partner would be good," Evan said, misery in every word. "But she's relentless. She's ten steps ahead of everyone and thinks we should all have her work ethic and her brain. I mean, I'd like to have a social life at some point. I'm looking down the end of forty soon."

"You're thirty-one, Evan. Relax."

"Ha. Easy for you to say."

"I'm thirty-four. If anything, I'm closer to forty than you are."

"Yeah, but you're your own boss."

"And I work harder because of it. You know that." They paused while the waitress dropped off their order of monster fries. Covered in shredded brisket, gouda cheese, and carb-loaded baddies, the treat was just the thing Reid needed to focus on work once more.

"I think the PR woman is right," he said, trying not to imagine Naomi in nothing but that fiery-red hair. "We need to manage our growth now before we're overwhelmed."

Evan nodded. "That makes sense. After you mentioned her, I googled her firm and made a few phone calls. It's small, like she said. But the companies she's worked with can't say enough good things about her."

Reid wanted to find some reason to turn her down. His attraction to Naomi bothered him. He had no room for a woman right now, not when so many lives depended on him. It had been bad enough when he'd felt responsible for Cash. But now he had Hector and Lafayette, Finley, Martin, Tim, and now Jordan relying on the business to pay the bills.

A familiar constriction made him tense, and he dropped his fork, no longer hungry.

"Relax, man. It'll work out." Surprised to see Evan so upbeat after his talk of hating work, Reid studied his cousin.

"What?" Evan asked and motioned for another drink.

"Why are you suddenly so relaxed? Was that soda spiked with something?" Reid shook his head. "Lightweight."

"Ass. No. I'm just excited about growing the business. See, if we do this right, I'll start tapering off at work, taking on more responsibility with you guys."

Evan's gray eyes, so like Reid's, brightened. "The thought of not filing hundreds of returns or enduring more meetings with Vanessa is making me giddy. I swear I'd almost rather go back out on a field op."

Reid chuckled. "Yeah, sometimes I miss the Marine Corps. Weeks spent out in the field. Qualifying on the range. Time overseas in a foreign country where they weren't firing back at us. Ah, those were the days."

"Tell me about it."

Reid studied his cousin. "Why'd you get out so soon after joining?"

"Reid, I was in for six years." Evan shrugged. "Being an officer had its perks. I loved the Corps, but life in logistics got tedious. I had planned to follow you two into the infantry, but it didn't work out that way."

"Radio recon, not infantry," Reid corrected him, as he always did when his cousin lumped him in with the ground pounders.

"Yeah, yeah, same difference. You know, at first, logistics appealed to me. I thought it would be a better job to transition from if I ever got out, even though I'd planned to make the Marines a career. But I never thought I'd get so tired of taking orders from people."

"What did you know about orders, Lieutenant?"

"That's Captain to you. But hey, life as lowly lieutenant, then captain, wasn't much better."

Reid didn't comment. Though he hadn't been frontline, Evan had caught some shit in the trenches and had the mental scars to prove it.

"So why accounting then?" Reid asked. "I always wondered that. Didn't Aunt Jane push you toward business?"

"Yeah. She and Dad were so determined that I get

my freakin' MBA it about drove me nuts. Dad was a business guy. Great. Didn't mean I had to be." He gave a ghost of a grin. "They had a shit fit when I followed you guys into the Marine Corps. Dad used to complain to Uncle Charles all the time about how you two were a bad influence." He sobered quickly. "Unfortunately, Uncle Charles always agreed." *Especially if it had to do with Cash* remained unspoken.

Reid didn't want to think about his father because his emotions were conflicted. It was tough to a love a man he'd also hated. "Don't we have better things to be talking about? Like what we can do with the budget?"

Evan groaned. "Not more numbers."

Sometime later, Reid returned home. Cash hadn't yet arrived, and Reid knew better than to stay up waiting for him. Though Cash was his older brother, Reid had always felt responsible for the poor guy whose father had hated him no matter what he did. Hell, Cash had only to breathe too loudly for their old man to pound a few "manners" into him. And Cash would take any beating, verbal or physical, to prevent Reid from getting the same.

Reid hated the memories. Hated that his mother had been too involved in her own little world to care for them the way she should have. Or that his parents treated him like the golden child while shitting all over Cash.

Reid felt too wound up to relax, so he threw on some workout gear and left on a run. The brisk May evening air did him good, and he increased his pace around the quaint neighborhood to Green Lake. Phinney Ridge was a better area than he and Cash could afford, but an old Marine Corps buddy owned a bunch of properties in town and had rented to them at a hell of a price.

Not too proud to take the offer, especially considering how Reid had helped the guy when he'd been in a jam during his time in service, Reid and Cash enjoyed the safe, genteel neighborhood while being within a few miles of both Green Lake and Ballard.

Putting on a burst of speed, Reid wondered what to do about his brother. On the outside, Cash had a lot going for him. Big, handsome, strong, a powerhouse at the gym and with the ladies. Yet on his own, he continually fucked up. Booted from one job or another because he scared his employers, refusing to be tactful when he saw screwups by pointing out wrongdoing without a care for repercussions.

That was Cash, a superhero without the sense to ease his way out of dangerous situations. He was a grenade that took out everything in its path, whereas Reid took care of problems one shot at a time. Only hitting the target, not everything within a fifty-mile radius.

The run did him good, and Reid was feeling it as he returned. The shower he took was even better, or it would have been if a stray thought hadn't entered his mind. Like what Naomi Starr would look like covered in nothing but running water.

He swore under his breath, now stimulated when he'd been trying to relax.

That damn woman had acted like lightning, awakening his body from a long hibernation. Sure, Reid dated occasionally. But not lately, with the business being all-consuming for so long. Taking care of Cash and the others, making sure Evan wasn't disappointed at believing in them. Sometimes he felt the weight of the world on his shoulders. He just couldn't handle having to be there for a woman as well.

Unless she only wanted a few orgasms. That he could handle.

A glance down at himself showed he could handle it all too well right now.

Naomi had worn her long, wine-red hair down, curling over her perfect breasts. She had to be at least a C-cup. He'd wanted badly to reach out and cup each mound in his hands. Not at all professional or civilized. But damn, he'd wanted to.

She had turquoise-blue eyes, a mysterious shade that had seemed to change while they'd spoken. Reid had always been a sucker for intelligence, and the woman had that in spades. Looks, smarts, a body to die for...

He groaned and took himself in hand, pleasuring himself to the fantasy of that gorgeous redhead on her knees doing anything he wanted.

Reid sagged moments later, wishing he had someone to help him get off. But his hand saved him a lot of aggravation in the long run. No one to disappoint if he didn't call or text enough. No one demanding his time when he was too damn tired to go out after a fourteen-hour workday.

And no one to be jealous when he went to help his brother out of yet another jam.

No, Reid didn't need to be involved with anyone at the moment. First, he had to get the business squared away. Then maybe he'd find a serious lover.

And it sure the hell wouldn't be one he worked with. He snorted. After all that talk warning Cash away from Jordan, would Reid make the same mistake?

No way in hell.

Chapter 4

No way in hell his body should be so keyed up at eight thirty in the morning sitting across from Naomi Starr.

Two days after first meeting the woman, Reid swore under his breath and subtly uncrossed his legs, growing uncomfortable. He looked away from Naomi at her desk in her tidy little office and took a moment to glance around.

The place fit her. Frames of local businesses accented the slate-blue walls of her office. Bold, clean lines in her furniture and in the way the small room seemed to be so much bigger than it actually was indicated a woman who knew how to show her best side. And that was to say nothing of the woman herself.

Naomi sat in a navy jacket and form-fitting skirt that reached her knees. Personally, Reid wouldn't have minded if she'd hiked the thing higher because damn, but she had some nice legs. The understated blouse she wore under the jacket covered her from the neck down while giving tantalizing impressions of the full breasts beneath.

Reid had always been a breast and leg man, and Naomi continued to tick off all the boxes on his "ideal woman" list.

Fortunately, a knock at the door interrupted them before Reid got caught staring.

"Sorry," her assistant apologized. "Naomi, I need your help with something that's urgent. It won't take long."

Naomi frowned.

"Take care of whatever you need to," Reid said to her and held up the decadent coffee she'd offered him. "I'm just going to nurse this for a while." Because he needed the caffeine. Who the hell scheduled appointments before nine if they didn't have to?

She gave him a tight smile. "I'm sorry about this. I'll be right back, and while I'm gone, take a look at my proposal." She pushed a blue folder toward him.

He looked through her ideas, agreeing with the direction she intended. Yet his concentration remained on the woman who'd left as well as the amazing cup of coffee he'd been given upon arrival.

In his office, when Reid had asked if he could get her something to drink, he would have offered her bottled water or some crap coffee from the tiny refreshment station he'd insisted they add to the office. It was a step up from car-dealer coffee but several steps down from Storyville, one of his favorite coffee bars in the city. Naomi could give them a run for their money with her gourmet coffee, served in a fancy ceramic mug. He'd also noticed the spring water in the hallway in a water cooler she no doubt paid through the nose for.

Probably why her fees were a little on the high side. To him, at least. According to Evan, she had more than reasonable prices for what she offered. Her clients couldn't say enough about all she'd done to help their businesses. The woman was a workhorse, no doubt about it. They had that in common. And, if he wasn't mistaken, a mutual attraction.

Or that could just be wishful thinking.

She returned, appearing as poised and put-together as she'd been before the interruption. "I'm so sorry for that. A new client panicked about something we'd already agreed upon then wouldn't speak to anyone but me about it." Naomi shrugged. "But it's no big deal. Now, back to you."

He watched her saunter back to her seat, enjoying the sight. When she sat and faced him, he kept his gaze above her chin at all times.

She nodded to the folder open in front of him. "This is the proposal I've outlined for you. Like I said, we'll do three months and revisit the terms. But I think this is what you need to get started."

He glanced back down at it. "Looks solid. I wanted to ask what you thought about TV ads too."

"They can be expensive but worth it. I'd definitely like to see your people on television. Cash and Hector stood out on the news because they sure as heck grabbed my attention. If I needed movers, I'd hire them from that segment alone."

Of course she would. Cash had that kind of presence about him. Competent, protective, mission-oriented... So long as he kept his big mouth shut, they might make things work.

"Yeah, about that. I've had a request for an interview, a spotlight on our company."

She grabbed a pen and pad of paper. "When did you schedule it for?"

"I didn't, not yet. Thought I'd see what you thought."

"Do it." She stared at him. "From the small group I saw at your office, you'll represent well. Now, if you're all photogenic too, we're golden. We know Hector and Cash look great on camera. Hector is much more charming than your brother. As appealing as your brother may be as the strong type, he's not exactly silent. A lot of censoring in that piece the news ran on your company."

"Tell me something I don't know." Her continuous stare made him a little uncomfortable. "Something wrong?"

"Hmm. I think we need to brand you as a family company first. You and your brother, together, would really work to sell Vets on the Go!"

"My cousin's also a partner. We all kind of look alike, so you'd see the family resemblance."

"Even better." She made a few notes. "So we highlight you three, then pepper the interview with your brawny, good-looking employees. And bam, you've already made an impression on the thousands of single women needing to move."

"Now we're targeting women?"

"Yes. And families and veterans themselves. You have an original appeal, and not just because you're handsome." She flushed and hurried to add, "And by you, I mean your team and your business."

"So I'm not handsome then?" he asked to tease her, loving that blush.

Naomi cleared her throat and said dryly, "I think you're well aware of your looks. My point is we use every weapon in your arsenal. You have fit, appealing employees who've served our country. That's three for three. Now looking at your rates…"

She swiveled her computer monitor so he could see

it. "Leo, our data guru, sent me a comparison to see who your major competitors are."

"We went through this before we started the company," he said.

"Bear with me." They went over more numbers, enough to make his head spin. In certain demographics, they seemed to hit the mark while missing entirely in others. "So you see, if you raise this rate but drop this fee, you'll still come out even."

"That's if this marketing works."

She gave him another of those penetrating looks that caused the sparks in his belly to start up and dance. "Oh, it'll work."

"Confident in your abilities, huh?"

"You know what, Reid? I am. Now, I've got the same issues as most women." Her charming smile disarmed him. "I often wonder, does this outfit make me look fat? Is my hair the mess I think it is? Will he call like he said he would?" She turned uber-professional between one breath and the next. "But one thing I'm not is deluded about my professional abilities. I won't promise what we can't deliver. I know how to help businesses grow and flourish, and yes, I'm *damn good* at what I do."

He believed her a hundred percent. "Okay then." He studied her right back, noticing the plump curve of her lips. The sparkle in her blue eyes.

He took his pen and signed the contract, then pushed the folder back to her, irritated that he had to work to maintain control, aware of his racing pulse. Reid was man enough to handle being attracted to a beautiful woman. Didn't mean he had to follow his dick where it led. "But for the record, the outfit is flattering, your hair is beautiful, and if he's dumb enough not to call back, he doesn't deserve you." He stood before he made a bigger fool of himself. "I'll set up the interview with the news station and let you know."

"Ah, right. Good." She cleared her throat. "Once I have that information, we can meet again to prep you for it. That, and I have a few more ideas I've been considering."

"Great." He just stared down at her.

"Any questions for me?" she asked, sounding way too perky.

"Yes." He stared some more, until that bright smile dimmed. He let her see his attraction, let her know that yes, he did find her smokin' hot.

"Your question?" she asked and licked her lips. Her gaze dropped to his mouth for a second before shooting back to his eyes.

Gratified to know she felt the same chemistry, he winked at her and saw her blush again. "My question is this… Where do you get your coffee? Because that cup I had was amazing."

———

Naomi stammered out a response, not sure exactly what she said. Reid nodded and tapped his temple. "Making a mental note." He glanced at his watch. "Oh crap. Look at the time. Gotta go. I'll talk to you soon." He left before she could pick up her jaw from the floor.

Good lord. That look he'd shot her had singed her ovaries. So it wasn't just her feeling that connection between them. What a terrible thing to learn. Then again, the man hadn't made a move. If he could remain strictly professional, so could she. So *would* she. Heck, she'd more than learned her lesson with Tanner.

Liz popped her head in the door. Thirty-seven, a frizzy blond, and a no-nonsense mother of five, the woman could manage a circus with one hand tied behind her back and one eye closed. "*That's* our client? Hold on while I wipe the drool." Liz exaggerated wiping the corner of her mouth. "And I thought the guys on TV were hot."

"I'm thinking of telling Reid he should open up a modeling agency instead," Naomi teased.

"No kidding." After Naomi shared a brief rundown of her notes, Liz nodded. "Oh yeah, for sure. If I had to pick someone to help me move, I'd call them. You're trusting a stranger with your prized possessions, you want to choose someone trustworthy. Good-looking doesn't hurt either."

"That's what I was thinking." She texted Leo and thanked him for his data, which had helped a ton. "Liz, after my talk with Natalie, did she calm down and let you help her?"

"Finally. You have the magic touch." Liz sighed and flopped into the chair across from her. "We really need to hire more help. We're getting busy, I mean, *really* busy."

"I know." Naomi felt the heat of excitement, the challenge to succeed driving her. For the first time in a long time, hope, not desperation, fueled her. She could feel it. Starr PR was ready to move to the next level. "I've talked to two possible candidates, friends from the old firm who want to jump ship." And didn't that give her the warm fuzzies.

"Best move I ever made," Liz agreed. "I probably

would have stayed at PP&R if Mike Rogers hadn't kept taking credit for all my work."

"He's such an ass."

"So is Tanner, I hear."

Naomi sat straighter. "Oh?"

Liz laughed. "Don't even try acting casual. You should hear what I'm hearing." Liz leaned forward. "Tanner's been having trouble with some of his new hires. The people there just aren't as competent as you and I were. Rumor has it the real talent is fleeing since no one seems to advance in the company unless they're related to the partners."

"That's too bad, and I mean that. PP&R was a good place to work. I blame myself for screwing up a good thing. Literally." Since Liz knew about Naomi's past, Naomi had no problem confiding in her friend and employee. Liz would have been a full partner had she been able to afford the buy-in. But then, she hadn't wanted the responsibility for the firm either. More than happy to play her part assisting with the clients, Liz was right where she wanted to be and a godsend Naomi intended to keep as happy as possible.

"Look, we both know it wasn't the smartest thing you could have done." Trust Liz not to sugarcoat anything. "But Tanner should have been more professional too. So you had a relationship? You were both handling it just fine until you started outperforming him at work. Then he turned into a sniveling worm who couldn't deal with a successful partner. Let's say you'd left on your own, separating work from your relationship. Do you really think he'd have been happy if you made it big, still outshining him?"

"Sadly, no." Naomi scowled. "But it's such a waste of a man. He had so much potential."

"Too bad he turned out to be a douche."

Naomi stared at petite, businesslike Liz with her no-frills black glasses and wiry blond hair and had to laugh. "Yeah, a total douche."

"Makes you wonder how a man like Reid Griffith would respond in the same circumstances though, doesn't it?"

"Yes. No," Naomi hurriedly denied. "I learned my lesson. No dating coworkers, clients, or bosses."

"Ever?"

"Ever."

Liz snorted. "Yeah, you keep telling yourself that. Good thing our new client didn't see you staring at his ass as he left."

"Hey, I can look. Just not touch."

"So sad." Liz shook her head. "And you, just squandering your best years. When's the last time you went out on a date?"

"Yes, yes, I'm lame and miserable." Naomi tapped her desk with her pretty red nails. "Now back to what's really important—has Tanner put on weight? Who's he dating? And who's planning to leave? We need to start making some calls."

Liz held up her phone and smiled. "Already ahead of you, boss. I have pictures too."

"Oh, nice."

"But one thing. That coffee you mentioned to Reid? Hate to break it to you, but that Jamaican Blue Mountain was nowhere near the Peet's blend you told him about." Liz gave her a sly grin. "Frazzled you, did he?"

"Oh shush and tell me Tanner got fat."

"Sorry to disappoint you." Liz showed her the phone with a picture of Tanner at a meeting. "But it's funny, looking at him, then putting his picture side by side with Reid, I can't tell who's better looking." Which was saying something, because Tanner, jerk that he was, had *fine* written all over him.

Naomi studied Tanner's picture. "On looks alone, I might have to give it to Tanner. Let's face it. He's beautiful. But on sheer sex appeal and personality, it's no contest—Reid. Then again, I'd award the Grinch over Tanner Michael Ryan."

Liz shared more gossip, but Naomi was stuck on how much more attractive she found Reid, when she shouldn't have been thinking about the man so much. And not when she had other clients to get to. Hmm. Maybe she should hand him over to Liz after all…

Reid met Cash at the gym for a workout. He'd tried several places when they'd gotten back to the States, but this one was run by a former Marine and it was close, in Green Lake. Cash liked it, and after turning in his membership at a pricier gym, Reid had signed on at Jameson's.

The members seemed normal, not too affluent and not thugs rolling people for money on the way out. Plus most of the men working out seemed to want to get in shape. He didn't notice a huge hookup atmosphere. Then again, Reid used the place to work out, not search for sex partners.

After sweating like a demon on a five-mile run that did nothing to cure him of the memory of Naomi Starr in that blouse, Reid moved to the free weights, only to find Cash arguing with some guy about training methods.

"Look, I know what I'm doing. We had this same argument a week ago," Cash growled at the guy.

Not as large as Cash but just as fierce in his expression, the man, wearing a Jameson's Gym red T-shirt, glared back. "I didn't say you don't know what you're doing. I'm only trying to help you, moron." Whoa, not great customer service at Jameson's, apparently.

"Fuck you."

"Back at ya, shit for brains. You're doing it wrong, Old School. Get a clue."

Cash took a step in the guy's direction and clenched his fists. "Say that again."

"Why? Need me to break down those small words into even smaller ones?" The guy smirked.

Reid hoped his brother wouldn't get himself kicked out of yet another place. Because Reid liked it here. "Cash, what the hell?"

Cash turned, and Reid noticed quite a few women alternating looks between him and the trainer...and now Reid. A few guys gave them wary expressions, and someone bolted down the hall. Probably to grab security.

"Oh, hey, Reid." Cash nodded to him, seeming not at all bothered. "Check out this asswipe. Thinks he knows more than I do about what I should be benching."

The guy scowled. "Again, not what I said." He turned and ignored Cash. "Hi. I'm Gavin Donnigan. I happen to *work here*, and I *train people* for a living."

Reid took his hand. "Name's Reid. I have no idea who this man is, giving you a hard time. I'm just here to work out."

"Reid, seriously?" Cash crossed his arms over his chest, showcasing a sweaty T-shirt and ever-growing biceps.

Gavin grinned. "Your last name wouldn't happen to be Griffith?"

"Nope."

Cash glared at him. "Fuck you too, Bro."

Gavin laughed. "Hey, man. I have a brother just like this one. Yeah, your best bet is to just pretend you don't know him."

Reid looked from Gavin to Cash, sensing he'd missed something. "You know Cash?"

"Met him overseas years ago. We hung out at some of the same shitty places."

"Ah. I'm guessing Marine Corps?"

"Yep. 1stMARDIV. 1st Recon Battalion. You?"

They made small talk about their time in the service, ignoring Cash, who moved away to exercise without Gavin's interference. Talk turned to Reid's workouts, and Gavin suggested a few moves Reid hadn't considered that would increase his mass without putting too much bulk on him. His shirts strained at the seams as it was.

"Yeah, that'll totally help you get stronger and leaner." Gavin nodded. "It's great for runners. Your brother—sorry, I mean, that guy you don't know—isn't sticking to the workout I set up for him. The one he asked me for a month ago, the dick. He's going to get even bigger than he is now."

"Is that possible?" Reid said, loudly enough to be overheard by his brother. "I mean, his head is so fat he can barely fit through the door as it is."

Cash grinned. "Ass."

Gavin chuckled.

A large, muscular man with a military-short haircut and angry glint in his eye entered the room and made a beeline for them. "What's the problem?" he barked. Reid looked from the guy to Cash and wondered who might come out on top if the argument turned physical.

Gavin held his hands up in surrender. "No problem, Mac. Just showing this talented Marine how to maximize his training."

Mac relaxed. "Oh great. Another devil dog. Hey, man." He introduced himself as the owner of the place and a retired Marine, though the guy didn't look that old. He must have read Reid's surprise because he said, "Medical discharge. Took a hit through the knee that never healed right."

"That sucks."

"Yeah." Mac looked over at Cash and raised a brow. "Who's that monster? Your brother?"

"Not according to rumor," Gavin teased.

Reid sighed. "He's all mine." He winced at their grins. "Listen, if he gets a little, ah—"

"Argumentative? Surly? Obnoxious?" Gavin said, his voice rising with each word until Cash looked over at him and gave him the finger.

"Yeah, all that. If he's a little much, just let me know, and I'll talk to him. We like this place. Hate to get kicked out because of a bad day and some attitude." He'd make sure to talk to Cash later, regardless.

"No problem." Mac clapped Gavin on the back, and the big guy shuddered. "If I didn't throw *this* guy out, I won't toss your brother. And trust me, Gavin was a mess."

Gavin gave Mac a sour look. "Thanks so much."

"No problem. Nice to meet you, Reid. Anytime you want to stop in and talk shop, my office is down the hall." Mac walked away, and Reid noticed a slight limp.

"He'd still be in if he hadn't gotten shot." Gavin shrugged. "What can you do?" The conversation turned local and to some people they both knew.

"Chris Jennings? He's a member too?" Reid asked. "He gave me a helluva deal on the house we're renting."

"Yeah. Guy is loaded now that he hit big in the tech field. But when I knew him, he was a nerdy little grunt." Gavin grinned. "I used to kick his ass on a regular basis on our daily runs."

"So did I." Reid laughed. "Hey, anytime you want to grab a beer, let me know."

"I will." Gavin paused. "Reid, you know, I think I saw your brother on TV the other night. Did he save some kid from getting knifed?"

"I did," Cash boomed. "Vets on the Go! kicks ass."

"Our moving company," Reid explained. "We only hire vets and do local moves. It's a win-win because I get to boss my big brother around and keep him in line at the same time."

Cash laughed. "Right. We all know I'm in charge."

Gavin leaned in and said, "Just let him think so. I do that with my brother all the time."

They shared a conspiratorial grin, then Reid was tortured by both Gavin and Cash as he tried to follow the workout Gavin had given his brother, just to test it out. A tall redhead walked by in short shorts and a tank top, bringing Naomi instantly to his mind. But the redhead didn't have the right color eyes or the right build. Didn't keep Cash from looking though.

"Reid, that's pathetic," Gavin said. "Lift like you got a pair, man. Or do you want people to think you were in the Air Force?"

Next to them, an older man frowned. "Hey."

"Sorry. I meant the Army."

"What's the difference?" Cash muttered, and Gavin did his best to calm a different older man down.

"And who said you could stop lifting?" Gavin asked.

"Ten more reps at this weight, Reid. Let's go." Cash watched with narrowed eyes.

Reid groaned. Nothing like getting heckled by Marines while trying to forget a certain PR professional's appeal.

He worked harder. And pulled a muscle.

Chapter 5

THE NEXT AFTERNOON, AFTER FITTING IN TWO MORE LOCAL moves for the week's end, Reid gathered Evan, Cash, the Jacksons, and Jordan in the conference room to meet with Naomi. He'd scheduled with the TV station to do the interview that evening, though it would air the following week, and Naomi wanted them all to be ready.

As usual, everyone looked to Cash until it became clear he intended to sit back and let Reid run the show. Reid didn't mind, because the headache that was to come would sound better coming from his mouth than his brother's.

"Thanks for coming, guys." Reid meant that. Though he'd be sure to pay them for their time, the evening hadn't been mandatory, especially not after a full day's work. "The shirts look good on you." Everyone had dressed in their Vets on the Go! T-shirts and jeans. Reid had to admit the team looked strong, professional. He liked Jordan being there as well. Naomi agreed, saying it made them appear more approachable, inclusive. And hell, Jordan was cute.

"Naomi's going to go over a few points." He glared a warning at Cash, who glared back. The big bastard hadn't wanted to be included in the promotional stuff.

Naomi smiled at everyone. She wore another suit that set off her killer body. Reid had assumed his "nothing matters but the business" face before joining the others.

But it took effort to pretend not to be affected by the woman. To his amusement, she seemed to be acting the same with him.

He felt an unspoken challenge lingering between them, as if to see who would cave to the attraction first. Or he might be deluded.

Either might be true at this point.

Before Naomi could speak, Cash said, "I don't see why we all need to be here. Reid, they want to talk to you, the face of the company."

"Yeah," Evan muttered, looking tired.

"We all know I'm best when I'm not talking."

"Ain't that the truth," Hector said, to which everyone had a laugh.

"You're here," Naomi hurriedly cut in, "because you're all necessary for the segment. I talked with the reporter interviewing you. She's a friend of mine. Together, we brainstormed a terrific piece that will not only get the station kudos for its public interest story, but will also generate your team more revenue with more clients."

"Just what we need," Reid said. "Oh, and Evan, don't let me forget to talk to you after the meeting about a few expenses."

"Of course I'll stay late. I apparently have no life." Evan popped an antacid and gulped it down with coffee.

"Gross." Cash made a face, then grinned at the finger Evan shot him.

Naomi looked from Evan to Cash to Reid. "You three are perfect. All Marines, correct?"

They nodded.

"And the rest of the team looks terrific. We'll take

you in for makeup and a little sprucing, but don't worry. We're just using the bulk of you for the photo op. Same with Evan and Cash, to an extent. Reid, you're the mouthpiece of the company. But in case the interviewer pulls any of the rest of you aside, I have some buzzwords you can throw around."

Jordan frowned. "Excuse me. Why am I here, exactly? I just started three days ago."

Naomi answered, "You're an attractive female who served her country and now works for Vets on the Go! We need you, Hector, and Lafayette to show yourselves as capable and friendly."

"Good luck with that," Cash chimed in.

Lafayette groaned. "Nah, man. She's meaning diversity. Get a shot of the black guys and the chick to be all inclusive."

"Shouldn't we have a token gay on the team then?" Cash grumbled.

"What am I? Chopped liver?" Lafayette asked.

Everyone paused.

Reid sighed. "Not now, Lafayette. You can hassle Cash about it later."

"Oh, okay."

Cash turned to Reid, his eyes wide. "You knew Lafayette was gay and didn't tell me?"

"Why is this relevant?" Reid didn't have the patience to deal with his brother now.

Lafayette and Hector nodded. "Exactly," Hector said, then turned to Cash with a more serious expression. "Is this a problem?"

"Hell yes, it's a problem!"

"Here we go." Reid pinched the bridge of his nose.

Out of the corner of his eye, he saw Evan grinning and Naomi and Jordan glued to the spectacle as if watching a horror movie. Unexpectedly, Lafayette relaxed while his brother tensed as if ready to throw down.

"What the fuck is your problem?" Hector growled.

"I should have been told, that's my problem." Cash completely ignored Lafayette as he started in on Reid. "You said I make all the decisions about personnel."

"So knowing Lafayette is gay would have impacted you hiring him?"

"No, jackass. But we don't keep secrets. Who cares if he's gay? He's not all that bright, but he's a hard worker."

"What?" Now Lafayette frowned, but Hector had lost his hostility.

"I mean, he and Hector could make more money working for one of the bigger companies, but they know we're better people."

"Explain 'not that bright.'" Lafayette glared.

Cash spoke over him. "You just look at the twins and you know they can lift a mountain without trying hard."

Jordan turned to Lafayette. "Is lifting mountains a thing?"

"Not in my world. In Cash's? Who knows?"

"But I should have known," Cash continued.

Naomi tried to intervene. "Perhaps we should get back on track—"

"No," Reid interrupted, amused and annoyed at the same time. "Look, Cash, you might be the muscle behind the operation, but I'm the brains."

Evan cleared his throat.

"Evan and I are the brains. Don't stress it that you

don't know Lafayette's sexual proclivities, Jordan's shoe size, or Finley's latest gambling fixation," Reid said, seeing Finley walk into the room as he apologized for being late. "And no, guys. You're not the diversity package. Naomi wanted all the pretty people for the shoot."

"Ah. So no on Tim and Martin," Hector said with a laugh.

"Actually, I had planned on using the whole team, but Tim and Martin didn't want to be included."

Cash frowned. "I didn't want to be included either."

"Oh my God." Evan rubbed his temples. "Shut up and deal, Cash. Can we please get on with this? I have more work to get back to after we wrap this up."

"This is going to take some time." Naomi frowned. "You do know the interview and photo shoot are tonight."

"Cash said the interview was Monday afternoon."

Cash paused. "I don't remember saying that. Oh, wait, I was talking about another interview, the one on that reality TV show I'm hooked on. That chick is going to be in Pioneer Square Monday afternoon. I'm totally going to see it. With any luck, she'll pop off and punch her sister in the mouth."

"What show is this?" Jordan asked, sounding interested.

Evan growled, and Reid fought a smile. It took a lot to rile his cousin. Once again, Cash managed the nearly impossible. He glanced at Naomi, wondering what she thought of the chaos, and took comfort in her large eyes and the questioning look she shot him.

He nodded. "Yep. It's always like this. You still sure you want to work with us?"

—◦◦◦—

Naomi had to fight not to laugh. In amusement or frustration, she couldn't be sure. God, did any of these people know the meaning of the word *focus*? Reid sat back with a wry grin as his brother regaled the table with the exploits of some real women of some random city she couldn't care less about. The issue of Lafayette's sexuality had come and gone faster than she'd been able to track. She'd been about to step in, and to step all over Cash's homophobia, when the big guy had shifted all his anger toward his brother for not telling him about the issue. Being gay didn't seem to matter at all, but not knowing something his brother did bothered Cash.

Huh. She didn't know how to process that yet.

Watching Jordan interact with the crew was telling. Instead of the calm, levelheaded feminine presence Naomi had been hoping for, Jordan seemed like one of the guys. Finley remained quiet but amused, a constant smile on his face as he studied everyone and flipped a coin over his knuckles, back and forth. He saw her watching and made the quarter disappear.

Then he opened up his other hand and showed her the coin.

"Great. We can hire you out for parties," she said.

He guffawed.

A sudden lull hit the table, and she hurried to speak before someone else found something not important to talk about for ten minutes. "Okay, everyone, focus."

"Hold all questions to the end," Reid added.

"Yes, that." Naomi stood, needing to feel bigger and thus in charge of this chaotic meeting. "All you people have to do is look trustworthy. Hector, Lafayette, smile a lot and flex those amazing muscles. Finley, look charming and don't stare overlong at women's breasts or butts."

"Hey." He bit back a grin.

"Jordan, just act sweet and professional."

"But—"

"I don't care. Pretend." Naomi turned away from Jordan and zoned in on Cash. "You. You'll stand with Evan and Reid and look brotherly and united. Don't ask, just do."

Cash closed his mouth on his question.

"Now, those buzzwords for you in case anyone asks." She rattled off a bunch of key phrases like *integrity*, *dedication*, *attention to detail*, all words she knew they understood having served in the military, and added more target marketing jargon to make them appear trustworthy and appealing.

"The photo shoot starts in an hour by the truck Finley should have pulled out back. The interview should actually air next week. Now, does anyone have any questions?"

"Wow, she's good," Lafayette said in a loud whisper.

Finley nodded. "Come on, guys. Let's leave the bosses to get lectured while we get the props ready."

Once the group left, she faced off with the Griffiths. Apart, they were impressive, but together, they could be overwhelming. Of the three of them, she found Reid the most appealing. Intelligence shone in his gray eyes, and his full lips curved in a smile that gave him a polished charm, complementing the strength in his tall, muscular frame. Smaller than Cash but no less attractive, Reid seemed confident and sexy all at the same time. Cash had a brooding intensity, all muscle and command. There was no denying his appeal. And Evan, despite not realizing they'd be taking pictures tonight, looked completely put-together gorgeous. He possessed a smoother, gentler charisma that would make any woman with a pulse take a second look, though he didn't seem to have Reid's intensity or Cash's boldness.

"Evan, thanks for coming. I'm so sorry for the confusion." She took in his attire—dark slacks and a white button-down shirt. The handsome executive personified. Though Reid wore a similar button-down shirt with blue jeans, he looked more dangerous somehow. Rougher and exciting.

And off-limits.

So sad she had to keep reminding herself of that.

"No problem." Evan gave her a tired smile. "Just tell me where you want me and what to say."

"See?" Reid turned to Cash. "*That's* how you deal with the situation. Follow some freakin' orders."

"Whatever." Cash grunted, then sat back, glaring at Reid and Naomi.

"Hey, don't give me that look," she said, amused and not at all threatened. For some reason, the Griffith brothers—and cousin—looked like they could take on an armed gang without a problem yet gave the impression they wouldn't hurt one whisker on a kitten. Fanciful, but she felt it all the same. "Okay, guys. Let's get this show on the road."

Cash gave a loud groan.

Once he and Evan walked outside the warehouse to join the others, Reid joined Naomi and stared down at her notes. "Any more advice for me?"

She shook her head and turned, caught unaware that they stood so close. She faltered when one of her heels wobbled, and Reid caught her.

They both froze, staring at the other. She wondered if he felt the heat between them and thanked God her blazer covered her now-erect nipples. What was it about this man that put her every nerve on alert?

His gaze slipped to her mouth before finding her eyes again, and she found his light-gray stare unnerving. Talk about intense.

"You okay?" he asked, his voice like silk.

"F-fine. Sorry." She went against every instinct she possessed and took a step back, disappointed he let her. "Thanks."

"Yeah." He continued to stare at her and tucked his hands in his pockets.

She refused to look down at his jeans, not wanting to know if he'd been as affected as she still was by that simple touch.

"Man, you are *really* pretty."

She felt her cheeks heat. "Reid."

"Just sayin'." He smiled, and she wanted to fan herself. "So, any advice, Starr PR?"

"Just be yourself." She smiled back, pleased when he seemed entranced. "Your interviewer is Rhonda Peters, and I'm sure she'll be in love with you five seconds after meeting you."

His grin turned cocky. "Oh?"

"Please. You're attractive, and you know it." *There, I got it off my chest.* "Which is terrific when trying to sell something. You see a commercial with a gorgeous woman who barely looks at a pair of jeans slung over the corner of her bed. But you remember that commercial for jeans because she stuck in your mind."

"Nah. If she's not wearing them, I'm not interested. Wait. I am, but not in the jeans." He laughed. "So, do you ever wear jeans?" He glanced at her suit. "I imagine you look great in anything."

Before she let herself be drawn into flirtation, she mentally backed away. "Perfect. Use that with Rhonda, but be careful, or she'll take you up on your offer."

"Offer?" His gaze cooled.

"That bedroom voice, the seduction. It's good, but you might want to throttle back how hard you push. Rhonda will be overwhelmed."

"But not you." He studied her. "What would it take to overwhelm you, Naomi?"

Hearing her name on those sexy lips threw her for a moment. Unfortunately, he noticed, because he gave her a sly smile.

"Me? Nothing. I never mix business with pleasure. Ever." Not anymore.

"Huh. Then it's a good thing you and I only have a three-month contract, isn't it?"

Wait. That hadn't gone as planned. "What?"

Reid laughed. "I'm kidding, Naomi. I agree. Sex and business don't go together. I'm just yanking your chain. You're too easy." He held up a hand. "To rile. Too easy to rile. Otherwise, you're a tough woman. Not meaning that in any way offensive either. Having to work for something makes it more worth it, you know?"

She scowled. "I'm losing track of this conversation. What exactly do you mean?"

Reid lost his smile. "Heck if I know. Look, in the

Marine Corps, fraternization is a no-no. You don't make friends with your boss, and you aren't supposed to sleep with him or her either. I get you. But Naomi, you're not my employee."

"You're my client," she said, working hard to mean what she said. "It's unprofessional to get romantically involved with you. I'm qualified for this job because I'm good at what I do, not because I'm pretty and can flirt a good game."

He frowned. "Don't think I ever said you weren't qualified."

She wanted to smack herself for going off on a tangent and blushed three shades of red. Her face hurt, it felt so hot. "God, ignore me. It's been a long day. I'm sorry for digressing. I just meant we need to keep things professional, that's all."

Reid studied her for a moment, then nodded. "Hey, I respect that." His voice gentled. "I respect you, you know. Don't worry. This will turn out just fine tonight."

She nodded, about to apologize for turning his comments into a diatribe about unfair work practices when Rhonda's team showed up.

Instead, she sighed. "Break a leg, Reid. And just remember, be yourself."

Unfortunately, he did just that and had Rhonda and half her team fawning all over him. The team photographed well, and the TV crew seemed enchanted with the twins and Jordan. Finley had the lead cameraman laughing and the sound guy demanding another trick with Finley's magical quarter.

Their outdoor shoot had also attracted several onlookers, and word spread that the heroic guys from that stopped burglary earlier in the week were on TV again.

The interview couldn't have gone better. The photographers loved working with everyone, and the large moving van advertised their contact number and name for everyone to see.

But Rhonda, damn her, was getting way too cozy with Reid. Which wasn't Naomi's problem.

Gah. What the hell is wrong with me? He's not a boyfriend or potential boyfriend. He's a client.

"Naomi, hey. How are you?"

She turned to see an old friend, one of the managers at the television station. "Morgan, great to see you."

She accepted a kiss on the cheek and gave him one in return.

A few years her senior, Morgan had taken her on two dates after her breakup from Tanner. Though he'd been a nice guy, there was no chemistry, and his kisses had been mediocre and rushed. Before anything went further, she'd broken it off, claiming too much on her plate to get serious.

Morgan had a terrific smile and a slender build. A nice guy. Maybe too nice. He grinned. "You get better looking every time I see you."

"Flatterer." She smiled. "So how have you been?"

They made small talk while she watched the Griffiths get their pictures taken and get interviewed. Cash put Reid in a headlock, which hadn't been in the script. But everyone laughed as more photos were taken. And of course, Cash's arms bulged while Reid slugged his brother in the gut where he could manage a punch.

The photo shoot turned into a huge party with

everyone enjoying themselves, then transitioned to Ringo's Bar down the street.

By that time, she'd agreed to meet Morgan there to talk some more. He claimed to have a lead on a business that needed her help, though his eyes told another story. But it made her feel better to put even more distance between herself and Reid, because she swore she could feel the man watching her with Morgan, even as she watched Rhonda not so casually wrap her hand around his arm.

Chapter 6

Reid couldn't decide what to do: take Rhonda up on her offer of no-strings-attached sex for the night or keep an eye on Naomi, who seemed way too distracted by the douche sucking up to her.

The guy looked like her type. A polished, smartly dressed, white-collar professional who would say all the right things. Not like Reid, who somehow sent Naomi messages that he didn't respect her and wanted nothing more than to do her and split.

Not that he didn't want to sex her up, but he'd never been an asshole when it came to women. Even Cash, as much of a Neanderthal as he could be, treated a woman like she mattered. They hadn't learned too much from their parents, but the *respect women* part had stuck.

"Oh wow. You're so built." Rhonda sat with him, singing his praises. She'd bought two rounds of drinks and continued to ask him personal questions. What did he like? Was he dating? Didn't he think blonds had more fun? And yeah, Rhonda was blond.

Sure, it felt good to know a woman liked the look of him. But Jesus, what was with all the groping? Cash would laugh his ass off if Reid complained about feeling like a piece of meat, but just because Reid was a guy didn't mean he didn't have personal boundaries.

He gave Rhonda a strained smile, doing his best

to focus on her and not on Naomi and bright-white-teeth guy at the bar. He didn't normally do bars on the weekends, but this particular Friday night was packed, which made it difficult to keep an eye on Naomi.

He'd started to think of this bar as his go-to. He and Cash had ventured to Ringo's a time or two after work, and some of the others had joined them. It was close enough to be convenient and a decent enough place to relax. Not too expensive, and he didn't stick to the floor when he walked or worry about getting rolled when he left.

He glanced around, saw Cash and the twins with Jordan, and didn't need to worry about Jordan being taken care of. "Little Army" would likely throw a fit to know Cash was looking out for her. Naomi, though, needed help. He didn't like the look of her "date."

"Would you like a refill?" Reid asked Rhonda. "On me this time, I insist," he said before she demanded to pay again.

Rhonda nodded.

"Be right back." He left and made his way to Naomi and the slobberer.

"Yeah, Ted is now trying to muscle in on me. I can't believe he thinks he can do a better job," the guy was whining.

"I agree. He's a weatherman. Why would he want to segue into upper management?" Naomi asked, her voice smooth, sultry.

He inwardly groaned, grateful for jeans that masked most of his arousal. Damn. He needed to get it together around the woman. He muscled in next to her, jarring a drunken frat boy out of the way. When the kid glared at him, Reid glared back, and the wannabe scary guy left in a hurry.

Reid gave the bartender his order, including a seltzer for himself. He was done drinking, trying to clear his head for what the rest of his night might look like. More desk work and part of the Mariners game at home if he could manage to stay awake long enough.

"Hey, I need to use the restroom. I'll be right back," Toothy said to Naomi, who nodded.

Once he left, Reid cleared his throat and leaned toward her to be heard over the noisy bar. "Your date for the night?"

She turned and blinked at him, and he wanted to stare into her eyes forever. They were so…blue. "Who? Morgan?" She laughed. "Nah. We're old friends."

The tension he hadn't been aware of carrying lightened.

"What about you?" She glanced over at Rhonda. "Enjoying yourself?"

"Eh. She's nice. But Rhonda's a little touchy-feely for my tastes."

Her eyes narrowed. "Oh?"

Naomi didn't seem to like that. But was that because she saw him as a client to protect or as a man she might consider something more than a friend?

Her respect speech had thrown him. He hadn't realized he'd made her feel uncomfortable, so he resolved to maintain his distance. Which made coming over here to talk to her a very bad idea. As were his thoughts about getting her naked and doing wicked things with her. So stupid, yet he couldn't keep himself from looking out for her.

I'm just taking care of my people. Naomi's nothing special, he told himself. Lying so very, very badly.

He let out a sigh.

"Do you want me to tell her to back off?" Naomi asked, her gaze hostile and centered on his table.

"Nah. I'm sorry for unloading. I don't want to ruin your date."

"It's not a date."

"Your meeting up with an old friend, then."

She shrugged. "It's no problem. I was getting ready to go home anyway." She stood from her bar stool and faltered on a heel, and he wondered just how much she'd had to drink.

Her date, Morgan of the Teeth, returned and frowned at Reid.

Naomi flashed a smile. "Morgan, meet Reid Griffith. Rhonda interviewed him tonight."

Morgan's frown left him, and he smiled. "Oh, hi. You know, your interview is going to generate a lot of business for you. That was terrific the way you guys helped Reva's grandson. We interviewed them as well."

"Great." Reid shook the guy's clammy hand. *So* not impressive. Reid had two inches on the guy too. Pathetic that that made him feel better, but, hey, he'd take what he could get. Morgan had a big job with a television station. Reid owned a floundering moving company.

"I'm going to save him from Rhonda." Naomi clutched Reid's arm for leverage, and he steadied her.

"Oh." Morgan frowned. "I can talk to her."

"I don't know that you should," Naomi said and bit her lower lip. "If you do, be careful."

Reid wished she wouldn't do that, because he was dying to kiss the sting away.

"Why shouldn't I talk to Rhonda?" Morgan asked.

Naomi leaned toward him and whispered something. Morgan brightened. "Yeah?"

"Jill's been throwing out hints too." She pointed to Rhonda's assistant nearby. "You've been warned."

Before Morgan could hustle to the table, Reid stopped him. "Could you take Rhonda her drink and apologize for me? I'm going to head out. My head's killing me."

"Sure, sure. No problem. Nice meeting you, Reid." Morgan grabbed the drink and left them both without a backward glance.

"What did you tell him?" Reid asked.

"That Rhonda, who he's had a massive crush on forever, is into him. I might have hinted that Jill wants him too, in case he strikes out with Rhonda."

"Really?"

"Really. Morgan's a popular guy at the station. And in my defense, though I like Rhonda, she can get a little clingy." Naomi glared at him.

"Hey, what did *I* do?" he asked, conscious of her hand wrapped around his forearm.

"She shouldn't have been all over you." Naomi sighed. "But that's Rhonda. She's a great journalist but a sucker for a pretty face."

He wondered if she realized what she was saying.

She continued, "I happen to know she really did used to like Morgan. Jill follows whatever Rhonda does, and she's had a thing for Morgan for years. The TV station is a little crazy, where everyone is sleeping with everyone." She grinned. "It's a hotbed for drama behind the cameras."

He laughed with her.

"Besides, Morgan is a nice guy. If Rhonda tells him no, he'll back off."

"Good. You know, if you ever told me no, I'd do the same." Hell. That had come off a little stronger than he'd intended.

"A gentleman too. Who'd have guessed?"

"Ha ha. Funny. Come on. I really do feel a headache coming on. Let me walk you out to your car."

They went first to his brother's table and watched Finley's antics while Jordan pointed out all his tricks. Finley pretended to be crushed that she'd caught on to him. Cash and Lafayette were having some deep discussion, and when Hector tried to butt in, they both told him to shut up. They smirked at him while Hector flipped them off before heading to the bar.

"I'm taking off," Reid announced. "Just wanted to say you guys did a great job. Cash has the schedule for this weekend. I'll be in and out if you need me."

Cash looked from him to Naomi. "You guys going home together?" Blunt as always.

The table grew quiet.

Naomi laughed. So much for Reid's ego. "Your brother thinks I need help to my car. So I'm letting him be a gentleman. It's good for his image."

Lafayette raised a brow. "Uh-huh. Sure. Image is key."

Jordan snorted. "Then maybe you should let Cash help you out. God knows he's one step above a troll. Reid though, he's cool. I don't think he's flipped anyone off all night."

The group found that amusing, though Cash didn't look so pleased with Jordan or his brother.

Reid had to laugh. "See? Jordan fits in perfectly. I made a good decision to hire her."

To which Cash replied, "*I* made the decision to hire her."

Jordan stared between the pair. "Cash did?" She snorted. "No way."

Cash turned back to her with a growl. Reid's cue to make his escape. He refused to get into an argument with his brother when he had a sexy redhead to take home. He just hoped she wouldn't give him too much crap when he insisted on driving. The take-charge types could be so touchy when a guy tried to do right by them.

Lafayette said something Naomi couldn't make out, but before she could ask, Reid turned them toward the exit with a backhanded *goodbye* to the others. Her damn heel had cracked, and she had the hardest time walking. The half beer she'd downed didn't help, not on an empty stomach, but it took a lot more than six ounces of pilsner to affect her sobriety.

"Evan's not here?" she asked, realizing she hadn't seen him since the interview.

"Nope. Poor guy had to head back to work at his real job. He's an accountant with McNulty, Campbell, Associates. And his boss is constantly busting his bal—ah, tail. Evan's always tired lately."

"You can say 'balls,' Reid. I've heard the expression before."

To her bemusement, he flushed. "Sorry. I was taught not to swear in front of women."

Reid, a gentleman at heart. She liked him more because of it. "Evan seemed fine earlier. Heck, he charmed everyone around him. I saw a few of the ladies in the crowd trying to get his attention."

He shrugged and steered her from a large man who nearly plowed into them. Having Reid by her side helped a lot. One, because she had trouble balancing in her stupid shoes, and no way she planned to take them off to walk around in the bar. And two, because he shielded her from the crowd. She felt safe with him.

Until she started thinking too hard about her handsome client and the fact that her heart refused to stop racing when near him.

The crowd thickened, and a rotund man jostled her, then apologized. Then a woman near them did the same.

Before she knew it, Reid had guided them to the exit, using his body to part the sea of people, and they left the bar. The crisp bite of the May evening had her shivering, and Reid pulled her into his side.

"I'd give you my jacket, but I didn't wear one."

"I'm fine." Her heel shifted, and she nearly tripped again. "Damn it."

He stopped them next to a dark-blue Charger.

"Nice car."

"Get in."

She looked up at him, saw the resolve on his face, and realized he intended to take her home. "Wait. What?"

"Naomi, it's late, and you can barely walk in those things."

"The heel's a little wobbly, but I can make it back to

the office. My car's there." With any luck, it would start on the first try.

Reid frowned and crossed his arms over his chest. "I'm not letting you walk by yourself in the dark."

"You're not *letting* me?" Was she a toddler that needed permission?

"Besides, I overheard you on your phone earlier. Something about your car not starting yesterday and again today? Even if you do manage not to kill yourself on the walk back, you'll end up waiting on a cab to take you home if the car doesn't start."

She glared. "You sure do seem to like listening to other people's conversations."

"Just get in." When she didn't, he glowered. "I can wait all night."

She stared back at him, a little alarmed when he closed the distance between them.

Then he shocked her by pressing her up against the car, full-body contact. The heat of him singed her. Suddenly, instead of feeling annoyed or scared, she wanted him in the worst way. *Whoa, momma*.

Reid ran a finger down her cheek. "I'm not letting you drive home."

His implacable resolve surprised her. "Seriously, Reid. I'm a big girl. I know how to get home without getting mugged."

He didn't move, and she didn't want to think about him pressed so *firmly* against her.

She didn't see herself winning this battle, and though it was ridiculous to think she needed rescuing from herself, she had to admit it felt nice to have someone looking out for her. "If you really need to drive me home, go for it. But you're going to feel stupid tomorrow when all that testosterone in your system wears off." She added in a lower voice, "Let me go. Please."

"I'd rather feel stupid than regret not helping you out." He moved back to unlock the car and opened the door for her, then waited for her to settle in. After joining her, he followed her directions home.

Naomi could have been angry about it, but his need to protect softened something inside her. Something she'd need to firm up before dealing with the man again. Reid sat far too close. She could smell alcohol and the faint scent of cologne on him, and it went straight to her head. Hell, maybe she was a little loopy. She really needed to get something to eat.

They arrived at her home in Greenwood, a cute little bungalow she'd refused to sell, even after losing her job with PP&R. She'd worked so hard for her home and had finally gotten the house exactly as she'd wanted it.

"You okay?" Reid asked as he parked.

"Yes, fine. You've done your duty. Go home."

"Keys."

Her purse was in his hands before she could grab it back.

"Damn it!"

He had her keys out and had already left the vehicle when she'd thrown open her door, only to have him help her out and up the sidewalk. A domineering yet polite gentleman.

He nodded at the house. "Nice place."

"Thanks," she said grudgingly, loving the homey two-bedroom Craftsman. Dark purple with white trim and a tidy little porch, the house had plenty of room for her and Rex, should he deign to come home. Probably out catting around like half the men in this town, she thought…cattily.

She snorted. "I suppose you want to come in."

"Just to make sure you're okay."

She rolled her eyes at him, but he ignored her. She heard his car beep, locked up tight, and she glared at him. If he had any intention of staying, she'd disabuse him of that notion right away. She watched him unlock the front door, then step back to hold it open for her.

Since Rex didn't greet her right away, she figured he was probably touring the neighborhood. With a little huff, she took the keys from Reid and walked inside. He closed the door behind them while she flicked on a light.

"It's you," he said. "Same blue in here as your office walls."

Huh. He'd noticed. What did that mean? That he had good recall or actually possessed an interest in her? And why did she care?

She nearly tripped again and swore, then kicked off her stupid heels.

"You want some water? I know I'm parched. It's been a long day." Reid stepped past her into her open living room that led into a dining area and farther into her kitchen. She refused to follow him inside and instead massaged her aching toes.

He returned with a glass for her.

"Make yourself at home, why don't you?"

He didn't say anything and handed her the glass. She took a sip and handed it back. "There. Now go home, please. Because of you, I'll have to get someone to take me to my car in the morning." Though if she was feeling industrious, she could walk the short distance to get it herself.

"I'll swing by and pick you up."

His bossy attitude that had somewhat charmed her before now annoyed her. "No, thanks." She watched him drink her water and grew even more steamed. "I'm not some silly little woman needing your help, Reid. I'm not drunk or impaired in any way. I'm tired and my feet hurt."

He gave a small smile.

"You find that amusing?"

He set the glass down on a coaster on her side table, and she hated that she couldn't nag him about that either. "You're cute when you're mad."

"And helpless, right?" She felt a little light-headed, which had nothing to do with exhaustion and everything to do with Reid. Around him, she felt more. Angry, annoyed, aroused. The three A's of danger drawing nearer as he smiled at her distress. The bastard.

"Want me to help you, you poor, fragile thing?"

She could do without the smirk. "Yes, please," she said, her voice sugary-sweet, then dragged him closer by the shirtfront, shocking him. "Isn't this what you want? To take advantage of a *helpless* woman?"

"Hell no." Finally, a bit of his anger. He glared at her. "I'm trying to help you out here, Naomi. Oh, forget it."

"Oh, so now, because I'm a little aggressive, I'm not good enough for you." She started to lose track of what she was saying, so close to Reid, to that firm chin with a hint of stubble, to that sexy smell of man and cologne, to the sheer breadth of him that seemed much bigger up close. Reid stood inches above her own height, their disparity even greater without her heels.

He tried to pry her hands free but stalled when he looked down into her eyes. "Y-you're mad?" He sounded hoarse, his gaze moving slowly over her face and stilling on her mouth. "Fuck," he muttered.

"Yeah, I'm mad. You're a menace, you know that?" Out of control and stirred to an angry passion by the man who refused to know she had her own mind, she yanked him down for an angrier kiss. The touch of his mouth on hers brought everything to a halt. An instant connection turned their burning chemistry into an all-out inferno.

She heard him moan but couldn't function past trying to get as close to Reid as possible. Her breasts ached, and she couldn't breathe while she devoured his mouth. That bar in his pants, which she could feel pressed so tightly against her, made it worse because her girl parts reacted by doing somersaults and flooding her body with need.

He wrapped his arms around her waist at some point and backed her against the wall as they continued to kiss.

When she knew she'd soon go past the point of no return, she broke the kiss. "There," she said after she remembered how to talk. "Now you've seen this 'helpless' woman back to her house safe and sound. Go home, Reid." That probably would have sounded better if she could keep herself from kissing him in between reprimands.

And if she could stop herself from touching his broad, muscular chest.

He was breathing hard as he stared down at her. "I don't think you know what you are."

"Oh?" Yet again presuming to know her own mind better than she did? The ass. The sexy, hung-like-a-horse jerk.

Only a coma patient would fail to notice his arousal. And Naomi had never claimed to be a saint. Presented with that much temptation, she resolved to teach him a lesson.

Her rationalizations threw all her reservations about Reid out the window. She'd never wanted a man so much, and she needed him to see she remained in charge.

Yeah, sure.

"Well, then. I probably don't know what I'm doing when I do this." She slid her hand down his chest to the fastening of his jeans, staring into his eyes as she went. His stare had darkened, and he watched her as if ready to pounce.

"You don't want to do this, Naomi." Yet he made no move to stop her...until she slid his zipper down.

He grabbed her hand. "Seriously. You should—*Fuck*."

She'd used her other hand to grip him, hard. "Let go. I wouldn't want to hurt you."

He quickly put his hands up on either side of her head on the wall. "Okay, now let go. Before I do something I shouldn't." He closed his eyes as she put her hands inside his underwear. "Jesus, Naomi. Stop."

And he was big.

She paused. "Do you really want me to?"

"Fuck, no." He gave an angry laugh. "But you don't have to—"

She interrupted him by using one hand to drag him down for a kiss while she pumped him with the other.

He tried to hold back, but she gripped him harder and

started jerking him off. Lost to everything but needing to own this man, she kissed him for all she was worth. She paused only to say, "I think maybe you're the one who's helpless. When it comes to me."

Then Reid turned the tables and took charge.

Chapter 7

REID KISSED LIKE A STARVING MAN. NAOMI TASTED *so good*. So fresh and pure and sinful, all in one mouth-watering punch. And the way she handled him. Hell, he was going to come too soon. But it had been so long, and the scent and feel of her turned his brain to mush.

She thought he was helpless? Hell yes, he was. And the little witch knew it.

She kept pumping him while she teased him with that tongue. Then she let out a sexy little moan as she tried to get closer, her full breasts pushed up against his shirt where her blazer had parted.

Reid kissed her, lost to desire, knowing she was all in as she stroked him faster.

He had no intention of taking advantage of her. But she kept saying she was fine, and damn if her anger hadn't turned him on past reason. Besides, no meek woman could handle him with such precision and *such hot little hands*.

He yanked his mouth away and warned, "Gonna come." He kissed her cheek, her neck. He sucked hard, wanting to leave a mark.

She moaned. "Then come. All over my hand." She nibbled her way across his cheek and stuck her tongue in his ear.

He shuddered, the sensation overwhelming. "Naomi…"

She jerked his dick and whispered, "Or would you rather come in my mouth?"

The image combined with the sensation...

Reid lost it. He came like a rocket, the release one that made him dizzy. It felt like it lasted forever while the pleasure took over his mind, body, and everything in between.

She wiped her hand on his belly under his shirt. "Good thing you're such a big, strong, capable man, isn't it?" She laughed low. "I'd hate to feel I took advantage of you."

"Oh, you did," he said, panting. "You...need...to pay for that." As he caught his breath, he didn't give her a chance to feel superior. Instead, he kissed her once more and inched her skirt up so he could slide a finger inside her panties.

Shit, she was wet, her panties drenched. *So hot*. He continued to kiss her, his fingers moving over her slick flesh, needing to feel that heat around him in some way.

It came as no surprise that he started to grow hard again. But Naomi, like Reid, was fast on the draw. Her little moans turned to full-out whimpers, then a cry as she came over his hand. He caressed her folds as she came down off her own climax, mesmerized by the sexy woman.

She leaned back against the wall, her eyes closed, her lips parted, looking like a damn fantasy come to life. He eased her skirt back down, then watched as her eyes opened, the blue so dark, it looked black.

He slowly put his finger in his mouth, tasting her and wanting more. Her eyes widened as she watched him.

Neither of them spoke, and he regretfully righted

his clothing, wincing at the mess on his belly and in his pants.

Man, he wanted her again. Right now. But he could already see the regret building. Knowing Naomi, she'd put up a million roadblocks between them. All that talk about not mixing business with pleasure she now too clearly recalled.

"Too bad you'll probably regret this in the morning," he muttered, trying to come up with some way to put things back on an even keel.

She frowned. "What?"

"I'll be by to pick you up and take you to your car. Is nine okay?"

"Nine?"

"In the morning."

"Um, yes, but—"

"Great, see you then." He kissed her because had to, and he left her dazed and staring as he closed the door behind him. Reid still had no plans to start a relationship. But after having that brief taste of Naomi, he knew he needed more.

And damn her, she needed it too. He just had to make her see that…somehow.

***

Naomi spent the night in a daze. After Reid left, she swore up and down, calling herself all kinds of fool while she threw herself into cleaning up the house, something to keep her hands busy while her mind ran wild. She'd never been so in lust with someone that she'd thrown all her rules away. Even Tanner had been thought out, a result of a stupid competition with her sister, but Naomi had been in control when she'd said yes to a relationship with her boss.

A relationship—not a hand job against the wall before being fingered to orgasm by the sexiest man alive.

Her cheeks heated as she remembered how brazen she'd been. She'd already been aroused by the guy, but then he'd made her angry. A bad combination for a woman like Naomi. Some people got hangry—a mixture of angry and hungry. Naomi, apparently, turned horny when she grew angry. *Horngry. How's that for a buzzword?*

She laughed hysterically at her bad choice, finished scrubbing her counters, put on some pajamas, then slumped into bed, knowing it would take forever for her to get to sleep.

The next thing she knew, someone hammered at her front door.

"What?" She stumbled out of bed and threw on her robe, alarmed to find it nearly nine. On her way down the hall, she nearly tripped over Rex, who wound between her ankles. "Oh, and nice to see you again, Romeo."

He meowed at her.

The person playing her front door like a set of well-used bongos continued.

"Hold on," she yelled, the events of the previous night coming back to her. She opened the door to Reid, who, as usual, looked amazing. Naomi, on the other hand, wore a ratty little silk robe, had bedhead and dragon breath, and might have forgotten to remove her eye makeup. She probably looked like a raccoon.

Reid broke into a full grin.

"Shut up." She turned and let him follow her. "Come on, Rex."

"Rex?" he asked.

The cat's meow answered him. She put some food in the cat's bowl and turned to see Rex purring in Reid's arms.

She scowled. "Huh. Guess he really can sense evil. Like to like, after all."

Reid laughed. "I see you slept in."

"I guess I did." She rubbed her head. "Ah, you're here to take me to my car?"

He gave her a thorough once-over, lingering on her breasts. "You look good, Naomi. In a suit or a robe."

"Oh, stop." She blushed.

"You want to shower? I can scrub your back," he teased, not sounding serious…much.

She held up a hand, not at all prepared to deal with Reid and what they'd done last night. God, what had she been thinking? Sex with a client?

"Look, you probably regretted last night the second I left your house," Reid started.

"I don't need you thinking for me, Reid, you big—"

"Because you're one of the most professional women I know," he said over her protests. "I respect you."

"Huh?"

"And I know you'd never date a client, even if I asked you out. So I'm just here as *a friend*," he emphasized and lifted a brow. "Last night never happened. I'd never make a colleague uncomfortable by coming on to her."

Was he saying what she thought he was saying? He had regrets too? Why did that feel awful?

"My point is we can both pretend last night doesn't exist. You didn't kiss me first, and I never kissed you back." Did he have to focus on her mouth like that?

She just stared at him, wanting to pounce on the out he offered but not sure why she hesitated. Kiss him *first*? *Well, hell. I did. But hey, he kissed me back. We're still tied.* Even as she thought it, her subconscious gave her a mental slap. *Jesus. We're not playing a game, Naomi!*

Reid frowned. "Okay?"

"Um, sure. Okay. I'm still so confused." She groaned. "What time is it again?"

He smiled, closed the distance between them, and put his hands on her shoulders.

They both froze.

She felt the heat of his palms straight to her skin, her silk robe and spaghetti-strap nightie no barrier at all. If he shifted his hands just so, he'd be able to feel her breasts, to take the hardened nipples into his palms. Or even better, his mouth.

Instead, Reid turned her around and marched her through her kitchen and down the hall. Her heart rate tripled by the time they reached the bedroom. Would he take her there? Make love to her and put them both out of their misery? Should she reject him? *Could* she reject him?

Reid gave her a gentle nudge. "Go shower. I'll wait out here with Rex. Mind if I make myself some coffee?"

"Go ahead," she said automatically. The door shut behind her, and she flopped face-first onto her bed, not sure she wasn't still dreaming. If so, this had the makings of a nightmare for sure.

After a moment, she went into the bathroom and got her second big shock of the day when she looked into the mirror.

Her hair was matted on one side and stood up on

the other, and she had dark smudges under her eyes. A definite raccoon. She groaned and hurried to wash. No wonder Reid had clarified he wanted to be just friends. He'd said he respected her now? And he didn't want to make her uncomfortable? Too late.

But she knew she had only herself to blame.

She agonized as she cleaned up, then told herself to stop thinking so hard and let it go. So what? She and Reid had made out and gotten touchy-feely. It was over and wouldn't happen again. For all she knew, Reid did that kind of thing with other women all the time. And didn't that make her feel special?

Naomi glared at her reflection in the mirror, then forced herself to forget it all. She'd add it to the list of things she wished she'd never done. *Make that people I wished I'd never done.*

Still, despite the embarrassing situation, Reid had shown up to take her to her car, and he'd been more than pleasant. Naomi could do the same. She'd gotten over Tanner. Surely she could move past one tiny blip of pleasure with Reid Griffith. She hurried to join him, wearing a pair of jeans and a soft, comfortable pullover.

Sipping coffee at her small kitchen table while glancing through his phone, Reid looked like an ad for male domesticity. She swallowed a sigh and glanced at his cup. "Is there more for me?"

"Sure." He made eye contact, even seemed approving of her outfit the way he smiled as he looked her over. Casual Saturday attire while she ran errands around town. She'd put her hair up in an easy twist, and her makeup was light. Nothing raccoony about her now.

He handed her the cup, and she doctored it before

sitting with him. Except as she sipped, she couldn't help remembering how big and hot he'd felt in her hands. How amazing it had felt to be touched by him…

Reid continued to glance at her, then he looked away, then back again. "Well, this isn't awkward at all," he muttered, and she laughed.

He laughed too, and then it wasn't awkward anymore. He rubbed his chin and said, "Let's put last night behind us, okay?"

"Agreed." And like that, it had never happened.

Or so she kept trying to convince herself.

The drive to pick up her car went without a hitch. Parked at the office, the car wouldn't necessarily give away the fact that she'd left it overnight.

"You aren't that far from Ringo's, are you?" he asked as he parked behind her. "Or from our office, actually."

"I'm close. Just a few blocks that way." She nodded back the way they'd come. "I tried to tell you last night that I didn't need a ride this morning, but you left so fast I didn't get the chance."

His lips quirked, and she had to fight not to trace his mouth with a finger, mesmerized by the sexy lines of his face. "Well, I didn't want to stay and freak you out more than I already had."

"I wasn't freaked out."

He snorted.

"I wasn't."

"Naomi, your eyes were huge, your fists clenched, and you looked at me like you planned on punching me or fucking me. Since I hadn't brought any condoms, I trucked on out of there before I did something stupid."

She gaped. "That is *ridiculous*. What happened

between us was a fluke. A one-time mistake. I had no intention of… And you! Didn't you say we weren't going to talk about this?" Her voice continued to rise.

"I'm sorry. It's just that you're so much fun to tease." He had the nerve to laugh. "Seriously, I swear, I won't bring it up again."

Annoyed that he seemed able to write her off so easily, she glanced down at his crotch, gratified to see his response. "Looks like it's up again right now, Mr. We'll-Forget-All-About-It."

He groaned and leaned his head back against his headrest. "I know. I'm sorry. You get me hard. I can't help it."

"Well, try to relax or something." *Before I jump you.* "We both agreed. We have to work together. We need to be professional. Remember your rule about not fraternizing."

"Right. So why don't you take that professional—not sexy—ass out to your car? I have to get to work. We'll talk this week, okay?"

"About work and the advertising proposal I gave you."

"Right." Before she left, he grabbed her by the wrist, holding her loosely but firmly. "Naomi, in all seriousness, I enjoyed the hell out of last night, but I'd never pressure you for more than you wanted to give, okay?"

She warmed. "Thanks."

He nodded and let her go, but his fingers brushed her wrist as he did so, starting a whole new mess of arousal to soak into her brain and pool there.

Naomi hurried from the car and lost herself in her many errands. It took her half the day, but she managed to put Reid in the rearview of her thoughts.

She finally settled down, chalked up her mistake to a lack of balance in her life, and did her best to focus on the next step to advancing her company. As she fetched her coffee from the barista of her favorite local place, she mentally reviewed her ideas for Starr PR and how to get an invitation to sit down with Chris Jennings to talk marketing.

Someone bumped into her on her way to a seat. When she glanced up from her phone to offer an apology, she ran into another headache that refused to fade from her sorry life.

"Hey, Naomi. How are you?" Tanner Ryan asked, standing next to the one person she'd hoped to never meet under strange circumstances—Chris Jennings.

—◦◦◦—

Reid had his hands full, literally, as he helped Hector move the Barkers. With Tim out due to the flu, they were short a man.

"You're not as bad as Cash said you'd be," Hector teased as the pair of them carried a large-ass sofa into the moving van.

"Well, you *are* as bad as I've heard."

Hector laughed. They'd gotten halfway done and had started making up for lost time as Reid rolled up his proverbial sleeves and *moved*.

"Man, you're quiet," Hector said an hour later.

Deep in his own thoughts, Reid hadn't realized how much time had passed in silence. "Don't you guys listen to a radio or something?"

"Nah. Too many different tastes in music. Now, if I'm with Lafayette or Martin, we're good. But Tim listens to country, and Finley is stuck in the eighties. We're not sure why, because he was born a decade later, but you know Finley—he's weird." Hector shook his head. "Your brother likes heavy metal or classic rock. I can stomach classic rock, but that head-bangin' shit gives me a headache."

"Me too." Reid sympathized. "So what do you listen to?"

"A lot, actually. I like rap, jazz, and dubstep."

"Eclectic."

Hector nodded. "Not like Cash, who does two styles of rock and that's it."

"Yeah, his taste sucks." Reid grunted as they set down a large dresser. "We're getting closer to being done."

Hector nodded, studying him.

"What?"

"You're here, working with me."

"And?"

"Cash talks a lot of shit about you and Evan. Says you two are too prissy to get your hands dirty." Hector grinned. "But then, Lafayette says the same things about me half the time. It's just funny that although you and Cash look alike, you're really different."

Reid sighed. "I've heard it all before. And for the record, all I've ever done is grunt work."

"In the Corps, maybe. But man, it's obvious you're all white-collar material. You had to take off your fancy shirt—on a Saturday—to put on a T-shirt. And you're quiet. Cash is loud and all over the place. Fancy he ain't."

They went back inside the house to grab more boxes. "You'd rather I ranted and raved all day?"

Hector chuckled. "Nope. This is a nice change."

They cleared out the Barkers' kitchen and dining room. A few boxes remained in the living area and hallway.

Reid liked Hector, and working with him, he'd come to learn that Hector had a real head on his shoulders. "So what do you do when you're not moving stuff?"

"I teach ballroom dance."

Reid stopped in his tracks. "What?"

Hector nodded. "It's fun, and it's a great way to pick up women."

Reid paused. "Hmm. That's not a bad idea."

Hector lifted two boxes, his muscles bulging. "I'm not just a pretty face, Reid. I'm full of good ideas too."

Reid huffed. "It's like I'm talking to my brother all over again."

Hector laughed and walked the load into the van. Reid added his as well.

"I also help at the local animal shelter," Hector added. "Not so much to get girls, but because I hate when people are mean to animals."

Reid was liking Hector more and more. "No kidding."

"You know, you should come down and join us sometime. We could use the help."

"If I had the time, I would. After the Barkers', I'm going to balance the books for a few hours." Reid felt the exhaustion of the week settle into his bones.

"Ladies like animal lovers."

"Uh-huh."

"And doing charity would help your image."

"Right." Reid straightened a few boxes, then got out of the van while Hector cinched some straps and tightened down the load for transport.

Hector closed the back and leaped out. "And you

know, I think it would be good for our image. Your PR lady would love you helping poor, defenseless kittens."

"Sure. Wait, what are you talking about?"

"You and Starr PR. Naomi's into you, man."

"She is not." *But damn if I don't want to be into her*.

"We were talking about you guys after you left Ringo's. Even Cash noticed, and he's pretty pathetic when it comes to talking up women."

"Cash?"

"Oh, he's popular, don't get me wrong. But his idea of seduction is to see who can drink the most, him or his date, then award himself as first prize."

They both laughed.

"Sadly, he's done that," Reid said. "Nah, Naomi and I are friendly. We work together. It's just platonic." Though that hand job said otherwise. "Sure, she's attractive."

"Hot." Hector nodded.

"Hot as fuck," Reid muttered.

"I heard that. So are you two involved or what? Will she give us a discount on her business if you keep her satisfied?" He winked.

"God, Hector. Not you too. Cash is bad enough. I thought you had sensitivity training in the Navy."

"I did." Hector flashed his pearly whites. "Didn't take."

"Yeah, right."

"Look, if you're not interested in that fine woman, I'd be happy to—"

"Try it and you'll lose some of those pretty teeth."

Hector smirked. "Thought so."

"Look. Naomi is like a coworker, someone I do business with. Fucking ruins relationships."

"Or makes them better."

"Why the hell are you asking me these questions anyway?"

"I like you, Reid. And I like this company. We're gonna hit big. Then you're going to need more upper management. That's my style. My brother's too. I don't want you messing things up because you don't know how to treat a lady."

Reid just stared at him, nonplussed by the surprising direction of the discussion with a man he didn't know all that well.

"And maybe your brother gave me twenty to give you some shit about her." Hector laughed. "If you could see your face." He laughed so hard, he cried.

Now that made much more sense. Freakin' Cash. "Asshole. Come on. Let's head back to the bay. You're driving."

"Sure thing, Mr. Griffith." Hector laughed some more. "Or should I say Lady Killer?"

Reid found himself grinning at Hector's smart-ass remarks and had to force himself to scowl. "Why is no one in this company in awe and terror of me? I'm a hard-ass boss!"

Hector just shot him a look, glanced from his own arms to Reid's, and raised a brow.

Reid sank into his seat and crossed his arms over his chest. "I'm a lot more lethal with a rifle."

"Good thing for me you don't have one."

"You're not kidding."

Hector drove them back to the office, but this time, the discussion turned toward the other Vets on the Go! employees. Hector had an able mind and grasp on who had what strengths. Oddly enough, Hector thought pairing Jordan with Cash on the next few moves would make more sense than sending out himself or his brother with the woman.

"They work well together. She keeps his huge ego in check, and he spends his time looking out for her instead of getting into trouble. If you put her out with me or Lafayette, it works, but my brother and I work well with everyone. Cash kind of needs more attention."

"You mean a keeper." Reid sighed.

"Nah, he just needs focus."

A nicer way of saying he needed a keeper.

"Jordan went out with me and Finley for half a morning, and she and Finley spent their time trying to out-harass each other. It was funny but a little much with our clients listening in."

"Ah, right."

"And then Cash put her on an easy afternoon pack-up with Martin and Tim. Apparently Tim never talked to her. Martin never shut up—Tim told me it was too much."

Reid had told Cash to make sure Jordan met everyone on their small team, worried at how she might interact with the others. But according to Cash, Jordan had no issues with anyone.

Hector put things into better perspective.

"Jordan doesn't get chatty with Cash or you guys?"

"Nah, man. She's perfect. She fits in with different temperaments. But with Cash…" Hector snorted. "They pretend they don't like each other. They taunt each other, but not like with Finley. Cash looks out for her when he's with her, and she defends him whenever we poke fun. It works; we've learned not to question it.

The one time Finley said something about them being a little *too* friendly with each other, Cash almost tore his head off."

"Hmm. I guess I'll make sure we change up the rotation then." Since that was Cash's domain, Reid would be sure to subtly manipulate his brother into it.

"Just take your time doing it. I don't want Cash or Jordan to think I talked to you about it. You didn't hear any of this from me. Don't know if you noticed, but your brother has anger issues."

"Tell me about it." Reid thought long and hard about all Hector had said. "I'll handle it, don't worry. And Hector? We expand so big we need more managers, you're hired."

"Thanks, boss."

"Quit playing suck-up, Jackson."

"Yes, sir, Mr. Griffith, sir."

"Ass."

Chapter 8

NAOMI SHOULD HAVE KNOWN TANNER WOULD MOVE ON the same clients she'd cherry-picked to work with. The blasted man had good taste and an eye for expansion.

He looked attractive, as usual. And a little tired, which surprised her. But he still commanded attention. Six foot three. Broad chest, polished looks with that square chin and those killer blue eyes. Not a clear gray like Reid's, but…God, just what she didn't need, to be thinking about Reid when dealing with Tanner.

"Wow, Naomi. You look great. I haven't seen you in forever."

She'd done her best to make it that way. "Yes."

When Tanner looked as if he'd lean closer for a kiss or hug hello, she hurried to stick her hand out between them. "Nice to see you again." She sounded stiff, and she knew it, but she had only seen Tanner once in the year and half since they'd parted. She'd cried the entire night after.

Now, with distance and time between them, she didn't miss him so much. She'd rather kick him in the balls for being a hypocrite and a bad boss than kiss him and beg him to come back to her.

Squaring her shoulders, she smiled into his eyes and squeezed his hand with appropriate tension, then gave a subtle tug when he held on a moment too long.

She turned to Chris. "Hello, I'm Naomi."

"I see that." Chris Jennings held out a hand and shook hers. He was cute, a little nerdy, and clearly intelligent. She could tell just by the way he sized her and everything up around him, and she had that added bonus of knowing all about him through her research. "So how do you and Tanner know each other?"

"We used to work together," Tanner answered.

"We did," Naomi said, wanting so badly to tell Chris what a putz her ex had been. But anything she did or said in this first meeting would leave a lasting impression, and she refused to come across as the bitter, unprofessional ditz who'd slept with her boss. Tanner admitting he'd slept with his employee wouldn't do him any favors either, so she didn't worry he'd spill the beans.

"Oh?" Chris looked from her to Tanner. "So you're a marketing whiz too?"

Before Tanner could answer that one, Naomi did. "Yep." She smiled, giving Chris all the wattage she could manage. "I love it. PR and marketing are so exciting. I worked with Paulson, Pierce & Ryan for a few years, then left to start my own firm. I crave a challenge."

He smiled back. Tanner's answering smile looked strained.

"I learned a lot from PP&R. They're a great company. But now I can focus on my clients more since we're a smaller firm." Enough work chat, now she had to act as if she didn't want to keep them. "I'm sorry. I'm really into my job and can go on and on about it. It was great to meet you, Chris. Tanner." She nodded at him, the handsome jerk, and saw his lips tighten.

Her mood perked. Great. She'd annoyed Tanner and had come across as polite.

"Naomi, would you like to join us?" Chris asked.

"She probably has things go do," Tanner tried, keeping that fake smile in place. "She always did work hard."

"Actually, I've gotten better about balancing my life," she said. "I was just going to sit down to enjoy my latte and relax on this beautiful Saturday." For once, Seattle had a sunny day, and the temperature remained warm. "I'd love to…if I'm not intruding." She looked from Chris to Tanner.

"Tanner and I ran into each other on the way in. And I'd rather not talk shop since I'm struggling to find balance between work and a life myself."

She nodded. "I know that feeling all too well." She sat with them and did her best to be cool but polite to Tanner.

The discussion turned from the weather to a few upcoming festivals in the city to the growing crime rate.

"I love it here, but the burglaries have been on the rise. Remember last year when they caught some lowlifes in Queen Anne? The guys had been knocking over businesses along the strip, then started on the residential area. An old lady and her boyfriend stopped them." Chris grinned. "Classic. Imagine being stopped by a woman in her eighties. That old lady made my day."

Tanner nodded. "It goes in waves. I think they just stopped a group who'd been targeting houses in Fremont last week. I saw something about that in the paper."

Chris brightened. "Oh yeah. I know those guys! A Marine I used to serve with years ago."

Naomi couldn't have dreamed of a better way to segue into the conversation. "That's so funny. I'm working with them."

Both Chris's and Tanner's eyes widened.

"Vets on the Go! They're a great group. The owners of the company are veterans who hire veterans. Reid, Cash, and Evan Griffith."

Chris's grin grew. "No kidding? Man, small world. I'm renting a house to those guys. So you met Cash, eh? What did you think?"

They shared a laugh and talked about the Griffiths with good-natured fun. Tanner nodded at all the right times, but she saw his frustration and wanted to cheer. *Take that, you backstabbing ass.*

"Oh man, I have to get going. I promised Teresa I wouldn't be late tonight," Chris said, and they all stood. "Great running into you, Tanner. I'll give you a call later this week about some ideas Jon had for you. See what you think." To Naomi, he said, "It was great meeting you. And hell, if you're not too busy, I'd love to talk to you about what you're doing for Cash and Reid. My company is growing faster than I'd anticipated, and we need some fresh marketing strategies. We're hoping to put together a tight PR team. Not sure if you're interested…?"

She forced herself to remain calm. "I know all about fast growth since founding Starr PR." Tanner's jaw tightened. She smiled, hoping she didn't look as excited as she felt. "Whenever you have the time, we're game. Like I said, I love a challenge."

"I'll have Jon contact you. Starr PR, right?" At her nod, he grinned. "You're right. It's catchy."

She waved goodbye and left with a spring in her step, uncaring about anything since she'd gotten her foot in the door—the same door Tanner Ryan would no doubt try to slam in her face. *Try it, pretty boy. I dare you.*

Now to make sure Reid gave her a good

recommendation. One that didn't include how skillful she was with her hands.

Unfortunately, she was so swamped with other clients that the few times she'd had to contact Reid, she kept missing him. They played phone tag for a few days before she finally managed to reach him.

She let out a relieved breath when he picked up the phone. "Oh my gosh, you're harder to reach than my father during baseball season."

He chuckled. "Sorry. We've been swamped. We've been circling around the decision to add on more personnel and another truck. Evan just bought the truck."

"Wow. Congrats."

"Yeah, and that web guy you mentioned was someone I'd considered working with before. I called, and he's designing a new website as we speak."

"Using a few key points I mentioned in your packet?"

"Yep. Hold on." He said something in a low growl to someone else. Cash's blunt words came through on her end, and she winced. "Sorry if you heard that," Reid apologized to her. "Just a minor dispute with a demanding employee."

"Employee?" Cash yelled. "Fuckhead. I'm on a break."

"Oh yeah, he's demanding." Reid sighed. "So, to what do I owe the honor of this call?"

"We had a few items we needed to discuss from last week. I've put together an email for you to read before we meet. Do you have time this week? I have a four thirty on Thursday or a nine Friday morning."

"Shit. I mean, shoot. No can do. We're still short people, so I've been filling in to give some of the guys a break."

"Who's managing the desk?"

"Dan Thompson, believe it or not. He's a retired vet we're moving in a few weeks." Reid sounded enthused. "And man, he's amazing. Guy was artillery back in 'Nam, and he's hell on wheels in admin. So at least the office is running smoothly."

"That's fantastic."

"Yeah. I'm one for three this week. I have a terrific, if temporary, admin chief. One of our trucks went down, so we had to scramble to get another, which led me to seeing the need for more in our fleet. Yes, Evan said we now have to call it a fleet."

"Listen to Evan."

"I'm trying, but half of what comes out of his mouth are complaints. He bitches and whines like a…ah, he's tired. I'll leave it at that."

She couldn't help laughing at his tone.

"I know, it sounds ridiculous. A broken-down truck, a bitchy accountant, and my jerk of a brother complains at the drop of a hat. He's not happy with the new rotation I set down for our movers. We have teams that work well together, and I like the unity of getting everyone on board with everyone else."

She could well imagine. "So he's working with Jordan?"

"Yep." Reid gave a tired laugh. "How's your week been going?"

"Busy. I had been wanting to sit down and talk with you about your strategy. We really do need to iron out a few points. Oh, and your interview will be live on the Friday night segment at six thirty."

"Yeah? Great."

"If you don't mind, I'll call your website tech and talk to him about highlighting your recent good press."

"That works. That way, I don't have to do it."

She made a note to do so. "Oh, and I meant to tell you. I met a friend of yours this past weekend."

"Chris? Yeah, he called. We talked. He's a great guy." Reid paused. "He asked how I liked working with you."

She curled her fists. "And?"

"I told him it was too soon to tell if you were effective, but that you know your stuff and you're easy to work with. All good marks."

"Thanks."

"Hey, I was honest. You screw up our business with crappy advertising, I won't hesitate to tell him that too."

"Thanks so much." She snorted. "It won't come to that. I know what I'm doing."

"I believe you or we wouldn't still be in business. SuzyTeaShine can't say enough good things about you. And if they can be in business with that stupid name, you gotta be skilled."

"Stop." She cleared her throat so as not to laugh. "Hey, it's Suzy's company. I just helped her market to the right people in the right venues."

"Uh-huh."

Sensing his distraction, she knew to wrap up the call. "I'll let you go. But you never answered me about our meeting."

"Hmm. This week is slammed. I can meet you this weekend or Monday. Your choice."

"Monday at ten?"

"Oh yeah. Nothing earlier than that." Reid sighed. "I'll go through what you send me beforehand. How about we meet for coffee and go over this? Sofa's is pretty decent in Green Lake."

"Sold." She loved their bear claws…a little too much. "I'll see you Monday at ten. Don't be late."

He laughed. "Ms. Starr, knowing I'm coming to see you, I wouldn't dream of it." Then he hung up.

She didn't know whether to be flattered or insulted. He wouldn't dream of being late because she was a stickler for punctuality or because he liked being around her?

The phone rang, distracting her, so she answered, "Hello?"

"A call from Mr. Tanner Ryan. Are you available to talk, Ms. Starr?" asked a perky young woman.

He has his secretary calling me? Power move for sure. "I can squeeze him in," she said, wanting to squeeze him in—by the throat. Better to get the call over with. She'd anticipated him contacting her much sooner. Had Chris given him a contract already? Jon hadn't called her, though he'd sent her an email requesting a meeting.

The phone clicked, and Tanner came on the line. "Hello, Naomi."

Familiar tingles lit her from the inside out, and she hated that his voice could still make her shiver. God, she wanted so badly to hate Tanner. "Hello, Tanner. What can I do for you?" Straight and to the point.

He laughed, the smoky sound of his amusement both painful and warming. She preferred painful.

"I always loved the sound of your voice. So soft yet sexy."

"I'm hanging up now."

"No, wait. Naomi, I'm just teasing. It was great seeing you Saturday."

She snorted. "I'll bet."

"Well, I'll admit it was a punch to the gut. I'm trying to schmooze Jennings, and there you are, still beautiful, funny, and intelligent. Made me realize I really did make the biggest mistake of my life by breaking up with you."

And that was why she found it so hard to hate the guy. He could be honest and apologetic and mean it. Tanner, despite having been an utter ass, had a core of decency to him.

He also had a tendency to remember things skewed to his benefit. "I'm sorry. Breaking up with me? You would have demoted me or fired me if I hadn't quit first."

"Not true. Well, not about firing you."

"Demoted me then. And how is that fair considering all the work I did to land you so many accounts?"

He sighed. "Naomi, I didn't call to rehash old times."

"I know why you called. You're threatened that Jennings wants to talk to me, and you want that fat juicy account all to yourself."

"Jennings Tech is blowing up. Their stock continues to rise, and the marketing they have in place has stagnated. Chris knows it, so does their team. Have you talked to Jon?"

"We've communicated."

"There's enough room for all of us to work together."

"Did Jennings tell you that?"

"No. Would you stop talking and listen for a minute?" Good, he sounded irritated.

"No, I will not shut up. I'm my own boss now, and I don't take orders from you." She paused, and when he remained quiet, she reached for the closure she'd been missing for so long. "I'm only going to say this once, and then we won't talk about it again. What you did hurt me. Deeply. I never did anything to interfere with your business. Everything was for PP&R and to help you. But you were threatened by my success and cut me out of things despite our results. You were both unprofessional and a shitty boyfriend. There. Now what did you want to talk about?"

He didn't say anything for a moment. "I'm sorry."

She pulled her phone away to look at it. "What's that?"

"I'm sorry. You're right, about all of it." He let out a breath. "I was getting pressure from the partners to build more, faster. Everyone kept looking to you, and it got to me. Plus you insisted we keep our relationship quiet, and that bothered me."

"*I* insisted? We both agreed it would look bad for the boss to be banging his assistant," she snapped, despite not planning to discuss the matter. "I loved you, Tanner. And you threw me away like trash."

"That's not true," he shot back. "I was having trouble at work, and you never saw it, basking in your own glory. The pride of the firm. Hell, I was dying, making sure everything stayed afloat while those pricks Pierce and Paulson were out golfing nine holes a day."

"You wanted a bigger part of the company."

"And I got it. All of it at once. Paulson's talking about leaving. So it'll just be me and Pierce. But depending on how this thing with Jennings goes, we could have room for another partner."

"Oh my God. Tell me you are *not* dangling a

partnership in front of me, as if I'll be so happy for the opportunity, I'll forget everything to reach up and grab it!"

"No. I'm merely stating that we're always looking for great team players. Naomi, I fucked up. You're the real deal, and I'm plainly stating I miss you."

"As an employee or girlfriend?"

"Both."

That shocked her to silence. "You're not dating anyone now?" Not what she'd heard.

"I am, but Mandy isn't you."

"I bet she'd love to hear that," she ended with an angry laugh. Of all the conversations she'd imagined having with Tanner, him crawling back to her hadn't been one of them.

The urge to say yes and forget the past wasn't strong, thankfully. That the urge existed at all made her feel sick. Naomi didn't cater to weakness, and the shallow character she'd seen in Tanner still dismayed her.

But she hadn't been kidding. She'd loved him—once.

An image of Reid swam in her mind's eye, another man she had no business involving herself with, yet she had.

And speaking of business… "You taught me a valuable lesson, Tanner. I don't mix business with pleasure." *Don't think about Reid, don't think about Reid…* "So if you're thinking about working together, that might be something to consider. You always were good at your job, at least."

He said nothing.

"But if this is some lame attempt to work your way into my good graces then undercut me with Jennings, forget it. I'll be talking to Jon again soon, and we'll see what he has to say about who Jennings Tech wants handling their PR. Until then, don't call me." She disconnected, trembling as she put her phone down.

Good Lord. Had that really happened? Tanner Ryan begging her to come back?

Liz popped her head in the door, her hair a wild corona of blond frizz that framed her narrow face. "Whoa. What the heck happened to you?"

"Tanner called." Naomi reached for her coffee and slugged it back. "I had just hung up with Reid, then my archnemesis had the nerve to suggest we not only get back together in business but in bed as well."

Liz gaped and took a seat across from Naomi. "No way."

"Yes way." She guzzled more caffeine. "It's like I'm in the *Twilight Zone* or something. He said his girlfriend, Mandy, 'isn't me.'" She ended in air quotes.

"But she is a redhead with blue eyes and a build similar to yours," Liz said. "I didn't tell you that before because I didn't want to freak you out. But she is. What do you make of that?"

"I have no idea." Naomi fiddled with her pen. "I kind of hate myself for thinking, for even a second, that I miss him."

Liz shrugged. "You were good together. It took me years to find Mitch. So when I had him, I refused to let him go. Even when that floozy Patsy tried moving in on him. I set her straight, set him straight when he got stupid, and finally have him trained enough that I can't imagine starting over."

"With five kids, you really can't afford to."

"Seriously." Liz grinned. "But it's not the expense, it's all the time training Mitch not to leave the toilet seat up, to get up early with the kids on Saturdays so I can sleep in, and getting him to do the laundry. That was a friggin' miracle, and I can't let that go."

They both laughed, knowing how much Liz and Mitch doted on each other. Naomi wanted that, a soul-deep connection with a man who would look at her the way Mitch looked at Liz, with love in his eyes.

Not suspicion or envy that she might outshine him at work.

She sighed. "He apologized for everything. Said he'd made a huge mistake."

"Good. He screwed up. Funny now that he's bidding for the same job you are, he's suddenly aware of his failings."

"Yeah, I noticed that."

"Keep noticing that," Liz said and grabbed the coffee cup off Naomi's desk. "I'm getting you an espresso. You need to focus on work and not on that man. He ruined your business, stole your clients, and started dating again not two weeks after that 'painful' breakup." Liz huffed. "He's not worth a moment of your busy day. Now Reid Griffith and his fine tush, *that* man is worth drooling over."

"Liz."

"I'm only human. Besides, he reminds me a little of Mitch. It's the tall, quiet ones you have to watch out for." Liz left.

Tall, yes. But Reid, quiet? He hadn't been so quiet when they'd been in her house kissing and…that other stuff. She still remembered his breathy moans. Just his voice turned her tingly in all the wrong places. The memory of his big hands, the scent of his cologne, it bothered her how much she'd fixated on those details.

Why the hell couldn't she stop thinking about him in that way? It had been all she could do to call and act with a professional detachment.

He was a client first, a man second. She would do well to keep reminding herself of that fact. With that firmly in mind, she returned to work and her espresso—*thank you, Liz*—and started adding to her folder on Chris Jennings.

Because when she landed that account, she wanted to be ready for anything.

Chapter 9

SATURDAY AFTERNOON, REID SAT NEXT TO HIS BROTHER ON the monthly drive to visit their mother. The assisted living home that she'd moved into last year was a step up from the home provider who'd been helping to care for her.

Apparently their mother needed a lot more than someone to check in on her a few times a week. Though she was only sixty-four, age and booze had taken their toll on the woman, and recently, she'd started forgetting who he was. Oddly enough, she always recognized Cash.

"I hate this," Cash muttered, staring out the passenger window.

"I don't like it any more than you do."

"I know." Cash groaned. "She was such a bitch growing up. Never gave two shits about me."

"No, she did." Reid had spent a long time thinking about his dysfunctional family. Something weird had occurred back then, an odd change in the mood around the house that Reid could never explain or understand.

Cash shrugged. He didn't like talking about the past, whereas Reid wanted to dissect it to make sure it never happened again.

"It was like some wacky switch was thrown," Reid said, trying to recall the exact moment. "Maybe things got weird before then, but remember? Around your birthday, when you got that football I was dying to throw."

"I'd turned seven," Cash said, so quiet.

"They argued, then Dad hit Mom. Only time that I can remember him doing that. He apologized later, but they were never the same. Treated you different. And Mom checked out."

"Yeah. Easier to live in the fantasy of a perfect family than with us assholes."

"When you say us, you mean you, right?" Reid tried to tease.

Cash only grunted. Sadly, he probably did mean himself. Verbally abused forever, with the occasional slap to the face or punch to the torso when a child, Cash had lived with the notion he was never good enough. But Reid had never understood why. Cash had been a top athlete if not a top student. Liked by adults and kids, he'd been on the road to a scholarship for football, no doubt. Then, in the tenth grade, their father had punched him, hard, for a mistake Reid had made. The punch turned to a beating, made worse because Cash had fought back, blackening their dad's eye.

Charles never laid a hand on him again, but the damage had been done. Cash turned brittle, hostile. His grades plummeted. He dropped out of sports and had little in the way of decent friends. He led a group of idiot kids into more mischief than was healthy and barely escaped juvenile detention.

At sixteen, he'd moved out. Four years later, once Reid had graduated, they joined the service together. And now here they were, visiting their mother the way they did every month, wishing for a past that could never be and a future that seemed to drag.

"An hour with Angela feels like a year," Cash mumbled.

"So why come?"

Again, Cash shrugged. Reid hurt for him, though he'd never say anything. His brother had the biggest heart in the world, buried deep beneath emotional trauma and a blustering ego. If Cash really thought about himself the way he bragged, he'd be president of the universe by now.

All the guy wanted was a little affection from his mother. With their father dead and gone, he'd never find it from Charles. Not that he would have if the old man had lived.

"Our family is totally fucked up," Reid commented.

Cash barked a laugh. "You got that right."

They drove in silence until Cash told him to slow down.

"Why?"

"Because your leggy PR chick is walking and I'm taking in the view." He whistled. "Day-um, son. I love a woman in shorts."

Naomi walked with a blond woman—Liz, he saw—on the sidewalk. He pulled up in an empty spot on the side of the road. Cash rolled down his window and whistled.

Reid rolled his eyes, hoping Naomi recognized the car and took the whistle as the compliment it was intended to be and not more harassment from some dumbass who should know better.

Liz waved at them. Funny, but her hair refused to be contained despite the bright orange headband holding the mass back. Naomi had hers in a ponytail. She wore a Sounders sweatshirt and shorts that showed off her long, *long* legs.

"She's hot. No doubt." Cash's seal of approval.

"She's off-limits."

"I meant for you." Cash laughed at him, the melancholy previously darkening his gaze lifting. "She's too brainy for me. Now if she'd just tell me how great I am while I was with her, that I could handle. But she's not the type to stay quiet."

No, she wasn't. She'd been moaning and whimpering when he'd kissed her, touched her. And that little cry at the end had been unforgettable. Hell, he was getting hard. Not cool with his brother in the car and Naomi walking to the window. He prayed the seat belt covered his arousal.

Naomi leaned over against the car. "Well, well. The Griffith brothers out and about on the weekend. No moving for you two today?"

Cash answered for him. "Nah. We have plans. A hot date with two smokin' babes."

Naomi glanced past him at Reid, her face calm while her eyes shot daggers at him. He would have crowed in triumph except he shouldn't want Naomi to feel possessive. And he really didn't want to see his mother.

Reid rolled his eyes again. "We're going to see our mother. Cash only wishes we had hot dates."

That took care of Cash's smirk.

Naomi blinked. "Oh, well, have fun."

"A word one never uses with Mom," Reid said dryly.

"No shit." Cash glanced past Naomi to Liz. "Hey. I'm Cash. Who are you?"

"I'm Liz, the woman who runs Starr PR. Naomi would die without me."

Naomi agreed, "All true."

Cash nodded. "Same here. I'm the backbone of our business. Reid's the image. My little brother tries, but there can be only one top dog, you know?"

"Oh my God. Your ego is almost as big as your biceps. Idiot." Reid sneered.

Naomi and Liz laughed. "We don't want to hold you up, so—" Naomi started to rise.

"No, stay." Cash sat up straighter. "Talking to pretty women is worlds better than visiting Angela."

Naomi patted him on the shoulder, and Reid didn't like the attention she gave him. At all. Cash was a good-looking guy. He had muscles and a brain hiding behind his big mouth. On top of that, he projected an air of confidence that caused others to effortlessly fall under his lead. If Cash tried, Reid was sure Naomi would fall for the guy.

He would have said something when he noticed Liz staring at him. "What's wrong?"

Liz blinked. "Oh, nothing. Just thinking you're so much better looking than Tanner Ryan."

Naomi turned pink. "Liz, really."

"Who's Tanner Ryan?" Cash asked.

"Some jerk Naomi used to work for. A real loser."

Naomi looked like she wanted to sink through the sidewalk.

"A loser, huh?" he asked her.

She smiled through her teeth. "A complete loser. Come on, big mouth. We need to walk. Later, guys." Naomi dragged Liz away, and he and Cash watched them walk at a brisk pace.

"Quit staring at her ass." Reid watched her until she and Liz disappeared from view.

"You first." Cash chuckled. "That was a nice distraction, but Naomi's right. We'd better go. Let's get this over with."

They drove for a while before Reid, unable to stop himself, said, "She's not your type. Not at all. Do us both a favor and stop flirting with her."

Cash turned to him with a big grin. "Flirting with her? Little Brother, when I'm flirting with a woman, she knows it. That was just me being friendly with Naomi."

"Well, quit it. We're working with the woman. Just working." He glared Cash into submission, surprisingly, then found the familiar road leading to their monthly trip to hell.

～～～

Cash left the car, following Reid. He was in no rush to see Angela, the woman who'd given birth to him, then left him to fend for himself while she drifted in la-la land, more content with movies, television, and books than taking care of her kid. She'd help Reid here and there, but even Reid had fended for himself when their father was busy.

Watching his brother with Naomi had been an eye-opener. Reid always had an air of cool competency. He'd bailed Cash out of more trouble than Cash could remember, and he had a knack for putting two bucks together and getting ten back.

But with Naomi, Reid had been nervy. A little frazzled, though he'd pretended to hold it together. And the way Naomi had eyed Reid, trying really hard not to look interested, definitely told its own story. The woman certainly hadn't liked the thought of them out with other women.

Cash grinned, wishing he could hold onto the good feeling for longer than it took to climb the stairs to his mother's floor.

Reid had been taking care of Cash for far too long. The guy had no social life. He threw his all into the business. It had been Reid's plans that made Vets on the Go! possible. Reid's knowledge of how to start the business, to get Evan's help, to delegate hiring and firing and the grunt work to Cash. Yet he'd still made Cash co-owner in the business though Cash hadn't had any investment capital.

Because Reid was like that. Family first. The poor bastard clung to a sense of duty and loyalty to the woman who'd given birth to him. Cash came to support Reid. He hated looking at Angela, loathed the sight of her.

But Reid needed him. For all that he had little to give, Cash would give Reid anything his little brother needed.

The journey to Angela Griffith's room happened way too fast.

They knocked and entered, finding their mother at the kitchen stove.

"This is for you," she said, glancing at Cash before turning back to her creation. She was cooking something for him, as she'd promised in her last phone call. God knew what the woman thought she was trying to prove. She hadn't given a damn about him for years. Now, for some reason, she sought to please him whenever possible.

And Reid, the good son, the one who'd stuck by her when Cash had turned into the rebel teen from hell, didn't seem to matter.

Angela opened her arms and waited for Cash to greet her. He endured a frail hug and turned his head before she could kiss him on the mouth. That always creeped him out. "Oh, sweetie. It's so good to see you." Then she gave Reid a kiss on the cheek. "You too, baby."

She looked like an angel. Such a contrast to the selfish woman he knew her to be. Angela had looks and charm. A vapid sense of self-importance. Her world had revolved around make-believe for as long as he could remember. Their father had tolerated her because he'd loved her no matter what—or so he'd claimed. But Cash thought the guy just liked the idea of a perfect little family.

With both Charles's and Angela's parents dead, it had only been Cash, Reid, and their parents left, not counting his dad's brother and family—Evan's parents, who they spent little time with. Then Charles had died. Now it was just Cash, Reid, and Angela. Dysfunction at its finest.

Reid gave a strained smile. "Hey, Mom. What are you making?"

"Cash's favorite." She looked at Cash or, rather, through him. Sometimes Cash didn't think she was all there. "He sure does love my stew."

Cash and Reid exchanged a glance. "Um, I'm partial to clam chowder."

Angela didn't seem to hear him and started humming while she stirred the pot. "Turn up the TV."

Cash did, not surprised to see her fixated on some soap opera from years ago. His mother fixated on drama of any kind, so long as it happened to other people, and she'd always been a *General Hospital* fan. He refused to admit it aloud, but he understood her fascination for other people's problems. He couldn't get enough of the *Housewives* on television. And TLC's *Love after Lockup*? A thumbs-up winner.

He sat at the table across from Reid and stared at his mother, wondering how much longer he'd have to make these monthly visits. Reid made small talk, engaging Angela because she liked to talk about herself.

Cash learned that her friend, Margaret, an actual living person, had visited on Friday and brought her the pink shawl sitting on the couch. He'd never seen the woman personally, but by all accounts, she was the only friend his mother had.

He watched his brother interacting with their mother, noted their similar facial structure and a few mannerisms, and wondered if he too shared anything with her. He certainly didn't get much from his father except for his size.

Charles Griffith had been a huge dickhead. Literally huge, six foot four, two-forty. All mean muscle and cruel attitude. Reid could do no wrong. Cash could do no right. Yet here, now, after the old man's death and his mother's decline into Crazytown, what really mattered?

He ate the stew that was supposedly his favorite. He listened to Reid tell their mother about their plans to expand their business and watched it all go over her head. She nodded and smiled, but she wasn't hearing Reid at all, her gaze affixed to Cash's face. Which truly made him uncomfortable, because he had the feeling she wasn't seeing him either.

Believing they had done their duty, Reid wrapped up their visit. "We have to go, Mom. We'll see you next month, same time, unless you want to see us before then?"

Cash hated the hopeful note in his brother's voice.

Angela, as usual, shook her head. "No, sweetie. You live your lives. I know you're busy. I'll be just fine here." She smiled. But this time she looked directly at Reid, and Cash sensed something different about her. "I always loved you, you know that?"

"Ah, sure, Mom." By the hesitance in Reid's voice, he sensed it too.

She gave Reid a kiss, then turned to Cash. He'd been standing by the kitchen doorway, more than ready to leave. She reached up to pat his cheek. "I wasn't there when I should have been, but you left me too soon." She looked so sad. Cash felt a pang of regret for not being what she wanted in a son. "I love you, honey. I always have."

"Sure. Love you too," he mumbled, hating that he meant it, hating how much he needed to hear her say it and mean it too. But he thought this time she might have, because her gaze was clear as she stared at him. "We'll see you in June, Ma."

"I don't think so." Her gaze turned cloudy again. "But that's okay, because Luke and Laura are getting married, and I have plans to make."

He and Reid shared a sigh. Their mother and her ancient recorded soaps—thirty or forty freakin' years old. Hell, did anyone even watch soap operas anymore? They had nothing on reality TV.

They left her to her shows and walked quietly to the car. Once inside, Reid sat there and tapped on the steering wheel, lost in thought.

And Cash hoped like hell he hadn't sounded like the lost little boy he'd always been, trying to win back his mother's love.

———⁓———

Reid didn't know what to make of Angela today. "She was off."

"Yeah."

Good. He wasn't the only one who felt it. "Do you think she's off her meds?"

"Who the hell knows?"

"You don't know what she takes, do you?"

Cash shrugged. "Why should I? She barely tolerates me. Hell, half the time we were there, I don't think she was seeing either one of us. Maybe she thought we were characters from her stupid soaps."

Reid agreed. "And what was with the stew? Your favorite?"

"Dad liked it. Maybe she thought I was him?" Cash grimaced. "God knows I'd rather be mistaken for anyone else but that fucker."

Reid said nothing to that, knowing his brother had a right to his feelings. Though Charles hadn't been a good man to Cash, he'd been supportive of Reid. Reid had worked hard to earn his father's trust. But no matter how many times he'd tried to talk to his dad about Cash, his father had refused to hear him out. Reid's efforts to heal their relationship had failed, and in time, Reid had come to dislike his father as much as he wanted to love him.

"Well, we're done with Mom for the month." The thought brought him no peace. His mother hadn't been herself. Maybe he'd go back next week to check on her. That was if he wasn't buried in broken trucks and clients out the ass. "You going out tonight?"

"Hell yeah. I'm meeting Hector and Lafayette for drinks at a bar downtown they like. You in?"

"I have work to do."

"Reid, take a day off, man. You need it. Dealing with Mom is never easy." Cash paused. "I don't know why you still do it."

"Why do you?"

Cash shrugged. "No one else will. I guess it's a tribute to the one thing the old man taught me that I could respect: protect women and take care of your mother. He wasn't worth squat, but he hit gold with those two pieces of advice."

"Guess so." Reid remembered his father playing catch with him in the backyard. His father teaching him and Cash how to ride bikes, back when his father had been civil to his oldest son. Other memories of Charles Griffith helping Reid with one thing or another. Yet those memories were muddied by recollections of his father constantly browbeating Cash. *A no-good loser. Nothing like your brother. A piece of shit I wouldn't touch if I didn't have to.*

What would make a once-decent man treat his own son like that?

"I know we've talked about this before, but do you think Charles wasn't your father?" Reid asked out loud, something they'd often talked about when the topic of Charles arose.

"Sure. But you and I look a little too much alike. And we don't exactly take after Mom."

"True. You're broader in the chest, not as handsome"—he ignored the finger Cash shot him—"and you have those ugly green eyes."

"Funny." Cash grinned, his mood seeming to lighten. "But these pretty green eyes and my broad, muscular chest score me lots of attention, Little Brother. Take a note."

"Please. At least I know how to treat a lady, and I date a woman more than once."

"Twice maybe."

Reid shook his head. "You find a woman who'll keep you for longer than a month, and then we'll talk."

Silence descended, and Reid realized what he'd said.

Fortunately, Cash just grunted at him, no ugly references to the woman Cash had once dated for *longer than a month*. Hell, Cash had once put a friggin' ring on her finger, and then Mariah had done the unthinkable. But Cash took Reid's joke for what is was, no mention of the ex-fiancée. Maybe time did heal all wounds. "Dream on. I haven't met anyone yet who could handle this fine mind and body."

"Yeah, there's that, isn't there?"

Pleased to have hurdled the past without Cash turning into a despondent, mopey zombie, Reid turned the talk to the Mariners recent game against the Blue Jays. Cash liked nothing better than to argue, so Reid let him.

After dropping his brother off at the bar, he drove to the office and put in a few hours' work.

Evan dropped by to compare notes, then left after insisting he refused to work on a Saturday night and planned to spend the evening with his mother.

"Tell Aunt Jane I said hi."

Evan brushed a hand over his hair. "Will do."

"And get a haircut, would you? You're starting to look like a civilian," Reid teased. Considering his own hair, short yet long by USMC standards, he knew better than to talk.

Evan snorted. "Yeah, right, you long-haired freak." He grinned. "I'm going home. You should too. Between the two of us, it's like we're competing for biggest loser of the year. Get a life, man. I plan to."

"Yeah? When would that be?"

Evan shrugged. "After I figure out what the hell I'm doing with my job. Next month, I think."

"What happened to your three-year plan?"

"I burned it. I can't keep up this pace and not go insane. I'm managing, but barely, and I know it." He stretched and yawned. "Besides, it's tough to have a relationship when you're never home. And since I can't use deployment as an excuse, it's up to me to give my mother grandchildren."

Reid liked his Aunt Jane, but she'd been on Evan's ass lately to settle down. More added pressure his cousin didn't need. "You sure you're up for that? You look weak to me."

"Thanks. All my working parts are in order, jackass. You should take your own advice and relax. Cut your hair, get laid, get a life. Follow Cash's plan."

"What? To leap without looking?"

"Why not? He seems happier than both of us."

"Yeah, yeah. Tell Aunt Jane I'll come by for dinner one of these nights."

Evan nodded. "Good. Then maybe she'll get off my ass and on yours."

Reid chuckled. "You wish. See you."

Evan left. Reid continued to work, took the forms Finley and Martin dropped off once they'd finished work, then finally closed up the office. A peek into the warehouse showed all the trucks locked up and accounted for, including their new vehicle that needed a wash, fresh paint, and their logo.

He drove home and changed into workout gear, not inclined to sit around and stare at the walls on a Saturday night. Only eight o'clock and he felt ready to sleep forever.

"I am so lame," he said to an empty room.

Reid ran a familiar route toward Green Lake, but instead of looping around the lake, he ran a different path, heading toward Naomi's part of town, actually. She did live close, and he liked the fact. Yet as the miles added up, he thought about catching an Uber home. He was near exhaustion. His muscles ached, and his mind was turning to soup, his thoughts vacillating from Naomi's smile to his mother's dismissive stare.

But as he rounded a corner and saw a young woman being harassed by two larger men, he decided he wasn't as tired as he'd thought.

Chapter 10

THE KNOCK AT NAOMI'S DOOR STARTLED HER. NINE ON A Saturday night? She glanced down at herself in yoga pants and a red tank top sans a bra. Not exactly dressed for company. She threw a zippered hoodie over her top and glanced through the peephole before opening the door wide.

Rex, the little punk, darted by her and nearly tripped Reid in the process.

"Reid?" She stood back to let him in and gaped at his bruised and bloodied face and ripped T-shirt. "What happened to you?"

"I'm really sorry to barge in on you like this. Would you mind giving me a ride ho—"

"To the hospital? Sure. Let me grab my keys."

"No." He stopped her by the arm. "A ride home. I just need to wash off my hands and I'll be fine."

She took hold of his arm and dragged him down the hall to her master bathroom. She pushed him not so gently onto the toilet. "You sit there. I'll fix you up while you tell me exactly what happened."

"Yes, ma'am." He winked, then winced. "Ow."

"Idiot." She grabbed a washcloth and gently wiped the blood from his right eyebrow. It wouldn't stop bleeding, and she started to panic.

"It's okay. Head wounds have a tendency to bleed a lot." He took the washcloth from her and pressed it to his brow.

"You have a bruise on your cheekbone and your shirt… It's done, I think." She helped him lift it over his head and tossed it into the trash. "Talk, Griffith," she ordered as she dabbed a tissue with some antiseptic.

The rest of him appeared fine but for a bit of bruising on his ribs. And then there were his knuckles, which had taken some knocks.

"I was out for a run."

"At nine at night?"

"Visits with Mom can be…stressful."

She didn't comment. She felt like eating tubs of ice cream after talking to her family, so she could relate.

"Cash went out, but I had work to do after our visit. When I finally got home, I was too tired to go to sleep, if you can believe that. I decided to go for a run."

"Around here?" She couldn't help feeling suspicious.

He chuckled. Fortunately, his gorgeous mouth hadn't been injured, though he groaned and clutched his ribs. "I live in Phinney Ridge. You're not very far from me or my office."

"Oh." Phinney Ridge was a nice area—then it clicked. Chris Jennings had mentioned renting a place to Reid. "That's a great neighborhood."

"I know. We're renting from a friend of mine who gave us a deal." He assessed her with a shrewd glance. "Chris Jennings owns the house."

"I know. He mentioned it at coffee last week."

"Yeah. He's got a girlfriend, you know."

She frowned. "So what?"

He shrugged carefully. "So if you're angling for a date, you might want to try elsewhere. Teresa doesn't share."

"You're an ass, you know that?" She wiped his knuckles a little too hard.

"Ow!"

"Baby. Now are you going to finish your story? Or do I have to get mean?"

He gave her an odd look. "Um, no. Don't do that. I don't think I can handle you being mean."

She made the mistake of looking down and saw his erection. "God, Reid."

"Well, it's your fault," he snapped. "I'm in pain, woman. Not here for your personal amusement."

She couldn't help it. She started laughing.

"It's not funny."

"It is." She tried to stop but couldn't. "You're bleeding and yet still 'standing tall.' I thought the Marine Corps slogan was *always faithful*, not *always hard*. Does that thing ever go down?"

He laughed, then groaned. "Stop it. I'm injured. I could be bleeding internally, you know."

"All the more reason to get you to a hospital," she said and turned to leave.

Reid reached out and grabbed the sleeve of her hoodie, tugging her back. "I'm fine. Just bruised a little, and the cut above my eye stings." He tugged again, and her hoodie parted. More accurately, the zipper fell off.

"Darn it."

"Sorry." He let her go.

"It's old. Was bound to happen sooner or later." She shrugged out of the thing and stepped closer to her injured patient. Removing his hand holding the washcloth, she saw that the wound had finally stopped bleeding. It didn't look as bad as she'd expected either. "You should probably get this stitched up."

"Yeah."

He sounded hoarse, and she glanced down, only to see him eye level with her breasts.

The tank top molded to her, and it was obvious she wore no bra.

"I wasn't expecting company."

He swallowed and leaned his head back against the wall, closing his eyes. "Right. Sorry. So, what happened... I was running a new route and came on two guys roughing up a woman. I tried to stop them, but apparently it was a setup and the woman was in on it. I got in a few punches and would have done more damage—not to the woman, mind you—if she hadn't pulled a knife on me. That distracted me. Next thing I know, one of the guys got up from where I'd planted him and socked me in the ribs. The other knocked me in the head. Bastards."

"You need to report this to the police." She dabbed his eyebrow and put some antiseptic on it, then covered it with a butterfly bandage. She did the same to his knuckles. She could do nothing for his bruises but get him some ice.

"The cops won't be able to do anything, but I did use a passerby's phone to report it. Unfortunately after all that, the bad guys got away." He sounded disgusted with himself. "Cash would have taken care of them with no problem. I got a beatdown. Man, promise you won't tell him about this?"

"I promise, but I'm pretty sure he's going to notice his brother with bruises all over his face."

"I'll make something up."

She didn't like how tired he looked. What if he'd suffered a concussion and didn't know it? "I still think you should go to a hospital to get looked over."

"No."

Stubborn man. She stared down into his gray eyes, amazed that even beaten up, Reid Griffith attracted her like no one ever had.

"What's that look?" Reid made no effort to hide the effect she had on him. He glanced down her body, zeroing in on her tight nipples. "Fuck, Naomi. You have an amazing body. And you're beautiful." He cupped himself, and the sight of Reid holding his cock seduced her right past her default thinking of "no."

She stepped closer, between his legs, and put her hands on his shoulders, her breasts now closer to his face. "You know this is a bad idea." She had to clear her throat to continue, especially when he put his hands on her waist. "We both know we need to have clear heads about this."

"Yeah." He licked his lips. "I want to touch you so bad. Need to kiss you, taste you."

Not exactly poetic, but the raw honesty in his words drugged her with desire. "I made a mistake like this before. Got involved with someone I worked with. It ended badly."

He blinked up at her, and she saw a man who'd gotten hurt doing the right thing. A Marine who protected, acted on instinct. A man who wanted her desperately. "I won't hurt you."

"You won't try to."

"Naomi, I'm so busy right now, a relationship is the

last thing I have time for. I won't lie to you. I want to fuck you like crazy. But it can't go further than that."

"Oh?"

"Look, I'm not after you because I'm in between women. I don't lie or cheat."

"Yeah? I don't either."

"I know." He groaned and gently slid his hand up her waist, over her shirt, to pause on her ribs. He watched her as he ran that large hand up and over her breast, cupping her before rubbing his thumb over her nipple.

She shuddered, her body like soft, willing putty in his hands.

"Yeah, that. We're attracted to each other, and we have some unbelievable chemistry. I don't normally get hard for a woman all the time. And I sure the hell don't come in three seconds, like I did the other night." He grimaced and arched his pelvis up. There was no question but that Reid was massively aroused.

"I don't either, though I admit it's been a long time for me."

"How long?" he asked, continuing to caress her.

Her knees felt weak. She clutched his shoulders, hoping she wasn't hurting him. "A y-year? Maybe more?" Had she been with anyone since Tanner? Frankly, she could barely remember her name right now.

"Months for me." He lifted his other hand up to cup her other breast, giving it the same attention and making her knees shake. "It's up to you, Naomi. Do you want this? You tell me no, I leave. It's not a problem, and working together won't ever be an issue. You tell me yes, I stay. I fuck you until you can't walk, and working together won't ever be an issue." He stared at her mouth with an intensity that left her breathless. "I don't kiss and tell either. You don't have to worry I'd ever screw with your reputation. But if you don't—"

She put her hand over his and squeezed her breast. "How's that for an answer?"

He pinched her nipple, and she couldn't stop the moan that left her.

"I didn't bring any protection," he confessed and stared at her without blinking.

"I have some. In the bedroom."

Reid wiggled on his seat, then frowned. "God. Am I really holding you while sitting on the can?"

She burst out laughing, feeling the sexual tension ease into a comfortable, if not easy, desire. "Let's not tell anyone."

"Ever," he said fervently.

They made it to the bedroom, and Reid watched her take out a condom. "Grab another one while you're at it."

She swallowed. "You sure? I don't want to hurt you."

"Naomi, the only way you could hurt me right now would be to tell me to get lost. But I'm a big boy. I'll recover if you change your mind."

She looked at him, seeing past the superficial bruising and gorgeous looks to a man of real character. Something in her shifted, but she didn't want to examine it. Not yet.

"You're not going anywhere." She lifted her shirt and tossed it aside. Now clad in her yoga pants and panties, she waited, proud, unafraid.

"Fuck me." Reid stared at her with reverence. "Might want to take out a third condom. You know, because I doubt I'll ever be soft around you again."

His chest and arms were things of beauty. Reid had a streamlined build, but he was by no means small. Several inches taller and much more muscular, the man was a living statue.

"Have I told you how much I like a well-developed chest?" She walked toward him and put her hands over his pecs, then ran her fingers over his hard nipples.

He swore softly, his erection prominent.

"Take those off."

He removed the rest of his clothes. "You sure? I might spontaneously come all over the place."

"Nice image."

He groaned when she licked her lips. "Don't do that. You're giving me all kinds of dirty thoughts."

"I'm not going down on you." No matter how much she wanted to, she didn't really know him. And despite not being that smart when it came to relationships, Naomi never messed with her health.

"I'm not asking you to, though I wouldn't say no if you begged." He stared as she slowly removed her yoga pants, leaving her in nothing but white panties. "It's a matter of trust. You mind if I want to go down on you?"

"Not smart. You don't know me." She found it hard to breathe at thoughts of him licking her up and eased her panties off.

"You told me it's been over a year. You won't go down on me because you don't really know me. And you're one of the most in-control women I've ever met. I know you, Naomi. Yeah, you're safe. The question is can I make you come before I do? Because you have to know, the first time's gonna be quick."

"But your injuries…" She watched him stalk toward

her. "Use a condom so you can come in me the first time." She turned to grab one for him and felt him plastered against her, his front to her back. She gasped, loving the sensation of closeness.

Carnal need overwhelmed everything.

"Fuck, yes, I'll use a condom the first time. I need to be inside you."

He turned her around and gave her a gentle shove back. Naomi fell onto the bed, her knees bent over the edge, spread on either side of him.

Reid donned the condom while watching her, then leaned down and lifted her up as if she weighed nothing. He scooted her back so that she lay fully on the bed and came down over her.

She expected him to fuck her fast. But he bent down and took a nipple in his mouth instead.

She gripped his hair, holding him close while he suckled. He moved to the other breast and teethed her, driving her wild. She felt his cock against her, pushing back and forth as he ground against her pelvis while loving her breasts.

Frustrated, she shifted and felt his cockhead brush her clitoris.

"Oh," she moaned and tried to move him closer.

Reid caught on, licking and sucking while he positioned himself to do the most good. He rode her clit, rubbing with delicious strokes but nowhere near to penetrating her.

"Reid, please."

He trailed kisses up her neck, across her cheek, to her ear and whispered, "Gonna fuck you so hard. Once won't be enough."

She agreed and arched into him, undone by the rough friction of his chest against her breasts. The feel of such a powerful man between her legs, undone by passion for her, was too much.

"In me. *Now*."

She yanked his mouth close and kissed him, sucking on his tongue the way she imagined to suck his dick at some point in the future.

He gasped and slid into her.

Finally.

They both moaned as he surged deeper, not giving her total fullness in a rush, as she'd wanted.

"More."

He kissed her back and seated himself fully. Then he leaned up and stared at her. "You're fucking gorgeous, you know that?"

He withdrew little by little, then just as slowly eased back inside.

She was going crazy with lust. He continued to give her tantalizing, tiny thrusts.

"I thought this was going to be fast," she complained. "Keep it up and I'll come without you." She was so close, every push and pull stirring her climax.

"You asked for it." He looked serious, determined. Excited. Reid withdrew again, then shoved deep inside her in one sudden push.

The shock of his intrusion pushed her into climax, and she cried out as he watched her, riding her with harder thrusts, the power of his penetration overwhelming. The orgasm was brutal and enveloped her completely, so when he shouted and stilled inside her, she felt his pleasure as intensely as her own.

Reid, so thick and full inside her, emptied into the condom, his arms shaky as he held himself over her. "Jesus, Naomi. I'm still coming."

"So maybe just once tonight?" she said, thoroughly sated. If she smoked, she'd be lighting up right now.

"Hell no. That's just the beginning."

He didn't pull out. Instead, Reid kissed her. Her lips, her cheeks, her neck. Then he started again on her mouth, making love to it. To her.

To her shock, he remained half-hard as he moved within her.

"I'll take it off and use a new one," he promised. "Just give me a minute."

"Take your time," she croaked, and he laughed.

Joy blanketed them both, the rush of pleasure swelling once more.

Naomi couldn't believe how good it was. Like a spiritual awakening with Reid, being the focus of his intensity.

He finally withdrew and left her to dispose of the condom.

Languid and satisfied on the deepest level, she just lay there.

He returned, bruised but not beaten, looking like a savage warrior come to take his prize.

"What's that look?" he asked her and leaned down to run a hand up her leg.

She spread her thighs wider, encouraging him. "What look?"

"That one. You seem happy to see me." He kissed his way up her leg and explored her with his hands and mouth. By the time he'd worked his way to her face, he was hard again.

"Need a condom," he managed.

She scooted under him to turn over, grabbed it, then handed it to him over her shoulder.

He put it on as she moved up on her hands and knees, aroused anew to have him take her from behind.

"Fuck. I'm coming in."

She laughed, and then she wasn't laughing as he entered her. The sensation of closeness was indescribable. He felt locked inside her body. And then he pulled back before slamming inside once more.

The rough taking excited her, and when he reached around to fondle her clit, she exploded.

He rode her through her climax into his own, the rough pounding more than welcome as he emptied once more.

Naomi had never felt so replete, and as she knelt before him, her head hanging low while he moaned and came, she knew a sense of peace.

Reid withdrew and came back to her moments later. Spent, she flopped, boneless, to the bed and just lay there. When he joined her, it felt only right to snuggle, chest to chest, before he left.

"God, Naomi. I don't think I can move. Give me a few minutes and I'll head home, okay? Can I get a raincheck on that third condom?"

She gave a muffled okay, then relaxed into his strong arms, loving the low chuckle that vibrated through his body. She laid her head on his chest and closed her eyes for just a second…

And woke to his fingers absently stroking her back, his erection pressing against her belly. It was dark, but she could see Reid's outline in the hint of moonlight peeking through her window. A moonbeam illuminated his face, and she saw his smile and eyebrows raised in question. She rolled onto her back, excitement bringing her wide awake.

He kissed her belly, then moved down her legs.

His mouth took over, and Naomi lost herself to his touch.

The next morning, she woke with a groan, feeling pleasantly sore.

She was alone this time, and not having to deal with an awkward morning after relieved her.

After a trip to the bathroom, she put on her silk robe and looked for Reid.

"Reid?"

She heard nothing and didn't know if she should remain relieved or be annoyed he'd darted off like a thief in the night. A three-time wham-bam-thank-you-ma'am?

Laughing at herself, she left the hallway to find a fresh pot of coffee in her kitchen along with a note.

Sorry. I didn't mean to fall asleep on you. But I did make good on that third condom.☺ I left so you didn't have to see my ugly mug so early this morning. (Trust me, I'm best with teeth brushed and a shower.) I'll see you tomorrow for coffee. And Naomi, this won't be weird unless you make it weird. Yes, YOU.

XO Reid

P.S. You're even beautiful when you snore. Ha.

She stared at the note, bemused at the warmth it engendered. Reid hadn't snuck out. Okay, so he kind of had, but his reasons were as valid as her need to look good when she saw him again. Oh God. She'd snored?

She reread the note several times and had to laugh.

Naomi had a meeting with her new lover the next morning. And like he said, it would only be weird if she made it weird. But could she see him and not think of him between her legs? Would she ever be able to have sex again and not expect such complete abandon? She'd come *three times*.

She could chalk up the first time to being needy. But the second and third? An unselfish lover, Reid paid attention to *her*, seeing to her needs before his own. Damn it. She was really coming to like this guy. Loyal. Sweet. Sexy. Unselfish. And a killer lover with some seriously talented equipment.

Naomi knew she'd have to do her best to mentally keep him in the friends-with-benefits category. Seeing him tomorrow would be a challenge. Would she be able to look at him the same?

She groaned. Once again, she'd ruined a good thing with sex.

Would she ever learn?

Chapter 11

MONDAY MORNING, REID SAT SIPPING HIS COFFEE ACROSS from Naomi. Fortunately, his eye hadn't turned black and blue. He just had a small cut above his brow that hadn't, in fact, needed stitches. His brother had accepted his scrapes with the excuse that he'd stopped a mugging. Not that uncommon in the city.

Reid had made sure to arrive at the coffee shop fifteen minutes early so he could be settled and ready to negotiate with his sexy PR expert. But she'd beaten him in and had turned the tables, watching *him* take *his* seat.

Nicely played.

He felt the tension, had known it would be there. The feisty redhead had no way of knowing he was a man of his word. It would take time for Naomi to trust that he meant what he said. He *did* respect her. He *did* want them to be professional about the business. He would never talk about what they'd done to anyone, because it was no one's business but theirs.

But Naomi had been burned before. He would need to prove she could trust him. And then, God willing, she'd use that talented mouth on him…everywhere.

He should have been too tired to be hard again, but nope. Just thoughts of Naomi turned him to stone, and sitting across from her didn't help. She wore a perfume that mixed with her natural scent and had him in mind of sex and spring.

He sipped his coffee and watched her, doing his best to clear his fogging mind. "You look lovely this morning."

She tipped her head. "So do you."

He watched her over his coffee. "My, my, Ms. Starr. Such a flatterer."

She grinned. "You started it."

"And I'm not even done with my first cup of coffee yet." He didn't have to work hard to come up with compliments. He noted the subdued green shirt with full cuffs she wore, the khaki pants and high heels. Naomi Starr was a knockout whether dressed to impress or in a worn robe with matted hair.

Frankly, he wasn't sure which look he preferred, and the thought amused him.

"Care to share the joke?"

And remind her of what he'd promised to bury behind a casual facade? No way. "Let's just say I'm impressed I'm talking before ten o'clock with so little caffeine in my system."

"Caffeine and sugar. Don't forget your pastry." She nodded at his plate.

"I like sweets. It's a weakness." He glanced at the half-eaten chocolate croissant on her plate. "But at least I'm in good company." He guzzled more coffee. "Now show me what you came up with for our campaign."

Fascinated, he watched her shift into all-work-no-play Naomi—the competent, take-no-prisoners businesswoman who knew her craft inside and out.

He had no doubt Naomi would take his business to the next level. Hearing her speak in such precise, knowledgeable terms while detailing a plan for success, he believed in her. And that had nothing to do with her looks and everything to do with her intelligence.

Unfortunately, those smarts made her even *more* attractive to him.

"I know web design takes time," Naomi was saying. "And you're working with Dennis, who's a genius. You're obviously not his only client. But I swing a lot of business his way, so he's going to put you at the top of his priority list. With a few more changes to your site, you'll be ready to maximize the interview's impact. I also reached out to a few local magazines and the paper, and we'll have you swamped in overlapping coverage for the next two weeks, a hard push to get your name out there.

"Then we'll back off, let the magic of your charm and your company do its work, then start pushing from an advertising perspective."

"Whatever you say." It all sounded good to him.

"In the meantime, I suggest you continue with your plan to hire more people. It's fine to keep a small firm small, but you've already mentioned you'd like Vets on the Go! to grow to meet recent demand. The larger you are, the more veterans you can hire, which helps the community."

"True, but hiring takes time. Don't get me wrong, I respect anyone who's served their country. But just because you wore a uniform doesn't mean you're not a dirtbag underneath. I've met plenty of those, trust me."

"You want your people to be beyond reproach."

"Exactly. I'm not going to hire some jackass just because he was Corps. I'm all about brotherhood, but not at the expense of the customers we serve."

"Good to know. And on that note, how is Dan Thompson working out?"

Reid grinned at the thought of the crusty old bastard. He loved the guy. "He's the right man for the job. I made him an offer, and he's planning to stay on part-time. I think he's bored with retirement. But that's our gain because the man's a god in the office. With him on board, I can hire less experienced admin assistants knowing Dan will train them. Things are coming together."

They discussed more options and a few things he hadn't considered for the company and should have. Though Naomi focused on PR and marketing, she'd worked with so many companies that she knew more about the business side of things than he'd have expected. And it wasn't like Reid had a business degree. He'd done his best to put together a business plan by looking at other models and with Evan's input. Naomi was helping tremendously with her suggestions.

He shook his head. "I can't believe your old boss ever let you go. I'd hire you after five minutes of talking to you. And not just because you're a knockout. You know your shit—ah, stuff." Sometimes he slipped when talking to her. Reid had been taught to respect women, and to him that meant no cursing around them. But he felt comfortable with Naomi, as much as his body felt *un*comfortable around her. It was an odd dichotomy, but then, so was she.

Naomi seemed both tough yet vulnerable. Sexy and sweet. He kept waiting to see the not-so-nice parts of her, which would make it easier to distance himself. He hoped. For all his talk about not having the time or energy for a girlfriend, he was finding it difficult to not want more from her.

He wondered if she had plans later... *Do not ask her to dinner, you moron. Give her what she wants—nothing but business.*

"Yes, funny to think I did so much for my company and then was let go. I wasn't, technically." She paused, studied him, then seemed to come to a decision. "I told you I was in a relationship with someone I worked with." She frowned. "I was stupid. I'd put him off for a long time, then I said yes when I should have said no. In my defense, Tanner was a nice guy...up until the time he wanted me gone because I outperformed him at work."

"Sounds like a real dick." Reid would never do something like that. At least, he hoped he wouldn't. He didn't think he had an excessively large ego. Not *excessively* large.

"He wasn't, and then he was." She blushed, then scowled. "Why am I telling you this?"

"You want me to know the score. Some guy at work dicked you over, but what really hurt was your *boyfriend* dicking you over. Sorry, Naomi, but he should have put you first, no question."

She gave him the most beautiful smile. "Thank you."

He flushed, not sure why. "Just stating a fact."

"Uh-huh. Anyway, I'm sorry I mentioned any of it after my lecture last week about keeping things professional. My only excuse is I haven't had my morning espresso." She held up her coffee cup. "Plain regular."

"Because our machine was bitchy, but it's better now," said a tall woman who looked like she could bench-press Reid's brother as she came to stand by Naomi.

The woman was toned, her sleeveless Blackstone Bikes T-shirt showing off her arms, and she handed Naomi a small cup of espresso. "On the house. Sorry."

Behind her at the counter a few feet away, a dark-haired man yelled, "Don't blame the machine because you're inept, Sadie!"

Customers around the place grinned, a few calling out to Sadie, their waitress.

The guy at the counter scowled. "Now get back here and make our customers happy, damn it!"

Sadie sighed and dragged herself back to the counter.

"Colorful coffee shop," Reid said. "I come in for the coffee and treats, but the entertainment is something else."

"Yeah." Naomi grinned as the counter guy made his way toward her. "Personally, I like the eye candy."

Reid had often seen the guy interact with customers. Friendly, flirty, and funny. But when he had the gall to kiss Naomi on the cheek, Reid wanted to punch him in his square jaw.

Naomi gushed. "Elliot, I missed you!"

"Ah, one of my favorite customers. I have a thing for redheads." He gave Reid a thorough once-over. "But then, I like them dark too." He held out a hand to Reid. "Elliot Liberato, owner of Sofa's. I've seen you around before. Nice to meet you."

Reid shook his hand, refraining from crushing it. "Reid Griffith."

Elliot's eyes widened, and he squeezed harder before letting go. "Hey, you're part of that moving company, aren't you?"

"Yes, but how did you—"

"A few friends showed me pictures, you know, of you guys having that photo shoot a week ago. They were there in the crowd trying to get phone numbers." Elliot winked. "I bet you're slammed with work now, aren't you?"

Reid did his best to forget the kiss Elliot and Naomi had shared. *So* not his business. "We're getting there."

"Well, Reid, I'm going to tell everyone about you guys. Give me a flier, and I'll put it up on our bulletin board."

"I was getting to you," Naomi said with a smile. Reid could tell she genuinely liked the guy. "We're working on Vets on the Go!'s branding now, but we're gearing up to start advertising. I'll get you a flier soon." To Reid she said, "We'll also put some in local gyms, supermarkets, libraries, places people frequent. But we'll target online with social media. You get much more exposure that way."

Elliot nodded. "Naomi helped us last year, brought us into a new sphere of production, so to speak. We now have an online shop for our cookies." Elliot beamed. Reid hated that he wanted to smash Elliot's perfect teeth in. The guy was too good-looking and too charming. And Naomi seemed to be eating him up.

"Congrats." Reid tried to act like he meant it.

"Hold on. Are either of you two allergic to peanuts?" When they shook their heads, Elliot dashed away and returned with two cookies.

He and Naomi took the cookies Elliot handed them. And damn, but they were delicious.

"Good, huh?" Elliot sounded smug.

"Amazing." Naomi groaned. "You are ruining my figure, Elliot."

"Bitch, please. You're gorgeous and you know it. Now this one…" He stared at Reid and sighed. "You think she's hot, don't you?"

Reid blinked. "Uh, yeah. I think you'd have to be blind or dead not to see that."

"I agree. You two enjoy and come back and see us." Elliot leaned closer to Reid. "And if you ever feel like coming over to the dark side, let me know."

He left whistling, returning to the back counter to argue with Sadie.

Reid was confused. "What did he mean by that? And why are you laughing at me?" he asked Naomi.

"That was Elliot not-so-subtly letting you know that if you wanted to ask him out, he'd probably say yes."

Reid stared at Elliot, who waved back at him. "He's gay?"

"Yep, and proud of it."

"Oh. *Oh*." Reid smiled, feeling better all of a sudden. "Good."

Now it was Naomi's turn to look confused. "Good?"

Reid couldn't explain a stupid attack of jealousy, so he tempered it with, "Good he feels confident to be out so publicly. I was in the military, and I know all about homophobes and morons. It's not the stereotypical 'we hate gays' theme anymore, but there are still those who have problems with it. Me? I don't care."

She smiled. "I've never had an issue either. Then again, my older brother is gay, so my parents were pretty accepting early on." She sighed. "So long as you get a great job and have a family and two kids by the time you're thirty, you're doing the Starrs proud." She groaned. "I'm the black sheep of my family."

"Yeah?" He grinned. "So they're all successful and coupled up and you're an old, ugly hag with a barely there company, is that it?"

She sipped her espresso and gave a blissful sigh, one that had his erection back in full force.

"Ben, he's the oldest, is a doctor with two kids. Peter's a lawyer, and he and his husband recently adopted an adorable little girl. Harley, my sister, just became VP of her company and is getting married this summer. She would have been married with kids by thirty, but her husband died a few years ago. It was really sad, but my sister never lets anything throw her. Now she's expecting, working her ass off, and about to be married to Mr. Perfect." Naomi smiled, showing bright-white teeth.

"So you fit right in," Reid said, sensing tension and not sure why. Naomi seemed to be one of the most capable women he'd ever met.

"Me? The woman who had to start over, lost her boyfriend and her job at the same time, and will probably never have kids or a husband because I have no time for a life and no intention of settling? Ha! Talk about a black sheep."

He snorted. "You think that's bad? My mother barely looks at me when we visit because she can't stop staring at my brother when she's not lost in some stupid soap opera, book, or movie. I might as well not exist."

She stared at him, her blue eyes wide, and he wanted to crawl under the table. How the hell had that slipped out?

Naomi reached out to touch his hand. "I'm sorry. That sounds terrible. But she's getting older, and older people can act strangely."

"Yeah." He sighed. "But she's always been distant."

"What about your dad?"

"He died years ago. He wasn't an easy man to love." Familiar feelings of guilt and anger surfaced at mention of the man. "It's just me and Cash. And Evan," he tacked on with a smile. "My cousin is a trip. His mom's still alive, but she's much older. She's more like a grandma than an aunt, but she's sweet."

"That's nice." She stroked his fingers.

They both looked down, then she slowly dragged her hand back. A rosy flush darkened her cheeks and made her eyes brighter. "Sorry."

He shrugged, pretending she apologized over his situation and not because she'd needed to touch him. "Hey, life is what it is."

They sat for a moment, finished their coffee and treats, and did their best not to look at each other. Reid would catch her glancing at him then looking away, and he'd do the same.

Finally unable to stop himself, he reached across the table and took her hand in his. Then he brought it to his mouth and kissed the back of it. "This was the most professional, businesslike, intimate breakfast I've shared with anyone." He smiled. "Let's do it again soon."

She laughed, looking relieved. "Yes. Let's."

They stood and left together, waving goodbye to Elliot, who was laughing at Sadie and her flailing hands.

"Place has character." He held the door for Naomi.

"I think you mean *characters*." She thanked him as she passed. "Sadie's engaged to Gear Blackstone, the bike guy."

Reid paused. "Gear Blackstone, the guy who had that

reality show *Motorcycle Madnezz*? I used to watch that. Man, his partner was such a tool—no pun intended."

"He was." She grinned. "I just watched whenever they'd feature Smoke working on a bike."

"Ah, you like them big, tattooed, and silent, eh?"

"Yep. Silence is golden."

He laughed, in a great mood as they walked to their cars. "I really hate to get back to work."

She sighed. "Me too. But the day waits for no woman. See you soon, Reid." She paused by her car door.

He wanted to kiss her goodbye. *Badly*. But he didn't want to break any more rules. So he gave a last wistful look at her lips and said, "Talk to you soon, Ms. Starr." He waved then turned to make his way to his car.

And couldn't help glancing over his shoulder at her one more time. The sun hit her dark-red hair, settling over the strands, making them appear on fire. Naomi wore a sweet smile, her blue eyes shining. Something in Reid changed. An emotion, a sensation of…fullness… grew and settled deep inside him.

He didn't know what to call it, but he liked the feeling. And he planned on telephoning her sooner than later. They had another meeting to work through. One where Reid set a few rules of his own.

Naomi watched Reid leave, wondering how she'd gone from making love to working to sharing herself with *her client*…who was so much more than that. Reid had turned into an honest-to-goodness friend. She was starting to trust him on a fundamental level. Though she must have trusted him already, because she'd had sex with the man.

Reid attracted her, no doubt. But every time they talked, she learned something new about him, and it made her like him even more.

Her phone buzzed, and she glanced down at it, only to see a number she could have done without. Tanner Ryan. She wondered if talking about him had somehow summoned him, an evil spirit of an ex she'd rather forget.

What had possessed her to mention him to Reid?

But Reid had shared something of himself. She couldn't forget his expression when he'd mentioned his mother. He looked the way she so often felt when dealing with her own family—loving but frustrated. It must be terrible to see his mother and think she preferred his brother over him.

The same way Naomi tired of constantly being second, third, and even fourth best when it came to her siblings.

Her phone buzzed again, and she glanced down to see a call from Harley. *Huh. Maybe this phone* is *cursed*.

"Hello?" she answered.

"Hey, Naomi. It's me, Harley."

"Yes, I have caller ID. I know."

"Guess what?" Harley bubbled with excitement. "Mom and I are coming for a visit at the end of the month!"

God, shoot me now.

"Would it be okay if we stayed with you for a few days? Ben is getting that award on the thirty-first. We didn't want to miss it. Dad and Peter can't come due to work, but Mom and I are planning to be there."

"Sure you can stay with me. I insist," she heard herself saying and immediately wanted to take back the words. "Do you need me to pick you up from the airport?"

"If you wouldn't mind. I'll shoot you the itinerary in a few days."

"Great." *No, no, no!* "What's Kyle going to do without you?"

"Oh, he's coming too. You do have space for us all, don't you? We can't stay with Ben because his in-laws are staying with them. They're flying in too. But it'll just be Mom and me, so two rooms. Kyle and I will be sharing a room, obviously."

"Sure." It hurt to keep the smile going. Perfect Kyle and perfect Harley were enough of a burden, too much happily ever after to go with Harley's pregnant glow. Add in Mom and her need to oversee her children's lives, and Naomi wanted to move out of the state, pronto.

"Great. I can't wait to see you and Tanner. It's been too long."

And then there was that little nugget Naomi had been hoarding. The fact that she and Tanner had broken up ages ago. Naomi had meant to let everyone know, but since her mother had pitched a fit about Naomi dating her boss way back when, Naomi hadn't had the heart to tell her she'd not only broken off with a poor choice for a boyfriend, but that she'd also lost her job. Left *my job. I left before I could be fired; there's a distinct difference.*

"Well." Naomi cleared her throat. "Tanner and I are no longer a thing."

"Oh, I'm so sorry." The worst thing was Harley meant it. Tack on *genuine* and *nice* to *business genius* and *domestic goddess.* "What happened?"

"The usual." Naomi did her best to keep her tone light. "We grew apart. Work got stressful, and I'd decided to leave. I've wanted to make it on my own for a while, and I finally did. I've been running Starr PR, and we're doing great."

"Oh my God. You broke up with Tanner *and* left your incredible job? When did all this happen?"

A year and a half ago, right after you announced your big promotion and engagement to Mr. Wonderful. "Not too long ago. I haven't mentioned it to Mom or Dad yet. But I'm happy and doing great," she said. "Even seeing a new guy," she added in a perky voice, needing to feel not so inadequate.

"Oh?" Harley laughed. "You really are doing great."

Didn't I say so? And it's not all because of Reid. Is it? Naomi's thoughts shot to Reid and his devastating smile. *Hell.* "He's a friend I met through work. We really hit it off. But I'm taking it slow. I'm so busy with the job that I don't have a lot of time for a boyfriend."

"I hear you. But life is short, Naomi. Take it from me, when you find someone special, hold on with both hands and don't let go."

Naomi gritted her teeth, tired of her older sister's wisdom, constantly handed down through a miasma of emotional pain and sad dignity. Naomi knew she was being petty, but she'd been getting unasked-for advice her entire life. The woman was only slightly less pushy than their mother when it came to telling Naomi what to do.

At least Peter and Brad wouldn't be coming. Her brother and his husband could be such know-it-alls, even worse than the rest of the family. The one person who never tried to boss her around, her father, remained at home in Walla Walla, no doubt glued to his phone for a teleconference about some corporate legal case or another.

Dad could always be counted on for a laugh. She wished he would have been able to come with the others. She got her sister off the phone after a few minutes with an excuse about work. Then she texted her father and received an answer she'd been dreading...

I know you and Tanner split a while ago. You stopped talking about him the way you used to, then altogether. Since you didn't tell your mother, I kept quiet. Now's your chance to confess. Love you. Good luck surviving your mother and sister! Better you tell them than I admit I knew and didn't tell. Ha! Love, Dad.

The traitor.

Naomi wondered how best to handle her family. On top of her mixed-up feelings for Reid, it seemed prudent to keep Reid and her family far apart. Not that easy to do considering she'd just mentioned she had a new man in her life.

With any luck, her family would never know her new "boyfriend" didn't really exist, and Reid would never learn she'd used him as a prop to keep her family off her back.

Talk about unprofessional to the extreme...

Chapter 12

"OH MY GOD. I'M IN HELL. KILL ME NOW." CASH GROANED and covered his eyes with his forearm. He sat kicked back in a chair in the conference room across from Reid and Hector.

Reid and Hector shared a look. Hector rolled his eyes and left to grab coffee, closing the conference door behind him.

Reid kicked his brother's chair.

Cash dropped his arm and glared. "Stop it, dickbag."

"Then quit being such a pussy and focus." Reid spoke in words his brother would understand. "We need four more people to round out the team. We have six working trucks. With Dan and Finley managing the front office and work picking up every freaking minute, we can't afford not to. Plus, we need people in case of injury. What if Jordan pulls a muscle and can't come in?"

"Is she injured?"

"I said *if*, moron."

Cash's eyes narrowed, and he sat straighter in his chair. "Call me a moron again, Little Brother, and I'll make you regret it."

Reid sighed. "Look, *idiot*, we need to get these people hired. Now."

Cash growled.

"Before Hector comes back, tell me what was wrong with the last two we interviewed." To Reid, they'd seemed reasonably intelligent and hard-working, according to their references.

"First off, Air Force Stan thinks he knows everything. That's wearing on a guy. I'd be more likely to punch him in the face than ask him to pass the packing tape."

"That's it?"

"He's obnoxious. I can't work with him."

Reid ground his teeth and wondered what his dentist would think the next time he saw her. "You work with Finley and Jordan just fine. And they're both obnoxious."

"Yeah, but they've grown on me."

Hector returned and handed Reid a fresh cup.

"Thank you."

Hector nodded and passed Cash a soda. "What did I miss?"

Reid answered, "Cash doesn't like Stan because he's obnoxious."

Hector frowned. "So are Finley and Jordan. Martin too."

"I forgot Martin." Reid nodded. "Right. So Stan's hired."

"Good," Hector said. "I liked him."

"Moving on," Reid said before Cash could argue. "What's wrong with Heidi? Her pre-interview last week went well. I thought we all liked her."

Cash and Hector exchanged a look.

"What?"

"You mean besides the fact that Heidi can break Lafayette in half?" Cash asked.

"Please. She can*not*." Hector glared at Cash, then added, "I like her, but she doesn't talk much."

Cash nodded. "Yeah, and what Hector said."

Reid sipped his coffee slowly. "A woman who's got muscles bigger than Hector, is quiet, and is willing to work for our wages?"

Hector drank his coffee and shrugged. "Reid's got a point, Cash."

"Great. More women in the place." Cash made a face, but Reid caught the sly look his brother shot him.

Hector choked on his coffee. "Um, yeah. You know, Reid, maybe we should give Heidi her second interview and let Cash take a pass. With Cash's big mouth—no offense, Cash."

"None taken."

"You're liable to be looking at a harassment suit once Tall and Charming here speaks."

Reid ran a hand through his hair. "Yeah? Well, this shit has to stop." He turned to Hector. "Mind giving us a few minutes?"

"Not at all." Hector must have been waiting to be excused because he bolted to the door. "Oh, and I need to help my brother on a job that looks like a three-man deal. Sorry. Good luck on the interviews." He darted out and shut the door fast behind him.

"Coward," Cash yelled.

Reid put his foot down. "Okay, Big Brother. No more excuses that you can't talk to people without offending them because that's the way you are. Screw that. We've worked too hard to make this business a go. You want out? Just say the word. You want to actually stick with something for more than a few months and start advancing? Maybe even make some friends and have a life?"

"That's rich, coming from you." Cash snorted, his

green eyes glowing, alive when brawling, even verbally. "You do nothing but slave over a desk all day long. Everything you touch turns to gold. Great. I'm so glad this is fulfilling for you. I'm tired of it."

"Of working?" Reid's temper continued to rise.

"Hell no. I like working. I actually enjoy physical activity on a daily basis. But this office crap is giving me hives." He scratched his arm as proof. The way a four-year-old would.

Reid wanted to bang his head on the table. "Look. I know you don't want to be here. But you're in charge of personnel. Now quit bitching, put on your big girl panties"—he ignored the finger Cash shot him—"and let's finish with the interviews. Heidi's passed the first, so let's get through this final one and make our decision."

Cash shot to his feet, swore under his breath some more, then yelled down the hall for Heidi Schneider. Reid poked his head out the doorway.

Unfortunately, their conference room sat between their main office and the clothing shop, which had opened its door early this morning. The computer and watch repair shops hadn't opened up yet, thank God.

So along with Heidi leaving their office and walking down the main hall like she owned it, a short, middle-aged woman with attractive features and distinctive blue eyes behind black glasses stormed toward them from the opposite direction.

Heidi reached them first and entered, passing Cash, who gave Reid a look after she moved by him. Heidi had to be six two because she'd nearly come eye to eye with his brother.

Heidi had short blond hair, plain if pleasant features,

and a clearly muscular build. She wore jeans and a sweatshirt that said "USMC Proud."

Reid raised a brow at it. "Hi, Heidi. It's nice to see you again. You remember Cash, my *charming* brother."

She didn't smile.

Okay then. He started to close the door to the conference room, but the woman—Miriam West, if he remembered right—hurried toward them and shoved her high-heeled foot in the door before he could pull it back.

"I need to talk to you two," she warned and pointed… something…at them.

Reid gaped. "Uh, is that a…a… What is that, Mrs. West?" Because to Reid, it looked like the older woman wielded a ten-inch dildo.

Cash stared as well, his mouth open.

Heidi took a seat and waited, no expression on her face.

"What do you think this is, Mr. Griffith? It's a dildo. And it's Ms. West, not Mrs."

Cash coughed.

Heidi just stared.

Reid tried to take control of the situation. "A large neon-blue dildo." This had to be some kind of joke. "Did Hector or Lafayette put you up to this? No. Wait. It was Finley, wasn't it?"

"I'm trying to conduct a class," she said, waving around the sex toy like a conductor preparing her orchestra. "You need to keep the noise down. My girls can't expect to reach the climax of success if you're bellowing every five seconds."

Cash's eyes widened. "Climax?"

Miriam turned to him, and Reid saw that the silk

dress she wore wasn't inspired to look like a robe, it *was* a robe. The heels she wore had a fuzzy red trim. She moved again, and he caught a flash of bare leg. *No*. No way she meant what she'd said to be taken literally. The sex toy had to be some kind of prop.

Heidi blinked but remained quiet.

"I run a liberating class on female empowerment," Miriam announced, set eyes on Heidi, and nodded. "You should check us out, honey. I'm right next door." She pulled a business card out of a pocket and put in on the table, then slid it to Heidi. "We're on chapter four right now. Experiencing the essence of what it means to be a woman. But all this hollering is distracting." She glared at Cash and Reid, but her expression soon turned calculating. "You know, if you wanted, you could come on over and help with a few demonstrations. Have you ever thought about showing women how they can help achieve oneness with themselves with the right support? A man's point of view would be so…stimulating." She smiled.

Cash had a shit-eating grin that didn't bode well.

"I have," Cash admitted.

"No," Reid said clearly, not caring what he'd said no to exactly. His brother's involvement in Miriam's group couldn't end well. "We're sorry for interrupting you. We'll keep it down."

"Well, if you don't plan on helping my class reach fulfillment, you probably should." She gave a lingering glance at Cash and Reid, then turned on her heel and left.

Reid stared after her, confused and slightly unnerved.

"I thought she sold vintage clothes," Cash rumbled. "That was…interesting."

"Very." Heidi had spoken, her voice surprisingly

light, though she had a slight accent. German, he thought but couldn't be sure.

They turned to see her sitting with her hands folded on the table. Miriam's card had vanished.

Reid didn't say a word and prayed Cash wouldn't. "So sorry about all that, Heidi. We usually have pretty uneventful days at Vets on the Go!"

She stared at him, and he felt dissected under that piercing gaze. "That's not what it looked like on the TV. I first heard about you there."

"That was all me," Cash said and crossed his arms over his chest. He leaned against the wall and stared down at her. "You passed the interview, and your background check came back clean. But out of all the applicants we've seen, why should we hire you?"

Reid sat across from Heidi. Not how he'd have started the interview, but Miriam had frazzled him.

Heidi considered Cash. "I'm a hard worker. I spent six years in the Navy, another seven in the Marine Corps. I got out so I could pursue my love of athletics."

"Says here you like to race?" Reid read.

"Yes. I'm a triathlete, and I travel a lot to compete. For fun."

Heidi didn't appear as if she knew what the word *fun* meant. She had yet to smile, but Reid liked her attitude and the competent vibe she gave off. "You've read what we're offering. You seem like a good fit. We'll work you on a trial basis for a month. If it's still working, you're hired. Any questions?"

He answered a few about benefits and time off as well as her need to be part-time during certain parts of the year while she trained.

"Sounds good. Anything else you'd like to share with us, Heidi?" Reid glanced at Cash, who'd been surprisingly quiet during the interview. Apparently he liked her as well.

"I'll work hard. I expect to be paid on time and treated with respect." She shot Cash a look, apparently sensing he'd be the one to watch.

Cash nodded to her.

"I like sports. I like people, but I do not like to talk."

"We'll get along just fine then," Cash said.

"And I like women. All kinds, really. I take it that won't be a problem?"

Cash frowned. "You like women?"

"I'm a lesbian." At Cash's continued frown, she added, "I like pussy. Understand?"

Hearing her speak so bluntly after being so polite and contained threw Reid once more.

Cash gave her a slow grin. "I like pussy and sports too. Sounds like you'll work, Heidi. Welcome aboard." Heidi stood, shook hands with Reid and Cash, then left.

Reid blinked. "Did she just say she likes pussy?"

"Yep." Cash chuckled. "What was I saying about not liking this admin shit? I'm freakin' loving it. Who's next?"

They interviewed a dozen more people, keeping the meetings short since those attending had already passed the first round of interviews a few days ago. More than half of their applicants were quick no-go's. A few of the applicants had potential, like the guy with a passion for reptiles and the other who loved music, so much that he whistled when nervous. Reid had liked him. Cash had said hell no, but Reid had decided to throw him a bone.

After a ten-minute lunch, they'd screened *more* people. They'd had to take a short break to air out the office after one applicant, who believed in a natural remedy to being dirty—and that didn't include bathing.

They'd finally reached quitting time, and Reid took a look at his notes. Out of the lot, four applicants looked fairly solid.

Stan and Heidi they'd hired. Funny Rob, a tall, muscular Asian man who hadn't cracked one joke, looked good to go as well. Cash had grunted his agreement on the guy. Mannie, their last interview, seemed the most normal of the bunch. Which wasn't saying much.

"I liked Mannie." Cash leaned back in his chair and sighed. "But those tats looked a little edgy. For all that his background check was clean, we should keep an eye on him."

"We need the help, and he looks good so far." Reid stood and stretched. "So we'll give him a shot. I think it's safe to say we put in a full day. I'm hungry."

"Yeah, let's get dinner."

Reid saw that the hour had reached six. The repair shops and Miriam's had likely closed. A glance to the left of the conference room showed the main office door still open, with Finley at the desk. He saw them walking and nodded to his right.

Once inside the office, Reid nearly ran into a giant. At first glance, the guy looked a lot like Cash. Same height, hair and eye color, even the same sneer.

"You guys Vets on the Go!?" the man asked, his voice deep and raspy.

Cash smirked. "Well, we ain't Miriam's Modiste, that's for sure."

Reid shuddered, remembering Miriam and her silicone dick.

The guy shot Cash a look filled with venom, and Reid took a closer step toward his brother. What the hell?

The man blinked, and Reid wondered if he'd seen things. Cash didn't seem put off by the guy at all.

What a long day. "Yo, Finley, thanks. You can go. I take it Dan left at four?"

"Yep." Finley leaped over the desk. "Later." He left.

Just Cash, Reid, and the stranger remained.

"So, I'm here for an interview." The guy looked from Cash to Reid, his gaze measuring, evaluating. Odd. But then, after the day they'd had, why should this applicant be any different?

As if reading his mind, Cash sighed. "Sure, why not? We can do it here since the office is empty."

He and Reid sat in the waiting area. The guy, Smith Ramsey, according to his application, remained standing. He looked down at them, and Reid tried but couldn't catalog the big guy's expression. He clearly had the build and demeanor of a warrior, though Reid would make sure they looked up the references he'd listed before possibly hiring him.

Reid read through the information on the application then handed it to Cash. "So you want a job with us?"

"Yep."

Silence.

Cash continued reading.

"Tell us a little bit about yourself."

The man stared at Reid. After a long pause, he spoke.

"Former Marine. Just got out after back-to-back tours in Afghanistan. Time to settle down. I'm not fragged or fucked up. Just a civilian needing a job."

Cash glanced up. "1st Battalion, 7th Marines? Saw some shit, eh?"

Smith shrugged.

Reid saw something strange in the way the larger man regarded Cash. He couldn't put a finger on it though. "So you're okay with an average wage and a job that's physically demanding?"

Smith snorted. "Same as when I was in. But there, they let me shoot a gun. They don't like you doing that in the civilian sector."

"No, I can't think they would."

"At least with you guys, I won't have to sit behind a desk all day listening to some sniveling asshole cry about his hard life working nine to five. Fuckheads have no idea what real work is." That sneer again.

"I feel that," Cash agreed, studying him. "You sure you want to work here? We're all fellow vets, and we hire all kinds. Men, women, black, white, gay, straight. You work here, you get along. You seem like an asshole."

Interesting Cash wasn't all over the guy, who seemed like a slightly younger version of himself. According to Smith's sheet, he was thirty-two years old.

Smith didn't break stride, that sneer still present. "Well, you're an asshole, and you seem to do well here. If you can do it, I'm sure I can fit it."

Great way to get a job, insulting your boss before you even have it.

Cash shot him the finger.

Smith crossed his arms over his chest. "Big words, big man."

Despite a sense he was missing something, Reid found himself kind of liking the guy. He choked back his laughter when Cash glared from Smith to him and cleared his throat. "We're still reviewing candidates, but we'll let you know. Just one question: why us?"

Smith stared Reid in the eye. "I need work. You hire vets, and you guys seem honest. That's all I'm looking for right now. An honest day's pay for an honest day's work. What you see is what you get. You want me, my number's there." He nodded to the application form. That said, he turned on his heel and left.

"Huh." Cash stared after him. "I don't like him. Besides, we already have four picked out, right?"

"We do... Why don't you like him?"

"He's a prick."

Reid thought it funny Cash didn't like the guy for being just like him. "Like looking into a mirror, eh?"

"Ha ha." Cash swore at him under his breath. "Can we get something to eat now? I'm starving."

They locked up and walked down the hall. But as they passed Miriam's closed door, they heard definite laughter within. And if Reid wasn't mistaken, what sounded like a moan?

Cash and he shared a glance, then Cash took a step closer to the door. "Maybe I should—"

"No." Reid grabbed him by the arm and dragged him down the hall. "Let's grab something to eat and get Evan in on this. Before my stomach is permanently stuck to my spine."

"No shit."

They ended up eating two large pizzas at home. Evan had work left to do but had agreed, via a phone call, with Reid's rundown of the day.

Reid felt physically and mentally drained and couldn't understand it. "I swear, today was harder than any day we've had so far, and that includes when I used to do the moving with you at the beginning."

"Lightweight." Cash mowed down his food as if he'd never get another meal.

"So what did you think of the last guy? Smith?"

"A ballbuster. He could be a real asset or a serial killer. I'm not sure which."

Reid chuckled. "I thought it was just me. I got a weird vibe off him too. But hey, we have the four we needed and two we can use part-time. That's it. I think we're done hiring for a while. And you know, we'll eventually have people coming and going. But if we can keep a core group, we'll do well." He and Evan had gone over the numbers to death, and they both knew that between insurance costs to cover the business and the employees, they would need to really *move* to make a profit. But hell, this venture was their own baby. They were the bosses; they made the decisions.

Reid glanced at his brother, now eyeing Reid's pizza. He shoved a few slices at Cash. "Go for it." Reid liked knowing that with Vets on the Go!, Cash had a job and a future. A way to build toward something more instead of always having to start over somewhere else with people who couldn't always appreciate his work ethic because his mouth got in the way.

Someone's phone buzzed. Reid checked his and found it clear.

Cash frowned at his phone, chewing. "Crap. Gotta go. See you later." He left without mentioning where he was headed or cleaning up. No surprise.

Reid leaned back and contemplated grabbing a beer. It wasn't too late, and though he wanted to relax, he had too much on his mind to chill just yet. Ever since he'd visited his mother last week, he'd needed to see for himself that she was still okay.

"We'll see you in June, Ma," Cash had said.

Her response, "I don't think so," still bothered him.

Reid drove to the assisted living home with an hour to spare. Visiting hours ended at eight thirty, so he hustled to his mother's room. And found it empty.

Concerned, he knocked again, then used a key to enter.

Inside, he found her gone.

A knock at the door distracted him, and he turned to see an older gentleman with a walker and an oxygen tank watching him.

"You the boy?"

"One of them," Reid said, trying to remain calm. "Any idea where my mother went?"

The old man nodded. "Angela had a seizure. They took her away this morning."

Reid tracked down an orderly. After a few phone calls—and a twenty—the guy rattled off the name of the hospital Angela had been taken to. Reid raced to the administration desk at the front. Getting confirmation that the orderly had been correct, he asked the question burning at the forefront of his mind.

"Why wasn't I told about this?" he asked the desk clerk.

The woman shook her head. "I'm sorry, sir. But according to your mother's instructions, she listed someone else as a contact."

"What? Who?"

"I can't tell you that. Our patients' privacy is important, and your mother was firm that her friend not be named."

What the fuck? In an icy voice, he answered, "She's my *mother*."

The lady looked sympathetic but refused to budge.

Reid at least had the information he'd needed. At the hospital, he learned she continued to go in and out of consciousness.

The head nurse, after seeing his identification, called Angela's doctor, who let Reid know that his mother likely wouldn't make it past the week. She'd had a stroke, and her organs had started shutting down. She also showed signs of malnutrition and confusion.

He'd known his mother hadn't been right and that of course someday she'd die, but the reality of it floored him.

Reid called Cash. "It's Mom. She's dying." He rattled off her room number and the name of the hospital.

"On my way." Cash disconnected.

Reid didn't know what to feel. A hazy relief that she might finally know peace mingled with guilt and anger. Now he'd never know the mother he'd always dreamed she could be. Hell, his asshole of a father had spent more time raising him than Angela ever had.

"Fuck." He wiped his eyes, furious to be crying over a woman more invested in soap opera weddings than her own sons.

Cash arrived, heard the prognosis, and responded with a much more stoic attitude. "Well, she's finally gonna get to go live with her telenovelas in the sky."

"Nice." Reid managed a chuckle.

Cash's smile was strained. "She say anything?"

"I haven't been allowed in to see her." Reid frowned. "She didn't list either of us as her emergency contact at the home. I only found out because I swung by tonight to see her."

"What the hell? Angela doesn't have any friends. Not real ones, anyway."

Reid ran a hand over his jaw. "I know." He stared at Cash. "Where were you, anyway?"

Cash shrugged and sat next to him. "Jordan had a problem I thought I could help her with." He grimaced. "Turns out she already had some guy helping her." The grimace turned into a scowl. "Some dick named Rafi. Sounds like a stuffed poodle to me."

Reid felt for his brother, but hadn't he warned Cash not to get involved with Jordan? *The same way he warned you not to get involved with Naomi?*

Reid wanted to call her so much, it alarmed him. The need to share with her, to hear her voice, see her sweet smile. He still remembered the feeling of her hand touching his as she offered comfort.

He forced himself not to call her, not even to respond to her work email either. He'd deal with her later, when he could function again.

"We should probably tell Evan. Unless it's Aunt Jane that Mom talked to."

Hell. Cash was calling her *Mom* now. The big bastard would go squirrelly when she passed. Reid mentally geared up for his brother needing him. Like the business needed him and Evan and the others needed him.

He'd be strong, keep it together. His grief could wait.

He tucked it deep down, right next to his dreams of a happy family and a future filled with laughter and fond memories. A future that would now never come to be.

Chapter 13

FRIDAY MORNING, NAOMI HAD HAD ENOUGH. REID HAD been terse with his texts and ignored her emails. She had no idea what she'd done to annoy him...and immediately stopped that way of thinking. Why did she have to be the one to reach out to him? He knew her number. Though they were friends, it seemed Reid had done the responsible thing and distanced himself from her personally. She should be grateful one of them had sense.

Instead, she missed him.

"Naomi, your sister is on line two," Liz called from the main office, eschewing their intercom system in lieu of going old school with a yell.

"Got it," Naomi yelled back, glad for Liz's sense of humor.

Without her work, Naomi sometimes wondered how she'd function. Everything revolved around her job. This week, she'd picked up another client and finally had a meeting with Jon from Jennings Tech. It had been an exciting look at what she might be doing in the future. Except that while discussing working alongside Jennings's PR people, she might also have to work with Tanner again, something she'd done her best not to contemplate.

Reid and Tanner had so much in common yet couldn't be more different. Both handsome, confident, and talented. In bed, they'd both been about pleasing her. But her chemistry with Reid was off the charts. Just thinking about him got her aroused. God, such a talented—

Stop it! She hated that she had to constantly tell herself to stop thinking about *her client*, Reid, every five seconds.

"Still on line two," Liz yelled again.

"God hates me!"

Liz chuckled.

Naomi bit the bullet and picked up the phone. "Hello, Harley?"

"You are impossible to reach." On purpose. "So did you get the memo that we had the wrong dates for Ben's award ceremony? It's not the thirty-first. It's next Thursday, the twenty-third."

"Okay." Would that mean her family would stay for less time? "Are you guys still flying in?"

"I don't know. Shoot. I have to go. We have a doctor's appointment today. We're finding out what we're having! I'm so excited. Love you. See you soon." Harley hung up, and Naomi did her best to restructure her calendar.

After conferring with Liz and moving meetings around, she glanced at her cell phone again. She checked her emails too. Still nothing from Reid.

"Screw this." She picked up her landline to dial Reid's office and ended up getting connected to someone else.

"Tanner Ryan's on line one," Liz yelled a little too late.

"Hello, Naomi?" Tanner said.

She closed her eyes and counted to ten in her head. "Yes, hello, Tanner. What can I do for you?"

"I'd like to talk."

"Go ahead."

"In person."

Not on your life, buddy. I'm busy. "I'm sorry, Tanner, but I—"

He knocked on her door, his cell phone at his ear. "You can spare a few minutes for an old friend, can't you?"

Shit.

She sighed. "Come on in. I can give you..." She checked her calendar. "Thirty minutes."

He smiled. "You're busy, as I knew you'd be. You're a star. No pun intended."

She didn't smile.

He sobered and took a seat across from her. "We need to clear the air."

"It's been cleared already."

"No, it hasn't." He shoved a hand through his thick blond hair, and she suddenly preferred it shorter and darker. Like Reid's. "I apologized. You didn't forgive me, and I can't blame you for it."

Liz wavered by the door, her gaze wide on Tanner. "Um, sorry, but Mr. Griffith is here to talk to you about his campaign?" She kept looking from Tanner to Naomi and bit her lip.

Naomi wanted to laugh hysterically. "Mr. Griffith, oh, right."

"I know he was scheduled for later, but he had something come up and needs to see you sooner. I can move your ten thirty so you can talk to him once Mr. Ryan's gone." Scheduled later? Reid hadn't been answering her calls. Now, apparently, he wanted to talk to her.

Naomi had confided in Liz how much she wanted to talk to Reid. Liz, bless her, didn't judge Naomi for lusting after the guy. Nor did she fault Naomi for liking him.

"Yes, do that." Naomi cleared her throat to stem her jumpiness at seeing Reid again. "Thanks, Liz. Tell him I'll see him then."

Liz nodded and, after Tanner glanced back at Naomi, mouthed, "*Oh, wow, two men,*" and gave her a thumbs-up. She shut the door with a quiet *snick*.

Naomi did her best to keep a nervous grin off her face. "Now, Tanner. Say what you need to say."

He kicked back and crossed an ankle over one knee. In a suit and tie, he still looked the epitome of the handsome, white-collar professional. Even though she knew him to be much less polished all the time. "I needed to say I'm sorry. I did that. But I wanted to explain. I was a jerk and an idiot."

"You said something to that effect the last time we talked." But she liked hearing it again.

He groaned. "It's all been shit without you. The business is good, but it's not fun anymore. Our people have great ideas, but they lack that sizzle you had. That flair for our clients' needs."

Hmm. He didn't seem to be concerned with losing her as a girlfriend so much as he'd lost her talent at work.

He shifted his foot to the floor and leaned closer, a familiar spark in his eyes. "We made a great team. I miss having you beside me." He sighed. "God, I miss you, Naomi."

She blinked. "Seriously? After a year and a half. After gutting my professional reputation and—"

"Whoa. I never did that. Everyone assumed you'd left because you wanted to. Not because I made you."

"Which you did," she said between her teeth. "So what Beth told me on my way out was crap? That everyone knew I'd slept with the boss and been fired for being a slut?" Not that she'd believed Beth, the pushy secretary who'd always had a thing for Tanner. But that some of her colleagues *might* think that had bothered her.

"No way. Beth always did love to spread rumors. She was fired, by the way."

"Before or after you slept with her?" A shot in the dark…that played out.

He flushed. "I told you I was wrong. I should never have allowed business and my personal life to intersect. I don't do that anymore."

Didn't he? "Good for you." She had to say it. "I worked my tail off getting this business together. And to think I'd imagined being a partner at PP&R one day."

"You still could be," he insisted. "You and me, together again. It would be amazing."

"Until I land a client instead of you, or they ask me to take on their business and you can't stand the thought of losing out to your ex-girlfriend. I'm sorry, Tanner. I just can't do that again."

"Not even if I asked you to come back to me in all ways? You know, us getting back together as more than just girlfriend and boyfriend, as more than colleagues." He had a funny look in his eyes. "Naomi, I loved you."

"I loved you too." Which had been why his betrayal had stung so badly. "But that's in the past."

"It's not."

She hadn't thought he'd go so low to win her back.

Flattering, sure, but a little creepy too. "Tanner, enough. I happen to know you're dating someone right now. What would she think about your confession?"

"She's a sweet woman." He kept staring at her. "But she's not you."

Remembrances of the good times they'd shared, of the way they could talk about work and laugh together, filtered past the bitterness, the hurt. "We did have some fun together."

The hope on his face felt…wrong.

"Tanner, no. I'm sorry. I'm not coming back to work for you. I might actually end up working with you if this Jennings deal pans out."

"Maybe." He sat back and shuttered his expression. "Jon seems to like what PP&R has to offer. I'm pretty sure he's going to hire us."

"Oh?"

"But if he did, and you also came on board, you'd have to work with us—with me, Naomi. I'm the lead on this account. It's going to be huge."

"If you get it."

"*When* I get it."

She didn't doubt he could pull it off. But she had an ace up her sleeve, and he was sitting outside in her waiting room. A back door into Chris Jennings's good graces.

"Best of luck to you. I've learned my lesson, Tanner. I might be able to work with, not for you. But that's all it'll be. Work."

He shrugged. "I'm not giving up on you yet." He forced a smile, and she felt a moment of sadness for what might have been. Might still be, some small part of her forced her to consider. "In any case, thanks for seeing me. I'll talk to you again soon. Bye, Naomi."

She stood when he did. "Goodbye."

She watched him leave, not sure how to feel. Triumphant that he'd come crawling back to her? Flattered he'd said all the right things? Suspicious he didn't mean a word of it? But why shouldn't he? Naomi was beautiful, smart, amazing at her job. He *should* want her back.

If only he'd said those words even six months ago. But something in her had changed. She no longer needed validation from Tanner.

No, she didn't.

Yet the feeling she had decisions to make lingered.

Reid filled her doorway, and all thoughts about Tanner fled her mind.

"Ah, Liz said you could fit me in?" He looked haggard, as if he'd walked under the burden of something heavy.

"Sure. Come on in." She smiled. "Would you like a coffee?"

"Liz already filled me up." He held up a cup and took his seat. "Sorry I've been slow getting back to you this week. We've been slammed."

"I know the feeling." They discussed a few updates she'd had for him, and he mentioned what had gone on the past week. A lot of moving parts in his moving company.

Yet something more had happened. She could sense it. Should she ask? *Oh, to hell with it.* "Reid, are you okay? You look more stressed than usual."

He gave a short laugh. "Besides my brother wigging

out, hiring the rest of our wacky crew, and my mother in the hospital, I'm great." He gulped more coffee.

She moved around her desk to sit next to him. "Oh, Reid. What happened?"

His gaze had a faraway look, and he wasn't acting like his usual self. "I went to visit a few nights ago. Cash and I usually see her once a month. She doesn't like too many visitors, but she allows us that monthly time," he said, his tone bitter. "When we spoke Saturday, she seemed...off. So I went back to check and found out she'd had a stroke. She's in and out of consciousness. They don't expect her to recover."

"I'm so sorry." She took his hand in hers and squeezed, settling the connection on her lap. "Is there anything I can do?"

He smiled, and the sweetness in his expression brought tears to her eyes. Sure, her family drove her crazy, but she couldn't imagine losing any of them. Reid not only had a tumultuous past with his mother and father, but his dad had died years ago. And now he was close to losing his mom.

"Nah. But knowing you want to help makes me feel better. Thanks, Naomi."

She leaned forward and kissed him on the lips, uncaring of her open door, being at work, or any of her preconceived rules about "clients."

"I know you've got a lot on your plate, but can I interest you in dinner tonight? I make a mean baked chicken."

He studied their clasped hands, then slowly raised his gaze to her face. "You know, I think I'd like that." He gently withdrew his hand from hers, set the coffee cup on her desk, then stood. "I'd better get back. I just wanted to let you know I wasn't ignoring you on purpose." He stared at her, brooding. "I wanted to see you."

Such a simple statement. Yet it said so much. "I missed you too" threatened to slip out and might have if Liz hadn't popped her head in the door.

"I'm so sorry to interrupt, but Devlin Sanderson is waiting for you, and we already moved his Skype appointment once."

"I'd better let you go." Reid's gaze traveled over her face like a lover's caress. "I'll talk to you later. Text me."

"I will. Take care, Reid." So much she wanted to say but didn't.

Feeling for him, she sat to take Sanderson's call, doing her best to focus on her client and not the man who kept stealing his way into her thoughts and heart, no matter how much she tried to keep him out.

Later that night, Cash waited in their mother's hospital room. He and Reid had been taking turns visiting. Cash still couldn't believe she was leaving them. He hated that he cared. Angela—Mom—hadn't been there for him for way too long. Yet one slip of affection, one smile from the woman, and he turned into that little boy constantly craving her attention.

"I would hate you if I could," he muttered, staring at her frail form.

She'd always seemed like a fairy, caught between reality and the fiction she lived in. It still amazed him his father had gotten her pregnant twice. Angela must have freaked the fuck out delivering his big ass. He grinned, but there wasn't much humor in it.

Reid was younger, so he didn't remember it as well as Cash did. But Cash could recall, to the day, time, and place, the moment he'd lost his mother for good. The first seven years of his life had been blessed. He had a younger brother who idolized him, a mother who loved the snot out of him, and a father who thought he could do no wrong.

And then, on Valentine's Day, after coming home from school with a special card made just for his mother, he'd found her crying while staring at a photograph of herself and his father. Her eye had looked purple, as if she'd taken a beating. His dad hadn't been home, and since Charles had never before been abusive, Cash had no reason to think his father might have done the damage.

He could still see himself racing to her side, only to have her look at him and cry even harder. She'd called him her All-In. Her little man. And then the joy had leeched out of her face, and she'd gone to sleep.

Reid had been scared, so Cash had taken care of him, waiting for their father to return. But when Charles came back that night, he'd been cold. So cruel to Cash, blaming him for everything and anything, though nothing made sense. But Reid he'd tucked into bed, keeping the young boy away from his "tainted shithead of a brother."

To this day, Cash had no idea what he'd done to deserve such wrath. Though the old man rarely smacked him, the verbal abuse had been crushing for years. Was it any wonder he'd left home as soon as he'd been able? But he'd always been able to count on Reid. Still the younger brother who idolized him, even now.

Or did he?

Cash frowned, wondering when Reid would say he'd had enough and call it quits. The moving business would never be a huge moneymaker, and they all knew Reid could be earning big bucks working some desk job. His brother had smarts and charm and knew how to talk to people. Not like Cash, who was only good for picking up shit or shooting it.

Regret that his time had been cut short in the Marines still bothered him. And that got him to thinking about Mariah again…

He stared at his mother, realizing he should have taken his cues about relationships from her. She hadn't loved him. Neither had his father. So what the hell had made Cash think Mariah might?

He felt stupid for having sniffed around Jordan at all. Like all the others, she saw the real him after spending some time with him. And Reid wondered why Cash preferred one-night stands to relationships. One night, some pleasure, then he was gone. He wouldn't give anyone a chance to get a chance to know and reject him.

"Cash, Reid…" Angela Griffith groaned and blinked open watery eyes.

"Mom?" Cash hurried to her side, leaning over her.

She reached out a weak hand to cup his cheek. "All-In. All-In…" Her hand slid away.

His eyes burned. Hell. She was really gonna die.

"My big boy. I love you, baby."

"I love you too, Mom," Cash admitted, ignoring the tears running down his cheeks.

"So sorry I didn't wait. Loved you so much."

"It's okay, Mom. You go if you need to." He'd had

buddies leave this world, knew the pain of holding on to friends when they did nothing but suffer. "Time to move on, Angela Griffith." He stroked her cheek.

She smiled and sighed. Then she looked right at him. He couldn't have said why, but he knew she saw *him* and not a memory or fantasy. "You have your father's eyes. Oh, how I loved him."

He watched her eyes close and let his hand slip from her cheek.

"Time for me to go back to sleep." She drifted, her breathing slow but steady.

But what she'd said bothered him more than he could say.

Charles Griffith had gray eyes, like Reid. Cash's were green.

Not like he hadn't imagined being some other man's bastard for years. But he and Reid looked too much alike, and he had his father's height and brawn. Plus, his father had never mentioned another man. And God knew Charles had hated Cash's guts. No way his father wouldn't have rubbed that in if Cash had been a bastard.

So what did Angela mean?

He settled in to watch her while the subtle beeps let him know she lived.

Reid had left his mother to Cash and took the evening for himself. Cash had asked for some time alone with her, and fuck knew, Reid needed the break.

The week had been seriously from hell. Between work, getting to know the new guys better, and ramping up promotion, he felt ready to burst. Adding in his dying mother didn't make much of a dent in his frazzled brain.

He'd been numb since learning she had little time left. Reid didn't know why it bothered him so much. He'd pretty much given up on both his parents in high school. His entire life, he'd strived to be the best. What had it gotten him? Nothing but vague smiles from his mother and never-ending pressure from his father to do better.

At first, Reid thought he could sway his father into behaving the way he used to. Reid would excel; Dad would be happy and welcome Cash back into his loving arms. Instead, his father constantly used Reid's accomplishments to belittle Cash even more.

So Cash started failing classes. He dropped off the football team. Stopped caring, barely came home.

Reid worked extra hard, trying to keep the family together. With him around, Mom and Dad at least pretended they had someone to care about. Cash came and went, but Reid always showed his brother he loved him.

Not that Cash believed himself worthy of that love.

Maybe now, with their mother finally passing on, Cash could let go of past hurts and open himself up. Maybe Reid could relax, no longer having to take care of the fucking world.

He parked his car in front of Naomi's house and closed his eyes. So tired, so lost. He didn't understand how Angela could still make him feel small and worthless. Such power she held over him, even after so many years apart.

He knew Cash felt the same. Reid wondered if he ought to spend time with his brother at their mother's bedside, in solidarity.

He mentally shook himself. Tonight, he needed Naomi.

Just the sight of her smile today made the world a brighter place. Corny as hell but true. His heart raced when around her. His senses seemed more acute. And now, as he left the car and walked up to her home, he felt himself beginning to smile for no reason.

She opened the door just as he knocked, and the scent of baked chicken and spice hit him hard.

She stared at him. "Is that your stomach I hear rumbling?"

He nodded.

Naomi laughed and tugged him inside. She took the bottle of wine he handed her and put it on the side table. Then she took a good look at him.

"Come here."

She pulled him to her, and as he eased into her surprisingly strong grip, he felt himself relaxing for the first time in days. He let out a long sigh, content to remain in her arms forever.

Stroking his hair and whispering that everything would be all right, she had him believing in something other than grief. He inhaled the fragrance at the crook of her neck.

"You always smell good."

She laughed, the vibration moving through her breasts pressed up firmly against his chest. "You sure that's not the chicken?"

His body turned rock-hard in a heartbeat. He knew she could feel it, and as they parted, he noticed her flushed cheeks. "Nope. It's all you."

"Come on, handsome. Let's feed you."

He took the hand she offered and let her lead him to

the table set with a tablecloth and candles. Shoot. He should have brought flowers.

"Naomi." He stopped her before she could pull away. Then he leaned close, staring into her ocean-blue eyes, and gave her a tender kiss. "Thank you."

"You're welcome." She kissed him back.

Then he ate the best damn chicken he'd ever had in his entire life.

Chapter 14

NAOMI DIDN'T KNOW WHAT TO THINK. REID HAD ENTERED her house looking like a shell of a man. But two helpings of chicken, sweet potato casserole, salad, and wine, and the man had regained some semblance of life.

He laughed and complimented her cooking, her house, her sense of style. They finished the meal and continued to sit together, talking while they sipped the wine he'd brought. He regaled her with some hilarious stories of his week that couldn't possibly be true.

"She did not wave a sex toy at you."

"Swear to God she did." He laughed harder. "Now every time Cash and I walk past her doorway, we think we hear moaning. I think she plays some kind of recording so even when she's not there, we're hearing it."

"I have to get back to your office."

He raised a brow and grinned, the spark of devilry in his gaze irresistible. "You thinking to get in on her female empowerment class?"

"Well, I'm all about women feeling powerful."

His eyes darkened, and he looked her over from head to toe. Or rather, from head to breasts, since the table blocked her lower half. "I like you feeling powerful too."

She knew for a fact it had been a very *long* six days since she'd felt Reid inside her. Watching him watch her, her entire body tightened up, his gaze sparking like a live wire.

"I, ah, did you want dessert? I made brownies."

"Chocolate. I like." He stood when she did and followed her into the kitchen. "How about you feed me some of those brownies?"

She swallowed around a dry throat and turned around. She knew what that look in his eyes meant. Like tinder about to go up in flames, she allowed herself to move closer to his heat.

She hurried to grab the plate of brownies and froze, trapped by the counter in front of her and Reid at her back. His arms wrapped around her waist, holding her in place while he rubbed a thick erection against her ass.

"Mmm." He leaned closer and pushed her hair out of the way so he could kiss up her neck. "Maybe that's what I taste. Chocolate." He licked her neck, and instead of being creeped out, she drenched her panties.

"Oh God. You feel good."

"Not as good as you do. I want to make love to you. Right here. Right now." He rubbed her ass through the skirt she wore. "You good with that?"

"Y-yes." Like she'd say no. She tried to turn around, but he stilled her.

"You stay right there and let me do all the work. Let me *empower* you to do nothing but feel sexy," he teased and turned her face, managing to find her mouth for a soul-shattering kiss.

She had no idea how he'd done it, but his hands were everywhere. Her boots, socks, and underwear lay scattered on the kitchen floor. He continued to ravage her neck as he unbuttoned her blouse, then teased her breasts, getting her so close to orgasm, she feared coming too soon. Having him behind her, in charge and out of reach, was shockingly hot.

"I love your tits," he murmured as he cupped her, pinching the nipples into hard points. "You get me so hard."

"You get me so wet."

"Yeah?" he rasped. "Let's see." He had such wonderful hands… Unfortunately, he didn't move them fast enough to suit her.

Reid slipped her shirt off and unfastened her bra but left her skirt on. He ran his hands up the sides of her skirt, across her bare legs. His clever fingers found their way between her thighs and moved higher. The cool air made her shiver, her nipples stiff, her flesh pebbled. But it was the sensations caused by Reid that had her moaning his name.

"Oh yeah. Let's feel you come," he muttered as he rocked against her ass while rubbing her clit, then sliding fingers inside her.

"I'm close," she warned, shocked she'd been so ready so fast.

Reid wouldn't let her wait. He bit her shoulder, then fucked her with those long fingers. "Yes, come, baby."

She shoved back against him, but he wouldn't give her any room to avoid the delicious pressure overtaking all sense.

He grazed her clit once more as he thrust his fingers, his other hand molding her breast while he plucked the firm bud and drove her out of her mind.

She keened as she climaxed, the pleasure a total joy of the senses.

As she came down, leaning over her kitchen counter, she felt him withdraw, then heard him unzip. The rip of a package, and then he was pulling her hips back and raising her skirt.

"I need to come inside you. Wearing a condom, I promise. But...*fuck*." He slid inside her, feeling incredibly large.

The sensation of Reid in her already sensitive passage lit her up all over again, and she shrieked as he pumped hard, gripping her hips as he fucked the breath out of her and her multiple orgasms.

Reid stilled soon after, groaning as he jerked inside her. "Naomi." He poured into her for a long time, it seemed. But when he withdrew, he left her bereft. Empty.

"Damn. I feel light-headed."

She sighed. "I'm wobbly."

"We can't have that. Stay right there." He disposed of the condom and returned, his jeans buttoned once more, to lift her in his arms.

"What the heck?"

He bobbled her, as if to drop her, and she clamped her arms around his neck, only to hear him laugh.

"Idiot."

He smiled. "Aw, you say the sweetest things after sex. Why, it's making me ready to go for round two already."

"Already?"

"Well, not yet. But I have a feeling if we snuggle together, I can probably manage another Naomi-sized hard-on soon enough."

"Naomi-sized, eh?" She loved the fact he carried her down the hall to her bedroom. What guy did that? Stereotypes in romance movies, that's who. "Weren't you a Marine? This feels a lot like that scene in *An*

Officer and a Gentleman." An iconic movie where the hero, a Navy sailor, carries his woman out of a factory.

"Never saw it. But if he's carrying her and it's all romantic, I'm thinking it's a chick flick."

"How very advanced of you."

He grinned and dumped her on her bed, then stood looking down at her. His shirt was untucked, and she thought him the sexiest man ever. "Man, you are one walking wet dream, you know that?" he asked as he stared down at her clad in nothing but her skirt. "How about you take that off now?"

She slid out of her skirt and laid back on the bed, feeling sensual and desired.

Reid lost his humor, hunger once more darkening his eyes.

"Now you," she ordered. "Take off your shirt and shoes."

He gave her a look but did as commanded. And the sight of his muscular chest took her breath away.

She spread her legs and touched herself, staring at him as she did so.

He groaned. "Oh yeah. Do that. I'm nearly there." He cupped himself.

"Show me."

Reid stripped out of the rest of his clothes, and she wasn't surprised to see him thick and hard for her. The man had stamina, and he clearly liked watching her.

As his big hand wrapped around his shaft, she had an urge to take over. Naomi left the bed to kneel at his feet. "Let me."

Reid nodded, unblinking, as she wrapped her fingers around him, then ran a pretty red nail down his cock.

"That is fuckin' hot," he rasped, his slit wet, his body rock hard. "Your nails are red, like your lips."

She licked her lips on purpose. She knew what he wanted. And damn it, she wanted to give it to him.

"Reid, I have to know." She leaned closer to blow a breath over his cockhead.

He steadied himself on her shoulder, one big hand gripping her. "Whatever you want. Ask."

"Are you clean?"

He nodded so fast, she worried he'd give himself a headache. She would have laughed if she hadn't been turning herself on so much. Being the object of such raw desire was an aphrodisiac. And there was no denying his arousal.

"I always use a condom. And there hasn't been anyone in months."

"Yeah? Me too." She leaned close and licked his slit.

He cupped her head, holding her close but not too close. "Sorry." He acted as if he meant to pull his hand away, but instead, he clenched it in her hair. "You feel like silk." He moaned.

She used her tongue to stroke his cock before nibbling back to his tip. Naomi cupped his balls, rubbing the taut sac.

Reid pushed himself against her lips. "Please, baby. Suck me. God, I want you so much. I swear, I'll do whatever you want. I just want to feel you..." He tapered off as she took him inch by inch between her lips, looking up at him as he stared down at her.

"Can't believe how good you feel," he managed before falling silent, keeping still as she bobbed over him.

He trembled and locked a hand over her shoulder,

holding tight. Reid moaned and pumped a few times before stopping himself. He tasted salty, excited, and she knew he'd come soon.

"No. In you," he growled and pulled her off him. He grabbed another packet from his jeans and sheathed himself in a condom, then tackled her to the floor.

Romantic it wasn't. Wild, fierce, and real it was.

He nudged her legs wide and thrust deep.

She cried out and locked her ankles behind his back. Reid fucked her, a savage stroking that hit the very center of her before he stopped abruptly.

"I'm so close," she moaned, shocked to see a mischievous look come over his face.

He looked like trouble and sexy as hell.

"But not close enough." He withdrew from her, ignoring her efforts to drag him bodily back down. Then he scooted down her body and set his mouth on her.

He licked her into an orgasm that had her floating in seconds. Then he was back, thrusting fast and hard.

Reid whispered her name as she finally stopped seizing around him. The beautiful man came, his face scrunched in ecstasy as he emptied into the condom.

For a brief, crazy moment, she wished he'd been coming into her, skin to skin, nothing between them but passion and affection.

Knowing herself to be nowhere near done with the man, she stroked his sides, his back, and accepted the kiss he gave her after he caught his breath once more.

"I have to say it," he said. "*Motherfuckin' A*. You sucked me dry."

"Oh? Too bad. I was hoping for another go," she teased, pleasantly exhausted.

He laughed. "Really? 'Cause you give me a few, and I'll be ready to go again." He paused. "But maybe some of those brownies would help rev my energy. Wait here." He left her before she could offer to fetch the gooey treats.

When he returned once more, naked and minus the condom, carrying a plate full of brownies, and wearing a sweet smile, she had a moment of clarity. A sticky knot of love began to fill the empty spaces inside her. That should have started a panic. But tired of thinking too hard, she accepted her growing affection and told herself she'd handle confusing emotions later. Reid needed her support…and she really wanted to know if he could go for a third round.

Reid lay with Naomi in his arms, determined not to fall asleep this time. Hell, being with her was better than anything, including her damn brownies, and he'd never had better. She was addicting. Strong and sexy, with a core of steel that refused to bend.

He stroked her hair, fingering the soft strands. Lazing next to him, she sighed and petted his chest. Had he been a cat, he would have purred. As it was, he sighed with contentment and kissed the top of her head. She lay over his heart, and he wondered if she knew it beat for her at this moment.

"We are really good in bed together," she mused.

He nodded.

"I felt that." She smiled against his chest, that magical mouth stirring the spark plugs in his belly once more. Naomi gripped his now-flaccid cock in hand. "You're always big, Reid. I mean, geez." In her hand, his dick started to thicken, and she let him go.

"Scared?"

"Yes."

He laughed. "I'm a shower, a grower, and an all-around mower." He grinned. "I sure *mowed* your sweet pussy, didn't I?"

She laughed, as he'd known she would. "That was just bad."

"I know." It reminded him of something said at work, oddly enough. He grinned. "Speaking of pussy, you might want to be careful of Heidi, our newest hire. She flat-out told me and Cash she likes it."

Naomi leaned up on her elbows. "What?"

"Pussy. She told us she likes pussy."

"She did not."

"Yep. Didn't say much in the interview. Told us she wants respect and her pay on time, doesn't like to talk much, and likes sports. Oh, and pussy."

Naomi gaped. "Seriously?"

He laughed. "Since Cash likes the same things, we decided to hire her on the spot."

"Just Cash, huh? So you're not a fan of pussy?"

"Hearing you say that makes me want to give you that round three right now."

She groaned. "Maybe I need a small break. You're like a marathon man."

"Better that than a minute man. Trust me."

"Good point." She leaned down to plant kisses on his chest. "You're not that hairy but still manly. I don't get the smooth chest thing."

"Models and swimmers shave. Not me. I'm too lazy."

She patted him. "Lazy can be good. I'm lazy. Feed me more chocolate, Gunnery Sergeant Griffith."

"Yes, ma'am."

As she chewed, she forced him to take a few bites as well. "Are you feeling better, Reid?"

"I am." He smiled at her, feeling so much, he didn't know how to put it in words. "So much better." He took her hand in his and squeezed, then laid it over his heart. "You make me feel good, Naomi."

"You do the same to me." She bit her lip. "I missed you this week. And I was annoyed with myself for it. We're just friends."

"Really?" He glanced down at her laying over his naked body.

She blushed. "Naked friends with benefits and… Oh hell. I don't know what to call us. I like you, a lot. But we work together."

"I'm just a client."

"That's work."

"You're fired."

"Reid." She slapped him.

He tugged her close for a chocolatey kiss, then set her back over him. He liked her lying on him, his sexy, redheaded blanket. "I know what you're thinking, but we're not like your past work relationship. I would never sleep with someone I worked with. You and I are mutual acquaintances who met through my moving company. Nothing you do has an effect on the people in my employ because I make the hiring and firing decisions. And nothing I do has an effect on those in your company. Right?"

"Well, I guess you have a point. But you pay me."

"Not for sex."

"Of course not, you jackass."

He laughed. "Stop trying to label us. We're good together. Can't you just go with that? I mean, damn, Naomi. I felt like hell all week. Two seconds with you and I'm happy. Not just relaxed, but actually happy. How can anyone not smile when they see your big blue eyes? You're so damn pretty, inside and out." He feared he was growing sappy, but he had to say something of what he was feeling.

She hugged him again.

"So what about you?" he asked. "Anything got you all stressed out that more sex can cure?"

She sighed. "I wish. My family is coming to town for some award my oldest brother's getting. And they're staying with me. My mom, pregnant sister, and her fiancé."

"The perfect older sister?"

"Yes." She sounded glum.

He looked down at her and was taken aback at her beauty. It wasn't just a physical attraction that held him in thrall though. He saw so much more every time he looked at her. "Tell me about it. You helped me by listening. I can listen to you."

She rolled her fingers on his chest, tapping. He found it soothing, though she was likely agitated. "Harley is everything I'm not. I get jealous and hate myself for being petty."

"So you're saying you're human after all."

"Very human." She grunted. "If my older brothers and sister would screw up once in a while, I'd be fine. But they're so damn perfect all the time. Ben is getting a doctor of the year award from his clinic. His kids are cute, and I like his wife." She sounded annoyed.

Reid found it adorable but didn't speak, letting her get it all off her gorgeous chest.

"Pete married the love of his life. They're both handsome as sin, with great jobs—lawyers, of course—and have a beautiful baby. And they never put a foot wrong. I mean, Pete knew Brad was the one after seeing him the first time."

He didn't comment, wondering if he and Naomi had really connected upon first meeting or if the great sex had warped his mind.

"And Harley." She snorted. "Her first husband was an amazing guy who died young. Left her a ton of money, a great house, and a gaping hole in her soul." Naomi sniffed. "I sound so bitchy."

"Ah, you're not crying, are you?"

"No." Her pitiful sob made him want to laugh and ball her up in his arms. So he did both. When she struggled against him, he held her tighter and stroked her back. "Shh. Relax, Naomi. Your perfect siblings sound annoying. It's okay to be jealous."

"It is?"

"Yeah." He wiped her tears and pushed her hair out of her face. Even crying, she looked better than any woman he'd ever seen.

"H-Harley met a second great guy, and now she's pregnant. I'm so happy for her, so why do I get so angry at them all?"

"Well, you did say your parents pressured you to—"

"And that's another thing. Mom and Dad have been married for *thirty-eight years*. Happily married. Gee, no pressure there! My mom's pretty and smart and fit. Dad's everyone's favorite guy. It's impossible comparing myself to these people."

"Okay." He kissed her cheek. She kissed him back, just a simple peck on his lips. And it felt as if his world finally made sense. *I am seriously doped up on endorphins.*

"Mom expects great things out of all of us. I'm the only who can't deliver."

"That's not true."

"I never told them I broke up with Tanner. Or that I left my job."

"How long has it been?"

She sighed. "A year and a half."

"Wow." A thought struck him. "Maybe you're not over him." The idea physically hurt, that she might be in love with someone else.

But Naomi only huffed and toyed with his chest hair, angrily staring at his pecs. "Oh, I'm over him. He still thinks he loves me. *Ha.* He loves the idea of Doormat Naomi working her ass off for his company. Of Weak-Willed Naomi gushing about how great he is. For years, I did all the grunt work so he—my boss—could look good. Then I get noticed and suddenly I'm bad for his image and need to leave the firm. Bullshit."

He'd tensed at "he loves me."

She must have sensed it because she paused. "I'm oversharing, aren't I?"

He shook his head, intent on erasing her memory of some douchebag loser *boss*. She'd only mentioned working with the guy. He'd been her boss?

Reid grew angry. And hard. He blindly reached for

one of several packets he'd placed on the nightstand, taking care not to move her too much. She didn't notice. Finding a condom, he shifted Naomi up and off him. "Let me hit the head real quick. Then you can tell me more about this loser."

"Hit the head?"

He flushed. "Use the bathroom."

She smiled at him, looking sexy as fuck.

He cleaned up in the bathroom and donned the condom, aroused at all he wanted to do with her.

He returned to see her sitting up and brooding, one big lump in the now-shadowed room. "I'm sorry for going on and on," she apologized.

The darkness hid his erection, and he slid into bed with her once more. He flicked on a side light, seeing her clearly.

"Hey, I turned that off."

"I need it on." He sat up, his back propped against the headboard, and dragged her up to straddle him. "Kiss me, baby."

She did, at first lazy, then with a seductive caress that had him more than ready to go.

"Now sit down."

She looked puzzled, but when he positioned himself at her entrance and guided her down over him, her eyes widened. She lowered herself fully, sitting on her knees as she took him all in.

"*Oh*. You feel so deep inside me."

"That's right." He urged her to rock up and down. "Now tell me about this loser who still supposedly loves you."

"Reid, that's…weird."

"Why?" He drew her to him for a passionate kiss that had her moving faster. "Because you want *me*?" The pathetic need to mark her as his in some way gripped him.

"Reid," she moaned and ground over him.

"This turning you on? Knowing you'll come for *me*, not him?" He grew angrier, more aroused, and sucked her nipples, biting so that she slammed harder over him. He nearly lost his mind when she pumped faster. *Jesus*. "*I'm* the one you think about when you come, aren't I, baby?"

"Yes, yes." She was frantic, seeking her release. But Reid wanted her to see *him*.

He switched positions, laying her on her back while he fucked her hard. She came with a cry as he took her with brutal passion, coming so hard, he saw black for a moment.

Exhausted, he watched her, satisfied in more ways than one. "That's right," he crooned. "I'm the one for you, Naomi. Not some douche who didn't know what he had until it was too late." He was dopey and stupid and saying all the wrong things, but his obsession to make her need him persisted.

"Wow." She stared at up him, her eyes huge. "You are *so hot* when you're taking charge."

He gave a weak smile and collapsed on top of her, done in.

"Oof." She struggled to get free, then gave up. "Great. Now we're both sweaty, He-Man."

He winced, praying she'd forget half the shit he'd said, and gave her room to breathe. "That was hot, wasn't it? I should boss you around more often," he teased, making light of his jealousy.

"Hmm." She yawned. "Can I interest you in a shower?"

"Hell yeah."

Which was how he found himself toweling off in her bathroom half an hour later, staring at Rex, who'd magically reappeared with a *meow*, when she left in a robe to answer her doorbell.

"Mom?" Naomi sounded shrill. "What are you doing here?"

Chapter 15

THE ONE THING NAOMI HAD NEVER IMAGINED WHEN SEEING her family again was this scenario—being somewhat wet and nearly naked after having had the most amazing sex of her life.

She stared blankly at her mother, her sister, and her sister's fiancé, all standing on her doorstep. They stared back.

"Did you not get my message?" her mother asked. "Can we come in?"

"What? No. I mean, yes, come in. No, I didn't get your message." She gave her mom and sister a weak hug, tried to ignore Kyle's amused grin, and did her best to escape. But her mother had an iron grip on her arm.

"We obviously caught you by surprise."

"You could say that." She cleared her throat and motioned them inside. "Come in, come in. Sorry. I didn't realize you'd be coming so soon."

Her mother laughed, though Naomi didn't see anything funny about any of it. "With the awards banquet a week earlier than we originally thought, your sister and I decided to come sooner. We'll be out of your way, we promise. But we…"

Her mother's words trailed off, and she let her go. Naomi heard footsteps behind her and knew they'd caught a glimpse of Reid. She wanted to sink through the floor. *Please, God, be wearing clothes*… It was as if the years had fallen away and she was sixteen again, caught kissing her boyfriend by the front door. Except she and Reid had done much more than kiss.

She turned to see him dressed and clean, his hair damp but not too noticeably. He grinned at her and stepped to take her under his arm. He kissed her cheek, a clear claiming and one she didn't know if she should respond to.

Harley beat her to it. "Oh, so this must be the new boyfriend. Hi, I'm Harley." She held out a hand, which Reid shook. "And this is my fiancé, Kyle."

More hand shaking.

Her mother gaped at them. "What happened to Tanner?"

It would have been too good to be true that Harley had filled their mother in, but no, Harley had this once kept Naomi's private life private. Loyalty never had stopped Harley from ratting her out for every infraction when younger.

"Tanner wasn't good enough for Naomi," Reid cut in, giving Naomi a warm squeeze. "Hi, Mrs. Starr. Reid Griffith. Nice to meet you." He neither confirmed nor denied the boyfriend part. Smart. She wanted to kiss him for that.

"We'll be right back," she said, dragging him away before her mother could interrogate him.

She heard laughter behind her as she raced with Reid back down the hall and shut them both in her bedroom. "Oh my God! It's like I'm living a nightmare."

He sat on the bed and watched her dress in a rush. "I'm a nightmare?"

"What?" She finished zipping up her jeans and had just fastened her bra. "Of course not."

He crooked his finger for her to come to him.

"I have to finish dressing…"

"Naomi, come here."

She huffed and stomped to him, feeling like a recalcitrant toddler and no doubt resembling the part.

His hug soothed as words wouldn't have.

They stayed that way for a moment, then Reid kissed her belly and pushed her back to look up at her. "Better?"

"A little." She smiled down at him.

He cleared his throat. "Might want to put on a shirt before I forget your family's in the other room."

Blushing, she threw on a T-shirt and sat to put on some socks. "I'm so sorry for all this."

He laughed. "I'm not. I'm seeing you frazzled for the first time. It's kind of fun."

She glared.

He laughed again. "I mean that in the nicest way."

"My family drives me nuts."

"You've met Cash, right? You think I don't know crazy?" He had her there. "Look. It's no biggie. I'll straighten your mom out that you and I are just friends and—"

"You will do no such thing." She stood so fast, she grew dizzy as she loomed over him. "I'm sorry for this, but I need you to do me a huge favor." She felt like an utter idiot. "Can you just pretend to be my boyfriend for a while? A few days at most? Just to keep them happy and off my back?"

—∿—

Reid watched as his usually calm, professional, composed lover turned into a nervous wreck right in front of him. He couldn't say why, but seeing her so out of her element amused and touched him in a way. Naomi needed his help, and he had no intention of refusing her.

"Sure. Just for you. But that means you'll owe me a favor back. I guess we're no longer just friends with benefits. Now we're friends with favors too."

"Friend with favors." She snorted. "How do I get myself into these situations?"

"It's happened before?" This he had to hear.

"No. I just mean…" She sighed. "I still have no idea how we got here. I stormed into your office to help your business help mine. I'm supposed to just be pushing your company to reach a new plateau. And now we're having sex and you're pretending to be my boyfriend so my mother won't give me a ton of crap about Tanner." She paled. "Please, whatever you do, don't tell her you're a client of mine. I'll never hear the end of it."

"I take it she didn't approve of you and Tanner?" He didn't either.

"No." She started pacing. "I know I'm thirty, a grown woman. But you have no idea how much haranguing I get when I talk to them. I could do without lectures from her, Harley, Kyle, and eventually Ben."

"No problem." When she passed the next time, he grabbed her hand to stop her, then tugged her with him out the door. "Besides," he whispered as they walked down the hallway toward her family. "We're already together, and we like it. Why not just polish the relationship up a little? My favor-friend? I mean, *girl*friend?" He kissed her ear, pleased when she gave a small shiver and playfully smacked his arm.

"Stop that," she growled. But her grip on his hand tightened, and she held him as if their connection meant more than a ruse.

Or maybe he was projecting.

In any case, they met her family once again, a united front. He noted the family resemblance among the Starr women, though her mother and sister seemed more blond than redhead. Kyle turned out to be a nice guy, protective of Harley and devoted to keeping the peace. He managed Naomi's sister easily and with respect and sat on the couch with her rubbing her feet while Naomi's mother gave Reid the third degree.

"So you own a moving company and you live with your brother near here?"

"Yes, ma'am."

"Hmm. Ma'am—you sound military. What branch?"

"The best." He grinned at Naomi's eye roll. "Marine Corps."

"And you met my daughter how again?"

"We ran into each other, and she recognized the name of my company. My brother was on the news stopping a burglary, and it's made us pretty popular lately. One conversation led to a coffee and then this. Us." He smiled at Naomi, wondering if she knew how hunted she looked.

Did that make him the big bad wolf? He sure as hell liked feeling as if he were a real boyfriend, talking to her mother, helping her deal with a tough situation. Usually, feeling needed left a sour taste in his mouth. He did whatever he could but felt tremendous pressure to keep everyone happy.

With Naomi, he wanted her to need him *more*. And

her contentment eased his mood, made the burden of care seem as natural as breathing.

"Call me Kim, for goodness sake, Reid." Mrs. Starr kept staring from him to Naomi. She paused a moment, her eyes like her daughter's. "So, I take it you're coming with us to Ben's dinner on Thursday?"

"If he can," Naomi hurriedly cut in. "He's been swamped at work lately."

"But I'll do my best to be there," he promised. And he meant it.

Naomi gave him a grateful smile.

Her mother continued to study them.

Naomi gave him a not-so-subtle nudge. "It's okay, Reid. I know you need to get back to Cash. Thanks for staying, but you don't want to be late."

His cue. He nodded. "Great meeting you all."

They waved and said goodbye. Naomi walked him to the door and murmured, "Thanks again for all this. I'll find a way to get you out of Ben's dinner."

"I want to go. It's okay."

She paused. "You do?"

"Sure. I like seeing this side of you."

She huffed. "The flaky, neurotic side?"

He grinned. "Yeah. It's cute."

She snickered. "Lame, but I appreciate the backup." She glanced over her shoulder, and he noted her mother watching them closely. "I've gotta go back and get grilled over you and Tanner. Guess I should let her know I've got a new business too."

"Oh, this keeps getting better."

"I know." She shook her head. Then she looked into his eyes and grabbed both his hands. "I'll be thinking about you and your mom. Please call me if you need anything. I mean it, Reid. We're more than pretend dates, you know."

Because he had to, he leaned close to kiss her. For her mother's benefit, he said, "See you soon, beautiful." In a lower voice, he added, "Can't wait to meet your perfect brother too."

She shoved him out the door, laughing as he went.

It wasn't until he was halfway home that he realized his mother's situation hadn't changed yet his acceptance of her decline had. And that Naomi was the reason he felt so relaxed about his changing future.

Upon his return home, he noted Cash's car missing.

Reid turned around and drove for the hospital instead.

———

The weekend passed without incident. Though Cash had been shaken by their mother's condition, it didn't stop him from hitting the gym or going out drinking with the Jacksons.

Reid met with Evan for a game of bowling, if only to drag his cousin out from under the thumb of the "blond dictator," his boss at work. Reid had to wonder if Evan really had that much assigned work to do or if he piled it on himself. His cousin did have a tendency to want to excel at everything. As bad as Reid with the need to come in first all the time.

Because second place was for losers.

Reid could almost hear his father saying those exact words Monday morning as he got himself his first cup of "office" coffee. He really did need to look into that coffee Naomi served at her place. After grabbing his cup, he headed down the hallway toward the conference room. A glance at his watch showed they had another twenty minutes before opening for business. Enough time to go over the weekly schedule.

In the conference room, an issue rose with one of the new guys. Doing his best to delegate responsibility, Reid nodded to Finley to handle things. Finley rolled his eyes, and Reid bit back a grin as he sat in the back.

Mannie ignored Reid and confronted Finley while the others waited around for their assignments. The only team not present were Lafayette and Hector, who were working a four-day move they'd started Friday.

"I don't see why I have to wait to go out. Just send me and Stan together," Mannie said to Finley.

Reid had to wonder if Cash had been present, would Mannie have been so quick to jump down Finley's throat? He tamped down a flash of resentment. Sure, everyone needed Reid to keep the books and the business straight, but as usual, they sought Cash when they wanted leadership. Usually Reid let it go, but sometimes it bothered him more than he liked.

"Look, man. I don't make the rules." Finley, at least, deferred to Reid without reservation. He rolled a quarter over his knuckles, while in the other hand, he held the master roster on a clipboard. "New guys always go out with our 'trainers.' It's policy."

"Whatever. I don't see…" Mannie paused when Cash walked in, arguing with Jordan.

The nice thing about having Jordan around, in addition to her having proven a quick study and a great team player, was that she took the brunt of Cash's attitude instead of Reid. Even better, she seemed to delight in receiving it and gave it right back. For sure, she and Cash worked well together, even if his brother refused to acknowledge the connection.

"It makes no sense. You're too small." Cash glared down at her.

"You're a jackass. I still don't see that as a major handicap. We just ignore it and move on." Jordan smiled through her teeth at him. When she saw Reid grinning at them, she made a beeline for him. "Your brother—"

"Is a jackass. Yes, I heard. Tell me something I don't know."

She looked taken aback, and Reid held back a laugh. Barely.

She shook off her unease. "Well, I'm just saying I don't always need to be paired up with him or Lafayette. I can go with another trainer. And I'm not tiny." She glared at Cash, who glared back. To Reid, she said, "I need to get to know the whole team. You should send me out with someone I don't know. Like maybe Tim. Even though we went out that one time, we didn't get to talk much."

Tim stood in the back with Martin. At mention of his name, the quiet ex-Ranger blinked at Reid. "What?"

"Hey, I'm fine with that. Tim, you want to head out on your move with Jordan today?" Reid didn't give Tim a chance to answer. "Great. Martin, you go with Cash and Mannie." He glanced at Mannie. "Okay?"

Mannie sighed. "Fine. I'm just itching to start, man. Gotta bring home money so my old lady knows I'm working for it."

"I hear you," Stan, another of their newbies, said.

"Great. So that's settled," Reid interrupted his brother before Cash could start.

Poor Tim looked like he'd rather be anywhere but paired with Jordan. Tim was an odd dude, but Reid liked him. The big man didn't speak much except to Martin. He had plain features, deep-brown eyes that looked almost black against his pale skin, and hated having to deal with strangers.

Martin, on the other hand, loved nothing better than to get under people's skin. He'd keep Cash occupied. A good thing, considering Cash's sleepless nights. Big Brother wasn't handling their mother's bad health well at all, and he refused to talk to Reid about it.

That would have to change, but not right now. Not when Reid had finally started to wrap his mind around the big changes happening in his life. His mother, Naomi…

"What's that shit-eating grin for?" Cash muttered, spotting Reid's smile.

"Nothing. Just excited for you and the gang to get us more business. Go out and stop some more burglaries, Gunny Helps-A-Lot."

Cash flipped him off.

The others laughed. Finley handed out assignments, and everyone dispersed. Before they left, Reid pulled Cash aside.

"What? I'm busy."

"You okay?"

"I'm fine." Cash sighed. "I'll *be* fine. I need to move. Activity lets me forget about our fucked-up family. Keeps me steady."

"Great. I hope Mannie being with you guys won't be a problem."

"Nah. I'll feel him out. He seems good to go, but he's a little too eager."

"Yeah. It's bothering me too. I'm not sure he's going to work, but maybe I'm wrong. There's a first time for everything."

Cash snorted. "You're always wrong. But if it helps you sleep at night, keep thinking you're not. Now I have to get to work. But one question for you—why aren't we taking Finley with us?"

"With Heidi not starting until next week, we're uneven."

"Well, not if she went out with Martin, and I—"

"Plus, I need Finley manning the admin desk. Dan's out today for some medical appointments."

Cash sighed. "Okay. But you really need to hire more admin jocks, and fast. We can't keep relying on Dan, who's only part-time. Finley's decent enough, and losing him to the office sucks."

"Deal with it."

Cash said some uncomplimentary things, but Reid ignored him until he said, "Ah, just one other thing. Did the computer repair guys talk to you?"

Reid paused. "No, why?"

"Uh, no reason. I have to get going. Later."

"Wait, Cash." Reid hurried after him only to see Cash darting down the hallway. "Damn it." He went back to the office to see Finley getting ready for the day, a stash of doughnuts and coffee by the front desk. "Don't make a mess or you'll piss off Dan when he's back."

"No problem." Finley sucked down a doughnut, whole.

"You know anything about a problem we might be having with the computer repair guys two doors down?"

Finley shrugged. "Probably something to do with Cash reaming the guys a new one when they took up half the hallway with some boxes."

"When did this happen?"

"Friday, I think. You were gone."

Probably out for that meeting with Naomi. "Fine. Do you know when they open?"

"Who?"

"Finley, focus past the sugar, man. The computer guys. When do they open?"

"How should I know?"

Reid went to grab his cup of coffee off the counter, needing the boost, and realized he'd left it in the conference room. "Damn it. I'll be back."

"Thanks for the warning, boss." Finley lifted a doughnut at him in salute.

Reid choked back a laugh and scowled instead. Finley couldn't care less. Reid sighed. "I'm surrounded by slackers."

Finley laughed. "Semper Fi has nothing on Semper Whatever, boss."

"Sounds like it should be the company motto," Reid muttered as he left to grab his coffee from the conference room. He shut the door after him, then decided to take care of the issue with the computer guys before Cash did any more damage.

He'd met the owners of the other shops in the building upon first moving in months ago. Only Miriam had been in the place longer. The computer repair place and watch repair shop were newer. The computers guys had seemed stereotypically nerdy but decent. The watch guy…weird.

Then again, he'd thought Miriam mostly normal. He'd had no idea she was up to sexual workshops along with selling vintage clothing. Were there vintage dildos? He wondered…

Since the door was locked and no one answered when he knocked, Reid bypassed the computer shop and decided to reacquaint himself with Wally the Watch Guy, as Cash had named him. Though he had a million other things to do, keeping Vets on the Go! in good standing with their neighbors could be nothing but good for business.

Unlike the Cool Computer Dudes, Wallace Newton didn't seem very outgoing. He had a reputation as being one of the best watch repair shops in the city for the price, but one couldn't tell that to look at him.

Pushing through Wally's door, Reid entered into a dim, dark little shop. The curtain covering the window concealed any hint of sunlight, and only the one working fluorescent light overhead illuminated the space.

A long glass counter showed off many watches for sale. Against the adjoining wall, a tall bookcase held some books, a stand of batteries, and a swiveling tower of watchbands.

Behind the glass counter, in the far corner, was a small desk with a bunch of tools and a magnifying glass held in some kind of vise, under which Wally studied a small timepiece.

The older man didn't glance up when Reid entered despite the small jingle of a bell.

After a moment, the man drawled in a southern accent, "Be right with you."

"No rush." Reid watched Wally work.

Wally carried an easy extra thirty to forty pounds around his belly. He wore jeans, no matter the weather, and either flannel or plaid cotton, long-sleeve, button-up collared shirts. His handlebar mustache, once black, had been threaded with gray, like his shaggy hair.

The man might as well have hung a Proud to Be Texan banner on the wall. Oh, wait, there it was. Reid grinned at the Lone Star State's flag mounted above Wally's workstation.

"Hello there." Wally stood and stretched his five-four frame. "What can I do you for?"

"Nothing, Wally. It's me, Reid Griffith, from down the hall? Vets on the Go!?"

Wally's brown eyes sharpened behind his glasses. "Ah, one of the brothers. Well, young man, let me tell you something about noise." Wally went off, in a calm, slow Southern drawl, about the merits of not cussing in the hallways, not stomping around like a herd of cattle, and not picking fights with the computer dudes, who were, by all accounts, a decent pair of brothers who had helped Wally just the other day fix his cell phone.

Reid felt a headache pressing. "I'm really sorry about all the noise, Wally. We'll do better to keep it down. And the cursing," he added before Wally could say anything. "I'll talk to Cash and the guys."

Wally frowned. "Wasn't your brother. I didn't recognize the man, come to think. Heck, he could have been a customer, really."

At least Cash hadn't been screwing with Wally. "Still, I'll make sure I remind everyone that we share the building. We've had a few new hires, so they aren't familiar with the business yet."

Wally's bushy brows went up. "New hires are good for business. Congrats." He smiled. "Meant to come down and congratulate you fellas. Saw you on the news last Friday."

"Oh, how'd it look?" In all the drama with his mother

and Naomi, Reid had completely forgotten about the segment.

"Seemed good to me. And the more business you get, the more they'll go by my door on the way to you guys." Wally nodded. "Now if you don't mind, I have a bunch of work to get to."

"Sure thing. Just wanted to stop in and say hello. And please let us know if you have any problems with our people. Come see me, and I'll handle it personally."

"Good to know." Wally turned back to his station. "Oh, and could you keep down the ladies with all their noise? It's distracting." Wally's ears turned bright red. "I'm all for equality, mind you. But if they can't lift a box without all that grunting and hollering, maybe they should find other work."

"That's not us, Wally. Talk to Miriam. She's giving… classes."

"Classes?" Wally frowned.

Reid heard movement next door, then a door opening and closing. "I'll let you go. Take care." He left, wishing he could be a fly on the wall when Wally talked to Miriam about the noise. His mood restored, he went to talk to the computer dudes.

And got more than an earful.

After reassuring the geeky pair that they had nothing to worry about from Vets on the Go!, he promised to talk to Cash about better communicating. No sense in pissing off computer people when Reid knew they'd need these guys' services at some point down the road. Having computer repair people so close was a boon, and he knew it.

"Hey, you guys ever need help with receiving goods, let us know. We'll help you carry stuff up. Until the freight elevator is repaired, we're all having to deal with two flights of inconvenience."

The more sociable dude, Tom, nodded. His brother, Luke, looked like the quintessential nerd, complete with the black oversized glasses. The highbrow, everyone-around-me-is-stupid attitude didn't help either.

"You know," Luke said, arrogance dripping from each word, "if your brother would spend as much time reading books as he does throwing them around like footballs, he'd probably be working at more than a minimum-wage job." Apparently books had been in that box Cash had kicked around the other day.

"Like I said, I'm sorry about that. But we do have customers who need to use the hallway."

"The UPS guy dropped it off," Luke snapped. "Should I speak slower so you can understand?" Damn, did the guy *want* someone to punch him, just because?

Next to him, his brother sighed, looking up for heavenly inspiration.

Reid thought it a wonder Cash hadn't dropped the guy after Luke had opened his mouth the first time. "You speak any slower and I won't need my brother to come back to translate for me. I'll fix the problem myself." Reid gave the guy an even more direct warning. "But hey, keep acting like a dick and I'll let Cash talk for us. I came here to make amends."

"I—"

"We accept the apology," Tom said for his brother and elbowed him when Luke would have spoken. "Sorry, man. It's early, and we've already dealt with some bitchy customers leaving us nasty messages." He glared at Luke. "But we're not out to piss off the world, are we?"

Luke muttered no and walked away, disappearing into a back room. Tom sighed. "Next time there's a problem, talk to me. Luke's great with computers, not so great with people."

"Same. You have any issues, let me know." He and Tom shook hands. One crisis averted. "And if we have computer problems, we'll come to you first."

Tom grinned. "Luke can be an ass, but there's no one better with tech." Tom paused. "Can I ask you something?"

"Sure."

"What's up with Miriam's Modiste? She never used to be in during the day, but lately, her hours seem to have switched. And I keep hearing weird stuff over there."

Reid knew he'd have to deal with Miriam before long, or they'd start losing customers before they even reached the office. "She gives classes. You should hop over and check it out. Maybe talk to her about the noise."

Tom frowned. "Classes?"

"I'd explain, but it's better if Miriam does. Sorry, I have to get back. Just wanted to clear the air."

Tom nodded. "Thanks. Think I'll see if I can get her to tone down the noise. I'll let you know how it goes."

"Good luck." Considering Reid had just dealt with three of his neighbors—one of them being Luke—he figured he was due a break. "Talk to you later." He left, wishing he could see Tom's face after Miriam explained her women's classes to him.

On his way back to the office, Naomi texted him an invitation to her brother's ceremony on Thursday night. He paused in the hallway to answer and heard Tom's exclamation just before he entered. *Miriam strikes again.*

Chapter 16

Naomi hadn't thought her Tuesday could get any worse. She'd accidentally overheard her sister and almost-brother-in-law having sex in the bathroom, of all places. Her mother had nagged her throughout breakfast and out the door about Reid. And Jon of Jennings Tech had just confirmed that Paulson, Pierce & Ryan had won Jennings's business to take over the PR campaign for their newest product, X-Tech71.

"That's great news," she told Jon over the phone, hoping she sounded sincere.

"It is, but only because we know how well you two work together. Tanner's said only good things about you. With our key personnel overseeing the X-Tech campaign and you and Tanner spearheading our advertising angle, I know we'll be increasing revenue in no time."

"We're super excited to work with you." Scoring her first big client with Starr PR, on her own. A tiny thrill made it difficult to sit still. The job was a boon to offset having to work with Tanner. "I'm sure we'll do just fine working alongside PP&R."

"It's not a problem, you and Tanner working together, is it? I know you left the firm, but I didn't sense any bad blood between you two." Jon sounded concerned.

"No, no, not at all. Tanner's a great guy. Smart and savvy about marketing. We'll have no problem working with him. That is correct, isn't it? We'll be working *with* him, not *for* him?" Because that would be a nightmare she wasn't sure she could handle.

"Exactly. I'm still overseeing our public relations department, but with all our growth, we're directing more work in-house and to contractors. Joanne Smith is project manager for X-Tech71." What she and Tanner would be promoting. "You and Tanner fall under her purview. I figured between you two and with Joanne's insights, we should have something up and running in a month's time."

"Sounds perfect. I'm so excited to begin working with Jennings Tech," she said again, choosing to concentrate on that win. It had really happened. She'd done it! Even Tanner couldn't put her down right now. She'd landed the job. She could do this.

Coming back down to earth, she cleared her throat. "Can I ask what decided you in our favor?"

"It was a lot of things. Your track record is stellar and your reputation as a small firm is glowing. In fact, Reid Griffith can't say enough good things about you."

"Vets on the Go! is our newest client. They've been great to work with so far." She had to thank Reid for this. She wondered if he had any idea what he'd done for her.

"Reid and Cash are great. They also happen to be friends with Chris," he said dryly. "So it's a good thing you've done well by them."

She chuckled. "Oh, that's good to know. But we treat all our clients like they're special."

"Outstanding. Take a look at the contract and get it back to us by Friday if you can. We'd like to get moving on this right away. Oh, and before I forget, you and your team will be receiving an invite, by courier, to the company party next weekend. Cash and Reid were invited too, so don't be surprised to see your clients there. Chris is celebrating the company's birthday, and everyone's invited. Since you're now a part of the team, we can't wait to introduce you."

"Thanks so much, Jon. We'll see you then." Naomi wrapped up the call, then bolted for the door. Seeing no one waiting by Liz's desk, she yelled for Leo, currently working in his office instead of telecommuting, as he did on days he attended specialty classes at a local college.

"You rang, great leader?" Leo asked. Tall and lean with a mop of blond hair, Leo loved numbers more than Naomi loved chocolate. *A lot.* He was reliable, a near-genius, and had a major crush on Liz's oldest daughter. Liz kept her eye on him, dangling poor Heather like pretty bait, not that Heather minded. Leo was quite a catch. A genuinely nice guy with a job who didn't mooch off his parents.

Liz looked up from the computer, her eyes wide. "What's with all the yelling? What did I miss?"

"We did it! We scored the Jennings account!"

The three of them did a happy dance before celebrating with the chocolate cookies Liz had been hiding in her secret stash.

"You had Grasshoppers and never shared? Liz, I'm crushed." Naomi laughed before biting into one.

"Well, the last batch of chocolate chips disappeared before I even got one." Liz shot her and Leo a suspicious look.

Leo didn't say a word, but Naomi knew he'd swiped them to share with Heather on a break.

"Sue me. I have a chocolate addiction." She winked at Leo, who blushed. "There's only one catch with this deal."

Liz groaned. "I knew it. What?"

"Tanner's going to be working with us." To Leo, she said, "PP&R."

"Hey, I know who Tanner is," Leo said. "The walls here are thin. I listen. So you'll be working with your ex. You good with that?"

"I'd work with Satan himself to get in with Jennings. Do you two have any idea how much this is going to help grow our business? With the money we generate from this deal, we'll be able to add on *two* more people, not just one, and take on more clients."

"So we'll have a marketing specialist soon?" Liz asked. "That would be great."

"Yes. And maybe a social media specialist. That would really help."

Liz nodded.

"You know what else would help? A new computer," Leo hinted, not so subtly.

She grinned. "Get me specs. You're all getting bonuses too. Man, this totally makes up for overhearing my sister having sex this morning."

"I once heard my parents doing it. Made me think about being a priest for a good year. But I didn't think I could go without…" Leo stared at Liz, who raised a brow. He turned beet red. "Ah, I'd better get back to my spreadsheets." He darted away and slammed into his office.

"Oh, that came out wrong."

"It did?" Liz looked intrigued.

"Not really. I was going to tell you about my morning

THE WHOLE PACKAGE 225

but didn't mean to share with poor Leo." She raised her voice, "Except I now know our walls are thin."

Alternative rock sounded loudly through his closed door.

She and Liz shared a grin before Liz said, "So you heard your sister? Ew."

"Tell me about it. I mean, she's pregnant."

"And?"

"Well, isn't it uncomfortable with a belly?"

Liz laughed long and loud. "Honey, I had a belly both before and after I gave birth. It's always good when your guy knows what he's doing."

"Liz." Naomi turned red. "Anyway, hearing that was bad. Then my mother nagged the crap out of me about Reid. I told you how she arrived early."

Liz laughed, again, at Naomi's expense. "Sorry. But that's too funny. At least she didn't catch you guys going at it."

"It was a close call."

"Hmm." Liz took off her glasses. "Seems to me you and Reid are really hitting it off."

"I like him a lot. More than I should." Naomi groaned. "This deal with Jennings Tech… I'm going to be working with *him* again."

"By him, you mean Tanner, your ex who's still in love with you?"

"Yes, Liz. Thanks. I needed to hear that."

Liz shrugged. "Maybe you did. Tanner claims he wants you back. Are you sure, I mean, a hundred percent sure, you're over him?"

"Yes." Naomi paused. "I think. Mostly. Oh, I should hate him. He was such a jerk at the end."

"But he wasn't always."

"No, he wasn't. When I'm with Reid, I wonder if I'm making the same mistake. I'm gaga over this handsome guy, and we work together."

"Not exactly."

"That's what Reid says. That he's not anything like Tanner."

Liz blinked. "You told him about Tanner?"

"I accidentally overshared after sex. He must think I'm an idiot. Especially since I'm thirty years old and unable to admit to my mother that I can make my own choices."

"That is pathetic."

"Thanks so much, Liz." Naomi glared.

Liz held up her hands. "Hey, don't shoot the messenger. Personally, I think you should use this flimsy excuse to get to know Reid better. I like him for you. He looks at you like he cares. He's not out to use you for anything. I mean, he's already paying you for—"

Naomi glared.

"I wasn't going to say sex," Liz hurriedly stated. "I meant for business. That's a done deal. And it's not like you sleep with all your clients."

Naomi groaned.

"Gee. That didn't sound good, did it?"

Naomi hid her face behind her hands while Liz laughed hysterically. When Leo poked his head out and saw Liz crying because she was laughing so hard, he ducked back inside his office.

Naomi threw her hands up. "I'm going back to work."

"To the office, ho! Or to the office, Ho." Liz laughed some more.

"Weirdo." Naomi got back to work, and the hours

flew by. She texted back and forth with Reid a few times during his lunch break, which he spent eating over his desk, according to her poor, overworked fake boyfriend.

Yet the more Naomi thought about it, the more she decided lying to her mother was stupid. Naomi had made bad choices in the past, yes. But Reid wasn't a bad choice. She liked him. He liked her. They had incredible chemistry, and she'd developed feelings for him.

Why shouldn't she date the man?

Pleased she'd come to a mature decision, she thought about calling him at the end of the day. Then she wondered if she'd do better to tell him in person. Through texts, they agreed to share dinner together at one of her favorite restaurants. But on her drive home, she received a phone call.

Hitting a button on her steering wheel, she answered, "Hello?"

"Naomi, it's Reid."

"Reid?" She frowned. "You sound terrible. Are you sick?"

"I'm going to have to cancel tonight. I'm sorry." He paused. "My mother died."

"Oh, Reid. I'm so sorry." She felt terrible. "Is there anything I can do?"

"No. It's been a long time coming. She's in a better place, and that's no bull. I really believe that." He sighed. "But Cash isn't taking it well. I have to go. I just didn't want you to think I was standing you up or anything."

"No, you do what you have to do. And please let me know if I can help at all."

"Thanks. I have to go." He hung up, and she drove home, feeling so bad for him.

When she arrived, she saw her family laughing and playing some silly board game while drinking her mother's famous cocoa. The sweet scent of chocolate wafted throughout the house.

Naomi realized that time was a fickle thing. None of them had as much as they might hope. So she kissed her mother, smiled at her sister and Kyle, and made the most of the time she had with them. Her mind on Reid all the while…

———ᴠᴠᴠ———

Reid felt a sad sense of relief that their mother, who hadn't been around much in life, had at least died peacefully in her hospital bed. Last night, she'd died in her sleep.

Cash looked lost as they drove to the funeral home their mother had planned to use.

"I can do this," Reid said to his brother as he parked in the lot. "You don't need to be here."

"I'm good." Cash cleared his throat. "It's not like it's a big deal. She was the way she was, never really there. Now she's really gone."

"One way to look at it." Reid didn't have any tears left. He'd cried them out last night in the privacy of his room.

"So we'll wrap this up and get back to work." Cash shrugged. His movements were stiff, his face unnaturally calm.

"You need to get it out or you'll lose it."

"What?"

"The anger, the sadness. She treated you like shit. She vanished and left us to Dad for too long. And he was awful."

"To me, not to you."

Reid wished he could read his brother's expressions. "Dad's dead. We both came to terms with that. Now Mom's gone. We have Evan; we have Aunt Jane."

Cash gave a ghost of a grin. "Her, I like."

Reid chuckled. "Me too."

After a minute, Cash added, "We still have each other."

"Yep. We've always had that, so really, nothing's changed."

Cash nodded, though they both knew their world had shifted.

They left the car to attend to Angela's last requests. Surprisingly, she'd been organized enough to leave clear instructions with the funeral home and arranged her final resting place, next to their father. All that was left was to cremate the body, then go over her last will and testament Friday with some lawyer.

After dealing with the details, they left and headed home.

"So what's with you and the redhead?" Cash asked out of the blue.

"What?" Reid's heart raced at mention of Naomi, which made him feel stupid. It wasn't like he planned to lie about their relationship. But sharing it with others felt intrusive. Plus, with the boyfriend ruse Naomi had created to satisfy her mother, he wasn't sure where they officially stood.

Cash turned in his seat to study Reid, life coming back to his eyes as he watched him. "You heard me." As Reid tried to decide what to say, Cash whistled. "So it's like that, eh? You and the redhead a thing or just bangin'?"

Reid groaned. "We're not 'just bangin'.' And Jesus, don't say that around Naomi, okay?"

Cash chuckled. "Sure, Bro. So what's the deal? You dating her or what?"

"Kind of. We're taking it slow."

"Slow can be good." Cash wiggled his brows, and to his mortification, Reid's cheeks heated.

Which caused Cash to laugh at him, long and loud.

"So glad I'm the cause of your good mood."

Cash punched him in the arm. "Oh man, I needed that. Thanks."

"Not to change the subject or anything, but how did it go with Mannie the other day?"

"Okay, I guess. He did his job. Martin never shut the hell up, so at least Mannie was there as a buffer. I still sense something off about the guy, though I can't put my finger on it."

"So keep pairing him with you or one of the Jacksons until we're sure."

"Yeah. Maybe it's just because he's Army. We already have too many of them."

They both had a good laugh over that. "Speaking of Army, how's Jordan doing?"

Cash shrugged. "Good, I guess. Haven't seen much of her lately."

"You were just out with her last week."

"Well, yeah. But she's been distracted." Cash frowned and stretched out his legs. "Personal problems, I guess. Unlike Martin, she doesn't talk me to death. I kind of miss her quiet."

"She didn't seem all that quiet to me." Reid shot his brother a look before concentrating on the road once more. "Seems like she tells you where to go about once a day. I like her."

Cash grinned. "Me too." His smile faded. "Doesn't it feel weird to laugh when Mom just died?"

"Cash, man, I don't think she'd notice what we did if she was here. What makes you think her spirit would care now?"

"You believe in spirits?"

Reid shrugged, a little uncomfortable with the conversation. "I believe in an afterlife, I guess. Spirits, ghosts? Nah. But I have a hard time thinking when you die you just disappear."

"Yeah, well, I hope wherever she is, she's not hanging with the old man. Talk about hell."

Reid didn't say anything, because he agreed. Conversations with Cash about family usually devolved into bitter diatribes about their father. They both knew their mother had been little better, but it felt somehow disloyal to call her on it. Until now, apparently.

Yet Cash obviously felt something, because he was calling Angela "Mom" again.

They didn't speak as Reid parked and they walked inside their house. Once in, he ordered some takeout and changed into sweats and a T-shirt. Cash did the same.

They crashed on the sofa, sitting next to each other.

"Same old shit," Cash said.

"Different day," Reid finished.

Then they watched the Mariners win while they waited for their Chinese food.

And Reid wondered if this wouldn't be as bad as he'd feared, that Cash would be able to deal. He saw a text from Naomi and smiled.

Cash saw him and grunted. "Naomi, right?"

Another ding. Her asking if she could do anything for them.

His heart grew fonder. Alarmingly fonder.

Reid shrugged. "She's just being nice, asking how we're doing."

"Yeah? Tell her we could use a couple of beers to go with the lo mein."

"You want me to invite her over?"

Cash shrugged. "Why not?" He planted his big feet on the table and kicked back. "Don't worry, Little Brother. I have no designs on your girl."

"Please. Like she'd look twice at you when she has me to fawn over." Naomi hadn't given off any vibes she liked Cash like that.

Nah. The one and only time he and his brother had had an issue over a woman, it hadn't been Reid's girl having second thoughts. It had been Cash's. But then, Mariah hadn't been too particular about men, sad to say...

Reid teased his brother about the harem Cash was building at the gym. Cash gave him shit back, and they spent the rest of the night sharing insults and egg rolls in between cheering on the team.

Yet Reid could never quite forget Naomi's kindness or the fact he wished he'd had the stones to ask her over. But what kind of douche made a move on a woman the night after his mother died?

He blinked away tears, handling Angela's passing just fine, and taunted Cash some more. And if he saw his brother's eyes looking a little shinier than usual, he didn't say anything.

Chapter 17

NAOMI HAD BEEN BESIDE HERSELF, NEEDING TO SEE REID yet not wanting to intrude on his grief. But sitting next to him at her brother's banquet felt weird.

She leaned in to whisper, "Are you positive you're okay being here?" They sat at a large table with her family, including Ben and his wife.

Reid whispered back, "If you ask me that one more time, I'll go down on you in the middle of this crowded dining room. I'm fine."

She flushed and pulled back, glaring at him.

He grinned, and she sighed. "I'm sorry. It's just... I don't know how I'd act in your place. I should be here for you, not the other way around. This is just a dinner. You're dealing with serious stuff."

"Hey, I got a free steak out of the deal. We'll call it even."

She glanced at their plates, now empty of filets, and had to admit they'd been well fed. Ben stood at the podium thanking his family and his peers for having nominated him for the clinic's award. She tuned out her brother, glanced at her family glued to his speech, and let herself slide closer to Reid.

He'd met her at the banquet looking dazzlingly handsome in a suit and tie. Good lord, but had she seen him dressed like that from the first, she might have embarrassed herself by jumping the man. Talk about tall, dark, and gorgeous. She wasn't the only woman to think so either. Reid had gotten second looks from many of the women, and a few men, in attendance. Had her sister-in-law, Donna, not been so happily in love with Ben, Naomi might have socked her one.

Reid clasped Naomi's hand resting on his knee. The warmth of that weight comforted, and she didn't know how it was that *he* was the one bolstering *her* through this evening. She'd been waiting to talk to him alone, but between work, giving him space, and her visiting family, she'd had no opportunity to talk to him before they were seated at their large table.

"Thanks again for doing this," she whispered and turned to watch him, enamored with the twinkle in his eyes. The color seemed so light, in direct contrast to his dark hair and naturally tan skin tone.

"My pleasure. Really, Naomi. This thing with Mom was coming sooner or later. She's no doubt happier where she is now. And so am I."

"Okay. I'll stop bugging you about it." She caressed his hand with her own.

"I like that you care."

"I do." Out of the corner of her eye, she saw her mother watching her. "Can we talk after this? It's too hard now with everyone around."

His eyes narrowed. "Sure."

"Nothing bad," she said to reassure him.

"That's what they all say."

"Shh," Naomi's mother hushed them.

Put in her place, Naomi turned back around and watched her brother finally step down from the podium. They all clapped and congratulated him, and as Ben returned to the table, she realized what a spectacular family she had. Yes, she hated feeling inferior, but that was on her, not them. Ben's big grin made her eyes fill with happy tears.

She wasn't the only one moved either.

Donna wiped her eyes. "Oh shoot. My mascara's running."

"Better catch it then," Ben teased.

"God, that was terrible," Harley said. "You might be an outstanding surgeon, but your sense of humor is on par with Gabe's."

To Reid, Naomi explained, "Gabe, their son, is seven."

Reid chuckled. "It's good Dr. Ben excels in other areas."

"Dr. Ben?" Ben took a seat next to his wife. "Seriously, Naomi. I hate when you call me that."

"Why? You're a doctor. Your name is Ben."

"Yes, but I'm *Dr. Starr*. Dr. Ben sounds like some dippy celebrity schmuck. Like Dr. Phil, Dr. Oz, Dr. Drew." He grimaced. "Don't get me started."

"Hey now, you're in good company, Dr. Ben," Naomi said. "Don't forget Dr. Who. And what about Dr. Dre? He's amazing."

"What about Dr. Dolittle?" Reid added. "Animals love him."

"Or Doc Holliday." Naomi was doing her best not to burst out laughing at her brother's pique. "He had such a cool mustache."

"Even closer to home, there's Dr. Scholl's. He seriously helps people walk, everywhere," Reid chimed in.

"You two are hilarious." Ben's expression said otherwise.

The others laughed though, and the conversation and drink continued to flow freely. A live band started playing, and couples gathered on the dance floor. When the medical people at the pricey clinic where Ben worked went big, they really knew how to celebrate.

"Would you like to dance?" Reid asked her.

Flushed with pleasure, she accepted, still aware of her mother watching her. The blasted woman had been studying her with Reid all night.

"You can dance?" she asked. "I thought macho types didn't like dancing."

"I'm macho?" He blinked in surprise as he led her to the dance floor and gathered her close. They swayed to a slow song, and Naomi sighed, feeling like she was dancing on clouds. They fit together so well. She wondered if she was the only one to notice it or if Reid felt the same.

"I guess not," she amended, staring up into his beautiful eyes. "I've never had a boyfriend who liked dancing." That hadn't come out the right way.

He lifted a brow.

She felt her cheeks get hot but ignored her embarrassment. "I'd planned to talk to you about this later, but I need to say something."

His amusement faded. "Go ahead."

The hand against the small of her back felt hot.

"It's just… I don't need to pretend anything for my mother. I'm thirty years old, and I'm not ashamed of how I live my life."

"O-kay," he said slowly. "So you want me to leave?"

"Wait. What?" She dragged him closer when he started to draw back. "No, you idiot. I'm telling you I'd like us to date, for real." She closed her eyes when she heard herself. "Ack. I'm not saying anything well tonight."

He chuckled and kissed her.

She blinked her eyes open.

"Baby, you're just fine. You can call me an idiot anytime you like. It might even fit now and then."

She smiled. "Just now and then?"

He kissed her again. Nothing inappropriate about the kisses, but they started giving her very inappropriate thoughts. And by the stiffness wedged against her belly, he felt the same.

"Now let's talk about something normal so I can manage to get back to the table without embarrassing myself."

She laughed. "This is all my fault, I take it?"

"Sure isn't mine. I was trying to behave." He leaned closer and murmured, "Your family has been staring at us all night. Isn't this Ben's big evening?"

She pulled him closer to talk into his ear, brushing his nape and reveling in his tiny shiver. "They haven't seen me with anyone but Tanner in a while. And it was six months ago the last time I saw them, and then I made excuses for being alone. I don't date much."

"Fair warning. Neither do I." Reid sighed into her neck, the warmth of his breath sweet with alcohol. "I might suck at this."

"You seem to be good at everything you do."

"Yeah, right." He sounded amused again. "Well, in truth, I am, but only because I work my tail off all the time. It's exhausting, let me tell you."

"I know. I do the same." She and Reid seemed like halves of a whole. They had family they cared about, jobs that sucked up a lot of time and effort, and a need to take care of others.

"I like your family," he said and pulled back as the next song sped up a little.

"Me too. It was nice to remind myself of that fact."

"Yeah, sometimes you don't know what you've lost until it's gone." He caressed her cheek. "And I'm not talking about my mother." He stared into her eyes, and as they danced, she felt as if only the two of them existed.

It took her sister cutting in to remind her to let go of her boyfriend. Reid.

"My turn." Harley pushed Naomi into Kyle's arms.

Over her shoulder, she saw Reid laughing at something Harley said and ignored a stupid twinge of jealousy. As if Reid would make a move on her pregnant sister.

That simply, the jealousy vanished. She had a lot more to learn about Reid Griffith, but one thing she didn't question—his core of integrity.

He winked at her and turned back to Harley.

"We like your boyfriend," Kyle said.

"I'm so glad. Now I get to keep him," she responded, her voice syrupy sweet.

Kyle chuckled. "Still such a smart-ass."

"You bet." She watched her sister and Reid dance. "How's Harley doing, really?"

Kyle sighed, and she studied him, aware he seemed… tired. "She's pretending everything's fine, but she's having trouble."

Naomi stared. "Harley?"

"Yeah. She's under a lot of pressure, you know."

"But she thrives on that."

"She pretends she does," Kyle said. "Truth is, your

sister is handling a promotion, a wedding, and a tough pregnancy, and it's starting to wear on her. But she'd never tell you or your mother that because Harley always thinks she has to stand taller than everyone else." He sounded exasperated. "She'll only lean on me so much. I'm worried about her."

"She does look a little thin." And tired, but Naomi had assumed that was due to being pregnant.

"She's had awful morning sickness." Kyle paused, and they danced in silence for a few steps. "I think she's missing David and thinks she should have had kids with him."

Naomi almost stopped right there on the dance floor. "Kyle. Why would you say that?"

Mr. Perfect suddenly looked downright miserable. "Never mind. I shouldn't have—"

Naomi pulled him off the dance floor while trying to act as if she wasn't dragging him away. They reached a corner by one of the small bars, and she faced him, keeping the rest of her family in sight. "Okay, buster, explain that."

"I shouldn't have—"

She poked him in the chest. "Kyle Proctor, you will tell me what the heck is going on."

He ran a hand through his hair. Not even mussing it a little. "I saw her looking at their old wedding photos. She was crying and saying his name." He looked sick. "She had her hand over her belly."

"Oh, Kyle. Of course she misses David. They were soul mates." Great, now Kyle looked even more dispirited. "Until she met you. I've never seen my sister so happy. I mean it."

"You think?"

"I know. I can't believe she managed to find not one but two perfect men when it's hard enough to find even one that's passable."

Kyle seemed to revive. "You don't think she's just settling for me since her 'soul mate' is gone?"

Naomi punched him in his rock-solid arm. "No, you doofus." Yes, men were stupid. "My sister has never settled for anything in her life. She sets impossible standards to live up to. Let's not even get into all my issues with being the loser of a little sister."

Kyle blinked. "What? That's nuts."

"Hey, we all have crosses to bear. In this family of overachievers, I'm constantly trying to keep up with everyone else. And the one I'm always behind is Harley. She's beautiful, getting to marry the second great love of her life—her words, not mine—and so incredibly happy to be having your baby. Kyle, she's going to mourn David. But that's natural. You are a real, vital, new beginning. Frankly, I'd be surprised if my sister hadn't snapped with all that's going on in her life."

"Naomi, you're the best." He hugged her until she squeaked.

"Hey, you have your own woman. I want mine back," Reid said from behind them.

Kyle let her go, laughed, and swept Harley into his arms. They moved away and danced together. Naomi could feel the love from where she stood, watching as Harley placed her head on Kyle's shoulder.

"God, I want that."

"Kyle?" Reid wrapped an arm around her shoulders.

"If I call you an idiot again, will you be offended?"

"Nah." He chuckled and placed a kiss to her temple.

"I meant *that*. That whole lovey-dovey feeling they have for each other."

"It is nice." He watched them, rubbing her arm with his hot hand, distracting her. "So what were you and Kyle talking about? Harley was concerned."

"She was?"

He nodded. "Said she always worried her hot younger sister would one day steal her man."

Naomi gaped up at him. "She did not."

Reid grinned. "Oh, she did. I told her not to worry. No way was I letting you get away. Then she told me how much better I was than Tanner could ever hope to be."

"She did?"

"Well, not in so many words. But she did say we looked good together. I extrapolated the rest."

Naomi continued to gape at him. "*Extrapolated*. You actually used that in a sentence. You are so getting lucky later tonight."

He laughed and kissed her. By the time he pulled back, he was breathing heavily. "Maybe best not to do that again. I need a few minutes to recover before we head back to the table."

Unfortunately, Ben had started toward them. "Better recover fast or Ben will think you're excited to see him."

He glared at her before turning to order them both wine.

She had already mentioned how much she liked the red she'd had earlier. Reid, of course, paid attention to details. Was that because the Marine Corps had made him into a detail-oriented person? Or had he always been like that?

The more time she spent with Reid, the more she wanted to know him. To no great surprise, his charm and looks made him that much sexier. She found all of him attractive, and she didn't think she'd ever felt that with Tanner. She'd been aware of Tanner's flaws before, during, and for sure after their relationship.

"What's that look?" Reid asked her as he handed her the glass of wine. Ben, fortunately, had been waylaid by several people with congratulations.

"Tell me something bad about you."

He paused in the act of drinking. "Ah, why?"

"Because you're charming me just by breathing, and I don't like it."

He grinned. "I can be crass. I sometimes forget that second *i* in *liaison*. And I hate chick flicks."

"Hmm. I can probably work with that. I mean, forgetting the second *i*. That's almost unforgiveable."

He laughed.

That sound wound its way into her head and into her heart. Naomi took a step closer to him, uncaring that she'd started to seriously fall for this man she still didn't know as well as she should. But she had plans to rectify that.

Tonight.

Reid hadn't thought he'd enjoy himself so much at a fancy award function with a bunch of snooty doctors. He'd done plenty of ceremonial dinners while in the Marine Corps. But the chance to be near Naomi had been too good to pass up. And Naomi's family cracked him up, all of them trying to outdo each other. Talk about competitive. No wonder Naomi felt like second best. Her family held pedigrees in success times twelve.

"I take after Mom," Ben was saying as Naomi sat with her mother and sister at the table. She'd ditched him to Ben and Kyle. Girls at the table, boys at the bar.

Worked for him.

Reid would think about all Harley had told him about his *girlfriend* later. Right now, he put on his work face, needing to hold tight to the fact he wanted to jump for joy because Naomi was into him. Like, *really* into him.

Fuck, he'd finally done something right. His mother had died without seeming to give two shits about him. Yet a woman he felt for felt something back.

"How exactly do you take after your mom?" he asked Ben.

Kyle snorted. "Try not to be overwhelmed. Kim's a surgeon at St. Mary's in Walla Walla. I'm sorry, she's *head* surgeon."

"Really?"

"Yep." Ben smiled. "She's the reason I got into medicine."

"So we have a doctor. Naomi mentioned your brother is a lawyer?" Reid asked.

Ben nodded.

"Harley is a big business type. What about your dad?"

"Corporate lawyer. Big money." Kyle shook his head.

"Wait. So what do you do?" Reid started to feel ill. Sure, Naomi had mentioned her amazing family. But he hadn't realized he fell far short of the mark in comparison. Not that money should make a difference, but when it came to collars, he fell on the blue side, not the white, no matter what the guys at work thought.

"I'm a nobody." Kyle smiled. "And I'm fine with that."

Ben snorted. "Don't let him fool you. Kyle owns a small tech firm that's designed some apps you might have heard of." He rattled off some of the more popular games even Reid had tinkered with on his phone.

"No shit?"

"Well, I can't take all the credit. My nephew started me doing it. I was really into coding and computers as a kid. Kind of nerdy."

"Yeah, I can see that." Reid did his best to shake off feelings of insecurity. Hell, he'd been in Cash's shadow most of his life. He'd learned to deal. So what that these guys had money?

Ben laughed, and Kyle made an impressive muscle before downing a beer.

"So what about you?" Ben asked. "My little sister's been pretty closemouthed about you. And I have to wonder why."

Ah. The big brother talk. He'd seen plenty of friends make the same speech to others interested in their sisters, but he'd never been up close and personal with one. Reid grinned. "If I tell you I'm actually married with seventeen kids and several outstanding arrest warrants, will we get into a fight right here, right now?"

Ben wasn't a big guy, but he clearly had some muscle. Reid could take him down with one, maybe two blows. Kyle would be easy. One thing that had never left him from his time in the Marines was the ability to detect physical weakness. Reid had been a hand-to-hand wonder during training, his skill with a sniper rifle near unbeatable. Of course, none of that was taking into consideration getting sucker punched by fake victims.

Now he was more aware. He continued to exercise, though he'd let his weapons training lapse.

Ben, though, wouldn't want to damage his skilled hands.

Ben snorted. "You and my sister clearly belong together. You're as warped as she is. Come on, Reid. Let me do my job."

"Let him do his job," Kyle parroted. At Ben's look, he shrugged. "Hey, you did it to me. Now I get to sit back and watch some new guy get the Dr. Ben glare."

"Shut up."

Reid laughed. "Sure, whatever you want to know. Just don't frown so hard at me. It's lethal."

"You shut up too. Well, I mean after you answer my questions. Now talk, Griffith. Tell me your life story." Ben crossed his arms over his chest, clad in a suit that had to have cost a pretty penny.

"It's no secret. I spent fourteen years in the Marine Corps. Did my time, liked it, but decided to get out to help my family. Dad and Mom are dead." He suppressed the pang that came with his mother's mention. "It's just me and my older brother. We own Vets on the Go!, a local moving company. That's how I met your sister. She helped me out with some business advice, then we hooked up. I mean, she's hot...er, super smart and pretty." He noted Kyle biting back a grin. Ben nodded to keep him talking. "I like her a lot. She likes me. Period."

"So no kids, wives, or ex-girlfriends in the wings?" The guy seemed a lot more concerned with Reid's personal life than his career.

"Ah, no." Reid frowned. "Has she had trouble with that before?"

"No, but that's because Pete or I scope out all her dates. Or we used to when she was younger, before she moved out here. I live in the same town and barely see her anymore." He sighed. "But she was smart to move. More to get out from under Mom's thumb than anything else, I think. My mother tends to be a little controlling."

Reid chuckled. "Must be where your sister gets it."

Ben nodded. "I know! She acts like she's so easy to get along with. Let me tell you, you think I'm bad? You should have seen Naomi when I started dating Donna. Girl was all over my wife with questions." Ben smiled. "Had to make sure Donna was good enough for her big brother. She can say it all she wants, as I'm sure she's told you we're *so* intimidating." He huffed. "Please. It's really the girls who are the problem in our family. Mom, Harley, and Naomi can be too assertive for their own good sometimes."

"You got that right," Kyle muttered. "So, ah, what did you do in the Marines? Or can't you talk about it? Is it classified?" he teased.

Some of his work had been. Reid shrugged. "Not really. I was in a recon unit. We used to gather intelligence for the data dinks to go over." He gave Kyle a once-over. "Guys like you."

Ben laughed. Kyle gave him a sour smile. "Funny."

"Hey, everyone has a job to do, and we know how to delegate."

"So you shot guns? Like, in combat situations?" Kyle asked.

"Kyle." Ben frowned. "He might not want to talk about it."

Unlike many of his comrades-in-arms, Reid had

come out of his time in service with a healthy attitude about what he'd done. He had no problem with his missions. Then again, his had been clear-cut. He'd been fortunate not to get dropped in the zones with civilian combatants in live fire. No, his teams had gone behind enemy lines but been very specific about verified targets.

"I can tell you that I can shoot pretty accurately. And I hit the gym a lot, so don't even think of going toe to toe with me in a ring." He held up a fist. "But I'd never hurt *you*, Kyle. Because I love Doodler Do way too much." One of his favorite games on his phone. "Ben, I know other doctors. Your future is up in the air."

Ben flipped him off, and Reid had to laugh. They continued to give one another a hard time until Kim signaled for them to return to the table.

"Uh-oh. Her majesty, the queen, wants us back." Ben waved.

"Poor Harley. I should have gone back to save her earlier." Funny, but Kyle didn't look sorry.

"She's fine. It's Naomi you should worry about," Reid said, defending his girlfriend. "She looks nervous surrounded by all those blood-thirsty Starrs."

"Whatever." Ben shook his head. "You poor fool. She's the worst one."

Which made Reid more than curious to see exactly how lucky he'd get tonight. What had Harley said about him?

For that matter, why was her mother scowling at him?

Chapter 18

ONCE BACK AT HIS HOUSE, BECAUSE NAOMI REFUSED TO go back to hers, he let out the laughter he'd been holding inside. He sat on the couch while his fierce redhead paced, in front of him like an angry tiger.

Naomi snarled, "Why the hell did you tell my sister you were falling in love with me?"

That had not been one of his smarter moments. But he'd been watching Naomi laugh, and Harley had caught him looking all swoony, so yeah, he'd admitted the truth. It had felt good, natural, to want a woman's love in a non-dysfunctional way. Almost a "take that" kind of gesture to his absent mother.

Hmm. Maybe he wasn't handling her passing as well as he'd thought…

"Reid, focus." She glared down at him, that gown on her absolutely stunning. Naomi wore a blue, silky dress that bared her arms and came to the middle of her calves. It hugged her figure in all the right ways, revealing a mouthwatering view of her décolletage.

He blinked up at her and gave her a lazy grin. "You look incensed, sweetheart. And yes, I can spell that. Aren't you proud of me?"

"Now they think we're way more serious than we are." She looked pissed. No, she looked worried. What the hell was that about?

Reid shifted on the couch. "Hey, you wanted me to fit

in. I had to make it look like we were serious, because Harley asked a lot of questions."

Naomi paused. "Like what?"

"Like how we met, what did I know about you, did I think I could ever feel for you the way she and Kyle felt for each other… That kind of stuff."

"She did?" Now Naomi looked horrified. She sat next to him, baring a bit of leg. Nice. "I'm so sorry. She was way out of line."

"I don't know. It was nice of her to look out for you. I didn't mind."

"She's always doing things like that." Naomi sighed. "You were so great tonight. I don't even know why I'm mad." She swallowed.

He stifled a groan, suddenly aroused.

"Because you know it gets me hot." He grabbed her and settled her over his lap, her knees braced on either side of his thighs.

"Reid." She blushed and looked around. "What if Cash comes back?"

"He won't until much later. He's out with the crew tonight." He ran his hands up her thighs, bunching the material. Her skin felt silkier than the dress, and he wanted to taste her everywhere.

She put her hands on his shoulders, and the movement emphasized her breasts. The thought of burying his face between them turned him to steel.

"Reid, I have to ask you something."

He didn't like her worried tone. "Sure, what?" He kept stroking her legs, needing her to sit down on him. His cock ached, so hard it hurt.

"Did I push you into something you don't want?

Asking you for more than a fake relationship when you were vulnerable wasn't ri—"

He cut her off with a kiss, so in lust with the damn woman, it wasn't funny. He hadn't intended to but lost himself to feeling and ground her over him, leaving her no doubt to his feelings. When the need for air outweighed the need for Naomi's mouth, he pulled away, gasping. "That a good enough answer for you?"

She stared down at him, her eyes like a tropical sea, her mouth red and slick from their kiss. "I did say you were getting lucky tonight…"

"How lucky?" He decided to push. God, he had to. He needed… He didn't know what he needed, but he knew what he wanted. "Naomi, I'm clean." He paused. "Are you protected?"

She stilled. "I am." She stroked his neck, knowing how much he loved that. It turned him on like crazy. "And I know I can trust you."

"I'd never, *ever* do anything to hurt you. I told you before, I haven't been with anyone in a long time. And I always use protection. I'm clean, but unless you're on something, I could get you pregnant."

"If you always use protection, why not use it with me again?" She watched him, and he felt so much, he didn't know what to think.

"I don't know. You're different." His heart threatened to pound out of his chest. "Fuck. Look. I shouldn't pressure you, but I want to come inside you so bad." Understatement of his fucking life. "I have condoms though. We can—"

This time, she interrupted him by kissing him. So lost in her kiss, he hadn't realized she'd freed him from his pants until her hot little hand wrapped around his dick.

"Shit. Oh yeah," he groaned as she started pumping him. "Hell, Naomi. Slow down, or I'll come too soon."

"Not yet." She let him go, then reached between them to pull her panties aside. "In me, Reid. Or have you changed your mind?" She arched a brow, a sassy look on her face.

He dragged her down for a kiss while angling himself at her hot, wet entrance. He thrust up just as she plunged down, and the electric feel of her body gloving his was as close to heaven as he'd ever come.

She moaned into his mouth, kissing him back with hunger.

He cupped her ass, moving her up and down, needing to slow down yet unable to stop, overloaded with sensation.

She pulled from his mouth and planted kisses on his cheek, his jaw. "You're so big," she hissed into his ear before nibbling his earlobe.

He was too close, and he knew it. "Gonna come too soon…"

She grabbed his hand and put it between her legs, rubbing her clit through her panties. "Me too." Naomi watched him as he fingered her to a quick climax. The sight of her in the throes of orgasm shattered his already loose control, and he pumped up twice more before coming.

The release destroyed him, and he flooded her as endorphins sent him somewhere else entirely. The scent of her perfume clung to him, the heady smell of Naomi and sex and affection grounding him.

"All in me, Reid," she whispered and moved over him, causing him to tremble.

He jerked again, apparently not done. *Fucking A.*

She kissed her way down his neck, sucking hard at his throat.

He could only sit there, hers to play with, as he finally finished. He hadn't engaged in unprotected sex but twice in all his years, and he knew it wasn't the lack of a prophylactic that made it so damn good. Naomi embodied every one of his fantasies, her body just a small part of what made her perfect for him.

"Not that I didn't lose my mind, but we need to move before things get messy," she said on a breath.

He laughed, then groaned. "Oh, that's not good. I'm falling out."

"Not yet." She left him on a shriek and raced down the hall toward the bathroom.

Reid lay there, so satisfied yet hungry for more of Naomi. He stared at his limp cock and gave it a thumbs-up. "You did good, buddy."

"What?" she asked from the bathroom.

He felt drunk. *Must be if I'm talking to my dick.* Reid shook his head, then stood and took off his shoes and socks. He shrugged out of his jacket and shirt, then said to hell with it and walked out of his pants and underwear.

"We're far from done," he said, his eyes wide when he saw her nude in the bathroom. "You look like a goddess." Not just flattering her but speaking the truth.

"Aw, and you already had me. You must be wanting more."

He grinned, loving this playful side of her. *Hell, I'm such a dip. I love* every *side of her.*

It was too soon, too weird, too scary. But there it was. She frowned. "Are you okay?"

"How the hell can you ask me that when I haven't had a chance to go down on you? Now who's an idiot?" he growled.

She lost her uncertainty, her smile like a wash of sunshine that kept him warm. Close. Safe. A strange thought to have, but with Naomi, Reid belonged.

He would have lifted her in his arms, but she slapped him away. "Just point in the direction, and I'll go."

He did, then followed from behind, watching her fine ass on the way to his room.

Once inside, he locked the door behind him. Whether Cash came home or not, Reid wasn't passing up this opportunity to have Naomi Starr all to himself.

"On the bed." He nodded to it. "Then spread your legs and get ready for some fun."

Fun? Is that what he called it? Naomi called it losing her mind. She'd never had so much pleasure, and they'd barely started doing it before she'd climaxed. The great thing about Reid, though, was that she could count on more romps after her first climax.

After that incredible lovemaking, he'd started kissing and petting her all over again, leaving her in a hazy state of arousal.

"You came inside me," she said, still amazed she'd let him have her like that.

Even with Tanner, it had taken more than six months, and a medical report, before she'd agreed to no condoms. He'd laughed at her hesitancy, but she'd shown him a clear report as well, to be fair. With Reid, she took him on faith.

Because despite not knowing all about him, she knew what mattered.

And to him, she mattered.

Calling her a goddess? She'd have called that over the top from anyone else, but Reid meant it. She could see it on his face, in the way he touched her, kissed her. He took pleasure when she did.

Watching him interact with her family had been eye-opening. He hadn't forced anything, the way Tanner had. And she hadn't felt the need to rescue him or make excuses for any comments he made. Reid had held his own. Even better, her family had liked him. She could tell. Ben had always been a hoverer. Even while he'd been away at college and medical school, he'd kept tabs on her. She knew she should be thankful her siblings cared about her, but she found their hovering intrusive. But knowing they approved of her choice gave Reid a new sense of importance in her life.

She didn't know if she should like that or not. They'd liked Tanner too, though it had taken a lot more convincing on her part.

Reid looked at her with clear satisfaction. "Yeah, and I plan on doing that again real soon." His wicked grin had her melting inside. God, he was gorgeous. So big, strong, and beautiful. Reid made her feel both safe and cherished as he lay with her on the bed, his chin resting on her belly.

She knew she was getting a little too emotionally invested in the man, but she couldn't help it. Naomi loved—er, liked—with intensity. Why bother dating a man if she didn't intend to share more than her body?

"I'm not just using you for sex, you know," she blurted.

His grin widened. "Too bad. I could go for that. But then I'm not just using you for sex either. Now I'm using you for your soon-to-be brother-in-law. I can't believe you held out on me."

"What?" How could he think about anything with his face so close to her sex? If he moved even slightly, his mouth would be right on top of her clit.

"Doodler Do is one of my favorite games." He ran his hands up the insides of her thighs. When he neared her folds, he'd move them back down again, then repeat the action. The distracting caresses turned her to liquid… and fired her up to have him once more.

How much time did he need to get hard again? She was ready to go right now.

"Wait. Kyle told you about that?" Her sister's mega-rich fiancé didn't confide in anyone about his job. "What did Ben have to say?"

"Only that you're as aggressive as the rest of the women in your family." He sighed, and the warmth over her girlie parts made her shiver. He smirked at her, knowing the effect he had on her. Damn him. "Oh wait. He said assertive, not aggressive." He ran his hands back toward her sex, and she sucked in a breath when his thumbs skimmed upward, tracing her slick folds.

"In me," she whispered, arching her hips.

"Shh. Not yet. We're talking." He kissed her clit, sucked the taut nub, then eased back. "Now where were we?"

"You're evil," she breathed out, "And my family apparently likes you."

"Of course they do. I'm charming." He proceeded to show her how charming he was for several minutes, licking her to a near-screaming state. Then he backed off, leaving her limp, excited, and frustrated all at once.

"I think I hate you."

"That's what they all say," he teased, then looked up at her. "I'm kidding. This, us, Naomi, is new. And I like it a lot." He kissed her again, making love to her sex and sucking her into a powerful orgasm.

Once she came back to earth, he settled over her, his erection thick and heavy against her belly. He rested on his elbows, wiped his mouth, then kissed her.

"I love the way you taste," he said after pulling away, his breath uneven. "You get me so hard." He angled his cock between her legs but didn't penetrate, just held himself between her folds. "You're so hot." He moaned. "And wet. Jesus, don't move. Let me just… That's good."

He kissed her again and again. Reid caressed her breasts, kissing his way to them. He had a thing for them because he spent a lot of time molding and pinching her nipples in between kissing them.

"I love your tits."

"So charming," she managed between pants.

"First time I saw you, I had to do my best to take my gaze from them. I knew if you caught me staring, you'd kick my ass." He sucked her nipple into a hard point. "I wanted to bend you over my desk and fuck you so hard." He moaned and withdrew from the clasp of her thighs, then eased back down again.

"Come inside me," she ordered. Well, more like begged. The man had stamina! She'd been ready to come again several times, but he continued to drag it out. He felt rock-hard, so she knew he'd more than recuperated from before.

"Oh, I will." He moved back to her mouth, one hand teasing her breast while he rested against her pelvis. That heavy weight felt so good…

They kissed some more, and Reid's hunger showed in the urgent movements of his hips. "Coming in you is heaven. You don't know how good you feel. How right." He watched her as he entered her—finally—and he was right. He felt divine.

She told him so, and he laughed.

"Divine, eh? And you were impressed I used *extrapolate* in a sentence." He lost his smile as he moved in and out of her. His movements hurried, rough, and so incredibly erotic.

"I love watching you fuck me," she said, knowing her dirty talk got him hot.

"Yeah. Your tits bounce, and I'm inside you. My cock in that hungry pussy," he growled. Taking her harder. "Love coming in you. So fucking good." He raised himself, his hands on either side of her head, his muscular arms braced as he pumped his hips.

She moaned as he hit something special inside her, rubbing against that spot again and again, so much that she exploded into ecstasy as he hammered inside her. So deep, so very, very good…

"Oh yeah. Fuck. *Naomi*…"

She managed to open her eyes to see him orgasm, and the knowledge he jetted inside her made everything so much better. Only she and Reid shared this connection, this honest trust and exchange.

Hell, he'd told her sister he was falling in love with her.

Hope unfurled, though she told herself not to be stupid.

When Reid finally sagged down on top of her, she hugged him to her.

He didn't stay long before hopping up to grab a towel to clean them both. He surprised her by taking care of her, wiping her clean, then himself.

"There you go." He winked. "But I'm still inside you."

She blushed, silly considering all they'd done. *Just think, if I wasn't on the pill, I could be getting pregnant right now.*

She froze, thoughts of a baby not meshing with her career plans. Not until she reached thirty-three at any rate. Naomi had timed it. Having children after thirty-five increased the baby's health risk. But three more years would give her the time to stabilize her job and be financially ready for a baby.

For Reid's baby?

The notion should have shocked her. Instead, she could too easily see a dark-haired little boy with Reid's eyes nursing at her breast. And she wanted it.

God, I'm losing it!

"Hey, you okay?" He watched her with warm eyes. "Too late now for regrets. And don't think we're not resting up for round three."

"You and your rounds. We're not boxing, Reid."

He grinned. "You'd rather we quit while we're ahead?"

She shrugged. "I didn't say that." She smiled, unable

to keep a straight face. "But don't worry. After round three, I'll take off. Don't want to overstay my welcome."

He joined her in bed after tossing the towel back in the adjoining bathroom. Drawing her into his arms, under the covers, he kissed her. "You're just fine, and right where you need to be."

She cuddled with him, feeling pleasantly sore, still needy for him, and gratifyingly close. Not just physically but emotionally. As many times as she told herself to keep it light, to leave it be, she couldn't. "So are you really okay about your mom?"

He didn't answer, and she wondered if he'd fallen asleep. With her head against his chest, she couldn't see him.

"No," he said after a moment, his voice quiet. "She was fucked up, Naomi. Never there for us as kids. She loved us, but she loved her escape more. Books and TV, I told you, her soap opera crap. Anything that wasn't her life. My dad was a prick, so I understood. But she left us to him."

"I'm sorry."

"So am I." He sighed. "Cash got the brunt of it. My dad hated him. We never knew why. I struggled to be the good son. To keep the peace. Was number one in everything to make up for Cash giving up. He's so much smarter and better than he thinks he is. Makes me feel bad that he doesn't believe he's a good guy."

She felt for him and remained silent, letting him get it all out.

"My mom wasn't always so whacked-out. When we were little, I remember her taking care of us. She'd bake us cookies and spend time with us. But then the mom I knew disappeared. I loved her. And sometimes I hated her."

She felt his breath hitch but said nothing, just stroked his chest while he got it all out.

"I had to be Cash's support. My dad's support. I took care of everyone to keep us together. But my dad didn't care. My mom just vanished inside her head. When I was deployed, I never had to see her. But since I've been back, nearly two years, I've visited regularly. I don't know why. Guess I thought that one day, she'd realize what she'd done. She never did."

They lay together, Naomi willing Reid to feel the comfort, the love, she had for him. "I'm so sorry, Reid."

"Me too." He scooted down so that his head lay on her chest. She felt his tears, and her heart broke for him. "I miss her. How fucked up is that?" His quiet grief felt all the more terrible because he wouldn't give it voice.

But Naomi didn't stir, wanting him to know he was cared for, if just by her being there.

They lay like that for a time, then Reid shifted and spooned her from behind. "Just a little rest, okay?"

She covered his arm around her midsection, holding him close. "Believe it or not, I could use a rest too. It's not just you, Reid."

He chuckled and kissed the back of her hand. "Yeah, sure. I know the quickest way to get a chick to leave is to be underwhelming in bed."

"No chance of that with you." She meant that.

"Good." He nestled his groin against her ass. "Just remember that we're dating now. I don't share. And I for damn sure won't let you use your family to scare me away."

"Hey. That's not what I did." She tried to turn over, but he held her in place.

His strength was unmistakable and extremely attractive. She settled back in his arms on a huff. "Believe me. If I wanted to scare you away, I'd do it myself."

He laughed. "That's my fiery Starr."

"Oh, stop." She joined his laughter, and they settled into an easy rest.

That turned into a full night's sleep.

Chapter 19

WHEN REID WOKE THE NEXT MORNING, IT WAS TO THE FEEL of soft, curvy skin against his body. He'd held Naomi through the night, and he'd never had such a good sleep.

She wriggled her ass against his groin and sighed, and his dick sprang to instant attention.

He'd fantasized about being able to have her this way, waking up to her in his arms, naked, willing.

Reid lay on his side with her, his dick so hard, he couldn't concentrate on anything but the soft woman in his arms.

Without doing more than giving into temptation, uncaring of the time, who might be around, or, hell, being late to work, he lifted her leg and draped it over his, giving himself room to make love to her. He paused, still debating the best way to wake her when she wriggled back against him and moaned, "Reid, yes."

He pressed his face against her back and kissed between her shoulder blades while he slowly eased into her warm, wet body. Christ, it was like fucking a dream. He entered her from behind, on his side, his penetration both satisfying and frustrating because at that angle, he couldn't get deep enough to suit him.

With a hand clenched around her breast, he held on as he thrust in and out, enjoying the hell out of her breathy moans and pleas for more.

Naomi met him thrust for thrust.

When he drew a hand down to play with her clit, she pushed his hand aside and did it herself.

"Yeah, baby. Get yourself off." He thought it sexier than hell that Naomi took her pleasure, not waiting for him but taking charge herself. And her rise to orgasm allowed him to take his.

He couldn't help groaning and grunting as he sought fulfillment. But only when she cried out and stiffened around him did he spill inside her, the climax one that gratified on every level.

He let her body milk him of everything he had left before easing out of her.

She flopped on her belly and moaned.

Reid heard the TV go on in the living room and paused. Hell. He'd left a trail of clothes out there, and Naomi had undressed in the hall bathroom. Any chance Cash wouldn't notice evaporated as he heard his brother's booming laugh, followed by a "Get some, Reid!"

He covered his face, praying his brother didn't alienate Naomi too soon. Not when Reid had finally found a piece of what he'd been searching for his whole life.

He did a quick cleanup and took care of business before throwing on a pair of shorts. "I'll be back with your clothes," he said and kissed her cheek. A glance at the clock showed him he hadn't woken too late. "It's only five thirty, so you have time to recover before work."

She groaned and yanked the blankets over her head. "Need. Coffee."

He grinned, feeling amazing. "Sure thing, sweetheart."

He left the room whistling and saw Cash looking hungover, draped on the couch.

The minute Cash spotted Reid, he bolted upright,

groaning as he clutched his head, but held out a thumbs-up. "You are the motherfucking man!"

"Shh." Reid glanced at the hallway. "Not so loud. And do not—at all—embarrass that woman, or I will kick your ass back to Afghanistan, dickhead."

Cash's dumbass grin didn't bode well for the morning, but he looked better than Reid had hoped, bleary-eyed but wearing pants and one sock. "So, Little Bro hits, he scores. The crowd goes wild." Cash plunked his half-dressed butt on a barstool and watched Reid make coffee. "Any chance you'd make some pancakes to go with the coffee? You know, to keep me civil and quiet when your redhead appears?"

Reid grunted and whipped together some pancake mix. "All you have to do is add water."

"I know, but it tastes better when you make it."

Reid rolled his eyes but, still in too good a mood to protest, made a dozen cakes. He dumped half on a plate and slid it to Cash. The rest he plated for his lover. His girlfriend.

Cash stared at him while he wolfed down breakfast and mumbled around his food, "You nailed her for sure."

"Shh." Reid glared at him and monitored the hallway for signs of life.

"Was it good?"

"You are not this big an asshole."

Cash shrugged and ate, still watching him while Reid poured himself some much-needed caffeine.

"The funeral is Sunday, right?" Cash swallowed his last bite. "Might as well enjoy life while you can."

"I'm not feeling guilty about this."

Cash blinked. "Huh? Why would you?"

"Then what are you saying?"

"Just that Angela's funeral service is in a few days. We need to find someone to cover my shifts this weekend. At least for Sunday."

"I'd have Evan do it, but he's coming to the service with Aunt Jane."

Cash frowned. "What about having Tim fill in? He likes Martin, and he can help keep an eye on Mannie for us."

Reid nodded. "I'll pay him time and a half for filling in if he'll do it. I'd ask one of the Jacksons, but they're out of town this weekend for some family thing."

"Their sister is getting married." Of course Cash would know. "They offered to leave the wedding party early and come to the funeral, but I told them not to. Hell, I'm not even sure I'm going."

"You're going."

"Yeah? What if I don't feel like it? Who's gonna make me? You?"

Reid had flashbacks to high school, when he'd nagged Cash to graduate. Back then, Cash had dwarfed Reid. Though he still did, at least now Reid knew how to fight. He'd still get his ass handed to him, but he'd get in a few licks before he lost. "Settle down, Gunnery Sergeant Asshole." He ignored the finger Cash shot him. "Neither of us wants to go, but we have to. Don't forget the will's being read today. Five o'clock. We can ride there together."

"I can't. I'm on a move with Jordan and Heidi. But I'll be there."

"Okay." Reid didn't push. Plus Cash being near Jordan would ease his brother's anxiety. Cash refused to admit it, but he liked Jordan. And he didn't like upsetting her. Reid would have a talk with her, to explain about Cash's potential moodiness, before Cash went into work. He prepped a tray with coffee, pancakes, and syrup.

"You do one thing to embarrass or freak her out, I will end you." Reid gave Cash the "not kidding" stare.

Cash sighed. "Whatever, man. You used to be fun. Now you're just a prick." In a lower voice, he added, "You'd think getting laid would make you happy."

Reid smirked over his shoulder and walked away. "Jealous?"

"Hell yeah."

Reid had a feeling his brother wasn't talking about Naomi personally. Oddly, they'd never been competitive with each other. And they'd never let a woman come between them, ever. Even the mess with Mariah hadn't severed their close bond. Because even then, Cash had trusted Reid over his fiancée.

Reid entered his bedroom to find it empty, the shower running. He left the tray on his dresser and returned with Naomi's clothing.

He was sipping coffee and reading the news on a tablet when she entered, clad in nothing but a towel. She had another wrapped around her head like a turban.

"How do women do that?" he asked, nodding at her head.

"It's a secret. I could tell you, but I'd have to kill you."

"That's my line."

She smiled, but her grin brightened when she spotted the coffee. "Oh, this is good." She spotted her clothes on the now-made bed and sighed. "Thanks. I didn't want to have to streak out there to get them."

"You wouldn't want to. Cash is home."

She flushed, as he'd known she would.

"Don't worry. He says one thing that annoys you, I'll beat his ass."

"Um, don't take this the wrong way, Reid. But he's enormous. And you're more normal."

"Excuse me?" He flexed, gratified when she stared at his physique.

"Oh stop. Yes, you're sexy as hell. And muscular. But he's steroid-huge."

"He is not." Reid could only imagine his rage-y brother on steroids. Talk about a real monster.

"Okay, he's not a steroid guy. But he's really big."

"I'm six four," came a shout through the door, which had both Reid and Naomi jumping.

"That ass," Reid growled.

Naomi shocked him by laughing.

"No sex. We have to get to work," Cash boomed, and Reid prayed their neighbors didn't complain about the noise. Again. "Gotta shower, so in case I don't see you, hi, Naomi."

Reid pinched the bridge of his nose.

"Hi, Cash," she yelled back, now cutting into her pancakes. She sat on the bed and put the tray in her lap.

"Love your taste in panties, by the way," Cash answered.

Reid headed toward the door. "That is it!"

Naomi heard scuffling outside, but starved for some food after her marathon sex with Reid, she ate the heavenly pancakes and washed them down with lukewarm coffee. The blend was just okay. She'd have to give Reid some of her favorite brand.

He came back, looking a little ragged but still in one piece. When he saw her finishing her plate, he nodded. "Good. You need to eat more. You're too skinny."

She would have loved him for that statement alone. If she'd loved him. Which she didn't. Not yet. Maybe she did. Oh no. She did.

Guzzling the coffee, she prayed he couldn't read her panic.

"Hey, your family isn't going to come down on you for staying here, are they?"

She froze. "Um, I doubt it." They sure the heck would tease her about it though.

"Good. Cash is just being Cash. Don't worry about him. And don't worry about me waving your panties in triumph either. Our relationship is ours alone. You can trust me."

He looked so earnest. She rose and crossed to him. "Sorry about this."

"What?"

She kissed him. "Coffee breath."

He kissed her back until both of them were moaning and grinding. "Shit. We can't."

"I'm all clean now. Plus I have to get to work."

"Yeah. Me too." But he pulled her towel open, and it dropped, leaving her naked.

She undid the towel holding up her hair. A glance down his front showed his shorts tented.

"Well, maybe a quickie."

He smiled. "Great minds think alike."

An hour later, at home as she dressed and put on her makeup for work, she knew a sense of relief that she hadn't run into her family yet. With any luck, they would think she'd been too tired in her bedroom to come out to say good night. Then again, she was a grown woman. If she'd spent the evening at her boyfriend's house, who should care?

Now dressed and ready to handle her Friday, she entered the kitchen.

And saw her mother guarding the coffeepot.

"Good morning, sleepyhead." Kim gave her a wide smile.

Naomi sighed. "Yes, I spent the night with Reid."

"Did I ask?"

"Can I have my coffee press back?"

Her mother laughed. "Of course. I was just waiting to share a cup with you. Think you can spare some time to show dear old mom around the office?"

"Sure." Not exactly what she'd had in mind, but Naomi had a loose schedule today. "How about I pick you up at ten thirty? I can show you the office then take you to lunch."

"That sounds perfect."

"What about me?" Harley asked on a yawn as she padded into the room.

"You can stay here and enjoy your fiancé." Kim hugged Harley and patted her belly. "I can't believe I'm going to have another grandson in three more months!"

Harley rubbed her belly, the glow of pregnancy lighting up her smile. "Yep. Then you'll be another aunt, Naomi. When are you going to give Mom some grandchildren?"

The memory of her imagined black-haired baby with

Reid came rushing back with clarity. "I'm in no rush. I'm taking it slow. Dating. Then long engagement. Then marriage. Years later, a baby or two."

"By that time, you'll be fifty," her mother muttered. "So what about Reid? I like him."

Naomi repeated, "You like him."

"Yep. So does everyone else. What are you waiting for?"

"How about for him to ask me?" Like it was a given they'd marry when they'd just become lovers? Not that her mom knew that, but Naomi hated assumptions about her life.

"Why not ask him? It's a new age, Naomi," Harley said, a twinkle in her eye.

Naomi pointed at her sister. "You, stop instigating." She turned to her mom. "And you, I'll be back at ten thirty to get you. And no talk about my love life, or I'm not coming."

"Fine, fine." Her mother gave an innocent shrug. "So sad that it's considered rude to ask after your own daughter's happiness."

Naomi refrained from rolling her eyes. "Shouldn't you be thinking about getting back home to work? How are they managing without you?"

"I'm going to retire soon."

"In a few years," Harley tacked on.

"But I'm trying to slow down in increments."

Behind her, Harley shot their mother a look of disbelief.

"I saw that, Harley."

"Meh. I'd argue, but the baby is using my bladder as a trampoline." Harley waddled away.

Her mother smiled. "I'll be here and waiting for you, my dear. Don't be late."

As if Naomi would think twice about ditching her mother. It might be worth it in the short run, but she'd never hear the end of it. Besides, her siblings always catered to the Starr matriarch, making it that much harder for Naomi to buck the system.

In that as well, she and Reid shared something in common. Both of them wanting the respect and affection of their parents. She figured it to be a natural extension of the parent-child mold. But she and Reid took it a step further. He did his best to gain the love of a woman who was lost in her own mind. Naomi had the love, but she wanted the respect her mother gave to the children who succeeded, whereas she'd always felt like the bottom of the ladder because of her many failures.

Sure, Naomi had overcome obstacles in her life. But it seemed like her siblings sailed through without a problem. Except for Harley losing her husband, she'd never failed at anything. And she hadn't exactly failed her marriage. David had died.

Terrible thoughts didn't make her day go by any faster, but they did prevent her from ditching her mother at ten thirty. Naomi swung by to pick her up, having delivered a warning to Liz and Leo about what to expect.

Kim behaved herself, asking questions about the business and keeping Naomi's personal life private, for which Naomi was thankful. Though her mother liked to harangue her at home, she could and did comport herself in public. As a respected doctor and VIP at work, Kim knew how to handle people.

Sadly, Naomi knew her mother manipulated her

with ease. Mostly out of love, which made it difficult to deny.

Seated at her desk, Naomi watched her mother studying the office. "You get me to do what you want pretty easily."

"I don't know what you mean."

Naomi grinned. "I use that tone myself. I think you know *exactly* what I mean."

Her mother sighed and sat down. "I only ask about you out of love. I worry. All of my children are happy. But you, you're always searching for something."

"Now *I* don't know what you mean."

Her mother laughed. "I know you'll hate to hear this, but we really are alike."

Naomi groaned.

"I guess it's time we had that talk." Her mother sat back, crossed her legs, and studied Naomi over clasped hands. "For years, you've spent your time competing with your brothers and sister. In school, college, the workforce. And you never needed to."

"I know that." Naomi shifted, uncomfortable with the direction the conversation had taken.

"Honey, please. I know you better than you know yourself. When Ben took karate lessons, you needed karate lessons. When Peter became the team goalie in soccer, you had to change positions and outdo him. Which was just silly because that boy is a genius at the sport."

"Mom."

"Then Harley. Your biggest rival for years. Another girl, the closest to you in age, and you both liked the same things. You had to go into business."

"Communications, Mom. Business came after."

"Right. I actually had high hopes when you moved to Seattle. That you might let go of all this nonsense about trying to compete with your brothers and sister."

Naomi stared. "You hated me moving away."

"I didn't. I just let you think that. Naomi, if I say black, you say white. I want you to stay, you leave. But that's okay, because I like for my children to be independent. For all that I want you to forget being competitive, it's part of who you are. And honey, I'm so proud of you."

Naomi felt the bottom of her world drop out from under her. "Oh my God. You're dying."

Her mother burst into laughter. "No, no. But won't your father get a kick out of that when I tell him about our talk. He's been after me to set your mind at ease for years. Apparently, I've been too pigheaded to listen. I see it now though. No matter what you do, who you date, or how many babies you have or don't have, I love you. I respect you. And I'm proud of the woman you've become."

Teary-eyed yet mystified, Naomi asked, "What brought all this on? Not that I haven't been dying to hear that *my whole life*, but what's up, Mom?" Coming on top of Reid losing his own mother, a sudden fear of missing out on Kim Starr's obnoxious yet loving insistence on giving advice made Naomi yearn to treasure every minute spent with her mom.

"It's seeing your sister getting married again. Your brother achieving a major medical award. More grandbabies. I don't know. I'm not getting any younger. I want you to be happy. Not for me, for you. I really am planning to retire next year, you know. I worked my butt off to get to this point. But I'm ready. I want to play, to see my children and grandchildren. And I want you to have children at some point—but only if that makes you happy." Her mother grinned. "And especially if they have yours and Reid's looks."

"Mom." She blushed.

"I liked Tanner because you liked Tanner. But I wasn't sold on him for a long time. There was something about him that never quite suited you. Then there was the fact he was *your boss*," her mother emphasized, like Naomi could forget. "I didn't want you to make a mistake that might cost you your job." Her mother gave her a strange look. "Now you've got your own business and a new man. One who looks at you like he can't see anyone else in the room."

"We just started dating, really." He looked at her like that? She felt tingly all over.

"I saw you looking his way too, young lady. This man is different."

"He's a good person." *He'd never fire me for doing a good job. And he wouldn't sleep with me if I worked for him. Well, was in his employ.* She hated that she had to keep splitting hairs with that minute detail. "Look, I'm just going to say it. I met Reid through work."

"I know."

"I mean, he's a client of mine."

"Yes, I know."

"I… What?"

Her mother huffed. "Seriously. We get the news, Naomi. Ben saw the article when it came out in the paper, and we watched the interview on TV. It wasn't hard to put two and two together, especially after Ben did a little digging."

Ben, you asshole. "Oh." Naomi felt like a moron for trying to hide it.

"But if you're dating him now, despite your work relationship, I can only gather that he means a lot to you. You're not stupid."

"Yeah? Well, dating Tanner didn't turn out well for me. We broke up because I was doing better with clients than he was, and he couldn't take it."

Her mother stared in shock. "Really?"

"Yes." It felt so good to get that off her chest. "He didn't fire me, but he would have if I hadn't quit. I started Starr PR because I needed a job. But I like being my own boss, and we're doing really well. Reid started out as a client too." She smiled. "Unlike Tanner, Reid likes and respects me."

"Why shouldn't he?"

"But Mom, Tanner and I are going to have to work together on a new project." She explained her hope for a future with Jennings Tech. "He says he loves me and wants me back."

Her mother scowled. "I hope you're not seriously considering that."

"No." Naomi paused. "But I never did get that closure I needed with him. Maybe working together will give that to me."

"What does Reid think of you working with your ex?"

She shrugged. "I don't know. I haven't told him, not that it's his business."

Her mother laughed. "Yeah, right. So it wouldn't bother you if he started working closely with one of his exes who confessed to wanting him back?"

"Well, ah…" She'd kick the woman's ass. Then she'd kick Reid's. "Hmm. I guess I should tell him."

"Tell me what?" Reid asked from the doorway. "Hey, Naomi. Kim. Harley suggested I surprise you ladies by taking you to lunch. Though I'm not sure who gave her my phone number."

Naomi had a feeling her big sister had snooped. Thank God Naomi had never tried sexting. But she'd thank her sister later for trying to soothe any potential ruffled feathers between their mom and her. Reid smiled at her, then crossed the room toward her. He looked so handsome in his trademark khaki pants and button-down shirt.

Before he reached her, a voice she could have done without added, "Did someone say lunch? Oh, hello, Kim." Tanner stood in the doorway. "You didn't get the message, Naomi? Jennings wants to take us to lunch today, for business."

"Who's this?" Reid asked.

Her mother's mouth thinned. "Hello, Tanner."

Reid's eyes narrowed. "The douche who couldn't handle a little competition?"

"*Reid*." Naomi couldn't believe the scene playing out in front of her.

Her mother choked.

Behind Tanner, Liz's eyes went wide. She mouthed, "*I'm sorry*," but didn't step away from the spectacle unfolding.

Tanner stared with suspicion at Reid. "Who the hell are you?"

"Naomi's—"

Not sure if he meant to say client or boyfriend, in

work mode, Naomi interrupted, "Client" at the same time her mother said, "Boyfriend. What's it to you?"

Tanner's slow smile made her want to bury her over-heating face under the desk. "Client and boyfriend, eh? This is a new thing, I take it." As if it was any of his business. "Vets on the Go! hasn't been a client for long." Great. He was keeping tabs on her now?

Instead of punching him in the face, which she kind of wished he would, Reid answered, "She's her own boss now, taking orders from nobody. And she doesn't sleep with cowards with tiny dicks. Just idiots with huge ones." Reid paused, glanced at Kim, and shrugged. "Sorry about that."

"Oh, no bother at all. We were just going to lunch, Reid. We'd love to join you, Tanner."

Tanner, grim-faced, waited. "We have business, Naomi, as much as I hate to intrude on your mom's visit." He ignored Reid as if he didn't exist.

"Did you say Jennings?" Reid asked.

Tanner didn't answer. Naomi nodded.

Reid brightened. "Great. He's a good friend of mine. Come on. He won't mind if Kim and I join you." So saying, he waited for Naomi to gather her coat and purse. "Where are we going, Banner?"

"It's Tanner, you dick."

"Tanner," Kim admonished. "Nice language."

He flushed. "We're meeting at Porcellos downtown." A trendy Asian fusion hot spot Naomi had been wanting to try.

"Great. We'll meet you there," Reid said for her, which started to annoy Naomi. As much as she didn't want to work with Tanner, she didn't need Reid fighting her battles for her, no matter how much her mother seemed to be enjoying everything.

"Fine." Tanner turned and walked away.

"I have a few questions to ask Liz before we go. I'll be out here when you're ready," Kim said and shut Naomi and Reid in her office. Alone.

Together.

They stared at each other before Reid calmly sat in one of the two seats facing her desk. "So...working with the ex again, eh? How'd that happen?"

Chapter 20

REID WAITED WITH EXAGGERATED PATIENCE. SEEING HER talking to that model-handsome fuckface had been like watching Cash's fiancée cozy up to strangers at a bar, then to Reid. Not at all welcome and a little sickening.

He couldn't help remembering how emotional Naomi had been, talking about Tanner. And Jennings had hired the guy and Naomi to work together? He wanted badly to talk to Chris about it. But he knew if Naomi ever tried to interfere in *his* business, he'd lose it. So he couldn't, in good conscience, ask Chris to fire the guy as a favor to him.

Still didn't mean he couldn't kick Tanner's ass though. If the guy could lift a manicured hand to fight back. What a waste. But was that the type Naomi was really attracted to? Some gel-haired, office-type narcissist who smelled of class and money? *Hell.*

"You seem awfully calm about this."

He shrugged and donned his calm-as-fuck face. The one he'd often worn to convince his superiors he had his unit together before reaming his subordinates a new one for dropping the ball he'd then put back in play. "Look, I realize that this is your business. But I care about you, and I thought we were dating. Isn't that something you tell the person in your life? That you're working with an ex? I'd tell you."

"Uh, well, yeah." She sighed and slumped against

her desk. "It's a sudden thing. I was so hot to get the Jennings account, I had no idea I'd have to work with Tanner too. Problem is he's good at his job. There was never any question of that."

"Okay." He forced himself to think. "Do you still have feelings for him?"

"What? *No*."

He studied her. "But it's uncomfortable working with him."

She gave a short laugh. "I'll say. I'm doing this to advance Starr PR. Not because I want to. It's Jennings's company. I have to prove I'm a professional."

He nodded. "I can respect that." He stood. "So let's go to lunch."

She looked uneasy.

"What? I can be a gentleman…when I try hard."

"Ha ha."

"I won't embarrass you or your mom. And I swear not to take Tanner's head off unless he asks for it."

"I doubt he's going to ask for that."

"He puts a hand on you, he's asking for it."

They both stood.

Naomi shook her head, smiling. "How can you be charming when talking about beating someone up?" She stepped into his arms. "And do you have any idea how nice it was hearing you call him a coward and a douche?"

He kissed her, hard. "Good." She couldn't still have feelings for the guy. No way.

He drove himself, following her and Kim to the restaurant. Someone must have called ahead to Chris because they had seven seats at the table.

"Reid." Chris lit up upon seeing him.

"Yo, man. What's going on?" Reid gave him a man hug and smiled at the guy. "Hey, you're putting on some muscle."

Reid hadn't seen Chris in a while, and Chris had changed.

Chris laughed. "Teresa's been on me to lose the gut." The guy barely had any body fat, but okay. "When Naomi called to let me know about her mother and a plus-one coming, I was thrilled. Until I heard it was you."

They razzed each other some more. Chris introduced Jon, his project manager, and Joanne.

Reid realized he'd seriously overstepped. Now that he'd calmed down a bit on the drive over, he felt like a jerk for insisting on coming with Naomi to a business lunch. Although her mother was visiting and would need a rescue as well... "You know, when I heard Naomi was going to lunch with her mom, I had no idea it was for business."

He ignored Tanner's scoffing.

"It's my fault," Chris apologized. "I thought I'd told my secretary about today, but I forgot to have her CC Naomi on it. Tanner's in the system, but we're still filling in Starr PR as a contact on our project."

"I can be on my way," Kim said.

"Me too," Reid agreed.

Chris frowned. "Not at all. It's been a while since we've talked. And I hate to take your mother away, Naomi. We can reschedule—"

"Nonsense," Kim cut in. She put a hand on Reid's arm, and the woman had a grip like a constrictor. "Reid and I are getting to know each other better. Honey, enjoy your lunch. I'll see you later. It was wonderful to

meet you all." She cooled considerably when looking at
Tanner. "Tanner."

"Bye, Kim." Tanner ignored Reid.

Chris, no one's fool, watched it all with curiosity.
Crap. Not great for Naomi. But Reid couldn't let her
go without saying something. "Thanks, Chris. Naomi,
your mom wanted to talk to me anyway about your
brother moving. So this is a great business lunch for me
as well. Enjoy your meal with this spaz." He elbowed
Chris, who let out an *oomph*.

Jon grinned. "He nailed you on that."

Joanne chuckled.

"Shut it, Jon." Chris wheezed and straightened. "See
you this weekend at the party, Reid. Cash too, I hope.
And anyone from the company you want to invite. I
want to hear more about Vets on the Go!"

"We'll be there." Reid shook hands with Jon, with
no idea about said party. To Tanner, he gave the look
of death. "Dickhead."

"Reid." Kim yanked him away, but he heard Naomi
groan and saw Tanner's flush.

"What was that about?" Chris asked.

"Well, this lunch has turned out to be more exciting
than the ones we normally have," Joanne joked.

Reid didn't get to hear the rest because Kim towed
him toward the back and flagged down a waiter. "We
need to sit far away from that group," she told the
man, who hurried to get them menus after seating
them. "That was awesome!" Kim laughed and laughed.
"Oh my gosh, if you could have seen the look on that
pompous ass's face!" she crowed. "Fire my daughter,
will he?"

Reid was grinning with her until she came to that last part. "Ah, so you know about that?"

"Naomi told me. *Finally*. Why that girl thinks she can hide anything from me, I'll never know." She stared at him. Or, more likely, *through* him. "You love my daughter, don't you?"

He sputtered, trying to figure out how to gracefully respond, when the waiter arrived to drop off menus and take drink orders. After he left to get their drinks, Kim wasted no time grilling Reid again.

The woman should have been an interrogator. "What was all that about business with my son moving?" she asked.

He prayed she'd forgotten about asking him if he loved Naomi. "I didn't want Naomi to be put on the spot. My relationship with her has nothing to do with Chris or her job."

Kim smiled.

"What?" She did have a shark's grin, something he'd overheard Naomi saying to her sister last night. He'd be sure to share that later.

"It's nice to see a man put his girlfriend's career ahead of his feelings."

"I didn't say that. Exactly." He cleared his throat. "I respect Naomi. She's brilliant at her job, and she shouldn't have to deal with personal crap from me or that asshole she used to date." Reid blew out a breath. "Christ, what did she see in him besides white-capped teeth?"

Kim laughed again. "Caps is right. That man spent more time on his wardrobe than Naomi. He seemed nice, but he didn't feel right for her."

"But I do?" Reid watched Kim, seeing in her the

woman his mother could have been. Kim protected those she loved, and she loved Naomi, no question. "Look, don't answer that. But tell me why Naomi feels so inferior." Was he talking out of turn? He didn't care. He loved Naomi, and he wanted her happy. *Oh hell. I'm out of my depth and I know it.*

"That's a great question. Hold on. My blood sugar's low." They chose items from the menu and ordered before she answered him. "Naomi is the youngest. It can't have been easy following in her brothers' and sister's footsteps. I'll just say it, and yes, I'm bragging. I have remarkable children."

"Seems to me like they have a remarkable mother."

She flushed, so pretty, a hint of Naomi to come in her later years. A familiar intelligence shone from her eyes, one he often saw in Naomi. "See, you're good."

"I know." He grinned.

She clapped. "Oh, my husband's going to love you. Don't panic. Yes, you should take it slow with Naomi. Of all my kids, she's the most stubborn."

"The most like you?" he hazarded a guess.

Kim nodded. "The girl refuses to acknowledge failure. Which is silly. We all have problems to get through. But why she never sees that, I don't know. It must have killed her to lose Tanner and her job." She eyed Reid. "She loved him, you know. My daughter doesn't just go from fling to fling. Her relationships have always been on the serious side. I like you, Reid. So I'm going to give you some free advice."

"I'm all ears."

"Trust Naomi. She's smart and loyal. And when she loves, she loves all of you. The good and the bad. She accepted Tanner's weaknesses, and that slime has many. That she hadn't had a decent relationship since that boy, in a whole year and a half, speaks volumes. Don't screw her over."

"I won't." A pledge he meant.

"I know you won't. You're a good man. Your parents must be proud."

"My parents are dead," he said gruffly, the pain of his mother's death blunted by raw feelings for Naomi. "And they weren't supportive like you. Naomi's lucky."

Kim reached across the table to pat his hand. "Yes, she is." She looked at him when she said it. "Now let's talk more about you."

He groaned. "Do we have to? I think I already told you my shoe size and my Social Security number at the banquet last night."

She gave an evil chuckle, sounding remarkably like Naomi. It was no wonder he liked her. "Tell me more…"

―⁓―

Cash lifted like a man possessed. The gym was packed, but he didn't care. He needed to let go. The thought that Reid, the only person he'd ever loved without reservation and who'd loved him back just as much, might not be his real brother tore at him.

It just figured the one person he loved most in this world would also be ripped away, thanks to his asshole parents.

Fucking Angela. He wiped sweat from his eyes and worked harder on the squats. He was pressing more than he normally did and felt the burn. But he needed it.

"Yo, man. You should have been done ten presses ago," some muscle-bound dick said, glaring at him.

Cash ignored him, thinking about all Angela had said and not said before she'd died.

They should have gone to the reading of the will today, but the lawyer had been called out of town on an emergency, so they'd have the reading when he returned. Reid had been around, but his brother had been preoccupied at home. Though Cash normally didn't see him while working, they checked in on each other. Of course, now that he was tapping fine-as-shit Naomi Starr, Reid was understandably distracted.

Except Cash needed him around. Not to talk, because Cash didn't like talking. But Reid made him feel safe.

And that shamed him.

He was older by two years. He'd protected Reid all his life, when he could. Being separated for a time while in the Marine Corps, knowing Reid might be going into danger without him, had been a huge deal. Probably part of what had made Cash snap, to tell the truth. He'd been in the right when his superiors had tried to cover up some unsanctioned action that had nearly gone sideways, but he'd insulted the wrong guys and gotten his ass nearly thrown out. He should be thankful they'd let him separate with an honorable discharge, but fuck them. He'd served his country proudly, never putting a foot wrong. Not legally. Sure, he'd raised hell. He was a guy, wasn't he?

Cash left the weights and moved to an upright bench. He grabbed two forty-pound bells and started curling. Each move burned, and he welcomed the pain, the repetition, numbing the realization of his brother's growing distance, of his father's constant disapproval, of his mother's final acceptance…unless she'd been thinking of someone else.

It hurt. It hurt so much that he'd never get that acceptance he craved. She'd died, and he had nothing but poor Reid left. The hapless younger brother who'd scrapped his own career in the military to come home to help his big, useless brother. Who'd risked his financial future so stupid Cash could have something worthwhile to do.

His eyes burned, more sweat making it hard to see. He grunted with the strain, needing a push.

"Hey, Griffith, you good?" Gavin Donnigan asked, staring down at him.

"Fine," he bit out.

"Okay. Yell if you need me." Gavin moved on.

He overheard the muscled jerk talking to his friends about Cash, heard Gavin go over to put a stop to it. Then he tuned them out and continued to train.

He had no idea how much time had passed, but he was aware of Gavin watching over him now and again. The back room had pretty much cleared out, all except for Gavin and the three big goons.

Cash needed a spotter for the large bar. Of course Gavin was no longer there. So Cash turned to the one guy who hadn't said much. "Yo, mind giving me a spot?"

The guy nodded. He had a broad chest, big arms, and a beer gut from hell.

The other two dicks kept talking about how annoyed they were that Cash was hogging their bench. But since neither had the stones to come ask him to move, Cash stayed put, in no mood to deal with passive-aggressive assholes.

"Ignore them," his spotter said. "I'm Doug. Jim and

Andy think they own the gym." Doug grinned at the pair, and Cash couldn't get a handle on their relationship. Was Doug friends with the guys or not?

"Cash," Cash said by way of introduction. "Appreciate the spot."

"Sure."

Cash benched three hundred pounds and felt each rep burn. Finally clearing his head, he managed his last three and needed help on the final. "A little help."

Doug just stared down at him.

"Look. Cut the shit. Help me out."

"Maybe you'll move from the bench if I do."

Cash glared. "Get some balls and ask to me move, and I might."

Doug raised a brow and continued to stare down at him. The bar grew heavier. Jim and Andy laughed at him, and one of them said, "Not so strong now, huh?"

Cash gritted his teeth to keep from lashing out. He needed to get into a better position to deal with the jerks. "You want to talk about the bench, we'll 'talk' once this is off me."

"Uh-oh. Look who's having a problem," said Jim or Andy. Frankly, Cash couldn't tell the assholes apart. Both balding and needing to prove they had something they were obviously missing, they clearly had issues.

One of them stood by the door. Looking out for Gavin, maybe? While his buddy neared to stand over Cash.

"You want help, dickless?"

"He said his name is Cash, Andy."

Andy shrugged. "Dickless wants help, he should say pretty please."

The pair just stood there while the bar put serious pressure on Cash's chest. He'd worked to muscle exhaustion, and he didn't have the energy to deal with these three. But bullies and Cash didn't mix.

"Pretty please lift this fucking thing off my chest."

"And next time, don't hog the weights." Andy put a hand over the bar, adding weight that hurt. "This is our bench."

"Won't…hog…weights."

Andy grunted. Doug and Jim laughed.

The bar eased up, and Cash worked to catch his breath. His tormenters stayed close by, fortunately. Cash eased into a sitting position on the bench, rubbing his sore sternum, and gave Andy and Jim a second look. They were big guys with tiny brains if they thought they'd intimidated him.

Doug might have had a brain though, because when Cash's gaze met his, he took a step back.

"We clear now, dickless?" Andy asked.

Cash slowly stood and tilted his head left and right, cracking his neck. He had a moment to notice Gavin and Reid standing at the entranceway, Gavin holding Reid back with difficulty.

Uh-oh. If Cash was bad when riled, Reid could fight like a demon. Little Brother didn't often get pissed, but when he did, look out.

Cash grinned at Andy. "You know what? Takes brass balls to hold down a helpless Marine, knowing he's gonna eventually get up and feed you said balls one by one. Do you guys do this to everyone?"

He caught Gavin's jaw going tight and thought that might be the case.

Then Reid pushed past him and moved right for Doug, the closest of the three to him.

Doug, who likely outweighed Reid by fifty pounds at least, turned with a frown. "Hey, don't—"

Reid hit him, one solid blow to the jaw that sent the fucker down.

Then Cash forced his tired body to work and brought Andy to his knees with a swift kick between his legs.

"Damn it. No fighting," Gavin growled. "No matter how much these assholes deserve it."

Jim looked alarmed at the sight of the Griffith brothers bearing down on him, so he grabbed a ten-pound disk.

"What a pussy," Reid snorted and showed no sign of backing off.

"Easy. His ass is mine," Cash warned.

"His ass is no one's," Gavin tried again. "Damn it. Listen to me. Enough is enough."

"Bullshit. We both saw that fucker hold my brother down with three hundred pounds across his chest!" Reid pointed to Andy, who whimpered on the floor. "And that dipshit helped." When Doug tried to stand, Reid went over and watched, bristling with hostility. "Come on, asshole. Stand up. I dare you."

"I'll sue your ass," Andy managed, still breathing hard.

Jim was texting someone. Cash shook his head. "Sorry. Are we boring you?"

"You're going to be sorry. My cousins are here."

Gavin threw up his hands. "Fine. Fuck all of you. Cash, Reid, I'm trying to help." He whipped out his phone and called Mac, the owner. "Got a problem here. Need you and your fists now."

"Yeah? You want to help?" Reid said to Gavin. "Call for an ambulance." Reid rolled up his sleeves. "I'll take this one. You get the cousins," he told Cash.

Cash frowned. "Excuse me? This prick is mine."

"I doubt that. He's too small for you. Too easy. Look at him. He's pissing his pants."

"Fuck you," Jim said and took a swing.

Reid ducked and waited. "That's it? That's all you got?"

Cash frowned. "Aren't you supposed to be the one calming me down?"

"Why? Because you're a special snowflake dealing with Mom's death?"

Gavin groaned.

"No, asshole. Because you're the rational one. I'm the crazy."

"Look. I got grilled by Naomi's mom all afternoon." Reid ducked another wild swing.

When Jim tried to rush him, Cash stepped in, grabbed low, and flipped the guy over onto his back. "You're lucky you missed those weights. Landing on them'd hurt like a bitch."

Jim groaned and rolled to stand.

By now, more people had gathered at the doorway to the weight room. Two large bodybuilders entered.

"You guys Jim's dickhead cousins?" Cash asked.

One of them frowned. The other sighed. "Not this again."

Frowning guy walked to Cash. "You want some pain, motherfucker?"

Jim snickered as he rose, and Reid waited until he stood, then put him down again with a leg sweep.

"Damn it. I said he's mine," Cash snapped.

Reid huffed and crossed his arms over his chest. "Please. At this rate, I'll be thirty-five before you actually do anything. I had a rough day; I need the release. What have you done except lift weights?"

Cash gaped at his normally even-tempered brother. So when the beefy guy swung, he made contact with Cash's gut.

"Damn it. That hurt." Cash returned the punch and took the guy down, wrestling style, into a headlock.

By that time, Mac had pushed through the growing crowd. "Gavin, get this cleared, would you?"

Gavin turned to the crowd. "Okay, everyone. Nothing to see here but two brothers arguing."

"But what about—"

"Nothing to see, I said." In a terrible impression of Obi-Wan Kenobi, he said, "These aren't the droids you're looking for."

The crowd dispersed.

Mac grunted as he knelt by Cash on the floor. "Cash, man, you break his neck, you're in a world of hurt. He's not the enemy, Marine."

Cash and Reid swung equally amused glances at each other before Cash remembered Reid had annoyed him. He glared, then turned that look on Mac. "I'm not having a breakdown, Mac. This asshole is a bully. And those dicks tried to shove a three-hundred-pound bar down on my chest instead of spotting me. Not cool." Cash held on a second more, feeling the jerk with no neck start to fade. He released him and pushed him away, then stood.

"It still hurts," he complained, rubbing his sternum.

"Let me see," Mac ordered, slowly getting to his feet.

Cash whipped off his shirt. "Happy now?" He glanced down to see a darkening bruise.

Mac swore under his breath. Then out loud. "Andy, Jim, and the rest of you assholes, my office. And if you think about refusing, I've got the cops on speed dial."

Everyone limped out of the room but Gavin, who kept an eye on Cash and Reid.

Cash shoved his brother back. "What the hell do you think you're doing? Both of those guys had at least forty pounds on you."

To Cash's surprise, Reid shoved him back.

"Uh, guys…"

They ignored Gavin.

"Did you not hear me?" Reid barked. "I was grilled by Naomi's *mother*. I also learned Naomi's got to work with her ex on Jennings's project. How the hell am I supposed to handle that?" He shoved Cash back again.

As much as Cash felt for the guy, he didn't like being pushed. "Stop it."

"Or what?" Reid huffed and put Cash in a wristlock before shoving him away. The sorry little bastard. Cash had shown Reid how to master that trick years ago. "And my brother, who's supposed to be my best friend, refuses to talk to me. Fuckhead, she was my mother too!"

"Oh hell." Gavin turned his back on them, standing in the doorway .

Cash winced, his wrist now sore. "Easy, genius. I'm sorry I'm not handling her death better. But damn, I don't have someone to ball on a regular basis to help me handle my emotions." He was better than this, but he found himself saying, "What? She not blowing you enough? You have to come to me to—"

Reid hit him with a left hook right in the face. Then he used some of that freaky jujitsu he'd learned in the Corps that Cash hadn't been privy to and put Cash on his ass. Now on the wrong end of being choked out, Cash struggled to get free and not break his brother in half in the process.

"Apologize," Reid growled.

"What the hell's going on now?" Mac asked.

Gavin sighed. "It's a brother thing. Let it play out."

Mac grumbled and left.

"You guys are in so much shit," Gavin warned.

Cash focused on his brother's aggravation. He'd deal with Mac later. Lashing out at Naomi had not been a good idea. Plus Reid, that little shit, had grown *strong*.

But not as strong as Cash. He felt for a weak spot, broke Reid's hold, then reversed the choke hold until Reid tapped the floor. Cash let him go, then wrestled with him a little more, exhausting himself until both he and Reid were spent.

He shoved his brother off him with a punch to his diaphragm. Then Cash stood and reached down to lift Reid to his feet. "Breathe, dumbass."

"Shut. Up." Reid bent over, trying to catch his breath.

"Man, you guys are ten times worse than me and my brothers." Gavin sounded cheery. "Also, if you're smart, you'll head out the back door and avoid Mac for a day or two. I'll talk him down." He grinned at Reid. "Man, you surprised me. I thought you were the calm one."

Cash dragged him out by his ripped shirt, ignoring Reid's attempts to get free. "He has his moments. Hey, can you hold onto my bag for me? It's in locker 17."

"Sure thing, Cash. Now go."

Cash yanked Reid with him down the hall and out the back. Since he'd kept his keys and phone on him, he didn't worry about getting his bag back right away. He hauled ass to his car and shoved Reid against it.

"Ow. Fuck! You hit like a Mack truck."

"Yeah? So do you. Finally manned up. Nice. Now what the fuck is your problem?"

Chapter 21

REID WANTED TO BE ANGRIER, BUT HE'D PRETTY MUCH blown his wad in the gym. Seeing someone threaten his brother, he'd erupted. Then dealing with all the stress of loving a woman most likely unresolved about her ex, in addition to trying to figure out why his mother hadn't loved him enough and why his brother was now avoiding him, it was no wonder he'd lost it.

"We should be helping each other through this. But you're avoiding me. What's going on?"

Cash sighed and took a step back. He studied Reid, then looked away. "I don't know, man. I'm fucked up about Angela."

No kidding. One minute, she was Mom. The next, Angela. And Cash didn't know an emotional up from down on a good day.

"Talk to me. We're it, Cash. You and me."

"I know." Cash reached up and gripped his hair, his arms bulging. He had to be cold in just his workout shorts and sneakers, his shirt still in the gym. The spring air grew chilly in the evening, and the sun had set an hour ago. "Shit. I'm freezing."

"Get in. We'll talk."

Cash shook his head. "We'll talk at home." He got in his car and left.

Reid hurried to his vehicle parked out front and paused before he could be seen. Unfortunately, Mac was leaning against it. But so was Gavin, who caught Reid's eye and coughed. "No, no."

"What?" Mac growled.

"No, I know where Cash might be. He likes to hang at the steam room. I bet he's back there. Oh hell, Mac. What if he's on a tear with our older guys? Just what we need, our Marine vet talking shit about the other services."

Mac swore up a storm and marched back inside.

Reid hurried to his car. "Thanks, I owe you one."

"No problem. But I never saw you leave. You get me?" Gavin headed for the front of the building, yelling at a fictional Reid he supposedly saw inside.

Reid raced home, wondering what to do about Cash. And about Naomi.

The talk with her mother should have calmed him down. Kim seemed to like him. She'd filled him in on Naomi's quirks after learning about all his own and didn't seem to have a problem with his employment, which, compared to the rest of her family, looked pitiful.

But now he knew he was in love with a woman for the first time in his life. And he had no idea what to do about it. Naomi was independent, too smart for him. Beautiful... She could have any guy she wanted if she put in the effort. He had to wonder what she was doing with him.

He pulled into the driveway at home and hurried inside. Only to find Cash asleep, clearly exhausted. He had dark circles under his eyes and had lost weight. The poor bastard.

So Reid kicked at his leg and yelled, "Reveille! Reveille!"

Cash jerked awake and fell to the floor, which started Reid laughing.

"Asshole." Cash gingerly sat on the couch once more and yawned. "What?"

"Explain."

Cash stared from under hooded lids. "I think we might have different dads."

"And?"

Cash blinked. "You knew?"

"Cash, Dad hated you for a long time. But not me. Of the two of us, I look a lot more like him. But you're big, have his size. I wondered about it, but his name is on your birth certificate. And in Mom's scrapbook."

"It is?" The hopefulness in his voice had Reid hurting for him.

"You are so stupid." He sat next to his brother and slugged him in the arm. Sadly, the blow did nothing. "Who cares if we're half brothers or not? And I still don't think that's the case. If Dad wasn't your dad, he'd have kicked your ass out years ago."

"True." Cash stared at the spot where Reid had hit him in the arm. "That hit sucked."

"So do you. What a pussy. Boo-hoo, I might have a different daddy." Yeah, he was acting cruel. But Cash needed a wake-up. "Look, I need you now. We're in this Vets on the Go! thing together. It's our future."

"Man, I'm thinking Naomi might be your future. You don't need me."

Reid hit him again, and this time, Cash jerked back.

"Cut it out."

"Then stop being a dick. I think I love Naomi. I don't think she loves me back."

"Yet," Cash said.

"Yet," Reid repeated and shocked himself by smiling.

For the first time since his lunch with Kim, he felt good. "She's gutted me and doesn't even know it. I have to figure out this Tanner guy, where he fits with her. And then I have to outmaneuver her."

Cash nodded. "Outflank her. Trick her into needing you."

"She's smart. She doesn't need anyone."

"Sure she does." Cash snorted. "Or aren't you any good at sex? Give her lots of orgasms and she'll stay."

Reid sighed. "We really need to work on your interpersonal relationships with the opposite sex."

"You first."

He nodded. "We get through Mom's funeral Sunday. Then the workweek. And Jennings is having a major party next weekend. We should go. He wants to ask about the business. He'll help spread the word."

"Good man." Cash rubbed his chest. They sat in silence. "So you really don't care if I'm your half brother?"

Reid wrestled him to the ground and put his brother in a mock hold. Cash couldn't stop laughing long enough to take Reid seriously, apparently, so Reid snarled, "Cut it out. I'm your brother, no matter what. Say it!"

"No matter what." Cash tossed Reid off him as if Reid weighed nothing.

His brother really was a monster.

"Now stop being a pussy and deal."

"Fine. Quit calling me a pussy."

"I will as soon as you stop acting like one." Reid waited for Cash's assent before adding, "And speaking of pussy, I'm putting Heidi with you and Jordan next week."

Cash groaned and lay flat on the ground. "Why me?"

"Because Tim threatened to quit if we pair him with

anyone besides Martin anymore." Reid sat on the floor, his back to the couch. "Or Hector. But that's it."

Cash sighed. "Fine." He paused. "I'm sorry I said Naomi might not be blowing you enough."

"Great."

"I'm sure she's blowing you just fine."

"Stop. Please."

"And I won't stand in the way when you guys decide to live together and shit. I'm good with that."

Reid heard the worry and groaned. "Slow down, okay? First I have to get the woman to admit she can't live without me. That's a tall order considering I don't know if she even likes me past my dick."

"Sure she does."

"And anyway, that's all moving way too soon. I barely know her."

Cash opened an eye. "Really?"

"No. I know her." *And I love her like crazy. But I'm desperate to not let her know and scare her off. Not yet.* But now he had to deal with not scaring off someone else he loved. "Look, dickhead."

"Hey."

"I'm never ditching you. Not for a woman, a man, a dog, nothing. I might fall in love. Hell, someday I might even have kids if hell freezes over. But you're always my brother. And if my woman can't handle that, she's not the one for me."

Cash closed his eyes, but Reid saw a tear escape before he wiped it away. "Yeah, right. You'll be whipped. Mark my words."

Reid heard the relief in them and smiled. "Whatever you say, Casanova. How is Jordan, by the way?"

He scrambled to safety when Cash caught his second wind and rushed after him.

———∿∿∿———

The funeral service had gone as expected. Aunt Jane and Evan showed, though they both came for Reid and Cash, not to mourn for a woman who'd never been there for her sons. To Reid's surprise, Naomi had shown up to offer her support as well. After the short service, where they'd placed Angela's remains next to Charles's, Evan and Aunt Jane left. Naomi had insisted on going home with Reid and Cash and had cooked them some meat casserole thing for dinner.

Reid had never had better. The home-cooked meal won Cash over. He couldn't say enough good things about Naomi after that, and they had passed the evening quietly, watching television together before they retired to bed. Naomi and Reid stayed in his room, and Cash crashed on the couch, as usual ignoring his own bed.

Reid had slept—and only slept—with her, too emotionally drained for sex. Naomi, bless her, had understood. Though he felt like a weak wreck, Reid felt surprisingly better having her near. During the funeral and after, she was there for him. And watching her interact with Cash in the days that followed showed him how right he was to care for her. Naomi gave Cash attention without a fuss, treating him as a friend. She teased Cash, drew him out, and insisted he prove himself by competing in everything from video games downtown to drinking contests at their favorite bar.

It wasn't just Naomi who helped. The entire team at work offered condolences. On Monday and Tuesday,

Jordan stuck to Cash like glue on the Johnson job despite him trying to shake her. Heidi had been a godsend, more efficient and hardworking than either he or Cash had suspected. And the Jacksons treated Cash like their long-lost brother. Giving him the space, and arguments, he needed to get right again.

Reid felt as if his team was coming together, not just as coworkers, but as family. Hell, half of them hung around after work, just because.

By Thursday, he sent Mannie out with Jordan and Heidi, figuring that between the women, they could keep Mannie in line. He worked hard but seemed to go off track if not watched.

"I don't know how much longer he's going to work here," Cash said to Reid Thursday afternoon as they caught up in his office. "When I took him out this morning, he took his breaks with some rough-looking guys. Not saying we're not all a little rough, but I'd swear they were casing the house."

"Shoot. Really?"

"Yeah, but I can't say for certain."

Reid frowned. "He passed his criminal check. I don't know. Let's keep an eye on him."

"Problem is we need him, and I don't have time to babysit the guy. Stan, Heidi, and Funny Rob—who's not that funny, actually—are good to go. Lafayette and Hector gave Funny Rob a thumbs-up. Finley okayed Stan." Cash grinned. "Heidi's my personal fave. You know she watches *Real Housewives*? Bro, she adds value to our team."

Reid sighed. "Great. How about we call that big guy, Smith Ramsey, and put him on standby?"

Cash frowned. "I didn't like him."

"I did. He called today to check in. He's a Marine, and he's responsible. At least on paper. His background check and references checked out. All had good things to say about him." Aside from the fact that he was a sarcastic prick.

"We don't have the space."

"We—"

Jordan knocked on the door. "Can I talk to you guys?"

"Sure." Reid glanced at Cash and saw his brother checking her out, subtly, but it was there all the same. Reid cleared his throat, and Cash glanced down at some papers on the desk.

Jordan entered and closed the door behind her. "We have a problem."

"What did Mannie do?" Cash asked.

She blinked. "Ah, how do you know I'm here about Mannie?"

Now it was Cash's turn to look surprised. "What? No way Heidi made a move on you!"

Jordan frowned, then blushed. "No, you idiot. I'm here about Mannie."

"Which is what I asked in the first place," Cash grumbled.

Reid hid a smile. "Jordan, what's this about Mannie?"

She sighed. "I saw him take something today, and when I called him on it, he said it happened to fall into a box he was moving. Reid, I know what I saw. He was stealing Mrs. Early's jewelry."

Cash straightened in his seat, his gaze intent. "What did Mannie say when you called him on it?"

She shrugged. "Said if I was smart, I'd forget about it. That I hadn't seen what I thought I had, and if I made trouble, he'd make trouble back." A mean look came over Jordan's cute face. "Excuse my French, but fuck him. I'm not going to get fired because he has sticky fingers. I won't work with him again, and if you're smart, you won't either." She glared at Cash, as if daring him to contradict her.

Cash nodded, and her ire seemed to fade. "Thanks, Jordan. Good work. We'll take care of him."

She took a step back. "Oh, well. Okay then." She looked to Reid for confirmation.

"We don't tolerate thievery or bullshit. And threatening a fellow vet over an accusation instead of coming to us about it? That's not cool."

She gave a relieved smile. "Good. Because I really need this job."

"You got it," Cash said gruffly, then playfully added in a teasing voice, "unless you start stealing too."

Jordan didn't find him amusing. She poked him in the chest, right over the spot healing on his sternum.

Cash winced.

"Suck it up, you big baby. And don't ever tease me about stealing anything. I don't do that shit. Ever."

"Sorry, sorry." He held up his hands in surrender. "Jesus. I was kidding."

Jordan just laughed. "You're in for it, Griffith. Just you wait." She cackled like a witch and hissed at Cash, then left.

"Damn, I like her." Cash beamed. "Now let's can Mannie before I rip his arms off."

Reid sighed. "Bring him here and let me do it. You

just stand around looking threatening. I'm not getting sued for wrongful termination because you beat him to death with his own arm."

"Hey, if he's dead, he can't sue."

"His wife can," Reid snapped, out of patience.

Cash, the bastard, chuckled and left to fetch Mannie. Naomi called.

"Hello?"

"Just wanted to say hi, Reid. And to remind you about Chris Jennings's party on Saturday."

"I'll be there." He paused. "Are we going as a couple or as work friends?"

She took a moment to answer. "Work friends, I think. I'm sorry. I'm not trying to hide us, but this account with Jennings is huge for me. And it's bad enough I have to work with Tanner, even though I know you hate it. I hate it too."

He refused to be that guy, the one who couldn't handle his girlfriend alongside her ex. He trusted her, damn it. But he didn't trust Tanner. "I'm cool. Like I said, he touches you, I'll gut him."

She laughed. She obviously had no idea he was serious. Good thing she hadn't seen him fight at the gym. She still thought him mostly a gentleman. He planned to keep it that way.

He'd seen her all week. The sex, as usual, was fantastic, their connection deepening. At least, on his part.

Reid hated being this way, hated that just hearing her voice made everything better. Since when had he ever depended on anyone or anything for his happiness?

"Sure, Reid," she was saying. "Sounds good. Are you doing okay?"

"I'm good." He coughed. "Great. Looking forward to the party."

"I wish I was." She sighed. "I know this will turn out okay in the end. I just hope Tanner doesn't think he can dictate how we approach our advertising strategy."

Reid heard voices coming closer. "Hey, sweetheart. I'm sorry, but I have to go. Work calls."

"Oh, I'm rambling. Sorry. See you soon." She disconnected, and he immediately felt depressed.

Sack up, he told himself.

Cash walked in with Mannie, both of them looking a little tense.

"You wanted to see me, Reid?" Mannie shot Cash a wary look.

"Come on in, and shut the door."

Mannie took a seat across from Reid's desk. Cash stood by the exit, leaning against the wall.

"What's up?" Mannie tried to act tough, but Reid thought he looked nervous.

Reid watched him, letting the silence build, wondering if Mannie would say anything.

"Hey, look, if this is about what Jordan thinks she saw, she's wrong." He tried to laugh it off. "Damn. I was moving shit from one room to the van. I swear, she thinks I was stealing. If I was stealing, why would I wrap the stuff in a moving box and put it on the damn truck?"

"Why would you move the customer's personal jewelry without her okay?"

"What? Hell, man. I don't remember all the rules. That's why I'm still a trainee, right?"

Cash snorted. "Bullshit. We went over that the first day. I remember because I told you. Get out."

Reid held up a hand. "Hold on. Mannie, you were seen taking jewelry from the customer's bedroom. When Jordan spotted you, you then suddenly turned to the van, as if to place it there. Then, after you were caught, you threatened Jordan not to tell."

"That's crap. I didn't do any of that."

"Really?" Cash opened the door and yelled for Jordan, who had insisted on being there to confront Mannie. Subtle his brother was not.

"Keep it down, son," Dan snapped. "I told you earlier I'd get her when you asked."

"Oh, sorry, Dan." Cash smiled at the older guy, then waited for Jordan to enter before closing the door again.

Jordan scowled at Mannie.

Mannie scowled back and stood to face his accuser.

Reid wished it to all be over. "Jordan, can you please tell us what Mannie said to you?"

"He said he wasn't stealing but—"

"No," Reid interrupted. "The part about where he threatened you."

She planted her hands on her hips and stared Mannie down. "He said if I was a smart bitch, I'd keep my mouth shut. Because he needed this job. And if I ratted him out, I'd pay."

"So he threatened you?" Reid said, cutting off Cash. "That's workplace harassment."

Everyone who came on to Vets on the Go! signed a harassment disclaimer, agreeing to immediate termination if found guilty.

Jordan's eyes narrowed. "Oh yeah, I was harassed. And Heidi heard it, if you need more proof."

Mannie didn't seem to like hearing that. His eyes narrowed, but he looked worried.

"As we have a non-harassment policy, one that you, Mannie, signed, what do you have to say?"

Mannie swore. "They're lying. They don't like me outworking them is all. Not my fault I'm a go-getter."

Jordan scoffed. "Please. The only thing you're likely to get is jail time for petty theft."

"Fuck you, Jordan. It's your word against mine."

"Don't forget Heidi," Reid reminded him.

"The big lesbo?" Mannie snorted. "Whatever. You ask me, she's not that bright. She barely talks and doesn't really know what she's doing anyway. She'll say whatever Jordan wants her to say because she hates men."

Cash blinked. "Now you have a problem with Heidi?"

Reid had heard enough. "Manuel Lorenzo, you're fired. Your final paycheck will be mailed to you by the end of the week. Cash will escort you from the premises."

Mannie looked ready to explode. "This is bullshit! I didn't do nothing!" He started going off in Spanish, and Reid caught a few words that weren't so good.

Then Jordan fired back at him in Spanish, the two of them engaging in a lethal battle of swearing and insults, if Reid was a good judge of facial expressions.

"Do it, *puta*. I'll make you wish you had the balls to." Mannie grinned.

The poor bastard didn't realize Cash understood a lot more than he'd let on. Cash said something in a low voice that had Mannie, and Jordan, staring in surprise. "Yeah, fucker, I know what you're saying. You and me, we're gonna have a nice long chat once you're off our property. You come near her, even to say hello, I'll rip off your dick and shove it up your ass. Just for fun." Cash took a few steps toward Mannie, who backed away, his eyes wide.

"Try it, *cabrón*. You might be bigger than me, but you're not bigger than a bullet." Mannie pretended to shoot him with his fingers. Cash grabbed those fingers and bent them backward.

Mannie shrieked in pain.

"Come on, bitch. Let's take your finger gun outside."

"Easy, Cash." Reid knew better than to say anything, but Mannie had to know threatening Jordan wouldn't go over well. "Take him outside, *then* break his hand."

Cash let him go. "Okay." He opened the door and shoved Mannie out of it.

Before Reid could join them, Jordan said, "I'll go with them, as a witness. Oh, there's Hector. I'll grab him too." She raced after Cash.

Reid worked another hour until he heard his phone alarm. Time to visit the lawyer to wrap up their mother's will. She'd kept most of her things at the old house, only a few personal items and her clothing at the assisted living home, which one of the nurses had boxed up for them.

Reid still thought it odd their mother had been lucid enough to arrange for her passing with such thorough attention to detail.

But after he and Cash left the lawyer's office a few hours later, he realized he'd never really known her at all.

Chapter 22

Naomi sat at her house, watching Reid pace. She wanted to cradle him to her, the way she had after his mother had passed. But not now. He seemed seriously freaked out.

"I'm telling you. Something's not right about all this. My mother lived in the damn clouds for most of her life. Now suddenly she's organized enough to divvy up her assets? Shit. I mean, shoot. It's not like I want her money. But Naomi, she left me out of everything." He blinked, swore, and kept pacing.

"That makes no sense. I'm so sorry, Reid." She felt for him. From everything he'd told her before, his mother had loved him. She'd all but ignored Cash. "You know she loved you. Maybe this is her way of righting the wrong she did your brother."

"Maybe." He abruptly sat next to her on the couch. "Why do I even care? Why does she have the power to hurt me? She's dead. There's nothing of hers I want." He paused. "Well, maybe a few pictures of me and Cash as kids. But her and my dad? It's hard to love them. Even now."

Yet he did. And that was why she loved *him* so much.

God, she had to keep repressing that emotion. Loving a man she'd met just a few weeks ago wasn't smart.

If she could live off sex alone, she'd keep him. But there had to be more than a physical attraction between them. She liked Reid. A lot. He appealed to her on every level. And his sense of humor and intelligence met her on an equal playing field. But they had their differences. They'd fought on occasion. And they both loved making up.

This relationship felt too soon because she felt too much. Did he feel it too? Had he really been joking when he'd told her sister he loved her?

Reid reached for her hand. He liked touching her, and that need for connection warmed her.

"I'm sorry. I hate unloading on you. You're just so easy to talk to." He leaned his head back. "Why don't you tell me about your day?"

"God, stop being so sensitive listening to me. Quit being nice." Great, now she sounded like a shrew. "I mean, you can have a bad day. You can be angry at your mom. It's okay, Reid."

"I know it's okay." He took the "quit being nice" to heart. "I was trying to not be so selfish with our time."

"Oh?"

He scowled. "I haven't seen you much this week. I guess that doesn't bother you."

"Oh, now we're bitchy. Okay. Run with that." She knew she was pulling a tiger's tail, but she liked this side of Reid.

"I'm being bitchy?" He yanked her to him and kissed the breath out of her. "Maybe you're being bratty."

"So what? You won't do anything about it." She nipped his lower lip.

Reid's breathing grew shallow. "Is there something you want me to do about it?" He squeezed her breast, then dropped his hand to her leg, sliding it up under her skirt and over her panties, stopping right where she wanted him.

"Oh, I see. You're wet for me. Why didn't you say so?" He unzipped his pants and pulled himself out, stroking his hardening cock. He returned his fingers to her panties, nudging them aside. "You hungry, baby?"

She widened her legs, and his nostrils flared. He knew exactly what she wanted. He shoved first one finger then a second into her, pumping in and out. She ground against him, needy.

It wasn't enough.

Abruptly, he withdrew his hand.

"Suck me off and I might give you what you want." He grabbed her by the hair and dragged her over him.

The forcefulness turned her on, this little game they played.

She did what he wanted, opening her mouth wide to take him in.

"Fuck yeah." Reid guided her head, using her hair like reins. "That's it. Take me deeper." He moaned as she cupped his balls, then snaked her tongue around him.

He tensed, gasping, and she knew he was close.

"Put yourself over me. Now, Naomi."

She pulled away, ripped off her skirt and panties, and sat on him.

Reid moaned and sank into her, riding his bliss as he fingered her to her own climax.

Coming with Reid inside her felt like perfection. Naomi owned him like this, and they both knew it. She could watch him take his pleasure, knowing she'd given it to him. And she took him inside her body, accepting all of him.

She shifted over him, and he groaned.

"No, baby. Don't move." He arched up into her. "God, you feel good. I swear, if I could bottle you and keep you close all the time, I would."

"For sex?" she teased.

He frowned at her. "For this." He just stared, then brushed a hand over her hair, a finger over her cheek. The kiss that came gentled, drawing her closer. He was hugging her, still inside her as he softened. She felt his sigh against her neck, heard him inhale her.

"You smell like spring." He smiled against her. "My favorite season."

"I love spring too," she said back, stroking his hair. *I love you.* But could she really love him so soon after meeting him? Her mother seemed to think so, but then Kim Starr wanted Naomi settled down. And she liked Reid.

"Reid?"

"Whatever you want," he muttered.

She grinned, loving how sated they made each other.

"I want you to always be honest with me." Unlike Tanner, Reid needed to put her first.

He opened his eyes. "Always? What if that dress really does make you look fat? You want me to say that?"

"What? No." She huffed. "I meant about important things."

"Okay."

She studied him. "Just okay?"

"Sure. What do you want to know? Give me a test." *Do you love me?* "Do you like me?"

He scowled. "What the hell do you think? I'm making love to *you*."

"You know, you only curse when you get really angry or really turned on."

"Stop." He flushed.

She found him adorable. "You are so cute when you're embarrassed."

"Cut it out." He tried to hide a grin by shoving his face in her neck.

"Why do you do that?"

"I get your scent that way. And you really do smell amazing. You're sweet, and you make me smile."

"Reid." He thought her sweet?

"It's true." He lifted his head to look at her, then cupped her cheeks. "Naomi, I see you, and I see everything I've ever wanted. You're so smart, so quick and funny. And you get me hard, no question."

She blushed. "I know. You're still inside me."

"Yeah." He gave a low, satisfied moan. "But it's not just because you're gorgeous; it's the whole package." The way he watched her gave her tingles. He seemed on the verge of saying something more.

Then his phone chimed.

"Hell." He sighed, glanced at the number, and set the phone back down. "It's Cash. I gotta go."

"Okay." They moved apart and cleaned up, and she walked him to her door.

"I don't want to go," he confessed. "Is that being too needy? I know chicks hate guys who are clingy."

"Yeah? Well, this chick wants to cling to you." She stroked his cheek, besotted. "Tell Cash I said hi."

"I will."

He was halfway out the door when he stopped suddenly. "Listen, this is probably stupid, but we fired Mannie today." She'd met him briefly. "He was stealing from a customer, but we caught him. He threatened Jordan, but she told him to stick it." Reid watched Naomi, his expression serious. "I doubt he'd do anything to you. But just in case. If anything ever happened to you, I don't know what I'd do."

Touched, she kissed him. And this kiss felt different. It felt like the prelude to more.

"I'll see you soon."

"Yeah." He stood in her doorway, then he sighed and turned to go.

"Reid?"

He stopped a few paces down the walkway.

"I, ah…" No way she could tell him she loved him first. Not if he didn't feel the same, because then the dynamic would change.

Bah. She hated second-guessing herself. But after Tanner, she didn't trust her judgment when it came to men.

"You okay?"

"I'm good. I'll miss you is all."

His joy lifted her with him. "Me too, Naomi. I think about you all the time."

That had to be love, right? So why didn't he say it?

"Me too." Lame but honest.

He smiled. Then quietly, as if waving goodbye, he said it. "I love you." He smiled and walked away.

Boom. Bomb dropped!

Naomi spent a restless night convincing herself he'd really said it, half hoping he hadn't. Love was serious. A big four-letter word that meant commitment.

It was what she'd wanted—or was it?

She needed to talk to him. But during the day, she was too chicken to call him and discuss their relationship over the phone. And the following night at the party, things didn't go as she'd hoped. She didn't get a chance to talk to Reid beforehand. Discussing this at the party didn't make sense. Naomi would *not* have a personal conversation of such magnitude at Chris Jennings's house. Plus this way, she could put off the discussion she had no idea how to have. She loved him, didn't she? But then, what did that mean? Would things change or stay the same?

Then Tanner and his girlfriend came into view, and it was creepy.

Next to her, Liz shuddered. "Oh my God, Naomi. She looks just like you. Naomi 2.0. Is she a clone?"

"Shh. He'll hear you."

"Come on. Even Jennings noticed. I heard him say something to Jon about it."

Naomi fought a blush. "Have you seen Reid and the others yet?"

"No, but I've been keeping my eye on Heather and Leo. Is it me, or does my daughter keep trying to get him into a dark corner? Well, well. The apple doesn't fall far from the tree."

"Liz."

Liz laughed, and so did Naomi as she watched Leo and Heather reemerge from the shadows of Chris Jennings's outdoor patio. The man lived in a mansion in Denny-Blaine, one of the most affluent areas in Seattle.

The patio had trees and shrubs and patches of color everywhere as his flowers overwhelmed rock walls and strategically placed pots.

"When are we interviewing that marketing specialist again?" Liz asked, nibbling from a plate of appetizers.

"Wednesday. He did well on the phone call, and you liked his résumé best, right?"

"Yeah." She and Liz continued to chat, Naomi keeping her distance from Tanner.

"You can't put him off forever. Might as well get it over with," Liz said.

"I know." Naomi sighed. "I just wanted to say hi to Reid first."

"I'll keep a look out."

"Okay." She waved at Tanner, who took that as a sign and made straight for her.

"Wish me luck," she muttered.

"Amen."

"Naomi, you look terrific." Tanner appreciated her spring dress, a lavender floral piece that hit her knees and flowed as if made specifically for her. The dress had cap sleeves and a square neckline, hinting at her bosom without accentuating it, making her look both modest and daring at the same time.

Leaving his date with Liz, Tanner guided them to an unoccupied area by an outdoor heater. The venue looked lovely, white lights strung over the trees, tall tables scattered around the paved patio, with heaters providing warmth and a bit of light.

The full moon overhead glowed, and light jazz music played over hidden outdoor speakers. The soft rush of running water from Chris's garden added to the serenity outside despite the many people in attendance. Everyone spoke in quiet tones, as if in reverence for Jennings's ability to harness the beauty in nature.

"I'm so glad you came tonight. I've been thinking about you." Tanner kissed her hand.

She pulled it back, confused. "Tanner, why are you doing this?"

He looked pained. "I miss what we had."

"You threw us away, remember?" She nodded to Liz and Naomi 2.0. "Does your girlfriend realize you're over here flirting? That's not cool, Tanner. Or respectful."

He flushed. "I can't help it. I still love you."

I love you, Reid had said, his voice quiet, honest, brimming with emotion.

"You love what we had. I miss that too, sometimes. Someone to work with, the way we worked together. But Tanner, it'll never be that way again."

He frowned. A spark of something came into his eyes.

They were distanced enough from the party to keep the conversation uninterrupted yet in view of some of the guests. A glance over her shoulder showed her that Liz and Tanner's date had disappeared, but she could still see Heather and Leo hanging out by the outdoor waterfall.

"Do you love Reid Griffith? Is that what this is about?"

"I…" Did she owe Tanner the truth? "My feelings for him aren't your business."

"Ah, so you don't love him. I didn't think so."

"You're one to talk about love." She snorted. "I gave you everything. I loved you, and I supported you."

"Loved, Naomi? Or still love?" Tanner moved closer. "Can you really turn it off so easily?"

Looking into his bright-blue eyes, staring over those

familiar features, she felt...something. But it wasn't love.

Her hesitation betrayed her, however. Tanner's satisfaction put her nerves on alert because he seemed focused, not on her, but on something behind her. *Don't be there, Reid, Please not now.*

She turned to see Reid watching her, his expression closed. He stood close enough to hear their conversation, but she had no idea how long he'd been standing behind her.

"I was looking for you and ran into a woman who looks just like you. Weird." Reid shook his head. When he looked at Tanner, he frowned. "Seriously? You break up with Naomi, then date a woman who could be her twin?"

Tanner's face turned red. "Mandy is none of your business."

"I guess not. And Naomi's and my relationship is none of yours." He nodded to Naomi, but the set of his jaw didn't bode well for their next conversation.

Before they could have one, Cash joined them and whispered something into Reid's ear, then the pair took off.

"That was rude." Tanner swallowed the last of his beer. "I'm not kidding, Naomi. I'm not using you for anything either. Hell, I already have the Jennings bid. PP&R is in no danger of going under. I'm being straight with you. I love you."

"You said that already." And now she was annoyed. "You deliberately baited me with Reid."

"So what? If he can't handle a little competition, do you want him in your life? We'll be working together in the near future. Can you handle being with someone who's so insecure, he can't handle your job?" Tanner gave a self-deprecating grin. "I made that mistake. Trust me, I know. A man who can't deal with his girlfriend's or wife's job isn't long for the relationship."

Naomi took what he said into account. "I have to go."

"I'm here, and I'm waiting."

"Don't hold your breath." She left, seeking out Liz, and ran into Jennings and his fiancée. "Hi. Great party."

They made small talk until Chris pulled her aside. "Hey, Naomi, is everything all right with Tanner? That lunch the other day was odd."

"It's fine. Tanner and I dated a long time ago. But we're just business acquaintances now. Reid and I are dating though." Feeling bad that they hadn't arrived together, Naomi wanted others to know he belonged to her. She felt guilty for having denied their connection.

Chris blinked. "Reid?" Then he smiled. "You traded up, Naomi. Not that I said that out loud." He cleared his throat. "I'd better—Oh, there's Cash. Let me say hi."

He left her. Cash and Chris shook hands. Near them, she saw a few familiar faces: Jordan and some huge guy with her and one of the Jacksons. Of Reid, she saw no sign.

She drifted closer and heard Jordan and the big guy arguing about something.

Once Chris left, Cash motioned Naomi over. "What's up?" she asked.

"We have a problem," he said in a low voice. "One of our ex-employees crashed the party. We think he's planning to steal from Jennings."

"No." She saw disaster written all over this. "That sure won't help Vets on the Go! look reputable."

"Uh, yeah, that's why we're here." Jordan shook her head. "Cash, we don't have time for this. Let's split up."

"Good idea. Naomi, want to help?"

"I insist."

"Who's she?" the big guy with Jordan asked.

Cash frowned. "Why did you bring him?"

"You said bring a date." Jordan shrugged. "I'm helping train him."

"And her car broke down. She needed a ride."

Cash glared. "You should have asked me. I'd have picked you up."

"Yeah," the guy said. "That's why she called me."

"Asshole."

"Prick."

"Boys," Naomi hissed. "Focus. Now who the hell is this?" she asked Jordan.

"This is Smith. He's new."

"Hey." Smith gave her a thorough once-over. "Nice dress."

She sighed. "Okay, so how do you know one of your guys—"

"*Ex*-guys," Cash was quick to correct her.

"—is going to steal something tonight?"

"Because I saw him sneaking in with a group," Jordan said. "I would have said something, but he was too far away, and I didn't want to make a scene. He wore a Vets on the Go! T-shirt to get in, and the security guards let him in because they were expecting us. Mannie's mad because I turned him in for stealing."

"Way to go, narc," Smith muttered.

"Shut the hell up," Cash snarled. "She's loyal."

"Easy, dude. I'm kidding." Smith didn't seem very afraid of Cash. He didn't seem all that intelligent either.

Jordan described Mannie's appearance.

Naomi nodded. "Okay. We should split up. I'll take—"

"No." Cash shook his head. "You keep an eye on Chris and let us know if he or his people come inside. Reid's already hunting down Mannie. We have to catch him first."

"You're damn right you do. Talk about a PR nightmare." Naomi crossed her arms over her chest and tapped her fingers. "Well? What are you waiting for? Go."

Chapter 23

REID COULDN'T BELIEVE HOW HIS MOOD HAD GONE FROM excited to dismal in the span of a few heartbeats.

Naomi hadn't told Tanner to back off, that she loved Reid.

That was the answer in itself. Tanner was right. She didn't love Reid, and she didn't know how she felt about Tanner. Fuck it all.

To make matters worse, a rogue employee was on the verge of sinking the business. Chris would never tell, but he wouldn't endorse their company to friends if one of Reid's own stole from him.

Reid had too much to lose to let Mannie get away with anything. He hurried inside, looking all around on the pretext of needing to use the restroom.

Fortunately, Chris wasn't a trusting soul and had security guarding the upstairs.

Which meant Mannie would head up there.

Reid wound deeper into the house before finding another set of stairs leading up. He moved, waiting to be told to stop, then continued past a distracted guard. Another looked doped up, and Reid had to wonder if Mannie had drugged them or somehow gotten lucky.

Hurrying quietly, listening for some telltale noise, he heard a faint scrape and followed the sound behind a set of double doors. He pushed the doors open and moved deeper into the bedroom, pausing at the doorway of the walk-in closet…and watched Mannie retrieve a small safe from on top of a dresser and set it on the floor. The safe was the size of a small bread box.

Though Reid thought he'd hidden himself behind the doorframe, Mannie turned, holding a gun. "Figures you'd show up to try to ruin my night. Firing me wasn't enough?" He motioned for Reid to move. "Quietly."

"Not like I want to draw attention. Love your shirt."

"It's a good color on me." Mannie grinned.

"This isn't right."

"Fuck you. All I wanted was a chance. You took that away."

"A chance to steal?" Reid scoffed. "We don't take from our customers. We help people. Hell, Mannie. Half of them could be any of us. Older retirees. People needing a helping hand, not someone to take from what they can't afford to lose."

"Save the sob story. This asshole can afford to lose a few gold watches. You just have no clue what I'm dealing with." Mannie gave a tired smile, one that didn't reach his eyes. "I left the Army with no prospects, but better to be out than doing time at Fort Benning."

So Mannie had been a criminal while in the Army. Funny, his background check had never mentioned that. "Why didn't we spot that in your background check?"

"Because I used my cousin's ID. We look enough alike it works."

"Okay, but Fort Benning's in North Carolina. What are you doing in Seattle?"

"Manfred, my cousin, lives out here. That's why we moved." Mannie motioned for Reid to leave the room. "The guard's out of commission on the stairwell. I gave him a few pills, but he'll be fine later, don't worry. Now you're gonna carry that out for me." He pointed at the safe still on the floor. "Wrap it in that blanket, and let's go."

"No."

"Do it, or I'll hurt your girlfriend." Mannie gave a mean smile. "Little Jordan isn't so nice, is she?"

Relief that Naomi hadn't been targeted couldn't replace the worry that Jordan had. "What is your problem? Jordan did the right thing, Mannie. She's fellow Army. Why turn on her?"

"She thinks she's better than me, and that bitch is anything but." Mannie calmed. "Look, grab that safe and we're out of here. No one learns it was us, and your company stays clean. You'll never see me again."

Reid weighed the odds. He didn't want anyone getting hurt. And he sure as hell didn't want Vets on the Go! involved. "Fine." He tucked the blanket Mannie had pointed to around the small safe and staggered when he stood because it was a lot heavier than it looked. It had to weigh close to forty pounds. He needed both hands to hold it, as it was slightly bulky.

They hurried down the back stairs, taking care not to be seen, and ran into Cash at the end of the otherwise empty hallway.

"Motherfucker." Cash stared.

"Not here," Reid said. Not too many people had ventured that deep into Chris's house, but anyone could if they wanted.

"He has a gun," Reid added, and Mannie stepped out from behind him.

"Shit." Cash looked murderous. Behind him, Jordan and Smith appeared. "Great. The gang's all here."

"Who the hell is that?" Mannie asked, waving his gun at Smith.

"Easy, dickhead," Smith growled. "That might go off."

Mannie sneered.

"The only thing you and I have in common," Cash told Mannie. "We both think Smith's a jerk."

Smith sighed. Before he could do a thing, two more men approached, dressed in suits and ties. Undercover cops, maybe? Reid could hope. Except the men didn't identify themselves as they moved past Cash toward Mannie and Reid.

"Finally." Mannie tossed the weapon to one of the suits, making Reid's heart skip a beat. "We gotta go." He reached for the safe.

"Car's out front," one of them said. The other one shifted, and Smith was already moving, taking the gun out of play by shoving the guy into Mannie, then clocking the suit in the face. Cash and Jordan were already diving for the other man, which left Reid to manage Mannie.

Just as Smith reached the weapon and stated, "Damn, it's not even loaded," Reid played tug of war with Mannie, not wanting him to get away with Chris's valuables. The silent struggle would have made him laugh if he hadn't been so furious. No one wanted attention, so they'd all been careful to keep the noise down.

"Fine. Keep it." Mannie tripped Reid and shoved the safe at him.

Off-balance, Reid lost his grip, and the safe slipped out of the blanket. He and the metal box went down, and in the fall, his hand took the brunt of the safe's weight when it hit the floor. Something snapped and numbness settled in, which was quickly replaced by blinding pain.

In his periphery, he saw Cash hit Mannie, taking him down with one punch.

"Reid? Are you here?" Naomi called from another room.

Cash stood over Mannie while Jordan pinned the other guy down, his hands cuffed with a zip tie, her knee in the small of his back. "I always carry one on me," she said when she saw Cash looking and winked at him.

In moments, Smith, Jordan, and Cash had three would-be burglars down and out. Hector arrived with Naomi.

"Damn, it's like déjà vu," Hector said as he and Cash stripped Mannie's shirt off him.

"We have to get these guys out of here, pronto," Reid said, gritting his teeth at the throbbing pain. He nearly passed out when he shoved the safe off his hand.

"Reid, oh my God. Are you okay?" Naomi looked horrified.

He refused to look at his hand, but the others stared in alarm. "I know," he wheezed and sat up slowly, cradling his wrist. "We can pretend I tripped or something. Jordan, Cash, put the safe back." He described where he'd found it, and they hurried back upstairs with the thing. "Hector, Smith, ditch these idiots. Tie them up and leave them outside with a note if you have to."

Smith disappeared and reappeared a moment later with a roll of duct tape.

"Hmm. I like it. It's got a dramatic flair." Hector grinned. Then he and Smith carried out the bodies, one at a time, each secured with duct tape. Where the hell had Smith gotten the tape? Reid felt woozy and wondered what he'd missed.

Naomi hurried to his side and helped him to stand. "Oh no. Reid, your wrist. It's awful!"

"I know." He felt shocky and forced himself to remain standing, not ready to pass out when he had work to do. "Go back in and make our excuses. Tell them it was a personal matter. Chris will understand."

"I need to come with you to the hospital."

Reid felt sick, both at what had physically happened and what he'd overheard. And God knew he didn't need Naomi seeing him at his worst, in pain. "No. Naomi, you're not sure how you feel about me. I get it. But I know how *I* feel. I need time. And so do you."

"But, Reid…"

Jordan and Cash reappeared.

"Let's go," Reid said to them. "Jordan, you, Smith, and Hector stick around, just so we don't look like we all took off. And somehow let security know to check for the losers outside."

Jordan nodded, and she and the guys departed the hallway.

"I'll call you," Naomi promised.

But Reid didn't have room to deal with more disappointment. Not now.

He nodded, then he and Cash left in Cash's vehicle.

"Hey, Big Brother?"

Cash looked grim. "Yeah?"

"Drive faster."

"You got it."

The pain from losing Naomi hurt worse than anything, and he allowed himself a few tears because of it.

If Cash thought he cried because of his stupid wrist, so be it.

⌁

Naomi hadn't seen Reid in four days, and she'd had enough. Wednesday morning, she scheduled a follow-up with Vets on the Go! at Reid's office.

She entered to a bustling center of activity after passing through a busy hallway.

In the office, Dan was keeping order. The seats in the waiting area were full, with Finley talking to people in the side office. She'd passed Hector and Lafayette talking with people in the conference room too.

"Hi, Dan. Is Reid in?"

Dan visibly relaxed when he saw Naomi. "Glad you're here. He's ornery as a bear." He nodded to Reid's office.

She entered and saw Reid wearing a Vets on the Go! navy polo and a bright-white cast on his wrist sporting several signatures. It covered his left hand, minus the fingers, and took up half of his forearm.

He was swearing at someone on his cell phone and pacing. He looked strained, tired, and so good, she wanted to cry. She'd missed him more than she could have imagined. The realization that a life without Reid could be so empty had thrown her into a tailspin.

She'd finally realized what he meant to her. Thinking of him dying and never seeing him again left a huge hole inside her that nothing but Reid could fill.

After days of soul searching, she thought she'd come to her answer.

"Hi."

He turned around and glared while speaking into his cell phone, "I've gotta go." And like the first time she'd met him, Reid wiped all emotion off his face and regarded her as he would a stranger. With a polite wave, he said, "Please, have a seat. What have you got for me?"

Fine. She could work in business mode. She went over the new plans for the advertising campaign.

He nodded. "Looks good. I think we're on track."

"We are." She showed him Leo's numbers and added Liz's analysis. They tweaked some fees to increase a marketing idea she'd had to better take advantage of the company's growing visibility.

Before she knew it, nearly an hour had gone by. "Wow. Time flies."

"Yeah." He drank coffee and sighed. "Ah, that's good."

They stared at each other. She thought he looked tired and wondered what he thought about her.

"Well, I guess I'll see you later," he said, giving her the brush-off.

She narrowed her eyes, got up, and locked the door behind her. "We don't need to be interrupted."

"Go ahead." Reid drank from his cup and watched her. Even injured, with that big white cast on his arm, Reid looked lethal. His eyes were bright. They flickered, and he appeared full of pain. Then…nothing.

"We need to talk."

"Go ahead," he said again.

"Fine. Be immature."

He tiredly rubbed his eyes. "Naomi, what do you want from me? I heard you at Chris's party. You don't love me."

"That's not true."

"Sure it is."

"Will you please stop telling me how I feel?"

"Fine. Say what you need to say."

Thanks so much. "What you and I have is no one's business but ours. I didn't want to talk to Tanner about us, okay?"

He nodded.

Progress. "I know *exactly* how I feel about Tanner. At one point, I loved him. Now? All I feel is disappointment. I got the closure I needed. He's not the man I thought he was. He's still an amazing communicator and social media expert. He and I do work well together. But that's all there is."

"Are you sure?"

"Positive." Naomi waited for Reid to pull her into his arms so they could go back to the way they'd been.

He didn't. He just watched her, looking somber. "I'm glad you got the closure you needed."

"Thank you."

Two strangers, watching the other for signs of… something.

"I'll say it since you can't bring yourself to," he said wryly. "And me, Naomi. How do you feel about me?"

"I love you."

"Uh-huh." He didn't look convinced.

She frowned. "I'm telling you the truth."

"I think you should go."

She didn't understand. "What's the problem? You love me, I love you. We're a couple."

"A couple of wishful thinkers." He shook his head. "I don't know what I was thinking. I fell hard for you.

Too fast, too much at once. Maybe it was an emotional storm from my mother that landed me with you. I don't know. I transferred the need to be loved from my mother to you, and I can only apologize for that. Now you're saying you love me, and I think you're doing the same. Feeling guilty or sympathetic for my pain." He held up his cast. "You don't need to. I'll manage, the way I always have. You have a life and a career on the fast track. Working with Jennings will open you up to a whole new level of business."

"What are you saying?" Fear that he would continue to pull away freaked her out. "Reid?"

"You need time to figure out your goals. And so do I. I'd only be in your way if we stayed together. You're made for a better man than me."

She had no idea where any of this was coming from, but she'd be damned if she'd grovel after what she'd just told him.

She stood and nodded, falling back on what she knew. The job. "If that's what you want, I understand." Her heart was breaking into tiny pieces.

"It's not what I want." He sounded beyond tired. "But it's all I can expect. I wish you only the best, Naomi. And I still want to be friends."

"Friends?" Was he insane?

No, he was an idiot. One who still loved her but had somehow gotten turned around.

She nodded. "Fine. We're still friends." Changing the subject to keep him on his toes, she asked, "On another note, what's with all the foot traffic today?"

He shrugged. "Somehow, the press got wind of us and Chris's burglars, though I'm not sure how. We've been dubbed Seattle's secret superheroes." He frowned. "It's annoying, inaccurate, and a pain in the butt."

He still tried not to curse in front of her, her sweet little idiot.

She saw him looking at her, all heartsick, before he donned that emotionless mantle of armor.

And she saw his retreat for what it was, a need to reconcile his feelings with what he could live with. She knew how rejection from someone she'd once loved had hit her. To find that same thing from one's mother, and then from the woman he loved?

It would take time to earn his trust again. But Naomi knew how to work a crowd. And she knew how to work the Marine she'd fallen hard for. Looking at him now, she wondered how she ever could have questioned her feelings for him. Reid needed her. Not for her business acumen or her connections. He needed her love.

"Why are you looking at me like that?"

She shrugged and called on her mother's favorite excuse. "Sorry. Low blood sugar. I need to eat. I'll see you in a week, okay? We'll go over more stats." She leaned over his desk, pleased when he tensed, then tried to mask it by pretending to be nonchalant. Naomi held out a hand.

Reid hesitantly shook it.

"Friends," she said with a smile.

His irritation pleased her. "Yeah, sure." He withdrew his hand, and she felt tingles all the way to her feet. They still connected, no matter what he tried to say.

"I'll be seeing you." She left his office and headed straight to Cash, who she'd just seen exit the office.

"Hey, wait up." She hurried to join him and stopped

when she ran into Smith instead. "Wow. You look like Cash from behind."

"That's just cruel."

She stared up at him, seeing their obvious differences. Smith looked hard, mean. Cash looked the same until she looked closer and saw a wounded man trying to hide himself from the world. Smith looked like he wanted to kick the world in the teeth just because.

"You want Cash?"

"Yes, I need to talk to him."

Smith nodded down the hallway to the stairs. "He was refilling supplies in the bay last I saw him."

She thanked Smith, hurried downstairs, and found Cash arguing with Jordan in the large supply room.

"I'm telling you. She clocks him. I'm betting twenty bucks she does it. She's got a thing for him."

"No way." Jordan huffed. "LaRhonda is not interested in Burke. She had a baby with Miguel, remember?"

Another woman, probably the infamous Heidi, added in a clear, light voice, "No. LaRhonda loves Burke. You can tell because they're always fighting. Hiding their true feelings behind a lot of arguments."

A pregnant pause, then Jordan and Cash told Heidi how full of crap that theory was before Jordan left the supply room and nearly ran into Naomi.

"Oh, hey, Naomi. Reid's upstairs."

"I know. I just need to talk to Cash for a second."

"He's in there." Jordan hiked a thumb over her shoulder before darting away.

Naomi entered to find Heidi and Cash hovering over a tablet. They were watching some reality TV show.

"Cash."

He jumped, and Heidi laughed.

"That's not funny, damn it." He stomped to Naomi. "Heidi, tell me what happens."

"Sure thing, boss."

"And stop calling me boss. It's Cash." He turned to Naomi. "She gets that boss shit from Jordan." He gave a half grin. "So what's up? You finally talk my brother into quitting all that sulking he's been doing?"

She sighed. "No. He's still sulking."

"It's the sex," Heidi said, a faint accent in her words. "Give him great pussy, he's yours for life."

Naomi gaped.

"No, no." Cash shook his head. "Heidi, you're gay; you have no clue about what a man really wants. Naomi, give him great *head* and he's yours for life."

"Ah, yes. Of course." Heidi gave her a sly wink. "But the pussy is good too."

"I'll drink to that." Cash clinked a bottle of cola against Heidi's water.

"You guys scare me."

"Cheers." Heidi drank her water down. "Cash, hurry. Zelda's back."

"Hot damn." He turned from Naomi, but she grabbed him by the arm to jerk him back around. "What?" he snapped.

"I need your house this weekend. Can you get lost until Monday? You can stay at my place if you want."

"Hmm. Do you have cable?"

"No, but I have Wi-Fi and streaming."

"Deal. What time?"

"Sixish. But I also need your help for a few other things before you take off for the weekend."

"Yeah?"

"Trust me. My relationship with Reid is more interesting than your reality TV."

"I'm in."

"Great. Thanks. Now enjoy Zelda."

Naomi left, happy again since she had a workable plan. Poor Reid. They really were a lot alike. The unfortunate man had no idea what was about to hit him.

Chapter 24

REID HAD LOST HIS ZEST FOR LIFE. FRIDAY AFTERNOON AT work, he went through the motions. Naomi's PR campaign was working. They had clients out the ass. Smith, surprisingly, fit in, and he now had a dream team.

He'd partnered teams up, and Smith went out with either Jordan or Hector each time. Cash pretended not to care, but Reid knew his brother hated when Jordan and Smith went out together.

Since the big bastard had stopped bugging him about Naomi, Reid figured he'd cut Cash some slack and stop assigning Jordan and Smith together. Petty yet satisfying. And he'd finally gotten Cash to leave him the hell alone.

He knew what Naomi thought. That he was being a passive-aggressive asshole because she'd taken too long to realize she loved him. But that wasn't it at all.

He loved her too much. Like Charles had loved Angela. No matter how much his mother retreated from the world, his father had remained close by to do whatever she wanted. Reid worried he might have a little too much of his father inside him for any woman to handle. Especially if that woman didn't love him like he loved her.

Because when the love wasn't there, children suffered. And why the hell was he even thinking of kids with Naomi when the woman didn't know how she felt about him?

Fuck. Okay. I'm hurt and pissed and bitter. I'm entitled.

His arm hurt all the time, and he hated the damn pain meds because they made him groggy.

Did she really expect him to just accept that she now loved him? What had changed?

He sighed and let himself in the house, taking an early day. The June weather had warmed nicely, and because running jarred his arm inside the cast, the pressure too much to bear just yet, he wanted a long walk.

After he'd taken a cold shower because, as usual, thoughts of Naomi got him hard despite his heartache. The red-haired, gorgeous, smart little witch.

He rubbed his eyes, tired of the sting making them water. He just couldn't accept Naomi's sympathy masked as love and run with it. He was too greedy. Wanted too much, buying into the dumb idea of a happily ever after.

Reid decided to take a nap. He roused a bit later and saw Cash leaning over him.

"Hey, man. I have to go talk to Mac. I owe him and Gavin a few beers for us messing up the gym. But we're square. Mac's a good guy. And Gavin, when he stops fucking talking, isn't bad either." He smiled, then sighed. "I have to go to Mom's place too. I wish you'd help me clear the rest out, but with that injury, it can wait, I guess."

Reid must have mumbled something. Cash eventually left.

He woke again, this time flat on his back and...tied to the bed? He tugged at his bad wrist and saw it lying on a pillow, his arm loosely tied to the headboard by the elbow. But his other wrist and ankles were spread and bound by silk scarves.

What the hell kind of kinky dream was he having?

"I know you're awake."

At the sound of her voice, his entire body came alive.

Reid gaped to see Naomi staring down at him. She wore a short pink nightgown. A sheer nightgown, because he could see her pretty nipples and the hint of her pussy.

He hardened as expected. Then a rush of cool air breezed by, and he realized he wore no clothes.

"Whoa. What the hell—heck?"

She laughed. "There's my Reid."

"Naomi, what are you doing?" His body wanted more, but his mind needed answers. Stupid mind.

"I'm done with you, Reid."

The hurt followed. "I'm done with you too."

"No, you're not. I'm done with your excuses, tired of you putting up obstacles because you're scared. We're all scared of committing, of loving someone who might leave or cheat or fall out of love. Hey, it happened to me. And yes, it happened to your mom and dad. But you and I aren't them."

"Maybe I am. Maybe I'm just like my dad."

"You aren't. You're funny and sexy and sensitive. And so smart. I love you, you big idiot. I have for some time. But of course you had to overhear at the party, when I was in no condition to talk about my feelings." She paused. "So you avoided me for days. Maybe I should do the same back to you. Leave you all tied up because of me."

"So go."

"You wouldn't care?" She closed the distance between them and ran a long fingernail from his navel to his left nipple.

His dick bounced on his belly, his need for her fierce.

"I'd care, but you have to do what's right for you." He swallowed.

"So you're not going to fight for me at all?"

He wanted to shout but instead gritted his teeth then said, "I'm not playing a fucking game. You want to go, go."

"But I don't want to leave you." Her fingernail moved back down again, passing his belly button to graze his shaft. "I want to love you."

He wanted to argue, but he'd missed her so much. "You have to *really* love me, Naomi. I can't do maybes or not sures. I need to know."

She didn't answer, though he hadn't expected her to. But he couldn't have anticipated that she'd take him in her mouth and blow him until he lost his ever-loving mind.

As pent up as he was, it didn't take long. All the light scratching with those nails, the way she rubbed her tits over his legs as she sucked him dry, had him coming so damn hard.

After he'd released down her throat, she pulled back and wiped her lips. "Hmm. How was that for convincing you?"

"I…I… *Fuck*. Naomi…"

"I plan to when you're ready to go again, sweetie."

He could only stare at her in awe, his goddess. "What if I say no?"

"Then I keep you and convince you to say yes."

"Why me?" he asked, no longer playing.

Then neither was she. "You're mine, Reid. You get me. You're smart and funny and handsome and brutal. You protect what's yours, and you love unconditionally. No matter how badly your parents treated you, you still loved them. And you've stuck by Cash through everything.

"I want that in my life. I need that. A man I can call my own, who'll stand by me, and who I can love, respect, and trust. That's you."

"Naomi. Are you sure? Once you commit to me, that's it." His voice cracked. "You can't take it back."

The little boy appeared and disappeared as quickly, that vulnerable aspect of Reid all too aware he needed protection. He hated it, but he couldn't help feeling that way.

"Oh, baby. I love you, Reid. With everything I have and am. What you see is what you get. I'm a neurotic overachiever with mommy issues." She kissed him on the mouth, and he tasted himself on her lips.

Hope lightened him, but he tried not to give into it yet. "Well, I'm no prince. I have a temper, though I'm slow to boil. I love hard and deep, and it doesn't go away. I'm loyal, but not like a dog. You kick me one too many times, and I'll bite back. I have no family but Cash and Evan, well, and Aunt Jane too. But Naomi, Cash and I are a pair. Together. You can't have me without him in our lives."

"I know." She stroked Reid's hair and kissed him again. "He's part of you. And he needs you. My family is full of can-do people. And I have a cat who sleeps around. Can you handle that?"

"I'm pretty sure I can." Reid smiled. "One more thing."

"Yes?"

He tugged at his restraints. "I don't mind this, but I'd much rather tie *you* up and have my way with *you*. I'm getting there." He glanced down at himself.

She smiled. "That could be arranged, I suppose."

"What'll it cost me?"

"Will you marry me, Reid? We'll have a long engagement, but when I see something I want, I take it. And I want you."

Reid stared. "You're asking me to marry you while I'm tied up and naked?"

"Yep." She sat by him and smiled. "And if you give me the right answer, I'll let you make love to me all night long."

"Hmm. I wonder. Do you want me to say yes or no?"

"A hint for you. I like my men easy."

"A yes it is." He grinned, so damn happy. And so confused at how she'd gotten him to give in so soon. "I was trying to be good and do the right thing by giving you space."

"You were being a martyr for no good reason."

He grinned. "Understood, ma'am."

She laughed. "I love the way you salute, Marine." She fondled him, and he sighed with pleasure.

"Great. Now before you untie me, how about you come sit on my face? Then I'll tell you about the talk I plan to have with Tanner about leaving you alone. He can work with you, but he can't fuck with your head. I'm civilized, but not that civilized."

She shook her head. "You have nothing to worry about with him."

"I know. And neither do you."

She removed the nightie and crept over him, her curves and heat bathing him in lust and affection. "I love you, Reid Griffith."

"Not half as much as I love you, Naomi Starr." He felt himself come back to life, one heartbeat at a time. "Now be a good girl and sit on my face."

"That's my heart and flowers Marine."

"Oh yeah."

"I thought you guys said oorah."

She climbed over him and sooner rather than later found out that *oorah* and *oh yeah* could sound very alike, depending on how one said it.

Sometime later, Reid hugged her to him, no longer restrained, and sniffed at her neck. Yep, the scent of his woman smelled oh so good. "So what do you think about changing your name to Naomi Griffith at some point?"

"Griffith PR?"

He cradled her to him, his precious fiancée. "Nah. Starr PR, headed by Naomi Griffith."

"Hmm. I could grow to like it. But first a long engagement. We're not rushing us, Reid."

"Exactly. Though you wouldn't be opposed to another sex marathon with your as-yet fiancé, would you?"

"I'm not an idiot." She grinned at him, her blue eyes shining.

"No offense."

"None taken."

Acknowledgments

I'd like to thank Cat C. for having such a great idea. Couldn't have done it without you! And to all the folks at Sourcebooks who make my books possible, I truly appreciate all of you.

About the Author

Caffeine addict, boy referee, and romance aficionado, *New York Times* and *USA Today* bestseller Marie Harte is a confessed bibliophile and devotee of action movies. Whether biking around town, hiking, or hanging at the local tea shop, she's constantly plotting to give everyone a happily ever after. Visit marieharte.com and fall in love.

Also by Marie Harte